William Faulkner

Knight's Gambit

William Faulkner was born in 1897 and raised in Oxford, Mississippi, where he spent most of his life. One of the towering figures of American literature, he is the author of *The Sound and the Fury*, *As I Lay Dying*, and *Absalom, Absalom!*, among many other remarkable books. Faulkner was awarded the Nobel Prize in Literature for 1949 and France's Legion of Honor in 1951. He died in 1962.

———————

John Duvall is the Margaret Church Distinguished Professor of English at Purdue University. He is the author of *Faulkner's Marginal Couple: Invisible, Outlaw, and Unspeakable Communities*, *The Identifying Fictions of Toni Morrison*, and *Race and White Identity in Southern Fiction*. He has also edited a number of books, including *Faulkner and Postmodernism* and *Faulkner and His Critics*.

INTERNATIONAL

BOOKS BY WILLIAM FAULKNER

KNIGHT'S GAMBIT

Knight's Gambit

SIX MYSTERY STORIES

WILLIAM FAULKNER

THE RESTORED EDITION
EDITED BY JOHN N. DUVALL

VINTAGE INTERNATIONAL
Vintage Books
A Division of Penguin Random House LLC
New York

CONTENTS

ACKNOWLEDGMENTS

This edition of *Knight's Gambit* would never have materialized if it weren't for two people. The first is Jay Watson, whose selection of the topic "Faulkner and Print Culture" for the 2015 Faulkner and Yoknapatawpha Conference gave me the opportunity to delve into Faulkner's appearances in *Ellery Queen's Mystery Magazine*. I had long wondered about the details of Faulkner's winning second prize for "An Error in Chemistry" in the magazine's first detective-story competition in 1946. I came to understand that the magazine's editor, Frederic Dannay, who during the 1940s not only published "An Error in Chemistry" but also reprinted two earlier Faulkner stories, had a significant hand in shaping Faulkner's postwar reputation. The other person is Leah Pennywark. In spring 2016 Leah, now the Humanities Editor at the University of Minnesota Press, was working on her dissertation on the role of detective fiction in the development of postmodern fiction. I had suggested archival research on *Ellery Queen's Mystery Magazine* might be helpful, since it not only was the most important postwar detective-fiction magazine but also was the first English-language publisher of Jorge Luis Borges. Before leaving to examine Dannay's papers at Columbia University, she asked me if there was anything I was interested in. I said I'd like to know if there was any material related to "An Error in Chemistry" in this archive. I hoped there might be a carbon of an acceptance letter to Faulkner lurking in some file.

When she returned she presented me with digital photos she'd taken of Faulkner's final submitted typescript of "An Error in Chemistry." Initially, I thought it was nice to have but nothing significant. After all, Thomas L. McHaney had published facsimiles of the manuscript material relating to *Knight's Gambit* in 1987, part of Garland's multivolume series reproducing Faulkner's manuscripts and typescripts. But when I examined the digital pages more closely, I was startled to see that they had Dannay's handwritten copyedits. Looking at McHaney's volume, I realized that the typescript reproduced there, part of the William Faulkner Collection at the University of Virginia, was shorter and significantly different than the one in Dannay's papers. McHaney had published an earlier draft of "An Error in Chemistry"; Faulkner's final submitted typescript was virtually unknown.

The more I looked at the final typescript, the more I saw that Dannay had edited out much of the southernness of Faulkner's story, including the racism of one of the main characters. Faulkner's final typescript, I came to see, mattered because the differences between it and the published version changed one's understanding not only of the story but also of the role of mass-market magazines in shaping Faulkner. Only then did I think, "If one lost Faulkner typescript turned up without anyone really looking for it, what other *Knight's Gambit* manuscript material might I find if I actively searched?" This edition is the result. But not, of course, without the help of lots more people.

Special collections librarians and the people working in digital production offices are the best. Thanks particularly to AnnaLee Pauls at the Manuscripts and Rare Books Library at Princeton's Firestone Library for her help not only with the "Monk" typescripts during my visit but also in checking some additional files after I'd returned to West Lafayette. Thanks also to Christina Deane, Manager of the University of Virginia's Digital Production Group, for her expedited treatment of my request for certain typescripts. Finally, thanks to Kristen Wilson at the Harry Ransom Center, the University of Texas at Austin. Although the archive was still closed to scholars because of COVID-19, in April 2021 she prepared digital copies for me of their copy of the uncorrected galleys of *Knight's Gambit*.

The community of Faulkner scholars was generous as always. My thanks to Tom McHaney, long retired, who responded graciously to my queries regarding manuscript material relating to *Knight's Gambit*. Jack Matthews weighed in on matters large and small that I ran by him. Ted Atkinson and Taylor Hagood gave me opportunities to present portions of this work at other conferences. I previously published an edition of "An Error in Chemistry," based on the final typescript, in *The Faulkner Journal*, vol. 31, no. 1 (Spring 2017), edited by Peter Lurie and Theresa Towner and published by Johns Hopkins University Press. Sarah Gleason-White and Pardis Dabashi included my contribution, "Faulkner and Print Culture," in their edited volume, *New Faulkner Studies* (Cambridge UP, 2022), and some of the comments I make there regarding the typescripts of "Monk" are repurposed in the introduction to this volume. I have similarly drawn on material from my essay that appeared in Jay Watson, Jaime Harker, and James G. Thomas Jr.'s edited conference proceedings, *Faulkner and Print Culture* (UP of Mississippi, 2017). My thanks to all these editors and presses for permission to use this material.

My Purdue colleagues Ryan Schneider, Bob Lamb, and Robert Marzec doubtless are pleased that they will no longer have to listen to me yammer on about the minutiae of house style at the mass-market magazines that first published the *Knight's Gambit* stories. Another former graduate student, Marc Diefenderfer, helped me check my transcription of "An Error in Chemistry" against the final typescript. And during the pandemic, when no one else was available to help me proof my transcriptions, my wife, Kathy Schroth, actually volunteered to engage in the same slow and laborious process of reading aloud my text against the manuscripts and typescripts of the other stories. If that's not love, I don't know what is. Sometimes I cast aspersions at Faulkner's copy editors, but mine was excellent: Lisa Williams helped me clarify information in the appendix and prevented a number of errors from making their way into the finished product.

The volume appears by permission of Penguin Random House LLC (USA), and Penguin Random House Limited (UK), and the Faulkner Estate. Finally, my sincere gratitude to Katie Keene, my editor at the University Press of Mississippi, for believing in my desire to re-ink a badly faded corner of Faulkner's little postage stamp of his native soil.

INTRODUCTION

Editing *Knight's Gambit*

This volume offers a new edition of *Knight's Gambit*, William Faulkner's 1949 collection of stories that focus on Yoknapatawpha's long-time county attorney Gavin Stevens—a man more interested in justice than the law. While *Knight's Gambit* is often referred to as a collection of six detective stories, Stevens actually solves crimes in only three of them—"Smoke," "Hand Upon the Waters," and "An Error in Chemistry." In the last of these, the solution to the crime actually falls into his lap through the criminal's blunder, not through Stevens's intellectual prowess. In the novella-length title story, "Knight's Gambit," Stevens prevents a crime, but in the other two stories—"Monk" and "Tomorrow"—he simply seeks to understand how and why some will use the rule of law to pervert justice.[1] Whether solving a crime or not, Stevens always wants to detect the hidden motives of others.

An important recurring character, Stevens appears in many of Faulkner's novels—*Light in August* (1932), *The Hamlet* (1940), *Go Down, Moses* (1942), *Intruder in the Dust* (1948), *Requiem for a Nun* (1951), *The Town* (1957), and *The Mansion* (1959). He first played a minor role in the 1931 story "Hair," which is reprinted in *Collected Stories*. His first appearance as the lawyer seeking justice, however, is in "Smoke" (*Harper's*, April 1932), the earliest of the reprinted stories in *Knight's Gambit*. Faulkner has Stevens reprise this role in the collection's other stories: "Monk" (*Scribner's*, May 1937), "Hand Upon the Waters" (*Saturday Evening Post*, 4 Nov. 1939), "Tomorrow" (*Saturday Evening Post*, 23 Nov. 1940), "An Error in Chemistry" (*Ellery Queen's Mystery Magazine*, June 1946), and "Knight's Gambit," the only new piece in the volume.

To some readers, doubtless even to some Faulknerians, a new edition of *Knight's Gambit* may seem about as idiosyncratic (and, less charitably, unnecessary) as a different scholarly project, a fictional one, Stevens's longtime respite from practicing law—his translation of the Old Testament from English into classical Greek. After all, don't these crime stories represent a middlebrow (or even a pulp) Faulkner and so stand as the lesser work of the creator of Yoknapatawpha County?[2] Such a view seems supported by Faulkner's decision to exclude the *Knight's Gambit* stories from *Collected Stories*, while including those from his earlier collections, *These 13* (1931) and (with the exception of "Smoke") *Doctor Martino and Other Stories* (1934). This perspective, however, overlooks the fact that it had been years since most of the stories in *These 13* and *Doctor Martino* had been available to the public. *Knight's Gambit* had been out less than a year when *Collected Stories* appeared in 1950. Why would Faulkner or Random House want to damage the sales of a 1949 hardback (to say nothing of the 1950 Signet paperback edition) by including material from *Knight's Gambit* in *Collected Stories*? Moreover, having the *Knight's Gambit* stories in a stand-alone collection makes good sense as a business decision, one building on the success of Faulkner's 1948 novel, *Intruder in the Dust*, which featured the detective work of Chick Mallison, whose mentor is his uncle, Gavin Stevens. The stories in *Knight's Gambit* reunite these two characters. Except for "Smoke" and "Hand Upon the Waters," Stevens's nephew is either the narrator or a character.

While I am not suggesting that *Knight's Gambit* belongs in the same category as *The Unvanquished* (1938) or *Go Down, Moses* (1942), there is something that links all three: each adds one entirely new story to previously published material. Certainly the shared subject matter of the *Knight's Gambit* stories—Stevens's attempts to understand the mystery of human motives—does give the volume a kind of coherence, and during the period of New Criticism, a few critics unsurprisingly sought to identify the underlying themes that would turn *Knight's Gambit* into a unified work of art.[3] Alas, any attempt to discover Faulkner's larger design in grouping the stories of *Knight's Gambit* runs up against the hard fact that with both *The Unvanquished* and *Go Down, Moses*, Faulkner revised (often substantially) his earlier stories to ensure that these books would feel more like novels. However, he makes no revisions whatsoever to the previously published stories of *Knight's Gambit*, and the only logic of their presentation is chronological: they simply appear in the order they were first published; the one new story concludes the collection. Frankly, it is hard to see how any amount of revision could have turned these stories into a novel, since each of Stevens's investigations is discrete, and there are unresolved discrepancies between stories. One of the most obvious of these is the age of Stevens's nephew. In "Knight's Gambit," set just before and shortly after America's entry into World War II, Chick turns eighteen, so he would have been born in late 1923 or early 1924. However, in "Tomorrow," published in 1940, Chick narrates in time present an event that happened more than twenty years earlier, when he was twelve. This would mean that Mallison was born around 1907.

But *Knight's Gambit* does not have to be a novel built on interconnected stories for it to be significant; in terms of understanding both Yoknapatawpha County and Faulkner as a short-story writer, this collection has been underestimated. Some of its stories are arguably as good as or better than a number of those in *Collected Stories*. Perhaps the best, "Tomorrow," through the orality of its various narrating voices, questions the primacy of biological family ("blood pride") and illustrates that the law is sometimes profoundly unjust; this story could serve as effectively as "A Rose for Emily" or "Barn Burning" to introduce students to Faulkner's north Mississippi. Even what is generally regarded as the collection's weakest story, "An Error in Chemistry," likely would work better in the classroom than "Golden Land," "Black Music," or "The Leg," all of which appear in *Collected Stories*. These last three are set outside of Yoknapatawpha County and explore matters largely unrelated to Faulkner's major fiction. "Golden Land" examines a dysfunctional wealthy family living in the glare of a Hollywood media scandal; "Black Music," set in the fictional country of Rincon (presumably somewhere in the Global South), tells of a New York architect and the bizarre circumstances that led him to flee the United States twenty-five years earlier; and "The Leg" is a World War I story set in England about a man who talks to his friend killed in battle and who is haunted by his amputated leg. (The ideas behind these three stories might have been handled more convincingly by, respectively, Nathanael West, Ernest Hemingway, and H. P. Lovecraft.) Even with its plot contrivance, "An Error in Chemistry" still reflects on who belongs and who is marginal to the white southern community.

The main reason why this new edition may shed more light on Faulkner's career as a short-story writer is quite simple: all previous editions of *Knight's Gambit* were based on that of the 1949 first edition, a text that is problematic for a variety of reasons.[4] In typesetting the first edition, tear sheets were used from the various magazines in which the stories first appeared, with one exception. The opening story, "Smoke," first published in *Harper's*, was subsequently reprinted in *Doctor Martino and Other Stories*; tear sheets from this story collection were used in typesetting "Smoke" for *Knight's Gambit*. Only the previously unpublished "Knight's Gambit" was set from Faulkner's typescript. As a result, in all previous editions of the collection, only "Knight's Gambit" uses Faulkner's preferred spelling and punctuation conventions.

Based on Noel Polk's work with Faulkner's manuscripts and typescripts, Polk and Joseph Blotner, in their five-volume Library of America editions of the novels (on which the current Vintage International editions are based), restore Faulkner's preferences. The most prominent of these are the following: 1) Faulkner did not use apostrophes in the contractions "dont," "wont," "aint," and "oclock"; 2) he followed British usage in omitting the period in such honorifics as "Mr," "Mrs," and "Dr"; and 3) he almost always used the British suffix "-ise" in words that end "-ize" in American English. Polk and Blotner, though, also discovered instances where Faulkner's prose had been trimmed during production in the name of concision and readability. Because their goal was to restore as closely as possible Faulkner's final intentions, the Library of America and Vintage International editions of Faulkner's novels now include words, phrases, and sentences that did not appear in the first editions. Polk and Blotner, of course, included Faulkner's two story-based novels, *The Unvanquished* and *Go Down, Moses*, but not *Knight's Gambit*, since it is merely a collection of stories. As a result, the text of *Knight's Gambit* has remained until now what it was at the time of its initial publication—a hodgepodge of different house styles with no consistency from story to story.

But the changes made in this new edition go well beyond minor spelling and punctuation issues. What my study of the manuscripts and typescripts of the *Knight's Gambit* stories makes clear is that some of the supposed accessibility of Faulkner's short fiction is not the author's conscious decision to write for a broader audience, but rather the work of editors (including copy editors) who made changes based on their ideas about their magazine's audience or because of specific design features of their magazines. Northern editors at times did not understand Faulkner's South. Copy editors impatient with Faulkner's long paragraphs and sentences sometimes broke them into smaller units (not always wisely) and at other times simply lopped off significant portions of paragraphs and sentences.

The typescripts reveal much about print culture and the editorial practices of mass-market magazines. The published version of each story crucially depends on where it was accepted. Whoever edited "Smoke" at *Harper's* allowed Faulkner a lengthy exposition, whereas the editing at the *Saturday Evening Post* almost seemed intent on turning Faulkner into Hemingway by removing about half of the exposition in "Hand Upon the Waters." The *Post* editorial practice clearly favored plot over the development of setting and secondary characters, so much so that it's hardly an exaggeration to say that until now, we've been reading an abridged version of "Hand Upon the Waters."

My guiding principle has been to present *Knight's Gambit* in a fashion consistent with the Library of America editions of Faulkner's novels. This means attempting, as Noel Polk put it, to "*de-edit*" the first edition in order to give the reader as nearly as possible what these stories looked like when they left the author's typewriter (6), before the many hands of magazine fiction editors, copy editors, and in some cases even Faulkner's agents changed the stories for house style, concision, or propriety.

Some of the stories that follow are substantially different from their previous appearance in print. Others are more minimally changed. With every story, the scope of my editing is constrained by the manuscript and typescript material that is available for each. In two cases ("Monk" and "An Error in Chemistry"), I work with previously unknown final and copyedited typescripts. This new material allows for highly authoritative restorations of Faulkner's final intentions for these stories. But even in the absence of such final typescripts, the material evidence of manuscripts, typescripts, and earlier publications allows reconstructions that move us closer to the way Faulkner thought these stories should appear. I present selected variants between this edition and the first edition in the appendix.

A note on two global decisions that complicate (without finally undoing) my principle of attempting to recover Faulkner's final intentions for these stories. What precisely constitutes a final intention becomes less clear when a story collection reprints material that originally appeared up to seventeen years earlier. In both instances, for the sake of consistency, I decided to privilege Faulkner's preferences at the time *Knight's Gambit* was published.

1) Quotation Marks for Dialogue. Following the first edition and Faulkner's most typical practice, I use single quotation marks for dialogue throughout, even though a couple of the extant typescripts actually use double quotation marks.

2) Capitalizing "Negro."

Print-culture conventions changed from 1932, when *Harper's* published "Smoke," to 1949. In the early 1930s, only a few print venues capitalized "Negro."[5] By the 1940s the convention had changed, and "Negro" was the norm. Unsurprisingly, Faulkner did not begin capitalizing this racial term in his typescripts until the 1940s. However, two stories he published in the late 1930s—"Hand Upon the Waters" and "Tomorrow"—appeared in *The Saturday Evening Post*, which by then always capitalized "Negro." As a result, in the first edition of *Knight's Gambit*, "Negro" is consistently capitalized only in the two *Post* stories and the last two stories, "An Error in Chemistry" and "Knight's Gambit." "Smoke" creates the biggest inconsistency in the volume. In the manuscript of "Smoke," as well as in its earlier appearances in *Harper's* and *Doctor Martino and Other Stories*, "Negro" is always lowercase. Even in the uncorrected galleys, "Negro" still is lowercase in every instance.

While the galleys sent to Faulkner for final correction are lost, someone (not necessarily Faulkner) must have registered the inconsistency between "Smoke" and the final four stories in the volume regarding this matter of capitalization. That is because in the first edition three of the seventeen lowercase appearances of "negro" in "Smoke" are capitalized. These capitalizations would show up in the first edition only if they had been changed on the author's galleys.

Taking Faulkner's practice in the 1940s as a form of final intention, I capitalize "Negro" throughout this edition. Clearly, if Random House had invested in a good copy editor to proof the galleys, "Negro" would have been capitalized throughout, because that was the convention of print culture in 1949, one that Faulkner followed. While I have not used the corrupt text of the inexpensive 1950 Signet paperback of *Knight's Gambit* in constructing this edition, it is worth noting that the Signet edition does follow the standard practice of the time, capitalizing all instances of "Negro."

For readers interested in a deeper dive into the specifics of my process, the following sections detail for each story 1) the sources I consulted in constructing this edition, 2) some historical context regarding the magazines in which Faulkner published, and 3) examples of significant changes I have made to the first edition based on the source material.

"SMOKE"

Texts Consulted

"Smoke," twelve-page holographic manuscript, William Faulkner Collection, University of Virginia, 6074, IIA:15a.

"Smoke," *Harper's*, April 1932, pp. 562–78.

"Smoke," *Doctor Martino and Other Stories*. Harrison Smith and Robert Haas, 1934, pp. 120–58.

"Smoke," *Ellery Queen's Mystery Magazine*, Nov. 1947, pp. 50–71.

"Smoke," *Knight's Gambit*, uncorrected galleys, William Faulkner Collection, University of Texas at Austin, Container 8.1, pp. 5–15A. [Note: "Smoke" begins on p. 5, but there is also a 5A, a 6, and a 6A, and so on.]

"Smoke," *Knight's Gambit*, Random House, 1949, pp. 3–36.

Rejected by both *The Saturday Evening Post* and *Scribner's*, "Smoke" was accepted by *Harper's* on January 18, 1932. *Harper's* paid $400 for the story. Although less than half what Faulkner would have earned from the *Post* and around $100 less than *Scribner's* rate, the payment from *Harper's* carried the intangible of prestige, since the magazine had a solid reputation for literary fiction, having published stories in previous decades by Henry James, William Dean Howells, Mark Twain, and Jack London.

Edited at the time by the Harvard-educated popular historian Frederick Lewis Allen, *Harper's* epitomized the upper-middlebrow. With its familiar orange cover displaying its table of contents, advertisements were segregated at the beginning of each issue from the magazine's content. The ads reveal an aspirational consumer who valued reading and education. Since they published the magazine, Harper & Brothers had six pages advertising their new books, but many of the other major New York publishers had full-page ads featuring their latest list. Each issue also included around ten pages of ads for prep schools and colleges. The magazine featured a mix of cultural commentary, short stories, and poetry. The lead article in the issue in which "Smoke" appeared is Lincoln Colcord's "The Realism of Japanese Diplomacy." Colcord was a well-known journalist at the time who wrote political analysis for a number of influential magazines.

Only an early draft manuscript of "Smoke" survives; production files for *Harper's* (archived at the Library of Congress) do not extend back to 1931, which means that Faulkner's submitted typescript of "Smoke" apparently no longer exists. However, in the absence of the final typescript, other textual evidence allows for a partial reconstruction of what this missing typescript must have looked like. Faulkner's holographic manuscript is too early to authorize wholesale changes in the text;[6] nevertheless, it confirms Faulkner's preferred British spellings and his typical omission of apostrophes in certain contractions. The original publication of the story in *Harper's*, of course, was based on Faulkner's missing typescript. Moreover, there are the reprints of "Smoke" in *Doctor Martino and Other Stories* and *Ellery Queen's Mystery Magazine* (*EQMM*). The versions in *Harper's* and *Doctor Martino* are virtually identical, save for some minor differences in the use of ellipses and one instance where the *Doctor Martino* version reverses the order of two words that does not change the sense of the sentence.[7] *EQMM* reprints the *Doctor Martino* version, so these two also are virtually identical. (The only difference is that *EQMM* capitalizes "Negro," as was conventional in print culture by 1947, while *Harper's* and *Doctor Martino* always use lowercase for the word.) Taken together, these earlier print appearances reveal that several errors were introduced during the typesetting of *Knight's Gambit*; since they were not caught at the galley stage, they became part of the first edition and subsequent paperbacks. Such errors, corrected in this edition, are especially obvious when a word is dropped that affects syntax, or a verb tense suddenly shifts in the middle of a paragraph.

"MONK"

Texts Consulted

"Monk," submitted twenty-six-page typescript, Princeton University, Archive of Charles Scribner's Sons, Box 1234, Folder 12.

"Monk," twenty-five-page copyediting typescript, Princeton University, Archive of Charles Scribner's Sons, Box 1234, Folder 12.

"Monk," twenty-five-page carbon of copyediting typescript for author's final corrections, Princeton University, Archive of Charles Scribner's Sons, Box 1234, Folder 12.

"Monk," *Knight's Gambit*, uncorrected galleys, William Faulkner Collection, University of Texas at Austin, Container 8.1, pp. 15A–22.

"Monk," *Knight's Gambit*, Random House, 1949, pp. 39–60.

When *The Saturday Evening Post* rejected a story, *Scribner's* was often Faulkner's Plan B.[8] If the *Post* was middle-class America's favorite magazine, *Scribner's* was upper-middlebrow, one of the "quality group" that included *Harper's* and *The Atlantic*, magazines—as Frederick Lewis Allen notes in his January 1937 piece in *Scribner's* celebrating the venue's first fifty years—that were edited for "the educated classes" (22). Between 1931 and 1937, Faulkner placed nine stories in this magazine, a venue that regularly published stories by Ernest Hemingway, F. Scott Fitzgerald, Thomas Wolfe, and Caroline Gordon.[9] Ironically, although the quality of fiction published in *Scribner's* during the 1930s may represent the pinnacle of its literary reputation, circulation was rapidly declining. *Scribner's* circulation peaked in 1912 at 215,000. By 1930 there were only 70,000 subscribers, and these numbers dropped steadily throughout the decade. Tired of subsidizing a magazine that was hemorrhaging money, Charles Scribner and Sons sold it in 1938, and it ceased publication the following year (Gaipa). "Monk," published in the May 1937 issue, was the last of Faulkner's nine stories to appear in *Scribner's*.

In March 2019 while working in the archives of Charles Scribner and Sons at Princeton's Firestone Library, I discovered three previously unknown full typescripts of "Monk" that guided my restoration of Faulkner's final intentions for the story.[10] The need for this restoration is made clear by an editorial comment made in cursive in the right margin of the first page of the copyedited typescript of "Monk" that meant this version was ready for typesetting: "Expurgated by Scribner Editors." Unpacking what is meant by this remark requires looking at all three typescripts.

The first is Faulkner's twenty-six-page accepted typescript with some holographic markings. Faulkner's corrections are made in blue pen. Another hand (presumably that of *Scribner's* fiction editor at the time, Marion Ives) makes a small number of corrections and adds a few question marks next to certain words in pencil. On the top of the first page, for example, there are some numbers that are this individual's attempt to calculate the story's word count. By multiplying an approximate word count per page by the number of pages, Ives estimates its length as 6,825 words; "Monk" actually is composed of 7,201 words. Running down the right margin is a red stamp that reads: "COPY SCRIBNER'S MAGAZINE." Some of the editor's penciled marks made on Faulkner's typescript are directions to the typist of the second typescript, the one used for copyediting. At the time the practice at *Scribner's* was to retype accepted work onto paper with wide left and right margins marked by red lines running down the paper vertically. These margins allowed copy editors plenty of room to make clear corrections for the typesetter.

The second typescript (though in terms of the publication process it becomes the third and final typescript given to the typesetter), then, is twenty-five pages long and is used for copyediting. This typescript bears the same red stamp across the top that appears on the first typescript: "COPY SCRIBNER'S MAGAZINE." The Scribner typewriter used a 10-pt serif font, allowing thirty lines per page (as opposed to Faulkner's twenty-seven lines per full page). The smaller font also means that each line of the copyedited typescript has two to three more words per line than Faulkner's. This explains why the copyedited typescript is one page shorter than Faulkner's final typescript. Not surprisingly, the act of retyping Faulkner's story introduced a number of typos not present in the accepted typescript (even as this typist corrects a few of Faulkner's obvious typos), which means that the copy editor in some instances merely changes the copyedited typescript back to what Faulkner had actually written. While making a number of new edits, the copy editor also incorporates the changes made on the third typescript.

The third typescript is a carbon of the copyedited typescript, which was sent to Faulkner's agent at the time, Morton Goldman. The carbon was intended for the author to make final corrections, based on editorial feedback. This carbon, however, never made it past Goldman's office. It bears two red stamps running vertically down the right margin: the first (which is closer to the right edge of the paper) is the same as on the other two typescripts, and the second reads: "PLEASE CORRECT AND RETURN IMMEDIATELY." Goldman adds a note in cursive in the upper right margin, "no bitches allowed—nor sons of bitches M," and passes the carbon on to a subordinate who writes in a different hand immediately below, "noted," which is underlined twice. In addition to making corrections on this typescript, this individual is tasked with getting rid of language that *Scribner's* editors felt their audience would find offensive. In one instance this person is unable to come up with an acceptable substitute and asks the magazine in a handwritten marginal note to "please supply substitute." A couple of pages later, during Gavin Stevens's conversation with the convict Bill Terrel, Goldman's subordinate makes a substantial cut. Faced with two instances of the interdicted word "bitch," this individual simply cuts forty-nine consecutive words—the final sentence of one paragraph and the beginning of the next one—and then runs in what remains of the second paragraph with the preceding one. The *Scribner's* copy editor accepts this deletion on the final copyedited typescript precisely as it was reworked on the carbon by Goldman's office.

The place where Goldman's office is unable to find a substitute occurs when Faulkner uses "bitch" as a verb. When the violent criminal Terrel assumes that he will be denied parole again and thinks Stevens is the one responsible for the denial, he says, "So you're the one that bitched me up this time." The irony of *Scribner's* feeling the need to censor this word is that we know from a different text of Faulkner's, *The Wild Palms* [*If I Forget Thee, Jerusalem*], that "to bitch" is the author's own form of self-censorship. From context it is clear how it becomes a more acceptable substitute for a word that Faulkner knew would be totally beyond the pale. Early in their relationship, Charlotte Rittenmeyer tells Harry Wilborne that she likes "bitching, and making things with my hands" (75). It becomes a refrain almost. As she's dying, she reminds him that they "had fun . . . bitching and making things" (241). After Charlotte's death Harry recalls her "broad thighs and the hands that liked bitching and making things" (272). Clearly, Faulkner substitutes "to bitch" for "to fuck." Terrel, by this logic, really is saying to Stevens, "So you're the one that fucked me up this time."[11] Changed in the last instance by a copy editor to "crossed me up," we see that the *Scribner's* text is beyond expurgated: it's bowdlerized.

"HAND UPON THE WATERS"

Texts Consulted

"Hand Upon the Waters," thirty-page typescript, University of Virginia, 6074, IA:15c.2.

"Hand Upon the Waters," incomplete thirty-page typescript (numbered 1–24, 27, 29–33), William Faulkner Collection, University of Virginia, 6074, IA:15c.3.

"Hand Upon the Waters," *Saturday Evening Post*, 4 Nov. 1939, pp. 14–15, 75–76, 78–79.

"Hand Upon the Waters," *Knight's Gambit*, uncorrected galleys, William Faulkner Collection, University of Texas at Austin, Container 8.1, pp. 22–27A.

"Hand Upon the Waters," *Knight's Gambit*, Random House, 1949, pp. 63–81.

The Saturday Evening Post paid significantly more than other magazines for short stories, so it was always Faulkner's top choice for submitting new work. The *Post* paid $1,000 for "Hand Upon the Waters." In all, Faulkner published eighteen stories in the *Post* between 1930 and 1957. During these years, the magazine's circulation increased from nearly 300,000 to over 450,000 (Hefner and Timke). The *Post* was simply the best venue for authors to get their work into readers' hands.

Accepted and copyedited typescripts submitted to *The Saturday Evening Post* from the 1930s and 1940s are apparently lost. This is understandable. Since the *Post* was a weekly, storing old production files for any length of time would have taken up a prohibitive amount of space.[12] Fortunately, the Alderman Library at the University of Virginia houses two thirty-page typescripts of "Hand Upon the Waters." The first is complete but is the earlier of the two. Faulkner included his name and "Oxford, Mississippi" only on typescripts he intended for submission, the information appearing in the upper left-hand corner of the first page. The complete thirty-page typescript lacks these identifying details. The second typescript, however, is clearly one Faulkner intended to submit, since it does have his name and hometown on the first page. The numbering indicates that it was originally thirty-three pages; however, pages 25, 26, and 28 are missing.[13] Even if it is not identical to the typescript Faulkner submitted to the *Post* (and there is no way of knowing), the second typescript is unquestionably closer to the submitted typescript. Both the earlier and the later Virginia typescripts show that Faulkner conceived of a much more leisurely exposition than what one finds in the *Post* version, and that exposition only becomes longer in the later typescript. (In this regard Faulkner's story as submitted was similar to "Smoke," another story with a slowly developing opening; in fact, the *Post* rejected "Smoke" precisely because of its lengthy exposition.) Even if there was a missing third and final typescript, Faulkner would not have trimmed the story's exposition from what one sees in the two extant typescripts. For Faulkner, revision did not mean cutting or condensing, but rather expanding.[14] He did not simply retype in order to add a few handwritten corrections; rather, he reinhabited the narrative voice, and that voice takes over, adding new words, phrases, and sentences throughout.

No copyedited typescript survives. However, comparing the published version and the later Virginia typescript indicates a heavy editorial hand that removed many of Faulkner's descriptions of character and setting in favor of a more plot-driven presentation. This is particularly evident in the story's opening, which reduces Faulkner's first two paragraphs to one, cutting 168 words to 62 in order to take the reader to first dialogue more quickly. This less-is-more kind of editing removes a number of lushly rendered details about the river bottom and its flora and fauna. Whoever edited the story wanted the minimum of descriptive details and seemed always to be asking of each sentence, "Does this push the plot forward?"

Here is one brief example of the difference between the *Post* version and the later typescript. At the beginning of part 2, the coroner discusses Lonnie Grinnup's death with Gavin Stevens, and Faulkner's typescript provides this bit of delineation of a minor character: "The Coroner was an old country doctor, with a snuffy moustache and the blurred eyes of an old man behind steel spectacles." The *Post* version reduces this to "The coroner was an old country doctor." In all, the version I present here restores over 3,300 words that were cut by the *Post*. The result is a story in which the narrative voice is decidedly more Faulknerian.

"TOMORROW"

Texts Consulted

Untitled twenty-page typescript of "Tomorrow" with holographic corrections, William Faulkner Collection, University of Virginia, 6074, IA:15d.

"Tomorrow," *Saturday Evening Post*, 23 Nov. 1940, pp. 22–23, 32, 35, 37–39.

"Tomorrow," *Knight's Gambit*, uncorrected galleys, William Faulkner Collection, University of Texas at Austin, Container 8.1, pp. 28–34.

"Tomorrow," *Knight's Gambit*, Random House, 1949, pp. 85–105.

"Tomorrow" is another story where the paper trail limits what I am able to do. As I pointed out in my comments on "Hand Upon the Waters" above, none of the accepted or copyedited typescripts for the *Post* stories survive. With "Tomorrow" there is only one typescript at Virginia with a number of handwritten additions. While this draft is fairly close to the published story, it is clearly not the submitted typescript, because it lacks Faulkner's name and "Oxford, Mississippi" on the first page, details that mark typescripts Faulkner intended for submission. In fact, this typescript even lacks a title. With "Tomorrow," then, I have hewn more closely to the first edition. In the absence of a final typescript, I have not felt justified in restoring complete paragraphs from the early typescript where the material has been slightly reordered in the *Post* version and, thus, in the first edition.

However, based on what I learned from working with "Hand Upon the Waters," I have been able to make several types of restorations. First, I assume that passages in the *Post* version of "Tomorrow" that remove words, phrases, or sentences from the extant typescript reflect the magazine's copyediting process. If Faulkner was following his typical practice when preparing the missing final typescript, he would have added but not cut material. For example, during Bookwright's trial, Gavin Stevens speaks to the jury. The published version omits the first three sentences of the typescript's rendering of his speech. I have restored these sentences, along with several parenthetical asides in other paragraphs that did not make it into the *Post* version. Second, I am confident in following the typescript in deleting a number of paragraph breaks. Faulkner favored longer paragraphs; however, the *Post* added breaks because they published in columns and did not want their readers confronted with an entire column of unbroken text. Finally, while largely honoring the punctuation changes of the first edition, I have restored the dashes that Faulkner uses in his typescript to render Pruitt's narrative about Fentry. The *Post* often changes Faulkner's dashes to periods before paragraph breaks. But periods change the effect, making it appear that Pruitt has paused his story; clearly, however, the loquacious Pruitt is not done speaking when Gavin jumps in with questions. Faulkner's dashes more clearly signal Gavin's need to interrupt Pruitt in order to process Pruitt's new information.

"AN ERROR IN CHEMISTRY"

Texts Consulted

"An Error in Chemistry" [1940], twenty-two-page ts, MSS 6074, -a, -b, -c, -d Box 3, William Faulkner Papers, Alderman Library, University of Virginia, Charlottesville.

"An Error in Chemistry" [1945], thirty-page ts, MS 0323, Frederic Dannay Papers, Columbia University Library, New York. [Faulkner's typescript is twenty-eight pages; the other two pages are Dannay's headnote.]

"An Error in Chemistry," *Ellery Queen's Mystery Magazine*, June 1946, pp. 4–19.

"An Error in Chemistry," *Knight's Gambit*, uncorrected galleys, William Faulkner
Collection, University of Texas at Austin, Container 8.1, pp. 34–41.

"An Error in Chemistry," *Knight's Gambit*, Random House, 1949, pp. 109–31.

In the third week of September 1945, Faulkner sent his agent, Harold Ober, a revised twenty-eight-page typescript of "An Error in Chemistry" for publication in *EQMM*. The whereabouts of this final typescript of the story were unknown to Faulkner scholars for more than seventy years.[15] It is part of the Frederic Dannay Papers at Columbia University's Rare Book and Manuscript Library; the typescript was copyedited by Dannay in preparation for publication in his magazine's June 1946 issue. The only typescript of "An Error in Chemistry" that previously had been available is the one Faulkner had originally sent to Ober in November 1940, but this earlier version had been rejected by all of Faulkner's preferred higher-paying venues, such as *The Saturday Evening Post* and *Collier's*.

When Dannay offered to buy "An Error in Chemistry," he asked "if [Faulkner] would clear up an ambiguity in the story" (Blotner, *Faulkner*, 1189). The most substantive addition Faulkner made to the 1940 typescript likely explains why other magazines had rejected the story as originally written. The key plot moment simply did not explain. Faulkner assumed that everyone knew how to make a cold toddy. As a result, Joel Flint's fatal error—putting a spoonful of sugar directly into the whiskey—does not account for Stevens's response. In the revised version of the climax, Faulkner spells it out with nineteen additional typed lines of text—one must mix the sugar with water first, because sugar will not dissolve in whiskey, knowledge passed down from father to son. The addition clarifies what the error in chemistry actually is so that the reader better understands why Stevens immediately leaps on Flint, the imposter, for his failure to make the toddy as Wes Pritchel surely would have.

Although Dannay helped clarify the climactic moment of the story, elsewhere a number of his editorial decisions are questionable. In particular, Dannay removed some of the southernness of "An Error in Chemistry." For example, Dannay changed every instance of the sheriff's form of addressing Wesley Pritchel: "Uncle Wes" in Faulkner's typescript became "Mr. Pritchel" in print. On one level this change is understandable, since the story already contains the character referred to as Uncle Gavin because Stevens's nephew narrates the story. While this edit eliminates a possible confusion for readers unfamiliar with southern honorifics (is Pritchel the sheriff's uncle?), it shows that Dannay did not understand Faulkner's attention to how white southerners of different classes spoke to one another. Only the sheriff refers to Pritchel as "Uncle Wes"; Stevens more formally addresses the character as "Mr Pritchel."

More troubling still, Dannay deletes not only the racism that is a part of Flint's performance of Pritchel's rural white southern identity but also the narrator's understanding of the virulence of Pritchel's racism. Notably, in this pre–civil rights moment, Dannay deletes Flint-as-Pritchel's use of the N-word, which appears elsewhere in *Knight's Gambit* ("Monk," "Tomorrow," and "Knight's Gambit"). Why was Dannay ahead of other editors in being troubled by this racial epithet? Growing up in New York as a member of a Russian Jewish family, Dannay (born Daniel Nathan) doubtless experienced antisemitism and heard racial slurs directed toward Jewish people. As an editor, he could edit out offensive words, whether because he was sensitized or because he felt such words might impact sales. But Dannay's other deletion of the existence of racism in the rural South goes too far. At the moment when Stevens's nephew notices the "strange Negro youth" behind the wheel of Pritchel's truck, Dannay deleted a reference to race that removes a clue that tells the reader that something doesn't add up with Pritchel's behavior. Like a number of other poor whites in Yoknapatawpha County, Pritchel was known to despise Blacks. In the printed version, the phrase that follows "strange Negro youth" is as follows: "strange because Old Man Pritchel had never had a servant of any sort save his daughter" (129). In Faulkner's final typescript, however, the phrase reads, "strange because Old Man Pritchel had never had a servant of any sort save his daughter, and no Negro at all on his land" (19). Quite simply, Pritchel's racism was previously so virulent that it is striking, almost inexplicable, that Pritchel would now have a Black servant. This is a clue that the man representing himself as Pritchel isn't in fact Pritchel.

Why did Faulkner, who wrote disparagingly of pulp magazines in *Light in August* and *The Wild Palms* [*If I Forget Thee, Jerusalem*], submit his story to a mass-market genre magazine? Family responsibilities and a contract dispute with Warner Brothers meant that he needed the money, and *EQMM* would pay $300 for the story. More importantly, it would be entered in the magazine's first detective-story contest, which boasted a first prize of $2,000 (or around $26,700 in 2020 dollars). Much to his dismay, Faulkner did not win but was awarded second prize. He complained about this in a letter of 5 January 1946 to Ober: "Thank you for the Ellery Queen check. What a commentary. In France, I am the father of a literary movement. . . . In America, I eke out a hack's motion picture wages by winning second prize in a manufactured mystery story contest" (Blotner, *Selected Letters*, 217–18).

But despite Faulkner's disparaging remark, *EQMM* was hardly a trashy detective rag. That is because Dannay had literary aspirations both for his magazine and for the genre of detective fiction, which he felt that the critical establishment unfairly disparaged. Along with his cousin Manfred Bennington Lee, Dannay began writing enormously popular detective fiction in 1928 under the pen name Ellery Queen. However, Dannay alone edited *EQMM*, which was established in 1941. He argued the case for the literariness of detective fiction in the headnotes he wrote for every story that appeared in his magazine, often connecting the stories he published to various literary traditions. Each month *EQMM* presented a mix of new and previously published fiction. At the time "An Error in Chemistry" appeared in 1946, Dannay had previously reprinted fiction by O. Henry, Mark Twain, Theodore Dreiser, Dashiell Hammett, Graham Greene, and even Faulkner. Dannay twice reprinted Faulkner stories: the January 1944 issue included "The Hound," and the October 1947 issue featured "Smoke." In each instance Dannay included a laudatory headnote about Faulkner's fiction. In many ways Dannay is as important as Malcolm Cowley in bringing Faulkner to the attention of postwar American readers. In addition to promoting Faulkner in *EQMM*, Dannay also reprinted Faulkner stories in several anthologies of detective and crime fiction that he edited in the 1940s and 1950s. Cowley's 1946 *Portable Faulkner* is unquestionably important to Faulkner's postwar reception, but far fewer readers picked up this volume than the more than 100,000 readers who eagerly devoured *EQMM* every month. Cowley helped construct high-culture Faulkner, but Dannay, who included stories by Agatha Christie in each of the three issues in which Faulkner's fiction appeared, imagined a Faulkner with broad cultural appeal, an author one might read for pleasure and not because of his relation to high modernism or his role as a southern moralist.

"KNIGHT'S GAMBIT"

Texts Consulted

"Knight's Gambit," 161-page typescript setting copy, with a number of rejected draft pages on versos, William Faulkner Collection, University of Virginia, 6074, IA:15g.16.

"Knight's Gambit," 228-page carbon of novella version on 157 sheets. Note: carbon differs from original because in some instances Faulkner, after copyediting, strikes certain passages and apparently inserts the original page (now without a carbon) into his typewriter and adds new material. William Faulkner Collection, University of Virginia, 6074, IA:15f.3

"Knight's Gambit," *Knight's Gambit*, uncorrected galleys, William Faulkner Collection, University of Texas at Austin, Container 8.1, pp. 41–75A.

"Knight's Gambit," *Knight's Gambit*, Random House, 1949, pp. 135–246.

The novella-length "Knight's Gambit" is a story that Faulkner had worked on for a number of years. He hoped to sell the initial twenty-three-page typescript version that he sent to his agent, Harold Ober, on January 19, 1942 (Blotner, *Faulkner*, 1097). Ober, however, was unable to place it. Even this early version contains most of the key plot points of the much longer published story: Stevens prevents Max Harriss from using a wild stallion he buys to kill Captain Gualdes (Faulkner later added an "r" to the name), the Argentine horseman who seems to be courting both Max's sister and widowed mother. Max enlists to avoid jail, Gualdes marries the sister, and in the end, Stevens reunites with the mother, his long-lost love. As was invariably the case, as Faulkner revised "Knight's Gambit," the story grew. By June, Faulkner told Ober that the story would probably end up between sixty and seventy-five pages. The final typescript, finished in May 1949, is 161 pages long. During revision Faulkner changed the narration. What was initially a first-person narration by Stevens's nephew (Chuck, rather than Chick) becomes in the novella a limited third-person perspective from Chick's angle of vision.

Because "Knight's Gambit" was typeset from Faulkner's typescript, one might assume that there would be almost no issues for a new edition to address. Numerous errors, however, resulted from the desultory copyediting of the setting typescript. Many of these errors were missed on the galleys. Faulkner's setting typescript has handwritten corrections by both the author and a copy editor. Faulkner's changes are printed, while the copy editor uses cursive. The copy editor is neither thorough nor consistent. Faulkner often omitted commas in a series of modifying adjectives. At times the copy editor inserts commas but at other times allows series without commas to stand. I have removed the commas only when I was certain that they were the copy editor's (and not Faulkner's) addition. Sometimes the copy editor changes "like" to "as" or "as though," which detracts from the orality of the narrative voice; I have restored "like." Faulkner drops the final consonant on a number of words, which he or the copy editor catches in some instances, but not nearly all. For example, in the first edition toward the end of Part II, Gavin says to Chick, " 'Thirty minutes ago you were on your way to be. I couldn't even stop you'" (191). But a few pages earlier, prior to the return of the young Harriss woman on the opening evening of the story, Chick had said he needed to go not to *be* but to *bed*. Even though the typescript uses "be," this is clearly a typo that never should have made it into the first edition. I have corrected this and a number of other obvious typos.

Perhaps the clearest index of how poor the copyediting of "Knight's Gambit" was is the inconsistency of the supposed corrections to "sitting room." Faulkner himself was not always consistent, sometimes using "sitting room," other times "sitting-room," and once—as an adjective—"sittingroom." But whatever Faulkner used the copy editor often changed in an almost random fashion. After allowing "sitting room" to stand a couple of times, the copy editor decided (after seeing Faulkner's "sittingroom" as an adjective) to change "sitting-room" to "sittingroom," except when this individual misses certain subsequent instances and "sitting room" reappears uncorrected in the typescript and thus also in the first edition. I have decided always to restore Faulkner's choices with notations in the appendix that allow the reader to see the comedy of errors that "sitting room" becomes.

NOTES

1. In "Monk" Stevens does discover that Monk shot the warden at Terrel's instigation, but it's not clear that Terrel's act, while morally reprehensible, is in fact criminal. Stevens's discovery changes nothing, since Monk already has been executed for the murder, and Terrel is released by a corrupt parole board for a different crime.

2. For a brief summary of the mixed and often harsh critical response to *Knight's Gambit*, see Michael Wainwright (23–24). Wainwright himself approves of the title story only: "'Knight's Gambit' succeeds, whereas the rest of *Knight's Gambit* flounders, because Stevens's sustained submergence in his personal dilemmas—embroilments that shed light on human relations in general—appears only when Faulkner's interaction with chess consistently and cogently informs his art" (24–25). Twenty-one years earlier, John T. Irwin anticipated Wainwright's valuation of "Knight's Gambit." Juxtaposing his dismissal of the locked-room mystery "An Error in Chemistry" with his positive view of "Knight's Gambit," Irwin claims, "It is only when Faulkner pushes the detective story to the limits of the short story form that he is able to bend it to his own artistic will, as he did with the tale that gives the collection its title" (104). The success of "Knight's Gambit," for Irwin, is accomplished precisely by Faulkner's "annexing the imaginary of chess to the detective story" (115).

3. For example, Jerome Klinkowitz in a 1969 article argues, "The community-outlander theme is the heart and strength of the *Knight's Gambit* collection. In all of the stories it figures prominently, and each story becomes more technically perfect and artistically powerful as it centers more directly on that theme . . . outsider from without the community, outsider from within" (99). Klinkowitz's claim works best with "Smoke," "An Error in Chemistry," and "Knight's Gambit," because there are outlanders—respectively, Anse Holland, Joel Flint, and Harriss—men who marry into the community and proceed to outrage the norms of Jefferson and Yoknapatawpha County. Klinkowitz is less convincing presenting the outsider from within. As the seducer of Bookwright's daughter in "Tomorrow," Buck Thorpe may fit the bill, but in the other two stories, the outsider designation rests on the shoulders of characters with cognitive disabilities: the eponymous central character of "Monk" and Lonnie Grinnup in "Hand Upon the Waters." Neither outrages the community, and Lonnie in particular both offers and accepts hospitality. In his 1987 book, Michael Grimwood claims that *Knight's Gambit* is an anthology novel similar (if inferior) to *Go Down, Moses*. For Grimwood, Faulkner's expansion of his unpublished story, "Knight's Gambit," into a novella creates a conclusion to the collection that "revises, or reverses, the formula of the other stories" (213).

4. In setting the Vintage International, a few obvious typos in the first edition were corrected, but the fundamental problems with the first edition remain.

5. W. E. B. Du Bois argued in written appeals to various newspapers and magazines for the importance of capitalizing "Negro," but *The New York Times* rejected his request in 1926 before changing their house style to capitalize the word beginning in 1930 (Coleman).

6. For example, the Holland family is the McGannon family in the manuscript.

7. Faulkner was not consistent in how he marked dialogue where the speaker is interrupted or fails to complete a thought. Sometimes he uses a dash; sometimes, an

ellipsis. The manuscript twice uses dashes to conclude a piece of dialogue where all print versions use ellipses. *Harper's* uses three-dot ellipses everywhere, including at the end of a sentence of interrupted dialogue. *Doctor Martino* uses four-dot ellipses at the end of interrupted dialogue but with a space before the first period. The first edition uses a period and three-dot ellipses at the end of interrupted dialogue. Since the difference seems insignificant, I have retained the usage of the first edition.

8. Faulkner had already submitted work to *Scribner's* twenty-six times by October 1931, as Meriwether notes (254).

9. Faulkner's eight other *Scribner's* stories are "Dry September" (January 1931), "Spotted Horses" (June 1931), "Death Drag" (January 1932), "There Was a Queen" (January 1933), "Mule in the Yard" (August 1934), "Skirmish at Sartoris" (April 1935), "Fool About a Horse" (August 1936), and "The Brooch" (January 1936).

10. Prior to my discovery, the only available typescript material for "Monk" was a three-page carbon fragment at the University of Mississippi, part of the Rowan Oak Collection; these carbons, we now know, are from Faulkner's submitted typescript.

11. Charlotte also uses the word as Terrel does when she says, "But Jesus, Harry, how I have bitched it for you" (41).

12. The *Post* suspended publication in 1969, and its parent company, Curtis Publishing, was purchased by an Indianapolis businessman, Beurt SerVaas, who moved some material from the *Post*'s Philadelphia office to Indianapolis. SerVaas hoped that he could make money licensing the Norman Rockwell images but came to realize that there was still money to be made in maintaining some semblance of the magazine, and so in 1971 he began publishing the *Post* as a quarterly. The *Post* still exists and is published six times a year. The current managing editor, Andy Hollandbeck, told me in an email the magazine has some paper records from the 1930s and 1940s, but that these consist only of 1) physical copies of published issues, 2) some contracts, and 3) a card catalog that indexed submissions.

13. Fortunately, the *Post* made many fewer edits to the story's dialogue. Since the missing pages come from plot-driven, dialogue-heavy sections, I am able to move seamlessly back and forth between the later Virginia typescript and the first edition. In the appendix, I mark the moments where gaps in the typescript mean that this edition must depend on the first edition.

14. Faulkner of course did famously cut some sections focusing on Horace Benbow in *Sanctuary* after the novel had been set in galleys (likely because he found this material cut too close to the bone), but this is the exception that proves the rule. As his stories progress from earlier to later drafts, Faulkner only adds new material to what he had previously written, and if a sentence is rewritten, it only becomes more ornate.

15. In his list of extant documents for *Knight's Gambit* at the end of his introduction to the facsimile volume, *William Faulkner Manuscripts* 18: Knight's Gambit, Thomas L. McHaney notes the existence of an electrostatic copy of the final twenty-eight-page typescript (xi), which he learned of in a letter from James B. Meriwether (19 Aug 1986) detailing his research into Harold Ober files at Princeton (xiv). The University of Virginia's Alderman Library shortly thereafter acquired this copy (accession number 10428-c) on 1 November 1986. However, since the location and ownership of the original were

unknown when McHaney published his volume in 1987, he was unable to reproduce this final typescript but does include Faulkner's earlier twenty-two-page typescript.

WORKS CITED

Allen, Frederick Lewis. "Fifty Years of Scribner's Magazine." *Scribner's*, Jan. 1937, pp. 19–24.

Blotner, Joseph. *Faulkner: A Biography*. Vol. 2. Random House, 1974.

Blotner, Joseph, editor. *Selected Letters of William Faulkner*. Random House, 1977.

Coleman, Nancy. "Why We're Capitalizing Black." *New York Times*, Times Insider, 5 July 2020, https://www.nytimes.com/2020/07/05/insider/capitalized-black.html. Accessed 1 Jan. 2021.

Duvall, John N. "An Error in Canonicity, Or, A Fuller Story of Faulkner's Return to Print Culture, 1944–1951." *Faulkner and Print Culture*, edited by Jay Watson, Jaime Harker, and James G. Thomas, Jr. UP of Mississippi, 2017. 121–36.

Faulkner, William. *Knight's Gambit*. Random House, 1949.

Faulkner, William. *The Wild Palms [If I Forget Thee, Jerusalem]*. 1939. Vintage International, 1995.

Gaipa, Mark. "*Scribner's* Magazine: An Introduction to the MJP Edition, 1910–1922." *The Modernist Journals Project*. Brown University and the University of Tulsa. http://modjourn.org/render.php?id=mjp.2005.00.111&view=mjp_object.

Grimwood, Michael. *Heart in Conflict: Faulkner's Struggles with Vocation*. U of Georgia P, 1987.

Hefner, Brooks E., and Edward Timke, editors. *Circulating American Magazines*. James Madison University. http://sites.jmu.edu/circulating/. Accessed 16 Apr. 2021.

Irwin, John T. "*Knight's Gambit*: Poe, Faulkner, and the Tradition of the Detective Story." *Arizona Quarterly*, vol. 46, no. 4, 1990, pp. 95–116.

Klinkowitz, Jerome F. "The Thematic Unity of *Knight's Gambit*." *Critique*, vol. 11, no. 2, 1969, pp. 81–100.

McHaney, Thomas L. "Introduction." *William Faulkner Manuscripts 18*: "Knight's Gambit": *Typescripts and Miscellaneous Typescript Pages*, edited by Thomas L. McHaney. Garland, 1987. vii–xiv.

Meriwether, James B. "Faulkner's Correspondence with *Scribner's* Magazine." *Proof*, vol. 3, 1973, pp. 253–82.

Polk, Noel. "Where the Comma Goes: Editing Faulkner." *Children of the Dark House: Text and Context in Faulkner*. UP of Mississippi, 1996. 3–21.

Tomek, Beverly. "*Saturday Evening Post*" *Encyclopedia of Greater Philadelphia*. https://phil adelphiaencyclopedia.org/archive/saturday-evening-post/. Accessed 16 Apr. 2021.

Wainwright, Michael. *Faulkner's Gambit: Chess and Literature*. Palgrave Macmillan, 2011.

KNIGHT'S GAMBIT

SMOKE

Anselm Holland came to Jefferson many years ago. Where from, no one knew. But he was young then and a man of parts, or of presence at least, because within three years he had married the only daughter of a man who owned two thousand acres of some of the best land in the county, and he went to live in his father-in-law's house, where two years later his wife bore him twin sons and where a few years later still the father-in-law died and left Holland in full possession of the property, which was now in his wife's name. But even before that event, we in Jefferson had already listened to him talking a trifle more than loudly of 'my land, my crops'; and those of us whose fathers and grandfathers had been bred here looked upon him a little coldly and a little askance for a ruthless man and (from tales told about him by both white and Negro tenants and by others with whom he had dealings) for a violent one. But out of consideration for his wife and respect for his father-in-law, we treated him with courtesy if not with regard. So when his wife, too, died while the twin sons were still children, we believed that he was responsible, that her life had been worn out by the crass violence of an underbred outlander. And when his sons reached maturity and first one and then the other left home for good and all, we were not surprised. And when one day six months ago he was found dead, his foot fast in the stirrup of the saddled horse which he rode, and his body pretty badly broken where the horse had apparently dragged him through a rail fence (there still showed at the time on the horse's back and flanks the marks of the blows which he had dealt it in one of his fits of rage), there was none of us who was sorry, because a short time before that he had committed what to men of our town and time and thinking was the unpardonable outrage. On the day he died it was

3

learned that he had been digging up the graves in the family cemetery where his wife's people rested, among them the grave in which his wife had lain for thirty years. So the crazed, hate-ridden old man was buried among the graves which he had attempted to violate, and in the proper time his will was offered for probate. And we learned the substance of the will without surprise. We were not surprised to learn that even from beyond the grave he had struck one final blow at those alone whom he could now injure or outrage: his remaining flesh and blood.

At the time of their father's death the twin sons were forty. The younger one, Anselm, Junior, was said to have been the mother's favorite—perhaps because he was the one who was most like his father. Anyway, from the time of her death, while the boys were still children almost, we would hear of trouble between Old Anse and Young Anse, with Virginius, the other twin, acting as mediator and being cursed for his pains by both father and brother; he was that sort, Virginius was. And Young Anse was his sort too; in his late teens he ran away from home and was gone ten years. When he returned he and his brother were of age, and Anselm made formal demand upon his father that the land which we now learned was held by Old Anse only in trust, be divided and he—Young Anse—be given his share. Old Anse refused violently. Doubtless the request had been as violently made, because the two of them, Old Anse and Young Anse, were so much alike. And we heard that, strange to say, Virginius had taken his father's side. We heard that, that is. Because the land remained intact, and we heard how, in the midst of a scene of unparalleled violence even for them—a scene of such violence that the Negro servants all fled the house and scattered for the night—Young Anse departed, taking with him the team of mules which he did own; and from that day until his father's death, even after Virginius also had been forced to leave home, Anselm never spoke to his father and brother again. He did not leave the county this time, however. He just moved back into the hills ('where he can watch what the old man and Virginius are doing,' some of us said and all of us thought); and for the next fifteen years he lived alone in a dirt-floored, two-room cabin, like a hermit, doing his own cooking, coming into town behind his two mules not four times a year. Some time earlier he had been arrested and tried for making whiskey. He made no defense, refusing to plead either way, was fined both on the charge and for contempt of court, and flew into a rage exactly like his father when his brother Virginius offered to pay the fine. He tried to assault Virginius in the courtroom and went to the penitentiary at his own demand and was pardoned eight months later for good behavior and returned to his cabin—a dark, silent, aquiline-faced man whom both neighbors and strangers let severely alone.

The other twin, Virginius, stayed on, farming the land which his father had never done justice to even while he was alive. (They said of Old Anse, 'wherever he came from and whatever he was bred to be, it was not a farmer.' And so we said among ourselves, taking it to be true, 'That's the trouble between him and Young Anse: watching his father mistreat the land which his mother aimed for him and Virginius to have.') But Virginius stayed on. It could not have been much fun for him, and we said later that Virginius should have known that such an arrangement could not last. And then later than that we said, 'Maybe he did know.' Because that was Virginius. You didn't know what he was thinking at the time, any time. Old Anse and Young Anse were like water. Dark water, maybe; but men could see what they were about. But no man ever knew what Virginius was thinking or doing until afterward. We didn't even know what happened that time when Virginius, who had stuck it out alone for ten years while Young Anse was away, was driven away at last; he didn't tell it, not even to Granby Dodge, probably. But we knew Old Anse and we knew Virginius, and we could imagine it, about like this:

We watched Old Anse smoldering for about a year after Young Anse took his mules and went back into the hills. Then one day he broke out; maybe like this, 'You think that, now your brother is gone, you can just hang around and get it all, dont you?'

'I dont want it all,' Virginius said. 'I just want my share.'

'Ah,' Old Anse said. 'You'd like to have it parceled out right now too, would you? Claim like him it should have been divided up when you and him came of age.'

'I'd rather take a little of it and farm it right than to see it all in the shape it's in now,' Virginius said, still just, still mild—no man in the county ever saw Virginius lose his temper or even get ruffled, not even when Anselm tried to fight him in the courtroom about the fine.

'You would, would you?' Old Anse said. 'And me that's kept it work-ing at all, paying the taxes on it, while you and your brother have been putting money by every year, tax-free.'

'You know Anse never saved a nickel in his life,' Virginius said. 'Say what you want to about him, but dont accuse him of being forehanded.'

'Yes, by heaven! He was man enough to come out and claim what he thought was his and get out when he never got it. But you. You'll just hang around, waiting for me to go, with that damned meal mouth of yours. Pay me the taxes on your half back to the day your mother died, and take it.'

'No,' Virginius said. 'I wont do it.'

'No,' Old Anse said. 'No. Oh, no. Why spend your money for half of it when you can set down and get all of it some day without putting out a cent.' Then we imagined Old Anse (we thought of them sitting down until now, talking like two civilised men) rising, with his shaggy head and his heavy eyebrows. 'Get out of my house!' he said. But Virginius didn't move, didn't get up, watching his father. Old Anse came toward him, his hand raised. 'Get. Get out of my house. By heaven, I'll. . . . '

Virginius went, then. He didn't hurry, didn't run. He packed up his belongings (he would have more than Anse; quite a few little things) and went four or five miles to live with a cousin, the son of a remote kinsman of his mother. The cousin lived alone, on a good farm too, though now eaten up with mortgages, since the cousin was no farmer either, being half a stock-trader and half a lay preacher—a small, sandy, nondescript man whom you would not remember a minute after you looked at his face and then away—and probably no better at either of these than at farming. Without haste Virginius left, with none of his brother's foolish and violent finality; for which, strange to say, we thought none the less of Young Anse for showing, possessing. In fact, we always looked at Virginius a little askance too; he was a little too much master of himself. For it is human nature to trust quickest those who cannot depend on themselves. We called Virginius a deep one; we were not surprised when we learned how he had used his savings to disencumber the cousin's farm. And neither were we surprised when a year later we learned how Old Anse had refused to pay the taxes on his land and how, two days before the place would have gone delin-quent, the sheriff received anonymously in the mail cash to the exact penny of the Holland assessment. 'Trust Virginius,' we said, since we believed we knew that the money needed no name to it. The sheriff had notified Old Anse.

'Put it up for sale and be damned,' Old Anse said. 'If they think that all they have to do is set there waiting, the whole brood and biling of them. . . . '

The sheriff sent Young Anse word. 'It's not my land,' Young Anse sent back.

The sheriff notified Virginius. Virginius came to town and looked at the tax books himself. 'I got all I can carry myself, now,' he said. 'Of course, if he lets it go, I hope I can get it. But I dont know. A good farm like that wont last long or go cheap.' And that was all. No anger, no astonishment, no regret. But he was a deep one; we were not surprised when we learned how the sheriff had received that package of money, with the unsigned note: *Tax money for Anselm Holland farm. Send receipt to Anselm Holland, Senior.* 'Trust Virginius,' we said. We thought about Virginius quite a lot during the next year, out there in a strange house, farming strange land, watching the farm and the house where he was born and that was rightfully his going to ruin. For the old man was letting it go completely now: year by year the good broad fields were going back to jungle and gully, though still each January the sheriff received that anonymous money in the mail and sent the receipt to Old Anse, because the old man had stopped coming to town altogether now, and the very house was falling down about his head, and nobody save Virginius ever stopped there. Five or six times a year he would ride up to the front porch, and the old man would come out and bellow at him in savage and violent vituperation, Virginius taking it quietly, talking to the few remaining Negroes once he had seen with his own eyes that his father was all right, then riding away again. But nobody else ever stopped there, though now and then from a distance someone would see the old man going about the mournful and shaggy fields on the old white horse which was to kill him.

Then last summer we learned that he was digging up the graves in the cedar grove where five generations of his wife's people rested. A Negro reported it, and the county health officer went out there and found the white horse tied in the grove, and the old man himself came out of the grove with a shotgun. The health officer returned, and two days later a deputy went out there and found the old man lying beside the horse, his foot fast in the stirrup, and on the horse's rump the savage marks of the stick—not a switch: a stick—where it had been struck again and again and again.

So they buried him, among the graves which he had violated. Virginius and the cousin came to the funeral. They were the funeral, in fact. For Anse, Junior, didn't come. Nor did he come near the place later, though Virginius stayed long enough to lock the house and pay the Negroes off. But he too went back to the cousin's, and in due time Old Anse's will was offered for probate to Judge Dukinfield. The substance of the will was no secret; we all learned of it. Regular it was, and we were surprised neither at its regularity nor at its substance nor its wording: . . . *with the exception of these two bequests, I give and bequeath . . . my property to my elder son Virginius, provided it be proved to the satisfaction of the . . . Chancellor that it was the said Virginius who has been paying the taxes on my land, the . . . Chancellor to be the sole and unchallenged judge of the proof.*

The other two bequests were:

To my younger son Anselm, I give . . . two full sets of mule harness, with the condition that this . . . harness be used by . . . Anselm to make one visit to my grave. Otherwise this . . . harness to become and remain part . . . of my property as described above.

To my cousin-in-law Granby Dodge I give . . . one dollar in cash, to be used by him for the purchase of a hymn book or hymn books, as a token of my gratitude for his having fed and lodged my son Virginius since . . . Virginius quitted my roof.

That was the will. And we watched and listened to hear or see what Young Anse would say or do. And we heard and saw nothing. And we watched to see what Virginius would do. And he did nothing. Or we didn't know what he was doing, what he was thinking. But that was Virginius. Because it was all finished then, anyway. All he had to do was to wait until Judge Dukinfield validated the will, then Virginius could give Anse his half—if he intended to do this. We were divided there. 'He and Anse never had any trouble,' some said. 'Virginius never had any trouble with anybody,' others said. 'If you go by that token, he will have to divide that farm with the whole county.' 'But it was Virginius that tried to pay Anse's fine that time,' the first ones said. 'And it was Virginius that sided with his father when Young Anse wanted to divide the land, too,' the second ones said.

So we waited and we watched. We were watching Judge Dukinfield now; it was suddenly as if the whole thing had sifted into his hands; as though he sat godlike above the vindictive and jeering laughter of that old man who even underground would not die, and above these two irreconcilable brothers who for fifteen years had been the same as dead to each other. But we thought that in his last coup, Old Anse had overreached himself; that in choosing Judge Dukinfield, the old man's own fury had checkmated him; because in Judge Dukinfield we believed that Old Anse had chosen the one man among us with sufficient probity and honor and good sense—that sort of probity and honor which has never had time to become confused and self-doubting with too much learning in the law. The very fact that the validating of what was a simple enough document appeared to be taking him an overlong time, was to us but fresh proof that Judge Dukinfield was the one man among us who believed that justice is fifty percent legal knowledge and fifty percent unhaste and confidence in himself and in God.

So as the expiration of the legal period drew near, we watched Judge Dukinfield as he went daily between his home and his office in the courthouse yard. Deliberate and unhurried he moved—a widower of sixty and more, portly, white-headed, with an erect and dignified carriage which the Negroes called 'rear-backted.' He had been appointed Chancellor seventeen years ago; he possessed little knowledge of the law and a great deal of hard common sense; and for thirteen years now no man had opposed him for reelection, and even those who would be most enraged by his air of bland and affable condescension voted for him on occasion with a kind of childlike confidence and trust. So we watched him without impatience, knowing that what he finally did would be right, not because he did it, but because he would not permit himself or anyone else to do anything until it was right. So each morning we would see him cross the square at exactly ten minutes past eight oclock and go to the courthouse, where the Negro janitor had preceded him by exactly ten minutes, with the clocklike precision with which the block signal presages the arrival of the train, to open the office for the day. The Judge would enter the office, and the Negro would take his position in a wire-mended splint chair in the flagged passage which separated the office from the courthouse proper where he would sit all day long and doze, as he had done for seventeen years.

Then at five in the afternoon the Negro would wake and enter the office and perhaps wake the Judge too, who had lived long enough to have learned that the onus of any business is usually in the hasty minds of those theoreticians who have no business of their own; and then we would watch them cross the square again in single file and go on up the street toward home, the two of them, eyes front and about fifteen feet apart, walking so erect that the two frock coats made by the same tailor and to the Judge's measure fell from the two pairs of shoulders in single boardlike planes, without intimation of waist or of hips.

Then one afternoon, a little after five oclock, men began to run suddenly across the square, toward the courthouse. Other men saw them and ran too, their feet heavy on the paving, among the wagons and the cars, their voices tense, urgent, 'What? What is it?' 'Judge Dukinfield,' the word went; and they ran on and entered the flagged passage between the courthouse and the office, where the old Negro in his castoff frock coat stood beating his hands on the air. They passed him and ran into the office. Behind the table the Judge sat, leaning a little back in his chair, quite comfortable. His eyes were open, and he had been shot neatly once through the bridge of the nose, so that he appeared to have three eyes in a row. It was a bullet, yet no man about the square that day, or the old Negro who had sat all day long in the chair in the passage, had heard any sound.

It took Gavin Stevens a long time, that day—he and the little brass box. Because the Grand Jury could not tell at first what he was getting at—if any man in that room that day, the jury, the two brothers, the cousin, the old Negro, could tell. So at last the Foreman asked him point blank:

'Is it your contention, Gavin, that there is a connection between Mr Holland's will and Judge Dukinfield's murder?'

'Yes,' the county attorney said. 'And I'm going to contend more than that.'

They watched him: the jury, the two brothers. The old Negro and the cousin alone were not looking at him. In the last week the Negro had apparently aged fifty years. He had assumed public office concurrently with the Judge; indeed, because of that fact, since he had served the Judge's family for longer than some of us could remember. He was older than the Judge, though until that afternoon a week ago he had looked

forty years younger—a wizened figure, shapeless in the voluminous
frock coat, who reached the office ten minutes ahead of the Judge and
opened it and swept it and dusted the table without disturbing an object
upon it, all with a skillful slovenliness that was fruit of seventeen years
of practice, and then repaired to the wire-bound chair in the passage
to sleep. He seemed to sleep, that is. (The only other way to reach the
office was by means of the narrow private stair which led down from
the courtroom, used only by the presiding judge during court term,
who even then had to cross the passage and pass within eight feet of
the Negro's chair unless he followed the passage to where it made an
L beneath the single window in the office, and climbed through that
window.) For no man or woman had ever passed that chair without
seeing the wrinkled eyelids of its occupant open instantaneously upon
the brown, irisless eyes of extreme age. Now and then we would stop
and talk to him, to hear his voice roll in rich mispronunciation of the
orotund and meaningless legal phraseology which he had picked up
unawares, as he might have disease germs, and which he reproduced
with an ex-cathedra profundity that caused more than one of us to
listen to the Judge himself with affectionate amusement. But for all
that he was old; he forgot our names at times and confused us with one
another; and confusing our faces and our generations too, he waked
sometimes from his light slumber to challenge callers who were not
there, who had been dead for many years. But no one had ever been
known to pass him unawares.

But the others in the room watched Stevens—the jury about the
table, the two brothers sitting at opposite ends of the bench, with their
dark, identical, aquiline faces, their arms folded in identical attitudes.
'Are you contending that Judge Dukinfield's slayer is in this room?' the
Foreman asked.

The county attorney looked at them, at the faces watching him. 'I'm
going to contend more than that,' he said.

'Contend?' Anselm, the younger twin, said. He sat alone at his end of
the bench, with the whole span of bench between him and the brother
to whom he had not spoken in fifteen years, watching Stevens with a
hard, furious, unwinking glare.

'Yes,' Stevens said. He stood at the end of the table. He began to
speak, looking at no one in particular, speaking in an easy, anecdotal

tone, telling what we already knew, referring now and then to the other twin, Virginius, for corroboration. He told about Young Anse and his father. His tone was fair, pleasant. He seemed to be making a case for the living, telling about how Young Anse left home in anger, in natural anger at the manner in which his father was treating that land which had been his mother's and half of which was at the time rightfully his. His tone was quite just, specious, frank; if anything, a little partial to Anselm, Junior. That was it. Because of that seeming partiality, that seeming glozing, there began to emerge a picture of Young Anse that was damning him to something which we did not then know, damned him because of that very desire for justice and affection for his dead mother, warped by the violence which he had inherited from the very man who had wronged him. And the two broth- ers sitting there, with that space of friction-smooth plank between them, the younger watching Stevens with that leashed, violent glare, the elder as intently, but with a face unfathomable. Stevens now told how Young Anse left in anger, and how a year later Virginius, the quieter one, the calmer one, who had tried more than once to keep peace between them, was driven away in turn. And again he drew a specious, frank picture: of the brothers separated, not by the living father, but by what each had inherited from him; and drawn together, bred together, by that land which was not only rightfully theirs, but in which their mother's bones lay.

'So there they were, watching from a distance that good land going to ruin, the house in which they were born and their mother was born falling to pieces because of a crazed old man who attempted at the last, when he had driven them away and couldn't do anything else to them, to deprive them of it for good and all by letting it be sold for nonpay- ment of taxes. But somebody foiled him there, someone with foresight enough and self-control enough to keep his own counsel about what wasn't anybody else's business anyway so long as the taxes were paid. So then all they had to do was to wait until the old man died. He was old anyway and, even if he had been young, the waiting would not have been very hard for a self-controlled man, even if he did not know the contents of the old man's will. Though that waiting wouldn't have been so easy for a quick, violent man, especially if the violent man happened to know or suspect the substance of the will and was satisfied and, further, knew himself to have been irrevocably wronged; to have had citizenship and good name robbed through the agency of a man who had already despoiled him and had driven him out of the best years of his life among men, to live like a hermit in a hill cabin. A man like that would have neither the time nor the inclination to bother much with either waiting for something or not waiting for it.'

They stared at him, the two brothers. They might have been carved in stone, save for Anselm's eyes. Stevens talked quietly, not looking at anyone in particular. He had been county attorney for almost as long as Judge Dukinfield had been chancellor. He was a Harvard graduate: a loose-jointed man with a mop of untidy iron-gray hair, who could discuss Einstein with college professors and who spent whole afternoons among the squatting men against the walls of country stores, talking to them in their idiom. He called these his vacations.

'Then in time the father died, as any man who possessed self-control and foresight would have known. And his will was submitted for probate; and even folks way back in the hills heard what was in it, heard how at last that mistreated land would belong to its rightful owner. Or owners, since Anse Holland knows as well as we do that Virge would no more take more than his rightful half, will or no will, now than he would have when his father gave him the chance. Anse knows that because he knows that he would do the same thing—give Virge his half—if he were Virge. Because they were both born to Anselm Holland, but they were born to Cornelia Mardis too. But even if Anse didn't know, believe, that, he would know that the land which had been his mother's and in which her bones now lie would now be treated right. So maybe that night when he heard that his father was dead, maybe for the first time since Anse was a child, since before his mother died maybe and she would come upstairs at night and look into the room where he was asleep and go away: maybe for the first time since then, Anse slept. Because it was all vindicated then, you see: the outrage, the injustice, the lost good name, and the penitentiary stain—all gone now like a dream. To be forgotten now, because it was all right. By that time, you see, he had got used to being a hermit, to being alone; he could not have changed after that long. He was happier where he was, alone back there. And now to know that it was all past like a bad dream, and that the land, his mother's land, her heritage and her mausoleum, was now in the hands of the one man whom he could and would trust, even though they did not speak to each other. Dont you see?'

We watched him as we sat about the table which had not been disturbed since the day Judge Dukinfield died, upon which lay still the objects which had been, next to the pistol muzzle, his last sight on earth, and with which we were all familiar for years—the papers, the foul inkwell, the stubby pen to which the Judge clung, the small brass box which had been his superfluous paper weight. At their opposite ends of the wooden bench, the twin brothers watched Stevens, motionless, intent.

'No, we dont see,' the Foreman said. 'What are you getting at? What is the connection between all this and Judge Dukinfield's murder?'

'Here it is,' Stevens said. 'Judge Dukinfield was validating that will when he was killed. It was a queer will; but we all expected that of Mr Holland. But it was all regular, the beneficiaries are all satisfied; we all know that half of that land is Anse's the minute he wants it. So the will is all right. Its probation should have been just a formality. Yet Judge Dukinfield had had it in abeyance for over two weeks when he died. And so that man who thought that all he had to do was to wait—'

'What man?' the Foreman said.

'Wait,' Stevens said. 'All that man had to do was wait. But it wasn't the waiting that worried him, who had already waited fifteen years. That wasn't it. It was something else, which he learned (or remembered) when it was too late, which he should not have forgotten; because he is a shrewd man, a man of self-control and foresight; self-control enough to wait fifteen years for his chance, and foresight enough to have prepared for all the incalculables except one: his own memory. And when it was too late, he remembered that there was another man who would also know what he had forgotten about. And that other man who would know it was Judge Dukinfield. And that thing which he would also know was that that horse could not have killed Mr Holland.'

When his voice ceased there was no sound in the room. The jury sat quietly about the table, looking at Stevens. Anselm turned his leashed, furious face and looked once at his brother, then he looked at Stevens again, leaning a little forward now. Virginius had not moved; there was no change in his grave, intent expression. Between him and the wall the cousin sat. His hands lay on his lap and his head was bowed a little, as though he were in church. We knew of him only that he was some kind of an itinerant preacher, and that now and then he gathered up strings of scrubby horses and mules and took them somewhere and swapped or sold them. Because he was a man of infrequent speech who in his dealings with men betrayed such an excruciating shyness and lack of confidence that we pitied him, with that kind of pitying disgust you feel for a crippled worm, dreading even to put him to the agony of saying 'yes' or 'no' to a question. But we heard how on Sundays, in the pulpits of country churches, he became a different man, changed; his voice then timbrous and moving and assured out of all proportion to his nature and his size.

'Now, imagine the waiting,' Stevens said, 'with that man knowing what was going to happen before it had happened, knowing at last that the reason why nothing was happening, why that will had apparently gone into Judge Dukinfield's office and then dropped out of the world, out of the knowledge of man, was because he had forgotten something which he should not have forgotten. And that was that Judge Dukinfield also knew that Mr Holland was not the man who beat that horse. He knew that Judge Dukinfield knew that the man who struck that horse with that stick so as to leave marks on its back was the man who killed Mr Holland first and then hooked his foot in that stirrup and struck that horse with a stick to make it bolt. But the horse didn't bolt. The man knew beforehand that it would not; he had known for years that it would not, but he had forgotten that. Because while it was still a colt it had been beaten so severely once that ever since, even at the sight of a switch in the rider's hand, it would lie down on the ground, as Mr Holland knew, and as all who were close to Mr Holland's family knew. So it just lay down on top of Mr Holland's body. But that was all right too, at first; that was just as well. That's what that man thought for the next week or so, lying in his bed at night and waiting, who had already waited fifteen years. Because even then, when it was too late and he realised that he had made a mistake, he had not even then remembered all that he should never have forgotten. Then he remembered that too, when it was too late, after the body had been found and the marks of the stick on the horse seen and remarked and it was too late to remove them. They were probably gone from the horse by then, anyway. But there was only one tool he could use to remove them from men's minds.

Imagine him then, his terror, his outrage, his feeling of having been tricked by something beyond retaliation: that furious desire to turn time back for just one minute, to undo or to complete when it is too late. Because the last thing which he remembered when it was too late was that Mr Holland had bought that horse from Judge Dukinfield, the man who was sitting here at this table, passing on the validity of a will giving away two thousand acres of some of the best land in the county. And he waited, since he had but one tool that would remove those stick marks, and nothing happened. And nothing happened, and he knew why. And he waited as long as he dared, until he believed that there was more at stake than a few roods and squares of earth. So what else could he do but what he did?'

His voice had hardly ceased before Anselm was speaking. His voice was harsh, abrupt. 'You're wrong,' he said.

As one, we looked at him where he sat forward on the bench, in his muddy boots and his worn overalls, glaring at Stevens; even Virginius turned and looked at him for an instant. The cousin and the old Negro alone had not moved. They did not seem to be listening. 'Where am I wrong?' Stevens said.

But Anselm did not answer. He glared at Stevens. 'Will Virginius get the place in spite of . . . of. . . . '

'In spite of what?' Stevens said.

'Whether he . . . that. . . . '

'You mean your father? Whether he died or was murdered?'

'Yes,' Anselm said.

'Yes. You and Virge get the land whether the will stands up or not, provided, of course, that Virge divides with you if it does. But the man that killed your father wasn't certain of that and he didn't dare to ask. Because he didn't want that. He wanted Virge to have it all. That's why he wants that will to stand.'

'You're wrong,' Anselm said, in that harsh, sudden tone. 'I killed him. But it wasn't because of that damned farm. Now bring on your sheriff.'

And now it was Stevens who, gazing steadily at Anselm's furious face, said quietly: 'And I say that you are wrong, Anse.'

For some time after that we who watched and listened dwelt in anti-climax, in a dreamlike state in which we seemed to know beforehand what was going to happen, aware at the same time that it didn't matter because we should soon wake. It was as though we were outside of time, watching events from outside; still outside of and beyond time since that first instant when we looked again at Anselm as though we had never seen him before. There was a sound, a slow, sighing sound, not loud; maybe of relief—something. Perhaps we were all thinking how Anse's nightmare must be really over at last; it was as though we too had rushed suddenly back to where he lay as a child in his bed and the mother who they said was partial to him, whose heritage had been lost to him, and even the very resting place of her tragic and long quiet dust outraged, coming in to look at him for a moment before going away again. Far back down time that was, straight though it be. And straight though that corridor was, the boy who had lain unawares in that bed had got lost in it, as we all do, must, ever shall; that boy was as dead as any other of his blood in that violated cedar grove, and the man at whom we looked, we looked at across the irrevocable chasm, with pity perhaps, but not with mercy. So it took the sense of Stevens' words about as long to penetrate to us as it did to Anse; he had to repeat himself, 'Now I say that you are wrong, Anse.'

'What?' Anse said. Then he moved. He did not get up, yet somehow he seemed to lunge suddenly, violently. 'You're a liar. You—'

'You're wrong, Anse. You didn't kill your father. The man who killed your father was the man who could plan and conceive to kill that old man who sat here behind this table every day, day after day, until an old Negro would come in and wake him and tell him it was time to go home—a man who never did man, woman, or child aught but good as he believed that he and God saw it. It wasn't you that killed your father. You demanded of him what you believed was yours, and when he refused to give it, you left, went away, never spoke to him again. You heard how he was mistreating the place but you held your peace, because the land was just "that damned farm." You held your peace until you heard how a crazy man was digging up the graves where your mother's flesh and blood and your own was buried. Then, and then only, you came to him, to remonstrate. But you were never a man to remonstrate, and he was never a man to listen to it. So you found him there, in the grove, with the shotgun. I dont even expect you paid much attention to the shotgun. I reckon you just took it away from him and whipped him with your bare hands and left him there beside the horse; maybe you thought that he was dead. Then somebody happened to pass there after you were gone and found him; maybe that someone had been there all the time, watching. Somebody that wanted him dead too; not in anger and outrage, but by calculation. For profit, by a will, maybe. So he came there and he found what you had left and he finished it: hooked your father's foot in that stirrup and tried to beat that horse into bolting to make it look well, forgetting in his haste what he should not have forgot. But it wasn't you. Because you went back home, and when you heard what had been found, you said nothing. Because you thought something at the time which you did not even say to yourself. And when you heard what was in the will you believed that you knew. And you were glad then. Because you had lived alone until youth and wanting things were gone out of you; you just wanted to be quiet as you wanted your mother's dust to be quiet. And besides, what could land and position among men be to a man without citizenship, with a blemished name?'

We listened quietly while Stevens' voice died in that little room in which no air ever stirred, no draft ever blew because of its position, its natural lee beneath the courthouse wall.

'It wasn't you that killed your father or Judge Dukinfield either, Anse. Because if that man who killed your father had remembered in time that Judge Dukinfield once owned that horse, Judge Dukinfield would be alive to-day.'

We breathed quietly, sitting about the table behind which Judge Dukinfield had been sitting when he looked up into the pistol. The table had not been disturbed. Upon it still lay the papers, the pens, the inkwell, the small, curiously chased brass box which his daughter had fetched him from Europe twelve years ago—for what purpose neither she nor the Judge knew, since it would have been suitable only for bath salts or tobacco, neither of which the Judge used—and which he had kept for a paper weight, that, too, superfluous where no draft ever blew. But he kept it there on the table, and all of us knew it, had watched him toy with it while he talked, opening the spring lid and watching it snap viciously shut at the slightest touch.

When I look back on it now, I can see that the rest of it should not have taken as long as it did. It seems to me now that we must have

known all the time; I still seem to feel that kind of disgust without
mercy which after all does the office of pity, as when you watch a soft
worm impaled on a pin, when you feel that retching revulsion—would
even use your naked palm in place of nothing at all, thinking, 'Go on.
Mash it. Smear it. Get it over with.' But that was not Stevens' plan.
Because he had a plan, and we realised afterward that, since he could
not convict the man, the man himself would have to. And it was unfair,
the way he did it; later we told him so. ('Ah,' he said. 'But isn't justice
always unfair? Isn't it always composed of injustice and luck and plati-
tude in unequal parts?')

But anyway we could not see yet what he was getting at as he began
to speak again in that tone—easy, anecdotal, his hand resting now on
the brass box. But men are moved so much by preconceptions. It is
not realities, circumstances, that astonish us; it is the concussion of
what we should have known, if we had only not been so busy believing what we discover later we had taken for the truth for no other
reason than that we happened to be believing it at the moment. He
was talking about smoking again, about how a man never really enjoys
tobacco until he begins to believe that it is harmful to him, and how
non-smokers miss one of the greatest pleasures in life for a man of
sensibility: the knowledge that he is succumbing to a vice which can
injure himself alone.

'Do you smoke, Anse?' he said.

'No,' Anse said.

'You dont either, do you, Virge?'

'No,' Virginius said. 'None of us ever did—father or Anse or me. We
heired it, I reckon.'

'A family trait,' Stevens said. 'Is it in your mother's family too? Is it
in your branch, Granby?'

The cousin looked at Stevens, for less than a moment. Without
moving he appeared to writhe slowly within his neat, shoddy suit. 'No,
sir. I never used it.'

'Maybe because you are a preacher,' Stevens said. The cousin didn't
answer. He looked at Stevens again with his mild, still, hopelessly
abashed face. 'I've always smoked,' Stevens said. 'Ever since I finally
recovered from being sick at it at the age of fourteen. That's a long
time, long enough to have become finicky about tobacco. But most

smokers are, despite the psychologists and the standardised tobacco. Or maybe it's just cigarettes that are standardised. Or maybe they are just standardised to laymen, non-smokers. Because I have noticed how non-smokers are apt to go off half cocked about tobacco, the same as the rest of us go off half cocked about what we do not ourselves use, are not familiar with, since man is led by his pre- (or mis-) conceptions. Because you take a man who sells tobacco even though he does not use it himself, who watches customer after customer tear open the pack and light the cigarette just across the counter from him. You ask him if all tobacco smells alike, if he cannot distinguish one kind from another by the smell. Or maybe it's the shape and the color of the package it comes in; because even the psychologists have not yet told us just where seeing stops and smelling begins, or hearing stops and seeing begins. Any lawyer can tell you that.'

Again the Foreman checked him. We had listened quietly enough, but I think we all felt that to keep the murderer confused was one thing, but that we, the jury, were another. 'You should have done all this investigating before you called us together,' the Foreman said. 'Even if this be evidence, what good will it do without the body of the murderer be apprehended? Conjecture is all well enough—'

'All right,' Stevens said. 'Let me conjecture a little more, and if I dont seem to progress any, you tell me so, and I'll stop my way and do yours. And I expect that at first you are going to call this taking a right smart of liberty even with conjecture. But we found Judge Dukinfield dead, shot between the eyes, in this chair behind this table. That's not conjecture. And Uncle Job was sitting all day long in that chair in the passage, where anyone who entered this room (unless he came down the private stair from the courtroom and climbed through the window) would have to pass within three feet of him. And no man that we know of has passed Uncle Job in that chair in seventeen years. That's not conjecture.'

'Then what is your conjecture?'

But Stevens was talking about tobacco again, about smoking. 'I stopped in West's drug store last week for some tobacco, and he told me about a man who was particular about his smoking also. While he was getting my tobacco from the case, he reached out a box of cigarettes and handed it to me. It was dusty, faded, like he had had it a long time, and he told me how a drummer had left two of them with him years ago. "Ever smoke them?" he said. "No," I said. "They must be city cigarettes." Then he told me how he had sold the other package just that day. He said he was behind the counter, with the newspaper spread on it, sort of half reading the paper and half keeping the store while the clerk was gone to dinner. And he said he never heard or saw the man at all until he looked up and the man was just across the counter, so close that it made him jump. A smallish man in city clothes, West said, wanting a kind of cigarette that West had never heard of. "I haven't got that kind," West said. "I dont carry them." "Why dont you carry them?" the man said. "I have no sale for them," West said. And he told about the man in his city clothes, with a face like a shaved wax doll, and eyes with a still way of looking and a voice with a still way of talking. Then West said he saw the man's eyes and he looked at his nostrils, and then he knew what was wrong. Because the man was full of dope right then. "I dont have any calls for them," West said. "What am I trying to do now?" the man said. "Trying to sell you flypaper?" Then the man bought the other package of cigarettes and went out. And West said that he was mad and he was sweating too, like he wanted to vomit, he said. He said to me, "If I had some devilment I was scared to do myself, you know what I'd do? I'd give that fellow about ten dollars and I'd tell him where the devilment was and tell him not to never speak to me again. When he went out, I felt just exactly like that. Like I was going to be sick."'

Stevens looked about at us; he paused for a moment. We watched him. 'He came here from somewhere in a car, a big roadster, that city man did. That city man that ran out of his own kind of tobacco.' He paused again, and then he turned his head slowly and he looked at Virginius Holland. It seemed like a full minute that we watched them looking steadily at one another. 'And a nigger told me that that big car was parked in Virginius Holland's barn the night before Judge Dukinfield was killed.' And for another time we watched the two of them looking steadily at each other, with no change of expression on either face. Stevens spoke in a tone quiet, speculative, almost musing. 'Someone tried to keep him from coming out here in that car, that big car that anyone who saw it once would remember and recognise. Maybe that someone wanted to forbid him to come in it, threaten him. Only the man that Doctor West sold those cigarettes to wouldn't have stood for very much threatening.'

'Meaning me, by "someone," ' Virginius said. He did not move or turn away his steady stare from Stevens' face. But Anselm moved. He turned his head and he looked at his brother, once. It was quite quiet, yet when the cousin spoke we could not hear or understand him at once; he had spoken but one time since we entered the room and Stevens locked the door. His voice was faint; again and without moving he appeared to writhe faintly beneath his clothes. He spoke with that abashed faintness, that excruciating desire for effacement with which we were all familiar.

'That fellow you're speaking of, he come to see me,' Dodge said. 'Stopped to see me. He stopped at the house about dark that night and said he was hunting to buy up little-built horses to use for this—this game—'

'Polo?' Stevens said. The cousin had not looked at anyone while he spoke; it was as though he were speaking to his slowly moving hands upon his lap.

'Yes, sir. Virginius was there. We talked about horses. Then the next morning he took his car and went on. I never had anything that suited him. I dont know where he come from or where he went.'

'Or who else he came to see,' Stevens said. 'Or what else he came to do. You cant say that.'

Dodge didn't answer. It was not necessary, and again he had fled behind the shape of his effacement like a small and weak wild creature into a hole.

'That's my conjecture,' Stevens said.

And then we should have known. It was there to be seen, bald as a naked hand. We should have felt it—the someone in that room who felt what Stevens had called that horror, that outrage, that furious desire to turn time back for a second, to unsay, to undo. But maybe the someone had not felt it yet, had not yet felt the blow, the impact, as for a second or two a man may be unaware that he has been shot. Because now it was Virge that spoke, abruptly, harshly, 'How are you going to prove that?'

'Prove what, Virge?' Stevens said. Again they looked at each other, quiet, hard, like two boxers. Not swordsmen, but boxers; or at least with pistols. 'Who it was who hired that gorilla, that thug, down here from Memphis? I dont have to prove that. He told that. On the way back to Memphis he ran down a child at Battenburg (he was still full of dope; likely he had taken another shot of it when he finished his job here), and they caught him and locked him up and when the dope began to wear off he told where he had been, whom he had been to see, sitting in the cell in the jail there, jerking and snarling, after they had taken the pistol with the silencer on it away from him.'

'Ah,' Virginius said. 'That's nice. So all you've got to do is to prove that he was in this room that day. And how will you do that? Give that old nigger another dollar and let him remember again?'

But Stevens did not appear to be listening. He stood at the end of the table, between the two groups, and while he talked now he held the brass box in his hand, turning it, looking at it, talking in that easy, musing tone. 'You all know the peculiar attribute which this room has. How no draft ever blows in it. How when there has been smoking here on a Saturday, say, the smoke will still be here on Monday morning when Uncle Job opens the door, lying against the baseboard there like a dog asleep, kind of. You've all seen that.'

We were sitting a little forward now, like Anse, watching Stevens.

'Yes,' the Foreman said. 'We've seen that.'

'Yes,' Stevens said, still as though he were not listening, turning the closed box this way and that in his hand. 'You asked me for my conjecture. Here it is. But it will take a conjecturing man to do it—a man who could walk up to a merchant standing behind his counter, reading a newspaper with one eye and the other eye on the door for customers, before the merchant knew he was there. A city man, who insisted on city cigarettes. So this man left that store and crossed to the courthouse and entered and went on upstairs, as anyone might have done. Perhaps a dozen men saw him; perhaps twice that many did not look at him at all, since there are two places where a man does not look at faces: in the sanctuary of civil law, and in public lavatories. So he entered the courtroom and came down the private stair and into the passage, and saw Uncle Job asleep in his chair. So maybe he followed the passage, and climbed through the window behind Judge Dukinfield's back. Or maybe he walked right past Uncle Job, coming up from behind, you see. And to pass within eight feet of a man asleep in a chair would not be very hard for a man who could walk up to a merchant leaning on the counter of his own store. Perhaps he even lighted the cigarette from the pack that West had sold him before even Judge Dukinfield knew that he was in the room. Or perhaps the Judge was asleep in his chair, as he sometimes was. So perhaps the man stood there and finished the cigarette and watched the smoke pour slowly across the table and bank up against the wall, thinking about the easy money, the easy hicks, before he even drew the pistol. And it made less noise than the striking of the match which lighted the cigarette, since he had guarded so against noise that he forgot about silence. And then he went back as he came, and the dozen men and the two dozen saw him and did not see him, and at five that afternoon Uncle Job came in to wake the Judge and tell him it was time to go home. Isn't that right, Uncle Job?'

The old Negro looked up. 'I looked after him, like I promised Mistis,' he said. 'And I worried with him, like I promised Mistis I would. And I come in here and I thought at first he was asleep, like he sometimes—'

'Wait,' Stevens said. 'You came in and you saw him in the chair, as always, and you noticed the smoke against the wall behind the table as you crossed the floor. Wasn't that what you told me?'

Sitting in his mended chair, the old Negro began to cry. He looked like an old monkey, weakly crying black tears, brushing at his face with the back of a gnarled hand that shook with age, with something. 'I come in here many's the time in the morning, to clean up. It would be laying there, that smoke, and him that never smoked a lick in his life coming in and sniffing with that high nose of hisn and saying, "Well, Job, we sholy smoked out that corpus juris coon last night." '

'No,' Stevens said. 'Tell about how the smoke was there behind that table that afternoon when you came to wake him to go home, when there hadn't anybody passed you all that day except Mr Virge Holland yonder. And Mr Virge dont smoke, and the Judge didn't smoke. But that smoke was there. Tell what you told me.'

'It was there. And I thought that he was asleep like always, and I went to wake him up—'

'And this little box was sitting on the edge of the table where he had been handling it while he talked to Mr Virge, and when you reached your hand to wake him—'

'Yes, sir. It jumped off the table and I thought that he was asleep—'

'The box jumped off the table. And it made a noise and you wondered why that didn't wake the Judge, and you looked down at where the box was lying on the floor in the smoke, with the lid open, and you thought that it was broken. And so you reached your hand down to see, because the Judge liked it because Miss Emma had brought it back to him from across the water, even if he didn't need it for a paper weight in his office. So you closed the lid and set it on the table again. And then you found that the Judge was more than asleep.'

He ceased. We breathed quietly, hearing ourselves breathe. Stevens seemed to watch his hand as it turned the box slowly this way and that. He had turned a little from the table in talking with the old Negro, so that now he faced the bench rather than the jury, the table. 'Uncle Job calls this a gold box. Which is as good a name as any. Better than most. Because all metal is about the same; it just happens that some folks want one kind more than another. But it all has certain general attributes, likenesses. One of them is, that whatever is shut up in a metal box will stay in it unchanged for a longer time than in a wooden or paper box. You can shut up smoke, for instance, in a metal box with a tight lid like this one, and even a week later it will still be there. And not only that, a chemist or a smoker or tobacco seller like Doctor West can tell what made the smoke, what kind of tobacco, particularly if it happens to be a strange brand, a kind not sold in Jefferson, and of which he just happened to have two packs and remembered who he sold one of them to.'

We did not move. We just sat there and heard the man's urgent stumbling feet on the floor, then we saw him strike the box from Stevens' hand. But we were not particularly watching him, even then. Like him we watched the box bounce into two pieces as the lid snapped off, and emit a fading vapor which dissolved sluggishly away. As one we leaned across the table and looked down upon the sandy and hopeless mediocrity of Granby Dodge's head as he knelt on the floor and flapped at the fading smoke with his hands.

'But I still dont . . . ' Virginius said. We were outside now, in the courthouse yard, the five of us, blinking a little at one another as though we had just come out of a cave.

'You've got a will, haven't you?' Stevens said. Then Virginius stopped perfectly still, looking at Stevens.

'Oh,' he said at last.

'One of those natural mutual deed-of-trust wills that any two business partners might execute,' Stevens said. 'You and Granby each the other's beneficiary and executor, for mutual protection of mutual holdings. That's natural. Likely Granby was the one who suggested it first, by telling you how he had made you his heir. So you'd better tear it up, yours, your copy. Make Anse your heir, if you have to have a will.'

'He wont need to wait for that,' Virginius said. 'Half of that land is his.'

'You just treat it right, as he knows you will,' Stevens said. 'Anse dont need any land.'

'Yes,' Virginius said. He looked away. 'But I wish. . . . '

'You just treat it right. He knows you'll do that.'

'Yes,' Virginius said. He looked at Stevens again. 'Well, I reckon I . . . we both owe you. . . . '

'More than you think,' Stevens said. He spoke quite soberly. 'Or to that horse. A week after your father died, Granby bought enough rat poison to kill three elephants, West told me. But after he remembered what he had forgotten about that horse, he was afraid to kill his rats before that will was settled. Because he is a man both shrewd and ignorant at the same time: a dangerous combination. Ignorant enough to believe that the law is something like dynamite: the slave of whoever puts his hand to it first, and even then a dangerous slave; and just shrewd enough to believe that people avail themselves of it, resort to it, only for personal ends. I found that out when he sent a Negro to see me one day last summer, to find out if the way in which a man died could affect the probation of his will. And I knew who had sent the Negro to me, and I knew that whatever information the Negro took back to the man who sent him, that man had already made up his mind to disbelieve it, since I was a servant of the slave, the dynamite. So if that had been a normal horse, or Granby had remembered in time, you would be underground now. Granby might not be any better off than he is, but you would be dead.'

'Oh,' Virginius said, quietly, soberly. 'I reckon I'm obliged.'

'Yes,' Stevens said. 'You've incurred a right smart of obligation. You owe Granby something.' Virginius looked at him. 'You owe him for those taxes he has been paying every year now for fifteen years.'

'Oh,' Virginius said. 'Yes. I thought that father. . . . Every November, about, Granby would borrow money from me, not much, and not ever the same amount. To buy stock with, he said. He paid some of it back. But he still owes me . . . no. I owe him now.' He was quite grave, quite sober. 'When a man starts doing wrong, it's not what he does; it's what he leaves.'

'But it's what he does that people will have to hurt him for, the outsiders. Because the folks that'll be hurt by what he leaves wont hurt him. So it's a good thing for the rest of us that what he does takes him out of their hands. I have taken him out of your hands now, Virge, blood or no blood. Do you understand?'

'I understand,' Virginius said. 'I wouldn't anyway . . .' Then suddenly he looked at Stevens. 'Gavin,' he said.

'What?' Stevens said.

Virginius watched him. 'You talked a right smart in yonder about chemistry and such, about that smoke. I reckon I believed some of it and I reckon I didn't believe some of it. And I reckon if I told you which I believed and didn't believe, you'd laugh at me.' His face was quite sober. Stevens' face was quite grave too. Yet there was something in Stevens' eyes, his glance; something quick and eager; not ridiculing, either. 'That was a week ago. If you had opened that box to see if that smoke was still in there, it would have got out. And if there hadn't been any smoke in that box, Granby wouldn't have given himself away. And that was a week ago. How did you know there was going to be any smoke in that box?'

'I didn't,' Stevens said. He said it quickly, brightly, cheerfully, almost happily, almost beaming. 'I didn't. I waited as long as I could before I put the smoke in there. Just before you all came into the room, I filled that box full of pipe smoke and shut it up. But I didn't know. I was a lot scareder than Granby Dodge. But it was all right. That smoke stayed in that box almost an hour.'

MONK

I will have to try to tell about Monk. I mean, actually try—a deliberate attempt to bridge the inconsistencies in his brief and sordid and unoriginal history, to make something out of it not only with the nebulous tools of supposition and inference and invention, but to employ these nebulous tools upon the nebulous and inexplicable material which he left behind him. Because it is only in literature that the paradoxical and even mutually negativing anecdotes in the history of a human heart can be juxtaposed and annealed by art into verisimilitude and credibility.

He was a moron, perhaps even a cretin; he should never have gone to the penitentiary at all. But at the time of his trial we had a young District Attorney who had his eye on Congress and Monk had no people and no money and not even a lawyer because I dont believe he ever understood why he should need a lawyer or even what a lawyer was, and so the Court appointed a lawyer for him, a young man just admitted to the bar, who probably knew but little more about the practical functioning of criminal law than Monk did, who perhaps pleaded Monk guilty at the direction of the Court or maybe forgot that he could have entered a plea of mental incompetence, since Monk did not for one moment deny that he had killed the deceased. They could not keep him from affirming and even reiterating it, in fact. He was neither confessing nor boasting. It was almost as though he were trying to make a speech, to the people who held him beside the body until the deputy got there, to the deputy and to the jailor and to the other prisoners—the casual niggers picked up for gambling or vagrancy or for selling whiskey in alleys—and to the J.P. who arraigned him, and the lawyer appointed by the Court, and to the Court and the jury. Even an hour after the killing he could not seem to remember where it had happened; he could not even remember the man whom he affirmed that he had killed; he named as his victim (this on suggestion, prompting) several men who were alive and even one who was present in the J.P.'s office at the time. But he never denied that he had killed somebody. It was not insistence, it was just a serene reiteration of the fact in that voice bright eager and sympathetic while he tried to make his speech, trying to tell them something of which they could make neither head nor tail and to which they refused to listen. He was not confessing, not trying to establish grounds for lenience in order to escape what he had done. It was as though he were trying to postulate something, using this opportunity to bridge the hitherto abyss between himself and the living world, the world of living men, the ponderable and travailing earth—as witness the curious speech which he made on the gallows five years later.

But then, he never should have lived either. He came—emerged: whether he was born there or not, no one knew—from the pine hill country in the eastern part of our county: a country which twenty-five years ago (Monk was about twenty-five) was without roads almost and where even the sheriff of the county did not go—a country impenetrable and almost uncultivated and populated by a clannish people who owned allegiance to no one and no thing and whom outsiders never saw until a few years back when good roads and automobiles penetrated the green fastnesses where the denizens with their corrupt Scotch-Irish names intermarried and made whiskey and shot at all strangers from behind log barns and snake fences. It was the good roads and the fords which not only brought Monk to Jefferson but brought the half-rumored information about his origin. Because the very people among whom he had grown up seemed to know almost as little about him as we did—a tale of an old woman who lived like a hermit even among those fiercely solitary people, in a log house with a loaded shotgun standing just inside the front door, and a son who had been too much even for that country and people, who had murdered and fled, possibly driven out, where gone none knew for ten years, when one day he returned, with a woman. That is, they learned that he or some man was there, with the woman—a woman with hard bright metallic city hair and a hard blonde city face seen about the place from a distance, crossing the yard or just standing in the door and looking out upon the green solitude with an expression of cold and sullen and unseeing inscrutability: and deadly too but like a snake is deadly, in a different way from their almost conventional ritual of warning and then powder. Then they were gone. The others did not know when they departed nor why, any more than they knew when they had arrived nor why. Some said that one night the old lady, Mrs Odlethrop, had got the drop on both of them with the shotgun and drove them out of the house and out of the country.

But they were gone; and it was months later before the neighbors discovered that there was a child, an infant, in the house, whether brought there or born there again they did not know. This was Monk; and the further tale how six or seven years later they began to smell the body and some of them went into the house where old Mrs Odlethrop had been dead for a week and found a small creature in a single shift made from bedticking trying to raise the shotgun from its corner beside the door. They could not catch Monk at all. That is, they failed to hold him that first time, and they never had another chance. But he did not go away. They knew that he was somewhere watching them while they prepared the body for burial, and that he was watching from the undergrowth while they buried it. They never saw him again for some time, though they knew that he was about the place and on the following Sunday they found where he had been digging into the grave, with sticks and with his bare hands. He had a pretty big hole by then and they filled it up and that night some of them lay in ambush for him, to catch him and give him food. But again they could not hold him, the small furious body (it was naked now) which writhed out of their hands as if it had been greased and fled with no human sound. After that, certain of the neighbors would carry food to the deserted house and leave it for him. But they never saw him. They just heard, a few months later, that he was living with a childless widower, an old man named Fraser who was a whiskey maker of wide repute. He seems to have lived there for the next ten years, until Fraser himself died. It was probably Fraser who gave him the name which he brought to town with him, since nobody ever knew what old Mrs Odlethrop had called him, and now the country got to know him or become familiar with him at least—a youth not tall and already a little pudgy, as though he were thirty-eight instead of eighteen, with the ugly, shrewdly foolish, innocent face whose features rather than expression must have gained him his nickname, who gave to the man who had taken him up and fed him the absolute and unquestioning devotion of a dog and who at eighteen was said to be able to make Fraser's whiskey as well as Fraser could.

That was all that he had ever learned to do—to make and sell whiskey where it was against the law and so had to be done in secret, which further increases the paradox of his public statement when they drew the black cap over his head for killing the warden of the penitentiary five years later. That was all he knew: that, and fidelity to the man who fed him and taught him what to do and how and when; so that after Fraser died and the man, whoever it was, came along in the truck or the car and said, 'All right, Monk. Jump in,' he got into it exactly as the homeless dog would have, and came to Jefferson. This time it was a filling station two or three miles from town, where he slept on a pallet in the back room, what time the pallet was not already occupied by a customer who had got too drunk to drive his car or walk away, where he even learned to work the gasoline pump and to make correct change, though his job was mainly that of remembering just where the half pint bottles were buried in the sand ditch five hundred yards away. He was known about the town now, in the cheap bright town clothes for which he had discarded his overalls—the colored shirts which faded with the first washing, the banded straw hats which dissolved in the first shower, the striped shoes which came to pieces on his very feet—pleasant, impervious to affront, talkative when anyone would listen, with that shrewd foolish face, that face at once cunning and dreamy, pasty even beneath the sunburn, with that curious quality of imperfect connection between sense and ratiocination. The town knew him for seven years until that Saturday midnight and the dead man (he was no loss to anyone, but then as I said, Monk had neither friends money nor lawyer) lying on the ground behind the filling station and Monk standing there with the pistol in his hand—there were two others present, who had been with the dead man all evening—trying to tell the ones who held him and then the deputy himself whatever it was that he was trying to say in his eager, sympathetic voice, as though the sound of the shot had broken the barrier behind which he had lived for twenty-five years and that he had now crossed the chasm into the world of living men by means of the dead body at his feet.

Because he had no more conception of death than an animal has—
of that of the man at his feet nor of the warden's later nor of his own.
The thing at his feet was just something that would never walk or talk
or eat again and so was a source neither of good nor harm to anyone;
certainly not of good, use. He had no comprehension of bereavement,
irreparable finality. He was sorry for it, but that was all. I dont think he
realised that in lying there it had started a train, a current, of retribution that someone would have to pay. Because he never denied that
he had done it, though denial would have done him no good since the
two companions of the dead man were there to testify against him.
But he did not deny it, even though he was never able to tell what happened, what the quarrel was about nor (as I said) later even where it
had occurred and who it was that he had killed, stating once (as I also
said) that his victim was a man standing at the moment in the crowd
which had followed him into the J.P.'s office. He just kept on trying to
say whatever it was that had been inside him for twenty-five years and
that he had only now found the chance (or perhaps the words) to free
himself of it, just as five years later on the scaffold he was to get it (or
something else) said at last, establishing at last that contact with the
old fecund ponderable travailing earth which he wanted but had not
been able to tell it because only then had they told him how to say what
it was that he desired. He tried to tell it to the deputy who arrested
him and to the J.P. who arraigned him; he stood in the courtroom with
that expression on his face which people have when they are waiting
for a chance to speak, and heard the indictment read: . . . . . . *against
the peace and dignity of the Sovereign State of Mississippi, that the aforesaid
Monk Odlethrop did wilfully and maliciously and with premeditated*—and
interrupted, in a voice reedy and high, the sound of which in dying
away left upon his face the same expression of amazement and surprise
which all our faces wore:

'My name aint Monk; it's Stonewall Jackson Odlethrop.'

You see? If it were true, he could not have heard it in almost twenty
years since his grandmother (if grandmother she was) had died: and yet
he could not even recall the circumstances of one month ago when he
had committed a murder. And he could not have invented it. He could
not have known who Stonewall Jackson was, to have named himself. He
had been to school in the country, for one year. Doubtless old Fraser

sent him, but he did not stay. Perhaps even the first-grade work in a
country school was too much for him. He told my uncle about it when
the matter of his pardon came up. He did not remember just when,
nor where the school was, nor why he had quit. But he did remember
being there because he had liked it. All he could remember was how
they would all read together out of the books. He did not know what
they were reading, because he did not know what the book said; he
could not even write his name now. But he said it was fine to hold the
book and hear all the voices together and then to feel (he said he could
not hear his own voice) his voice too along with the others by the way
his throat would buzz, he called it. So he could never have heard of
Stonewall Jackson. Yet there it was, inherited from the earth, the soil,
transmitted to him through a self-pariahed people—something of bitter
pride and indomitable undefeat of a soil and the men and women who
trod upon it and slept within it.

They gave him life. It was one of the shortest trials ever held in our
county because, as I said, nobody regretted the deceased and nobody
except my uncle Gavin seemed to be concerned about Monk. He had
never been on a train before. He got on, handcuffed to the deputy, in
a pair of new overalls which someone, perhaps the sovereign state
whose peace and dignity he had outraged, had given him, and the still
new, still pristine gaudy-banded imitation panama hat (it was still only
the first of June and he had been in jail six weeks) which he had just
bought during the week of the fatal Saturday night. He had the window
side in the car and he sat there looking at us with his warped pudgy
foolish face, waving the fingers of the hand, the free arm propped in
the window until the train began to move, accelerating slowly, huge
and dingy as the metal gangways clashed, drawing him from our sight
hermetically sealed and leaving upon us a sense of finality more irrevocable than if we had watched the penitentiary gates themselves
close behind him and never to open again in his life, the face looking
back at us, craning to see us, wan and small behind the dingy glass yet
wearing that expression questioning yet unalarmed, eager, serene, and
grave. Five years later one of the dead man's two companions on that
Saturday night, dying of a complication of pneumonia and whiskey,
confessed that he had fired the shot and thrust the pistol into Monk's
hand, telling Monk to look at what he had done.

My uncle Gavin got the pardon, wrote the petition, got the signatures, went to the capitol and got it signed and executed by the Governor and took it himself to the penitentiary and told Monk that he was free. And Monk looked at him for a minute until he understood, and cried. He did not want to leave. He was a trusty now; he had transferred to the warden the same doglike devotion which he had given to old Fraser. He had learned to do nothing well save manufacture and sell whiskey, though after he came to town he had learned to sweep out the filling station. So that's what he did here; his life now must have been something like that time when he had gone to school. He swept and kept the warden's house like a woman would have, and the warden's wife had taught him to knit; crying, he showed my uncle the sweater which he was knitting for the warden's birthday and which would not be finished for weeks yet.

So Uncle Gavin came home. He brought the pardon with him, though he did not destroy it because he said it had been recorded and that the main thing now was to look up the law and see if a man could be expelled from the penitentiary like he could from a college. But I think he still hoped that maybe some day Monk would change his mind; I think that's why he kept it. Then Monk did set himself free, without any help. It was not a week after Uncle Gavin had talked to him; I dont think Uncle Gavin had even decided where to put the pardon for safe-keeping, when the news came. It was a headline in the Memphis papers next day, but we got the news that night over the telephone: how Monk Odlethrop, apparently leading an abortive jailbreak, had killed the warden with the warden's own pistol, in cold blood. There was no doubt this time; fifty men had seen him do it and some of the other convicts overpowered him and took the pistol away from him. Yes. Monk, the man who a week ago cried when Uncle Gavin told him that he was free, leading a jailbreak and committing a murder (on the body of the man for whom he was knitting the sweater which he cried for permission to finish) so coldblooded that his own confederates had turned upon him.

Uncle Gavin went to see him again. He was in solitary confinement now, in the death house. He was still knitting on the sweater. He knitted well, Uncle Gavin said, and the sweater was almost finished. 'I aint got but three days more,' Monk said. 'So I aint got no time to waste.'

'But why, Monk?' Uncle Gavin said. 'Why? Why did you do it?' He said that the needles would not cease nor falter, even while Monk would look at him with that expression serene, sympathetic, and almost exalted. Because he had no conception of death. I dont believe he had ever connected the carrion at his feet behind the filling station that night with the man who had just been walking and talking, or that on the ground in the compound with the man for whom he was knitting the sweater.

'I knowed that making and selling that whiskey wasn't right,' he said. 'I knowed that wasn't it. Only I. . . . . . ' He looked at Uncle Gavin. The serenity was still there, but for the moment something groped behind it: not bafflement or indecision, just seeking, groping.

'Only what?' Uncle Gavin said. 'The whiskey wasn't it? Wasn't what? It what?'

'No. Not it.' Monk looked at Uncle Gavin. 'I mind that day on the train, and that fellow in the cap would put his head in the door and holler, and I would say "Is this it? Is this where we get off?" and the deppity would say No. Only if I had been there without that deppity to tell me, and that fellow had come in and hollered, I would have. . . . . . '

'Got off wrong? Is that it? And now you know what is right, where to get off right? Is that it?'

'Yes,' Monk said. 'Yes. I know right, now.'

'What? What is right? What do you know now that they never told you before?'

He told them. He walked up onto the scaffold three days later and stood where they told him to stand and held his head docilely (and without being asked) to one side so they could knot the rope comfortably, his face still serene, still exalted and wearing that expression of someone waiting his chance to speak, until they stood back. He evidently took that to be his signal, because he said, 'I have sinned against God and man and now I have done paid it out with my suffering. And now—' they say he said this part loud, his voice clear and serene. The words must have sounded quite loud to him and profoundly irrefutable and his heart uplifted, because he was talking inside the black cap now: 'And now I am going out into the free world, and farm.'

II.

You see? It just does not add up. Granted that he did not know that he was about to die, his words still do not make sense. He could have known but little more about farming than he could have about Stonewall Jackson; certainly he had never done any of it. He had seen it, of course, the cotton and the corn in the fields, and men working it. But he could not have wanted to do it himself before, or he would have, since he could have found chances enough. Yet he turns and murders the man who had befriended him and whether he realised it or not, saved him from comparative hell and upon whom he had transferred his capacity for doglike fidelity and devotion and on whose account a week ago he had refused a pardon: his reason being that he wanted to return into the world and farm land—this, the change, to occur in one week's time and after he had been for five years more completely removed and insulated from the world than any nun. Yes, granted that this could be the logical sequence in that mind which he hardly possessed and granted that it could have been powerful enough to cause him to murder his one friend (Yes, it was the warden's pistol; we heard about that: how the warden kept it in the house and one day it disappeared and to keep word of it getting out the warden had his Negro cook, another trusty and who would have been the logical one to have taken it, severely beaten to force the truth from him. Then Monk himself found the pistol, where the warden now recalled having hidden it himself, and returned it)—; granted all this, how in the world could the impulse have reached him, the desire to farm land have got into him where he now was. That's what I told Uncle Gavin.

'It adds up, all right,' Uncle Gavin said. 'We just haven't got the right ciphers yet. Neither did they.'

'They?'

'Yes. They didn't hang the man who murdered Gambrell. They just crucified the pistol.'

'What do you mean?' I said.

'I dont know. Maybe I never shall. Probably never shall. But it adds up, as you put it, somewhere, somehow. It has to. After all, that's too much buffooning even for circumstance, let alone a mere flesh-and-blood imbecile. But probably the ultimate clowning of circumstance will be that we wont know it.' But we did, he did. He discovered it by accident, and he never told anyone but me, and I will tell you why.

At that time we had for Governor a man without ancestry and with but little more divulged background than Monk had; a politician, a shrewd man who (some of us feared, Uncle Gavin and others about the state) would go far if he lived. About three years after Monk died he declared, without warning, a kind of jubilee. He set a date for the convening of the Pardon Board at the penitentiary, where he inferred that he would hand out pardons to various convicts in the same way that the English king gives out knighthoods and garters on his birthday. Of course all the Opposition said that he was frankly auctioning off the pardons, but Uncle Gavin didn't think so. He said that the Governor was shrewder than that, that next year was election year and that the Governor was not only gaining votes from the kin of the men he would pardon but was laying a trap for the purists and moralists to try to impeach him for corruption and then fail for lack of evidence. But it was known that he had the Pardon Board completely under his thumb so the only protest the Opposition could make was to form committees to be present at the time, which step the Governor—oh, he was shrewd—courteously applauded, even to the extent of furnishing transportation for them. Uncle Gavin was one of the delegates from our county.

He said that all these unofficial delegates were given copies of the list of those slated for pardon (the ones with enough voting kin to warrant it, I suppose)—the crime, the sentence, the time already served, prison record, etc. It was in the mess hall; he said he and the other delegates were seated on the hard backless benches against one wall while the Governor and this Board sat about the table on the raised platform where the guards would sit while the men ate, when the convicts were marched in and halted. Then the Governor called the first name on the list and told the man to come forward to the table. But nobody moved. They just huddled there in their striped overalls, murmuring to one another while the guards begun to holler at the man to come out and the Governor looked up from the paper and looked at them with his eyebrows raised. Then somebody said from back in the crowd: 'Let Terrel speak for us, Governor. We done 'lected him to do our talking.'

Uncle Gavin didn't look up at once. He looked at his list until he found the name: Terrel, Bill. Manslaughter. Twenty years. Served since

May 9, 19--. Applied for pardon January, 19--. Vetoed by Warden C. L. Gambrell. Applied for pardon September, 19--. Vetoed by Warden C. L. Gambrell. Record: Troublemaker. Then he looked up and watched Terrel walk out of the crowd and approach the table—a tall man, a huge man, with a dark aquiline face like an Indian's except for the pale yellow eyes, and a shock of wild black hair—who strode up to the table with a curious blend of arrogance and servility and stopped and, without waiting to be told to speak, said in a queer high singsong filled with that same abject arrogance: 'Your Honor and honorable gentlemen, we have done sinned against God and man but now we have done paid it out with our suffering. And now we want to go out into the free world, and farm.'

Uncle Gavin was on the platform almost before Terrel quit speaking, leaning over the Governor's chair and the Governor turned with his little shrewd plump face and his inscrutable speculative eyes toward Uncle Gavin's urgency and excitement. 'Send that man back for a minute,' Uncle Gavin said. 'I must speak to you in private.' For a moment longer the Governor looked at Uncle Gavin, the puppet Board looking at him too, with nothing in their faces at all, Uncle Gavin said.

'Why, certainly, Mr Stevens,' the Governor said. He rose and followed Uncle Gavin back to the wall, beneath the barred window, and the man Terrel still standing before the table with his head jerked suddenly up and utterly motionless and the light from the window in his yellow eyes like two matchflames as he stared at Uncle Gavin.

'Governor, that man's a murderer,' Uncle Gavin said. The Governor's face did not change at all.

'Manslaughter, Mr Stevens,' he said. 'Manslaughter. As a private and honorable and honored citizen of the state and as a humble servant of it, surely you and I can accept the word of a Mississippi jury.'

'I'm not talking about that,' Uncle Gavin said. He said he said it like that, out of his haste, as if Terrel would vanish if he did not hurry; he said how he had a terrible feeling that in a second the little inscrutable courteous man before him would magic Terrel out of reach of all retribution by means of his cold will and his ambition and his amoral ruthlessness. 'I'm talking about Gambrell and that halfwit they hanged. That man there killed them both as surely as if he had fired that pistol and sprung that trap.' Still the Governor's face did not change at all.

'That's a curious charge, not to say serious,' he said. 'Of course you have proof of it.'

'No. But I will get it. Let me have ten minutes with him, alone. I will get proof from him. I will make him give it to me.'

'Ah,' the Governor said. Now he did not look at Uncle Gavin for a whole minute. When he did look up again his face still had not altered as to expression, yet he had wiped something from it like he might have done it physically, with a handkerchief. ('You see, he was paying me a compliment,' Uncle Gavin told me. 'A compliment to my intelligence. He was telling me the absolute truth now. He was paying me the highest compliment in his power') 'What good do you think that would do?' he said.

'You mean. . . . . . .' Uncle Gavin said. They looked at one another. 'So you would still turn him loose on the citizens of this state, this country, just for a few votes?'

'Why not? If he murders again, there is always this place for him to come back to.' Now it was Uncle Gavin who thought for a minute, though he did not look down.

'Suppose I should repeat what you have just said. I have no proof of that either, but I would be believed. And that would——'

'Lose me votes? Yes. But you see, I have already lost those votes because I have never had them. You see? You force me to do what, for all you know, may be against my own principles too—or do you grant me principles?' Now Uncle Gavin said the Governor looked at him with an expression almost warm, almost pitying—and quite curious. 'Mr Stevens, you are what my grandpap would have called a gentleman. He would have snarled it at you, hating you and your kind; he might very probably have shot your horse from under you someday from behind a fence—for a principle. And you are trying to bring the notions of 1860 into the politics of the nineteen hundreds. And politics in the twentieth century is a sorry thing. In fact, I sometimes think that the whole twentieth century is a sorry thing, smelling to high heaven in somebody's nose. But, no matter.' He now turned, back toward the table and the room full of faces watching them. 'Take the advice of a well-wisher even if he cannot call you friend, and let this business alone. As I said before, if we let him out and he murders again, as he probably will, he can always come back here.'

'And be pardoned again,' Uncle Gavin said.

'Probably. Customs do not change that fast, remember.'

'But you will let me talk to him in private, wont you?' The Governor paused, looking back, courteous and pleasant.

'Why, certainly, Mr Stevens. It will be a pleasure to oblige you.'

They took them to a cell, so that a guard could stand opposite the barred door with a rifle. 'Watch yourself,' the guard told Uncle Gavin. 'He's a bad egg. Dont fool with him.'

'I'm not afraid,' Uncle Gavin said; he said he wasn't even careful now, though the guard didn't know what he meant. 'I have less reason to fear him than Mr Gambrell even, because Monk Odlethrop is dead now.' So they stood looking at one another in the bare cell—Uncle Gavin and the Indian-looking giant with the fierce yellow eyes.

'So you're the one that bitched me up this time,' Terrel said, in that queer almost whining singsong. We knew about that case too; it was in the Mississippi reports, besides it had not happened very far away and Terrel was not a farmer either. Uncle Gavin said that that was it, even before he realised that Terrel had spoken the exact words which Monk had spoken on the gallows and which Terrel could not have heard or even known that Monk had spoken them: not the similarity of the words but the fact that neither Terrel nor Monk had ever farmed anything anywhere. It was another filling station, near a railroad this time, and a brakeman on a night freight testified to seeing two men rush out of the bushes as the train passed, carrying something which proved later to be a man and whether dead or alive at the time the brakeman could not tell, and fling it under the train. The filling station belonged to Terrel, and the fight was proved, and Terrel was arrested. He denied the fight at first, then he denied that the deceased had been present, then he said that the deceased had seduced his (Terrel's) daughter and that his (Terrel's) son had killed the man and he was merely trying to avert suspicion from his son. The daughter and the son both denied this and the son proved an alibi and they dragged Terrel, cursing both his children, from the courtroom.

'Wait,' Uncle Gavin said. 'I'm going to ask you a question first. What did you tell Monk Odlethrop?'

'Nothing!' Terrel said. 'I told him nothing!'

'All right,' Uncle Gavin said. 'That's all I wanted to know.' He turned and spoke to the guard beyond the door. 'We're through. You can let us out.'

'Wait.' Terrel said. Uncle Gavin turned. Terrel stood as before, tall and hard and lean in his striped overalls, with his fierce depthless yellow eyes, speaking in that half-whining singsong. 'Send that son of a bitch away.'

'Son of a bitch yourself, fellow,' the guard said. 'You aint out of here yet.' But Terrel paid no more attention to the guard. He was looking at Uncle Gavin, speaking again in that voice in which the abjectness was completely false. 'What do you want to keep me locked up in here for? What have I ever done to you? You, rich and free, that can go wherever you want, while I will have to——' Then he shouted. Uncle Gavin said he shouted without raising his voice at all, that the guard in the corridor could not have heard him: 'Nothing, I tell you! I told him nothing!' But this time Uncle Gavin didn't even have time to begin to turn away. He said that Terrel passed him in two steps that made absolutely no sound at all, and looked out into the corridor. Then he turned and looked at Uncle Gavin. 'Listen,' he said. 'If I tell you, will you give me your word not to vote agin me?'

'Yes,' Uncle Gavin said. 'I wont vote agin you, as you say.'

'But how will I know you aint lying?'

'Ah,' Uncle Gavin said. 'How will you know, except by trying it?' They looked at one another. Now Terrel looked down; Uncle Gavin said Terrel held one hand in front of him and that he (Uncle Gavin) watched the knuckles whiten slowly as Terrel closed it.

'It looks like I got to,' he said. 'It just looks like I got to.' Then he looked up; he cried now, with no louder sound than when he had shouted before: 'But if you do, and if I ever get out of here, then look out! See? Look out.'

'Are you threatening me?' Uncle Gavin said. 'You, standing there, in that striped overall, with that wall behind you and this locked door and a man with a rifle in front of you? Do you want me to laugh?'

'I dont want nothing,' Terrel said. He whimpered almost now. 'I just want justice. That's all.' Now he began to shout again, in that repressed voice, watching his clenched white knuckles too apparently. 'I tried twice for it; I tried for justice and freedom twice. But it was him. He was the one; he knowed I knowed it too. I told him I was going to——' He stopped, as sudden as he began; Uncle Gavin said he could hear him breathing, panting.

'That was Gambrell,' Uncle Gavin said. 'Go on.'

'Yes. I told him I was. I told him. Because he laughed at me. He didn't have to done that. He could have voted agin me and let it go at that. He never had to laugh. He said I would stay here as long as he did or could keep me, and that he was here for life. And he was. He stayed here all his life. That's just exactly how long he stayed.' But he wasn't laughing, Uncle Gavin said. It wasn't laughing.

'Yes. And so you told Monk——'

'Yes. I told him. I said here we all were, pore ignorant country folks that hadn't had no chance. That God had made to live outdoors in the free world and farm His land for Him, only we were pore and ignorant and didn't know it and the rich folks wouldn't tell us until it was too late. That we were pore ignorant country folks that never saw a train before, getting on the train and nobody caring to tell us where to get off and farm in the free world like God wanted us to do, and that *he* was the one that held us back, kept us locked up outen the free world to laugh at us agin the wishes of God. But I never told him to do it. I just said 'And now we cant never get out because we aint got no pistol. But if somebody had a pistol, we would walk out into the free world and farm it because that's what God aimed for us to do and that's what we want to do. Aint that what we want to do?' and he said, 'Yes. That's it. That's what it is.' And I said, 'Only we aint got nara pistol.' And he said, 'I can get a pistol.' And I said, 'Then we will walk in the free world because we have sinned against God but it wasn't our fault because they hadn't told us what it was He aimed for us to do. But now we know what it is because we want to walk in the free world and farm for God.' That's all I told him. I never told him to do nothing. And now go tell them. Let them hang me too. Gambrell is rotted and that batbrain is rotted and I just as soon rot under ground as to rot in here. Go on and tell them.'

'Yes,' Uncle Gavin said. 'All right. You will go free.' For a minute he said Terrel did not move at all. Then he said,

'Free?'

'Yes,' Uncle Gavin said. 'Free. But remember this. A while ago you threatened me. Now I am going to threaten you. And the curious thing is, I can back mine up. I am going to keep track of you. And the next time anything happens, the next time anybody tries to frame you with a killing and you cant get anybody to say you were not there nor any of your kinfolks to take the blame for it——You understand?' Terrel had looked up at him when he said Free, but now he looked down again. 'Do you?' Uncle Gavin said.

'Yes,' Terrel said. 'I understand.'

'All right,' Uncle Gavin said. He turned; he called to the guard. 'You can let us out this time,' he said. He returned to the mess hall, where the Governor was calling the men up one by one and giving them their papers and where again the Governor paused and the smooth inscrutable face looking up at Uncle Gavin. He did not wait for Uncle Gavin to speak.

'You were successful, I see,' he said.

'Yes. Do you want to hear——'

'My dear sir, no. I must decline. I will put it stronger than that: I must refuse.' Again Uncle Gavin said he looked at him with that expression warm, quizzical, almost pitying, yet profoundly watchful and curious. 'I really believe that you never have quite given up hope that you can change this business. Have you?' Now Uncle Gavin said he did not answer for a moment. Then he said,

'No. I hadn't. So you are going to turn him loose? You really are?' Now he said that the pity, the warmth vanished, that now the face was as he first saw it: smooth, completely inscrutable, completely false.

'My dear Mr Stevens,' the Governor said. 'You have already convinced me. But I am merely the moderator of this meeting; here are the votes. But do you think that you can convince these gentlemen?' And Uncle Gavin said he looked around at them, the identical puppet faces of the seven or eight of the Governor's battalions and battalions of factory-made colonels.

'No,' Uncle Gavin said. 'I cant.' So he left then. It was in the middle of the morning and hot, but he started back to Jefferson at once, riding across the broad heat-miraged land, between the cotton and the corn of God's long-fecund remorseless acres which would outlast any corruption and injustice. He was glad of the heat, he said; glad to be sweating, sweating out of himself the smell and the taste of where he had been.

HAND UPON THE WATERS

1.

The river was low, at mid-July level. The current ran brown and rich as chocolate among the willows where the moccasins lay in the sun, and where the sun struck the path between the willows and the jungle itself, it was dusty. But inland, among the gum and cypress and holly and cane, the ground was still wet, dark, because here it never got completely dry; here you walked carefully indeed, watching your feet.

But the two men followed the path, though not to avoid the snakes and not because there was something other than even water moccasins abroad in the bottom on this hot summer morning, because they did not know this yet. They followed the path because the walking was better in it and because it led where they wished to go. One of them carried a clean gunnysack; it had been washed and it looked as if it had been ironed too. The other was a boy, less than twenty years old by his face. 'He ought to been catching fish in this water,' he said.

'If he happened to feel like fishing,' the one with the sack said. 'Him and Joe run that line when Lonnie feels like it, not when the fish are biting.'

'They'll be on the line, anyway,' the youth said. 'I dont reckon Lonnie cares who takes them off for him.'

They went on in single file, following the path, the youth, who was in front, glancing downward from time to time. A blue crane crossed the river, flying deliberately, its long legs trailing. Presently they came in sight of their destination. The bank rose to a cleared point almost like a headland—a point cleared apparently not so much by design and any labor as found comparatively free of undergrowth and further cleared by subsequent usage. In it sat a conical hut of such a harlequin appearance as to be almost camouflaged—generally round, with a pointed roof, built partly of mildewed canvas and odd-shaped boards and partly of oil tins hammered out flat. A section of stovepipe projected crazily above it and the two windows in view were set at different levels, sashless; no sash made to any angle would have fit them. There was a meagre woodpile and an axe, and a bunch of cane poles leaned against it; then they saw, on the earth before the open door, a dozen or so short lengths of cord just cut from a spool nearby, and a rusted can half full of heavy fish-hooks, some of which had been already bent onto the short cords. But there was nobody there.

'The boat's gone,' the man with the sack said, meaning that by that token the owner of the camp was somewhere on the river, doubtless close by, since if he had gone outside for the day, or for two or three weeks as he sometimes did, the skiff would have been drawn up out of the water and chained to its tree below the hut. He found at the same time that he was speaking to himself too, since the youth had gone on without stopping, along the path and past the camp. So he drew in his breath and was just about to shout when suddenly a man rushed out of the undergrowth and stopped, facing him and making an urgent whimpering noise—a man not large and not even quite as thick as he at first seemed, an adult yet with something childlike about him, about the way he ran, barefoot, in battered overalls and with the urgent eyes of the deaf and dumb.

'Hi, Joe,' the man with the sack said, raising his voice as people will with those whom they know cannot comprehend them; 'where's Lonnie?' He held up the sack. 'Got some fish?' But the other only stared at him, making that rapid whimpering sound, then turned and scuttled on up the path after the youth, who at that moment shouted:

'Just look at this line!'

So the older one followed too, for fifteen or twenty feet along the bank, to where the youth leaned eagerly out over the water beside a tree from which a light cotton rope stretched downward into the water. The deaf-and-dumb man stood just behind him, still making his urgent whimpering and lifting his feet rapidly in turn, though before the older man reached them the deaf-and-dumb one turned and scuttled past him again, back toward the hut. Now the older one could see the line

too where it slanted tautly down into the water. At this stage of the
river the line should have stood clear of the water, stretching from
bank to bank between the two trees with only the baited hooks of the
dependent cords submerged. But now it slanted sharply down into the
water from either end, with a heavy indicated downstream sag, and
even the older man admitted to the youth's excited reiteration that
the cord had more of movement than the current should have given it.

'It's big as a man!' the youth cried.

'Yonder's his boat,' the older one said. The youth looked where he
pointed. The boat was on the other side of the river and slightly below
them, floated in among a willow clump just inside a bend.

'What's he doing over there?' the youth said.

'I dont know,' the older man said. 'Cross and get it and we'll see
how big this fish is.'

'What'll Lonnie do if he finds the boat gone?'

'We aint going nowhere. He can holler to us when he comes back.
We're just going to take that fish off for him. Go and get it.'

So the youth stepped out of his overalls, lean in his shirt, and
removed the shirt and kicked off his shoes and waded out and began
to swim, holding straight across to let the current carry him down. The
older man leaned as the youth had done, against the tree the line was
fastened to, reaching out over the water, feeling the weight of the line,
the fish, in his hands. But he was still watching, or at least he could
see, because the youth (instead of crossing he shoved straight away
from the bar as if he intended to stay on the far side of the stream) had
scarcely moved the skiff when the other said,

'Come back over here.'

'I'll run it from this end and meet you at the bank,' the youth said,
staring upstream at the heavy sag of the line.

'No you aint,' the other said. 'Come back over here. We'll both work it.'

So the youth crossed, driving the home-made double-ended skiff,
still watching the invisible line near the center of which they could
see from time to time a faint commotion just beneath the surface. He
brought the skiff in below the older man, who at that moment discovered the deaf-and-dumb man just behind him again, still making the
rapid urgent sound, who now tried to get into the skiff the moment it

reached the bank. 'Get back,' the older man said, pushing the other back with his arm. 'Get back, Joe!'

'Let him come,' the youth said. 'He's done run this line a heap more than you and me ever will.'

'No,' the other said. 'He's too excited. He'll turn the boat over. I dont aim to get wet.'

'Hurry up, then,' the youth said, staring eagerly at the water where the line sagged beneath it. 'There's something on there, or there aint a hog in Georgia. It's big as a man, too.'

The older one stepped into the skiff, not carefully exactly, just gingerly, as men past forty enter small boats. He had never released his grasp on the line so they did not need the paddle, drawing the boat hand over hand along the line itself. Suddenly from the bank behind them the deaf-and-dumb man began to make an actual sound. It was quite loud.

2.

'Inquest?' Stevens said.

'Lonnie Grinnup.' The Coroner was an old country doctor, with a snuffy moustache and the blurred eyes of an old man behind steel spectacles. 'Two fellows found him drowned on his own trot-line this morning.'

'No,' Stevens said. 'Poor damned feeb. I'll come out.'

Later, in his own car—that car which contrived somehow to look exactly like him: never quite new, always a little shabby, a little light-looking, yet always sturdy and serviceable enough even though he did drive it too fast—he never once thought that actually he had no business there, could have had no business there merely as County Attorney even if it had not been an accident. He just thought, as everybody else in the county thought: "Nobody would hurt Lonnie Grinnup" and drove on to observe what was to be a purely sentimental moment—that instant when he and the dead man should be for the last time dramatically juxtaposed before the other's irrevocable obliteration among all the nameless and faceless of limbo. He did not know that in that instant the dead man's now blind and tongueless face was going to demand justice of him, as if it had known that he would come, that nobody there but himself could hear it and perhaps nobody there but himself could have responded.

It was still early afternoon. The distances were blue with heat, the land itself rich and heavy with the imminent harvest. Hay was already being cut and the corn stood in full tassel. Soon it would begin to fire, and the cotton was laid-by, square bloom and boll, which in another month would begin to open. Then, across the long flat where the road began to parallel the river bottom, he saw the store. By ordinary it should have stood as solitary and lonely as a milepost beside the empty road, but now he could already see the battered and topless cars and the saddled horses and mules and the wagons clotted about it. He drew in beside the car which he recognised as the Coroner's, and he could see the men too in their clean Saturday overalls and shirts and heavy hats—the quiet, grave country faces given not very much to speech and wedded to the laborious turn of physical days. There was not one of them he did not know by name and (better still) which did not know him—not warmly, because they did not quite understand him any more than they did the Harvard Phi Beta Kappa key on his watch chain, but with real respect, voting for him year after year and (some of them) calling him Judge when they did not always give that designation where it rightfully belonged. They greeted him quietly, not surprised to see him here, as they would have expected him to attend any of their deaths, as they expected to attend his. 'They got him in the grist mill,' one said.

This was a shed beside the store, where Ballenbaugh, who ran the store six days and on the seventh preached in the church two miles back in the hills, on Saturday afternoons ground meal. But the mill was not running now, and before the open door the overalls were densest and quietest. But they made way for him to enter, and he did—a dim, floorless space powdered everywhere with the clean white dust of meal and smelling of the clean, sweet, dry smell of it. There was a table and a chair or so where the Coroner and a few witnesses sat; Stevens noticed a man of about forty carrying a clean gunnysack folded and refolded until it was about the size of a book, and a youth whose face wore an expression of weary yet indomitable amazement. The body lay under a quilt on the flat low platform of the mill. The quilt was incredibly clean. It didn't even look hot, it just looked bright and gay and quiet in its myriad, tedious, beautifully stitched pattern over which whatever young hands or old hands gnarled with labor had drawn the endless thread. He crossed quietly to it and raised the corner, and the moment for which he had driven eight miles in the heat of the July afternoon had come.

There had been in the county not one pioneer but three simultaneous ones. They came together, on horseback, from the Cumberland Gap and the Carolinas, into the country when Jefferson was still a Chickasaw Agency post, and bought land in old Issetibbeha's patent and established families and flourished and then vanished: so that now, a hundred years afterward, there was in all the county they helped to found but one representative of those three names. This was Stevens, because the last of Doctor Holston's descendants had died before the end of the century, and the Louis Grenier lying under the bright quilt had never even known that he was Louis Grenier. He could not even spell the Lonnie Grinnup he called himself—an orphan too, like Stevens, a man a little under medium size and somewhere in his middle thirties, whom the whole county knew: that face almost delicate when you looked at it again, equable, constant, always cheerful, with an invariable fuzz of soft golden beard which had never known a razor and light-colored peaceful eyes—'touched,' they said, but whatever it was had touched him lightly, taking not very much away that need be missed—living year in and year out in the hovel he had built himself of an old tent and a few mismatched boards and flattened oil tins, with the deaf-and-dumb orphan whom ten years ago he had taken into his hut and raised and fed and clothed and who had not even grown mentally as far as he himself had. Actually the strip of river bank on which he squatted and ran his trot-line and fish-trap was almost the exact center of the thousand and more acres which his ancestor had owned. But he never knew it. Stevens believed that he would not even have cared; that even if he had still owned that original thousand acres he would have ignored them, not declined to be bothered with them but would have refused to accept the idea that any one man could or should own that much of the earth which belongs to all, to every man for his use and pleasure—in his own case, that thirty or forty square feet where his hut sat and the span of river his line stretched across, where anyone was welcome at any time, whether he was there or not, to use his gear and eat his food as long as there was food to eat; and at times he would quit his camp, only wedging the door shut against prowling animals, and with his deaf-and-dumb companion he would appear without warning at houses or cabins ten and fifteen miles away, where he would remain for weeks, always pleasant, equable, tactful, demanding nothing and without servility, sleeping where it was convenient for his hosts to have him sleep—in the hay of lofts or in beds in rooms saved for company, while the deaf-and-dumb youth lay on the porch or the ground just outside where he could hear him breathing.

The moment had come and Stevens had served it; now he could return to town. He laid the corner of the quilt back and turned, already on his way back to his car when, out of deference to the old doctor and to the people, not who voted for him but whom he knew, and the solemnity of their court, he realised he could not depart at once. So he moved over among the men who stood along the wall, their hats in their hands, to wait until the business was finished. It did not take long. He heard the two men tell of finding the body, he watched the Coroner uncap and shake violently out a fountain pen and write steadily for a moment, his mouth working beneath the snuffy moustache, and sign the paper and put the pen back into his pocket and Louis Grenier and Lonnie Grinnup both had ceased to be, and Stevens knew that he was not going back to town.

'I reckon that's all,' the Coroner said. He glanced toward the door. 'All right, Ike,' he said. 'You can take him.'

So he did not return to town. He moved aside with the others, with his thin face and his thoughtful nose and his mop of hair more white than brown and his bright dark eyes which read Descartes and Plato and the Latin poets for pleasure, and watched four men enter, carrying their hats and looking at nobody, and move toward the quilt, walking stiffly; he saw that they were walking on tiptoe. 'You going to take him, Ike?' he said.

The eldest of the four glanced at him for a moment. 'Yes. He had his burying money with Ballenbaugh.'

'You, and Pose, and Matthew, and Jim Blake,' Stevens said, naming the other three.

'We can make up the difference,' the other said.

'I'll help,' Stevens said.

'I thank you,' the other said. 'We got enough.' Then the Coroner was among them, speaking testily:

'All right, boys; all right. Give them room.'

With the others, Stevens moved out into the air, the afternoon again—the grave, sunburned faces, the combed heads with their neat, white razor-lines of Saturday neck-shaves. There was a wagon backed up to the shed now, its tail-gate open, the wagon bed filled with straw, which had not been there before. He watched them put their hats on and then see the wagon and remove them again and stand as the four men emerged and carried the quilt bundle to the wagon and began to put it into the wagon, a little clumsily, too careful, as if the quilt contained nitroglycerin or as if it weighed a thousand pounds or as if four men had never before attempted to handle one object, nothing of inherited instinct or of muscular capacity to guide them. Three or four more moved forward to help and Stevens touched the youth's shoulder, seeing again the expression of spent and incredulous wild amazement. "He wont sleep tonight," he thought. Then he corrected it: "No. He's going to get drunk."

'You went and got the boat before you knew anything was wrong,' he said.

'That's right,' the youth said. He spoke quietly enough at first. 'I knowed something was on the line, I could see that. So I swum over and got the boat and rowed back, I could see the line swagged down into the water with something pulling——'

'You mean you swam the boat back,' Stevens said.

'—and pulling—Sir?'

'You swam the boat back,' Stevens said. 'You swam over and got it and swam it back.'

'Swam it back?' The youth glared at him, wild and unflagging. 'No sir. I rowed it back, I tell you! I never suspected nothing! I rowed it straight back, I could already see them fish—'

'What with?' Stevens said. The youth glared at him. 'What did you row it back with?'

'With the oar! I got in the boat and picked up the oar and rowed it right back up there and all the time I could see them flopping around in the water. They didn't want to let go, they held right on even after we hauled him up on the hook, still eating him. Fish were! I knowed turtles would, but these was fish. Of course it was fish we thought was there! It was! Eating him! I wont never eat another one! Never!'

The body was in the wagon at last, decently on the hay. The quilt was spread again now as if to give it air. Stevens turned swiftly and went on back to his car. It had not seemed long, yet the afternoon had gone somewhere, taking some of the heat with it, and he got into the car and sat, his hands on the wheel, looking out at the wagon which was now about to depart. The man called Ike and another were on the seat; the other two were just coming up on saddled mules. "And it's not right," Stevens thought. "It doesn't add. Something more that I didn't see. Or something that hasn't happened yet——" The wagon began to move, across the dusty banquette toward the road. His hand dropped to the switch. The car was already in gear; it came into motion with the sound of the engine. It was already going fast when it passed the wagon.

He drove for a mile down the road and turned into a dirt lane which led across the levelling sun now, back toward the hills. Presently it began to rise, the sun intermittent now, for in places among the ridges sunset had already come. The road rose among its looped curves, then it forked. In the V of the fork stood a church, white-painted and steeple-less. Beside it, unfenced, a straggle of meagre marble headstones and other graves outlined only by rows of inverted glass jars and crockery and broken brick, wandered down the slope. He did not hesitate. He turned from the road and drove up beside the church and turned and stopped the car. He could see both branches of the fork, and the road he had come over where it curved away and vanished, descending, then reappeared in the valley below, in the sun again. But because of the curve, he could hear the wagon long before he expected to see it. Then he heard the truck. It was coming down out of the hills behind him, quite fast. It came around the curve below the church and into sight—a cab, a shallow bed with folded tarpaulin in it—and drew out of the road at the fork and stopped. He became aware that it was dusk, that the sun had left the valley too. Then the wagon and the two rid-ers came around the curve, and there was a man standing in the road beside the truck and Stevens recognised him: Tyler Ballenbaugh, a distant kinsman of the man who owned the store—a farmer, married and with a family, with a reputation for self-sufficiency and violence, who had been born in the county and had gone West and then returned and married and bought land, bringing with him like an effluvium tales of sums won gambling, who no longer gambled at cards but on certain years would mortgage his own crop and take the money and buy or sell cotton futures—standing there in the road beside the halted wagon, tall in the dusk, talking to the men in the wagon without raising his voice or making any gesture. Then there was another man beside him, in a white shirt, whom Stevens did not recognise nor look at again, because once more his hand dropped to the switch. Again the car was in motion with the sound of the engine. He flashed the lights on as he dropped rapidly down out of the churchyard and into the road behind the wagon, where the man in the white shirt leaped onto the running board, shouting at him, and Stevens recognised him too—a younger brother of Ballenbaugh's who had gone to Memphis years ago, where it was understood he had been a hired armed guard during a strike but who for the last two or three years had been at his brother's, hiding it was said, not from the police but from some of his Memphis friends or later business acquaintances. It was understood that his brother made him work about the farm, and now and then his name would make one in brawls and fights at country dances and picnics, and once he had been subdued, drunk, and thrown into jail by two Jefferson officers.

'Who the hell you spying on?' he shouted.

'Boyd,' the other Ballenbaugh said sharply. 'Get back in the truck.' He had not moved, standing yet beside the wagon—a big, somber-faced man who stared at Stevens out of pale, cold, absolutely expressionless eyes. 'Howdy, Gavin,' he said.

'Howdy, Tyler,' Stevens said. 'You going to take Lonnie?'

'Does anybody here object?'

'I dont,' Stevens said. He got out of the car. 'I'll help you swap him,' he said. They all moved then, gathering about the end of the wagon, directing one another in brief monosyllables. The quilt was fading too in the dusk, yet it still retained that quality of bright, spotless, impregnable serenity, as if indeed whatever lay beneath it would be impervious to grief or pain. It vanished still with that quality when Ballenbaugh spread the tarpaulin over it. Stevens got back into his car. The wagon moved on. The truck backed and turned, already gaining speed; the two faces fled past—the younger one which Stevens saw now was not truculent but frightened, the older one in which there was nothing at all save the pale, still, expressionless eyes. The cracked tail-light vanished over the hill. 'That was an Okatoba County license number,' he thought.

Lonnie Grinnup was buried the next afternoon, from Tyler Ballenbaugh's house. There were a lot of people present, since almost everybody in the county knew him, including a few from Jefferson. Stevens was not among them. 'Joe wasn't there either, I suppose,' he said. 'Lonnie's dummy.'

'No. He wasn't there. The folks that went in to Lonnie's camp Sunday morning to look at that trot-line said he was still there, hunting Lonnie. But he wasn't at the funeral. When he finds Lonnie this time, he can lie down by him all right. But he wont hear him breathing.'

'No,' Stevens said.

3.

He was in Mottstown, the seat of Okatoba County, on that afternoon. He had had the license number of the truck to prompt him, but even without this he would probably have started his search in Mottstown. Okatoba County lay just across the river—the other end of Lonnie Grinnup's trot-line was fastened to it—and there were other men besides Tyler Ballenbaugh who owned property in one county and owned their cars and banked their money in the other: this after the country fashion of doubting just a little the inherent soundness of anything—bank or government—which must function enclosed by paved streets and lit by electricity, and so would divide what they owned. And although it was Sunday, and although he would not know until he found it just what he was looking for, he found it before dark—the agent of the company which eleven years ago had issued to Lonnie Grinnup a five-thousand-dollar policy, with double indemnity for violence, on his life, with Tyler Ballenbaugh as beneficiary. It was quite correct. The doctor had never seen Lonnie before, but he had known Tyler for years, and Lonnie had made his mark on the application and Ballenbaugh had paid the premium and kept them up since. There seemed to have been no more secrecy about it than countrymen usually show in their business affairs. In fact, it did not need defending, as Stevens told the agent:

'I know it's done, oftener than people think, between folks no nearer kin than Lonnie and Tyler Ballenbaugh. Lonnie visiting around like he did, spending weeks and months and welcome in the homes of people who really could not afford that extra mouth to feed and who would have taken care of him if he got sick the same way. So why shouldn't they risk a few dollars every year against the chance of something happening, just as if he were a brother or cousin? And Tyler Ballenbaugh's a gambler to start with.'

'Then I'm not to notify the Company yet?'

'No. I want you to accept the claim when Ballenbaugh comes in to file it, explain to him it will take a week or ten days to settle it, wait three days and send him word to come in to your office to see you at nine oclock or ten oclock the next morning. Then telephone me at Jefferson when you *know* he has got the message.'

'What'll I tell him when he comes in?'

'Sell him another policy,' Stevens said.

He returned home. Early the next morning, about daybreak, the heat-wave broke and he lay in bed watching and hearing the crash and glare of lightning and the rain's loud fury, thinking of the drumming of it and the fierce chanelling of clay-colored water across Lonnie Grinnup's raw and kinless grave on the barren hill beside the steepleless church, and of the sound it would make, above the turmoil of the rising river, on the tin-and-canvas hut where the deaf-and-dumb youth probably still waited for him to come home, knowing that something had happened but not how, not why. "Not how," Stevens thought. "They fooled him some way. They didn't even bother to tie him up. They just fooled him."

It continued to rain intermittently through the rest of the week while he went about his affairs, following the established routine of his days, outwardly his pleasant and inscrutable self. On Wednesday night he received a telephone message, with enough circumlocutory mystery and secrecy about it to have attracted not only the attention but the suspicions of anyone who happened to be awake at either end, not to mention the telephone girls, from the Mottstown agent that Tyler Ballenbaugh had filed his claim.

'Speak up, speak up,' Stevens, in his slippers, said heartily. 'Only us girls here.'

'What? What's that?'

'I said, thank you. And let me know when you know he has gotten your message.' "I am playing stud poker with a man who has proved himself a gambler, which I have not," he thought. "But at least I have forced him to draw a card. And he knows who is in the pot with him." So when, on the following Monday afternoon, the second message came from the Mottstown agent, he knew only what he himself was going to do. He had thought once of asking the Sheriff for a deputy, or of taking some friend with him. "But even a friend would not believe that what I have is a hole card," he told himself, "even though I do: That one man, even an amateur at murder, might be satisfied that he had cleaned up after himself. But when there are two of them, neither one is going to be satisfied that the other has left no ravellings."

So he went alone. He owned a pistol. He looked at it and put it back into its drawer. "At least nobody is going to shoot me with that," he told himself. He left town at dusk. It was raining again. He drove through the bright lancing of the rain, behind the nervous frenzy of the windshield wipers. He passed Whiteleaf store, dark in the rain, and went on. The lane into which he had turned nine days ago lay like a wet yellow straw crossing the gray highway. This time he turned to the right and drove for another quarter-mile, the car slipping and whining in low gear between the yellow and running ditches, and turned out of the road and into a littered yard, where the headlights fell full upon a dark cabin across which the rain lanced and lanced. He did not turn off the lights. He walked full in the beam of them, toward the house, shouting:

'Nate. Nate.' After a moment a Negro voice answered, though no light showed. 'It's Mr Stevens,' Stevens said. 'I'm going in to Mr Lonnie Grinnup's camp. If I'm not back by daylight, you better go up to the store and tell them. Do you hear?' There was no answer. Then a woman's voice said:

'You come away from that door!' The man's voice murmured something, indistinguishable. 'I cant help it!' the woman cried. 'You come away and let them white folks alone!' "So there are others besides me," Stevens thought, thinking how quite often, almost always, there is in Negroes an instinct not for evil but to know evil at once when it exists. He went back to his car and took his flashlight from it and snapped off the headlights.

He found the truck. He had already seen the chain-marks in the mud of the road, and he could smell the bottom, the jungle—a heavier, denser, more somber smell than the open country under the rain. Then he found the truck, drawn out of the road. In the close-held beam of the torch he wiped the mud from the license plate and read again the number which he had watched nine days ago flee over the hill in the dusk. He snapped off the light and put it into his pocket.

Twenty minutes later he realised that he need not have worried about the light. He was in the path then, between the black wall of the jungle and the constant sound of the risen river. He could see now, despite the rain. It was as if the roiled and frothed and phosphorescent water running almost bank-full beside him were giving back to the air all the drowned light which the rain and the flooded creeks had carried into it during the day. Then he could see something, though it took him a second or two to realise what it was because he did not know he had come that far yet. It was a light inside the wet canvas wall of Lonnie Grinnup's hut. He was so near it that he could already hear the two voices, the one cold and level and steady, the other harsh and high, from within the hut. Now it was as if that faint glow beyond the wet canvas had taken from the air the light which the river had given to it. He stumbled over the woodpile and then over something else. He found the door and flung it back, entering also the devastation of Lonnie Grinnup's house—the shuck mattresses dragged out of the wooden bunks, the overturned stove—where Tyler Ballenbaugh stood facing him with a pistol and the younger one stood half-crouched above an overturned box of crude knives and forks and cooking vessels.

'Stand back, Gavin,' Ballenbaugh said.

'Stand back yourself, Tyler,' Stevens said. 'You're too late.'

'What do you mean, too late?' the younger one said. Then Stevens saw recognition come into the other's face. 'Well, by——'

'Is it all up, Gavin?' Tyler said. 'Dont lie to me now.'

'I reckon it is,' Stevens said. 'Put your pistol down.'

'Who else is with you?'

'Enough,' Stevens said. 'Put your pistol down, Tyler.'

'Hell,' the younger one said. He began to move; Stevens saw his eyes go swiftly from him to the door behind him. 'He's lying. There aint anybody with him. He's just spying around like he was the other day, putting his nose into business he's going to wish he had kept it out of. Because this time it's going to get bit off.' He was moving toward Stevens, stooping a little, his arms held slightly away from his sides.

'Boyd!' Tyler said. The other continued to approach Stevens, not smiling, but with a queer light, a glitter, in his face. 'Boyd!' Tyler said. Then he moved, too, with astonishing speed, and overtook the younger and with one sweep of his arm hurled him back into the bunk. They faced each other—the one cold, still, expressionless, the pistol held before him aimed at nothing, the other half-crouched, snarling.

'What the hell you going to do? Let him take us back to town like two damned sheep?'

'That's for me to decide,' Tyler said. He looked at Stevens. 'I never intended this, Gavin. I insured his life, kept the premiums paid—yes. But it was good business: If he outlived me, I wouldn't have had any use for the money, and if I had outlived him, I would have collected on my judgment. There was no secret about it. It was done in open daylight. Anybody could have found out about it. Maybe he told about it. I never told him not to. And who's to say against it anyway? I always fed him when he came to my house, he always stayed as long as he wanted to, come when he wanted to. But I never intended this.'

Suddenly the younger one began to laugh, half-crouched against the bunk where the other had flung him. 'So that's the tune,' he said. 'That's the way it's going.' Then it was not laughter any more, though the transition was so slight or perhaps so swift as to be imperceptible. He was standing now, leaning forward a little, facing his brother. 'I never insured him for five thousand dollars! I wasn't going to get——'

'Hush,' Tyler said.

'—five thousand dollars when they found him dead on that——'

Tyler walked steadily to the other and slapped him in two motions, palm and back, of the same hand, the pistol still held before him in the other.

'I said, hush, Boyd,' he said. He looked at Stevens again. 'I never intended this. I dont want that money now, even if they were going to pay it, because this is not the way I aimed for it to be. Not the way I bet. What are you going to do'?

'Do you need to ask that? I want an indictment for murder.'

'And then prove it!' the younger one snarled. 'Try to prove it! I never insured his——'

'Hush,' Tyler said. He spoke almost gently, looking at Stevens with the pale eyes in which there was absolutely nothing: 'You cant do that. It's a good name. Has been. Maybe nobody's done much for it yet, but nobody's hurt it yet, up to now. I have owed no man, I have taken nothing that was not mine. You mustn't do that, Gavin.'

'I mustn't do anything else, Tyler.'

The other looked at him. Stevens heard him draw a long breath and expel it. But his face did not change at all.

'You want your eye for an eye and tooth for a tooth.'

'Justice wants it. Maybe Lonnie Grinnup wants it. Wouldn't you?'

For a moment longer the other looked at him. Then Ballenbaugh turned and made a quiet gesture at his brother and another toward Stevens, quiet and peremptory, and then they were out of the hut, standing in the light from the door while the rain murmured steadily in the leaves overhead, and again Stevens received that impression, illusion, of space and even light from the river beyond the trees beneath which they stood. At first he didn't know what Ballenbaugh was about. He watched in mounting surprise as Ballenbaugh turned to face his brother, his hand extended, speaking in a voice which was actually harsh now: 'This is the end of the row. I was afraid from that night when you came home and told me. I should have raised you better, but I didn't. Here. Stand up and finish it.'

'Look out, Tyler!' Stevens said. 'Dont do that!'

'Keep out of this, Gavin. If it's meat for meat you want, you will get it.' He still faced his brother, he did not even glance at Stevens. 'Here,' he said. 'Take it and stand up.'

Then it was too late. Stevens saw the younger one spring back. He saw Tyler take a step forward and he seemed to hear in the other's voice the surprise, the disbelief, then the realisation of the mistake. 'Drop the pistol, Boyd,' he said. 'Drop it.'

'So you want it back, do you?' the younger said. 'I come to you that night and told you you were worth five thousand dollars as soon as somebody happened to look on that trot-line, and asked you to give me ten dollars, and you turned me down. Ten dollars, and you wouldn't.

Sure you can have it. Take it.' It flashed, low against his side; the orange fire lanced downward again as the other fell. "Now it's my turn," Stevens thought. They faced each other.

'Run while you can, Boyd,' Stevens said quietly. 'You've done enough. Run, now.'

'Sure I'll run,' Boyd said. 'You do all your worrying about me now, because in a minute you wont have any worries. I'll run all right, after I've said a word to smart guys that come sticking their noses where they'll wish to hell they hadn't——'

"Now he's going to shoot," Stevens thought, and he sprang. For an instant he had the illusion of watching himself springing, reflected somehow by the rain or by the light from the river, in the air above Boyd Ballenbaugh's head. Then he knew that it was not him—that figure which had no tongue and needed none, dropping with its arms extended and its body curved and shaped with silent and deadly purpose toward Boyd Ballenbaugh, which had been waiting nine days now for Lonnie Grinnup to come home. "He was in the tree," Stevens thought. Then the pistol glared. He saw the flash, but he heard no sound.

4.

The doctor kept him in the hospital only one day, though Tyler Ballenbaugh would be there longer than that. That evening, his unruly hair bursting above the neat surgeon's bandage about his head, he was sitting with two friends on the veranda of the house where he rented two rooms and a kitchen and bath, when the Sheriff of the county came up the walk—a big man too, pleasant, with eyes even paler and colder and more expressionless than Tyler Ballenbaugh's. 'It wont take but a minute, Gavin,' he said. 'Or I wouldn't have bothered you at all.'

'We'll go inside,' Stevens said.

'No no,' both the men said. 'We'll walk down to the gate and see if the weather's changed.' So they departed, and the Sheriff lowered one thigh to the veranda rail.

'Head feel all right?' he said.

'Feels all right,' Stevens said.

Then the Sheriff said:

'I reckon you heard where we found Boyd Ballenbaugh.'

Stevens looked back at him just as inscrutably. 'I may have,' he said pleasantly. 'Haven't had much in my head today but an ache.'

'You told us where to look. You were conscious when I got there. You were trying to give Tyler a drink of water. You told us to look on that trot-line.'

'Did I?' Stevens said. 'Well, well, what wont a man say drunk or out of his head. Sometimes he's right, too.'

'You were. We looked on the line, and there was Boyd hung on one of the hooks, dead, just like Lonnie Grinnup was. And Tyler Ballenbaugh with a broken leg and a bullet in his shoulder, and you with a crease in your skull you could hide a cigar in. How did he get on that trot-line, Gavin?'

'I dont know,' Stevens said.

'All right. I'm not Sheriff now. How did Boyd get on that trot-line?'

'I dont know.'

The Sheriff looked at him; they looked at each other. 'Is that what you answer to any friend that asks you?'

'Yes. Because I was shot, you see. I dont know.'

'All right,' the Sheriff said. He took a cigar from his pocket, though he didn't light it. 'Joe—that deaf-and-dumb boy Lonnie raised—seems to have gone away at last. He was still around there last Sunday, but nobody has seen him since. He didn't have to leave. He could have stayed around there. I dont reckon anybody would have bothered him.'

'Maybe he missed Lonnie too much to stay,' Stevens said.

'Maybe he missed Lonnie.' Now the Sheriff bit the end from the cigar and took a match from his pocket. 'It's too bad though he dont know about last night. It might make him feel better. It ought to make somebody feel better.'

'Maybe it does,' Stevens said. 'You dont get a whole lot out of this earth except the privilege of going back into it quiet and lying quiet after you get there. All men deserve that.'

'Oh; Lonnie,' the Sheriff said. 'What about the men who are killed in wars?'

'There's always a lot of them at one time, all together, all victims at one time of one general injustice, one roman holiday of lust and greed and folly; there were eight million of them, all with one set of emperors and kings and presidents and admirals and generals to curse. But Lonnie was by himself. Those others died to make the earth safe for Lonnie and his lot. They made all the earth safe for everybody else but Lonnie. It's like all the lepers jeering at the man who lost his leg, you see.'

'Ah,' the Sheriff said. He rose, and struck the match. 'Did that bullet cause you to forget this too? Just what was it made you suspect something was wrong? What was it the rest of us seemed to have missed?'

'It was that skiff,' Stevens said.

'The skiff?'

'Didn't you ever run a trot-line, a trot-line right at your camp? You dont paddle, you pull the boat hand over hand along the line itself. The paddle was in that skiff when that boy found it. Lonnie never used his paddle when he ran his line: he even kept the skiff tied to the same tree his trot-line was fastened to. That paddle stayed in his house. If you had ever been there, you would have seen it.'

TOMORROW

M y Uncle, Gavin Stevens, had not always been County Attorney. But the time when he had not been was more than twenty years ago and it had lasted for such a short period that only the old men remembered it and even some of them did not. Because in that time he had had but one case.

He was a young man then, twenty-eight, only a year out of the State University law school where, at Grandfather's instigation, he had gone after his return from Harvard and Heidelberg; and he had voluntarily taken the case, persuaded Grandfather to let him handle it alone, which Grandfather did, because, due to the victim's known character and the circumstances, the trial would be a mere formality even if the defendant had not had self-defense to plead.

So he tried the case. Years afterward he still said it was the only case, either as a private defender or a public prosecutor, in which he was convinced that right and justice were on his side, that he ever lost. Though actually he did not lose it—a hung jury and a mistrial in the autumn court term, an acquittal in the following spring term—the defendant a solid, well-to-do farmer, husband and father, too, named Bookwright from a section called Frenchman's Bend in the remote southeastern corner of the county; the victim a swaggering bravo calling himself Buck Thorpe and called Bucksnort by the other young men whom he had subjugated with his fists during the three years he had been in Frenchman's Bend; kinless, who had appeared overnight from nowhere, a brawler, a gambler, known (Uncle Gavin learned this only while preparing his case, since into that corner of the county even sheriffs seldom penetrated and in it people were born and died and were buried without certificates from county authorities) to be a distiller of illicit whiskey and caught once on the road to Memphis with a small drove of stolen cattle, which the owner promptly identified. He had a bill of sale for them, but none in the country knew the name which was signed to it. And the tawdry story itself was old and unoriginal enough—the country girl of seventeen, her imagination fired by the swagger and the proven physical prowess and the daring and the tongue glib with explanations, the father who tried to reason with her and got exactly as far as parents usually do in such cases; then the interdiction, the forbidden door, the inevitable elopement at midnight; and at four oclock the next morning Bookwright waked Will Varner, the Justice of the Peace and the chief officer of the Beat, and handed his pistol butt-first to Varner and said, 'I have come to surrender. I killed Thorpe two hours ago.'

And that was all he said or would say, even after Uncle Gavin saw him in jail and arranged his bond. It was a neighbor named Quick whom Bookwright had notified first who found the half-drawn pistol in Thorpe's dead hand where he lay in the road beside the empty buggy; all that Bookwright would say even when, a week after the brief account was printed in a Memphis paper, a woman appeared in Frenchman's Bend who claimed to be Thorpe's wife, and with a wedding license to prove it, trying to claim what money or property he might have left, so that not even Uncle Gavin ever discovered how Bookwright had managed to learn about the wife.

I can remember yet our surprise that the Grand Jury even found a true bill; when the clerk read the indictment, the betting was twenty to one that the jury would not be out ten minutes. The District Attorney himself did not even appear but conducted the case through an assistant, and it did not take an hour to submit all the evidence. Then Uncle Gavin rose, and I remember how he looked at the jury—at the eleven farmers and store-keepers, and at the twelfth man, who was to ruin his case—a farmer, too, a thin man, small, with thin gray hair and that appearance of hill farmers—at once frail and work-worn, yet curiously imperishable—who seem to become old men at fifty and then become invincible to time. And I can still hear Uncle Gavin's voice, quiet, almost monotonous, not ranting as criminal-court trials had taught us to expect; only the words were a little different from the ones he would use in later years. But even then, although he had been talking to them for only a year, he could already talk so that all the people in our country—the Negroes, the hill people, the rich flatland plantation owners—understood what he said.

'I wont talk anymore about the deceased. He is dead; let the dead bury him. And I'm not talking about self-defense. The defendant did not have to force this issue to the point of taking life. He could have stayed at home that night and let what he could not otherwise stop, come to pass. All of us in this country, the South, have been taught from birth a few things which we hold to above all else. One of the first of these—not the best; just one of the first—is that only a life can pay for the life it takes; that the one death is only half complete. If that is so, then we could have saved both these lives by stopping this defendant before he left his house that night; we could have saved at least one of them, even if we had had to take this defendant's life from him in order to stop him. Only we didn't know in time. And that's what I am talking about—not about the dead man and his character and the morality of the act he was engaged in; not about self-defense, whether or not this defendant was justified in forcing the issue to the point of taking life, but about us who are not dead and what we dont know—about all of us, human beings who at bottom want to do right, want not to harm others; human beings with all the complexity of human passions and feelings and beliefs, in the accepting or rejecting of which we had no choice, trying to do the best we can with them or despite them—this defendant, another human being with that same complexity of passions and instincts and beliefs, faced by a problem—the inevitable misery of his child who, with the headstrong folly of youth—again that same old complexity which she, too, did not ask to inherit—was incapable of her own preservation—and solved that problem to the best of his ability and beliefs, asking help of no one, and then abode by his decision and his act.'

He sat down. The District Attorney's assistant merely rose and bowed to the Court and sat down again, and the jury went out and we didn't even leave the room. Even the Judge didn't retire. And I remember the long breath, something which went through the room when the clock hand above the Bench passed the ten-minute mark and then it passed the half-hour mark, and the Judge beckoned a bailiff and whispered to him, and the bailiff went out and returned and whispered to the Judge, and the Judge rose and banged his gavel and recessed the Court.

And I remember how I hurried home through the dry vivid heat of that September noon and ate my dinner and hurried back to town, to Grandfather's office. It was empty. Even Grandfather, who took his nap after dinner, regardless of who hung and who didn't, returned first; after three oclock then, and the whole town knew now that Uncle Gavin's jury was hung by one man, eleven to one for acquittal; then Uncle Gavin came in fast, and Grandfather said, 'Well, Gavin, at least you stopped talking in time to hang just your jury and not your client.'

'That's right, sir,' Uncle Gavin said. Because he was looking at me with his bright eyes, his thin, quick face, his wild hair that was already beginning to turn white. 'Come here, Chick,' he said. 'I need you for a minute.'

'Ask Judge Frazier to allow you retract your oration and then let Charley sum up for you,' Grandfather said. But we were outside then, on the outside stairs that led down to the hot Square, Uncle Gavin stopping halfway down, so that we stood exactly halfway from anywhere, his hand on my shoulder, his eyes brighter and intenter than ever.

'This is not cricket,' he said. 'But justice is accomplished lots of times by methods that wont bear looking at. They have moved the jury to the back room in Mrs Rouncewell's boarding house. The room right opposite that mulberry tree. If you could get into the back yard without anybody seeing you, and be careful when you climb the tree——'

Nobody saw me. And there was the hot dry afternoon wind shaking the mulberry leaves too. I looked out through the windy leaves into the room; I could see and hear them too—the nine angry and disgusted men sprawled in chairs at the far end of the room; Mr Holland, the foreman, and another man standing in front of the chair in which the little, worn, dried-out hill man sat. His name was Fentry. I remembered all their names, because Uncle Gavin said that to be a successful lawyer and politician in our country you did not need a silver tongue nor even an intelligence; you needed only an infallible memory for names. But I would have remembered his name anyway, because it was Stonewall Jackson—Stonewall Jackson Fentry.

'Dont you admit that he was running off with Bookwright's seventeen-year-old daughter?' Mr Holland said. 'Dont you admit that he had a pistol in his hand when they found him? Dont you admit that he wasn't hardly buried before that woman turned up here and proved she was already his wife? Dont you admit that he was not only no-good but dangerous, and that if it hadn't been Bookwright, sooner or later somebody else would have had to, and that Bookwright was just unlucky?'

'Yes,' Fentry said.

'Then what do you want?' Mr Holland said. 'What do you want?'

'I cant help it,' Fentry said. 'I aint going to vote Mr Bookwright free.'

And he didn't. And that afternoon Judge Frazier discharged the jury and set the case for retrial in the next term of court in the spring; and the next morning Uncle Gavin came for me before I had finished breakfast. 'Tell your mother we might be gone overnight,' he said. 'Tell her I promise not to let you get either shot, snake-bit or surfeited with soda pop. . . . Because I've got to know,' he said. We were driving fast now, out the northeast road, and his eyes were bright, quick, not baffled, just intent and eager. 'He was born and raised and lived all his life out here at the very other end of the county, thirty miles from Frenchman's Bend. He said under oath that he had never even seen Bookwright before, and you can look at him and see that he never had enough time off from hard work to learn how to lie in. I doubt if he ever even heard Bookwright's name before.'

We drove until almost noon. We were in the hills now, out of the rich flat land, among the pine and bracken, the poor soil, the little tilted and barren patches of gaunt corn and cotton which somehow endured, as the people they clothed and fed somehow endured; the roads we followed less than lanes, winding and narrow, rutted and dust choked, the car in second gear half the time. Then we saw the mailbox, the crude lettering: *J. A. Fentry*; beyond it, the two-room log house with an open hall, and even I, a boy of twelve, could see that no woman's hand had touched it in a lot of years. We entered the broken gate, then a voice said, 'Stop! Stop where you are!' And we hadn't even seen him—an old man, barefoot, with a fierce white bristle of moustache, in patched denim faded almost to the color of skim milk, smaller, thinner even than the son, standing at the edge of the worn gallery with a shotgun, holding the gun across his middle in both hands and shaking with fury or perhaps with the palsy of age.

'Mr Fentry——' Uncle Gavin said.

'You've harried and badgered him enough!' the old man said. It was fury; the voice seemed to rise suddenly with a fiercer, an uncontrollable blaze of it. 'Get out of here! Get off my land! Go!'

'Come,' Uncle Gavin said quietly. And still his eyes were only bright, eager, intent and grave. We drove again, not fast now; the next mailbox was within the mile, and this time the house was even painted, neat and white, with beds of petunias beside the steps, and the land about it was better, and this time the man rose from the porch and came down to the gate.

'Howdy, Mr Stevens,' he said. 'So Jackson Fentry hung your jury for you.'

'Howdy, Mr Pruitt,' Uncle Gavin said. 'It looks like he did. Tell me.' And Pruitt told him, even though at that time Uncle Gavin would forget now and then and his language would slip back to Harvard and even to Heidelberg. It was as if people looked once at his face and knew that what he asked was not just for his own curiosity or his own selfish using.

'Only Ma knows more about it than I do,' Pruitt said. 'Come up to the gallery.' We followed him to the gallery, where a plump, white-haired old lady in a clean gingham sunbonnet and dress and a white apron sat in a low rocking chair, shelling field peas into a wooden bowl. 'This is Lawyer Stevens, Ma,' Pruitt said. 'Captain Stevens' son, from town. He wants to know about Jackson Fentry.'

'Yes,' Uncle Gavin said again. 'Tell me.' So we sat, too, while they told it, the son and the mother talking in rotation.

'That place of theirs,' Pruitt said. 'You seen some of it from the road. And what you never seen dont look no better. But his pa and his grandpa worked it, made a living for themselves and raised families and paid their taxes and owed no man. I dont know how they done it, but they did. And Jackson was helping from the time he got big enough to reach up to the plow handles. He never got much bigger than that neither. None of them ever did. I reckon that was why. And Jackson worked it, too, in his time, until he was about twenty-five and already looking forty, asking no odds of nobody, not married and not nothing, him and his pa living alone and doing their own washing and cooking, because how can a man afford to marry when him and his pa have just one pair of shoes between them. If it had been worth while getting a wife a-tall, since that place had already killed his ma and his grandma both before they were forty years old. Until one night——'

'Nonsense,' Mrs Pruitt said. 'When your pa and me married, we didn't even own a roof over our heads. We moved into a rented house, on rented land——'

'All right,' Pruitt said. 'Until one night he come to me and said how he had got him a sawmilling job down at Frenchman's Bend——'

'Frenchman's Bend?' Uncle Gavin said, and now his eyes were much brighter and quicker than just intent. 'Yes,' he said. 'Tell me.'

'All right,' Pruitt said. '—A day-wage job. Not to get rich, just to earn a little extra money maybe, risking a year or two to earn a little extra money, against the life his grandpa led until he died between the plow handles one day, and that his pa would lead until he died in a corn furrow, and then it would be his turn, and not even no son to come and pick him up out of the dirt. And that he had traded with a nigger to help his pa work their place while he was gone, and would I kind of go up there now and then and see that his pa was all right——'

'Which you did,' Mrs Pruitt said.

'I went close enough,' Pruitt said. 'I would get close enough to his fields to hear him cussing at the nigger for not moving fast enough and to watch the nigger trying to keep up with him, and to think what a good thing it was Jackson hadn't got two niggers to work the place while he was gone, because if that old man—and he was close to sixty then—had had to spend one full day sitting in a chair in the shade with nothing in his hands to chop or hoe or drive nails with, he would have died before sundown. So Jackson left. He walked. They didn't have but one mule. They aint never had but one mule. But it was just about thirty miles. He was gone about two and a half years, then one day—'

'He come home that first Christmas,' Mrs Pruitt said.

'That's right,' Pruitt said. 'He walked them thirty miles home and spent Christmas Day, and walked them other thirty miles back to the sawmill——'

'Whose sawmill?' Uncle Gavin said.

'Quick's,' Pruitt said. 'Old Man Ben Quick's. It was the second Christmas he never come home. Then, about the beginning of March, about when the river bottom down at Frenchman's Bend would be starting to dry out to where you could skid cypress logs through it again and you would have thought he would be settled down good to his third year of sawmilling, he come home to stay. He didn't walk this time. He come in a hired buggy. Because he had the goat and the baby——'

'Wait,' Uncle Gavin said.

'We didn't know how he come home,' Mrs Pruitt said. 'Because he had been home over a week before we even found out he had the baby——'

'Wait,' Uncle Gavin said. And they waited, looking at him, Pruitt sitting on the gallery railing and Mrs Pruitt's fingers still shelling the peas out of the long brittle hulls, looking at Uncle Gavin's bright intent eyes. They were not exultant now any more than they had been baffled or even very speculative before; they had just got brighter, as if whatever it was behind them had flared up, steady and fiercer, yet still quiet, as if it were going faster than the telling was going. 'Yes,' he said. 'Tell me.'

'And when I finally heard about it and went up there,' Mrs Pruitt said, 'that baby wasn't two weeks old. And how he kept it alive and just on goat-milk——'

'I dont know if you know it,' Pruitt said. 'A goat aint like a cow. You milk a goat every two hours or so. That means all night too.'

'Yes,' Mrs Pruitt said. 'He didn't even have diaper cloths. He just had some split flour sacks that the midwife had showed him how to put on. So I made him some cloths and I would go up there; he had kept the nigger on to help his pa in the field and he was doing the cooking and the washing and nursing that baby, milking the goat every two hours to feed it; and I would say, "Let me have it, Jackson. At least until it can be weaned. You come stay at my house, too, if you want," and him just looking at me—little, thin, already wore-out something that never in his whole life had ever set down to a table and et all he could hold—saying, "I thank you, ma'am. I can make out."'

'Which was correct,' Pruitt said. 'I dont know how he was at sawmilling, and he never had no farm to find out what kind of a farmer he was. But he raised that boy.'

'Yes,' Mrs Pruitt said. 'And I kept on after him: "We hadn't even heard you was married," I said. "Yessum," he said. "We was married last year. When the baby come, she died." "Who was she?" I said. "Was she a Frenchman's Bend girl?" "Nome," he said. "She come from downstate." "What was her name?" I said. "Miss Smith," he said.'

'He hadn't even had enough time off from hard work to learn how to lie either,' Pruitt said. 'But he raised that boy. After their crops were in in the fall, he let the nigger go, and next spring him and the old man done the work like they use to. He had made a kind of satchel, like they say Indians does, to carry the boy in. I would go up there now and then while the ground was still cold and see Jackson and his pa plowing and chopping brush, and that satchel hanging on a fence post and that boy asleep bolt upright in it like it was a feather bed. He learned to walk that spring, and I would stand there at the fence and watch that durn little critter out there in the middle of the furrow, trying his best to keep up with Jackson until Jackson would stop the plow at the turn-row and go back and get him and set him straddle of his neck and then take up the plow again and go on. In the late summer he could walk pretty good. Jackson made him a little hoe out of a stick and a scrap of shingle, and you could see Jackson chopping in the thigh-deep cotton, but you couldn't see the boy at all; you could just see the cotton shaking where he was.'

'Jackson made his clothes,' Mrs Pruitt said. 'Stitched them himself, by hand. I made a few garments and took them up there. I never done it but once though. He took them and he thanked me. But you could see it. It was like he even begrudged the earth itself for what that child had to eat to keep alive. And I tried to persuade Jackson to take him to church, have him baptised. "He's already named," he said. "His name is Jackson and Longstreet Fentry. Pa fit under both of them."'

'He never went nowhere,' Pruitt said. 'Because where you saw Jackson, you saw that boy. If he had had to steal that boy down there at Frenchman's Bend, he couldn't 'a' hid no closer. It was even the old man that would ride over to Haven Hill store to buy their supplies, and the only time Jackson and that boy was separated as much as one full breath was once a year when Jackson would ride in to Jefferson to pay their taxes, and when I first seen the boy I thought of a setter puppy, until one day I knowed Jackson had gone to pay their taxes and I went up there and the boy was under the bed, not making any fuss, just backed up into the corner, looking out at me. He didn't blink once. He was exactly like a fox or a wolf cub somebody had caught just last night.' We watched him take from his pocket a tin of snuff and tilt a measure of it into the lid and then into his lower lip, tapping the final grain from the lid with delicate deliberation.

'All right,' Uncle Gavin said. 'Then what?'

'That's all,' Pruitt said. 'In the next summer him and the boy disappeared.'

'Disappeared?' Uncle Gavin said.

'That's right. They were just gone one morning. I didn't know when. And one day, I couldn't stand it no longer, I went up there and the house was empty, and I went on to the field where the old man was plowing, and at first I thought the spreader between his plow handles had broke and he had tied a sapling across the handles, until he seen me and whirled and snatched the sapling off, and it was that shotgun, and I reckon what he said to me was about what he said to you this morning when you stopped there. Next year he had the nigger helping him again. Then, about five years later, Jackson come back. I dont know when. He was just there one morning. And the nigger was gone again, and him and his pa worked the place like they used to. And one day I couldn't stand it no longer, I went up there and I stood at the fence where he was plowing, until after a while the land he was breaking brought him up to the fence, and still he hadn't never looked at me; he plowed right by me, not ten feet away, still without looking out at me, and he turned and come back, and I said, "Did he die, Jackson?" and then he looked at me. "The boy," I said. And he said, "What boy?"'

They invited us to stay for dinner. Uncle Gavin thanked them. 'We brought a snack with us,' he said. 'And it's thirty miles to Varner's store, and twenty-two from there to Jefferson. And our roads aint quite used to automobiles yet.'

So it was just sundown when we drove up to Varner's store in Frenchman's Bend village; again a man rose from the deserted gallery and came down the steps to the car. It was Isham Quick, the witness who had first reached Thorpe's body—a tall, gangling man in the middle forties, with a vague, dreamy kind of face and near-sighted eyes, until you saw there was something shrewd behind them, even a little quizzical.

'I been waiting for you,' he said. 'Looks like you made a water-haul.' He blinked at Uncle Gavin. 'That Fentry.'

'Yes,' Uncle Gavin said. 'Why didn't you tell me sooner?'

'I didn't recognise it myself,' Quick said. 'It wasn't until I heard your jury was hung, and by one man, that I associated them names.'

'Names?' Uncle Gavin said. 'What na— Never mind. Just tell it.'

So we sat on the gallery of the locked and deserted store while the cicadas shrilled and rattled in the trees and the frogs boomed and brunted and the lightning-bugs blinked and drifted above the dusty road, and Quick told it, sprawled on the bench beyond Uncle Gavin, loose-jointed, like he would come all to pieces the first time he moved, talking in a lazy sardonic voice, like he had all night to tell it in and it would take all night to tell it. But it wasn't that long. It wasn't long enough for what was in it. But Uncle Gavin says it dont take many words to tell the sum of any human experience; that somebody has already done it in eight: He was born, he suffered and he died.

'It was Pap that hired him. But when I found out where he had come from, I knowed he would work, because folks in that country hadn't never had time to learn nothing but hard work. And I knowed he would be honest for the same reason: that there wasn't nothing in his country a man could want bad enough to learn how to steal it. What I seem to have underestimated was his capacity for love. I reckon I figured that, coming from where he come from, he never had none a-tall, and for that same previous reason—that even the comprehension of love had done been lost out of him back down the generations where the first one of them had had to take his final choice between the pursuit of love and the pursuit of keeping on breathing.

'So he come to work, doing the same work and drawing the same pay as the niggers done. Until in the late fall, when the bottom got wet and we got ready to shut down for the winter, I found out he had made a trade with Pap to stay on until spring as watchman and caretaker, with three days out to go home Christmas. And he did, and the next year when we started up, he had done learned so much about it and he stuck to it so, that by the middle of summer he was running the whole mill hisself, and by the end of summer Pap never went out there no more a-tall and I just went when I felt like it, maybe once a week or so; and by fall Pap was even talking about building him a shack to live in in place of that shuck mattress and a old broke-down cookstove in the boiler shed. And he stayed through that winter too. When he went home that Christmas we never even knowed it, when he went or when he come back, because even I hadn't been out there since fall.

'Then one afternoon in February—there had been a mild spell and I reckon I was restless—I rode out there. The first thing I seen was her,

and it was the first time I had ever done that—a woman, young, and
maybe when she was in her normal health she might have been pretty,
too. I dont know. Because she wasn't just thin, she was gaunted. She
was sick, more than just starved-looking, even if she was still on her
feet, and it wasn't just because she was going to have that baby in a
considerable less than another month. And I says, "Who is that?" and
he looked at me and says, "That's my wife," and I says, "Since when?
You never had no wife last fall. And that child aint a month off." And
he says, "Do you want us to leave?" and I says, "What do I want you
to leave for?" I'm telling this from what I know now, what I found out
after them two brothers showed up here three years later with their
court paper, not from what he ever told me, because he never told
nobody nothing.'

'All right,' Uncle Gavin said. 'Tell.'

'I dont know where he found her. I dont know if he found her somewhere, or if she just walked into the mill one day or one night and he
looked up and seen her, and it was like the fellow says—nobody knows
where or when love or lightning either is going to strike, except that
it aint going to strike there twice, because it dont have to. And I dont
believe she was hunting for the husband that had deserted her—likely
he cut and run soon as she told him about the baby—and I dont believe
she was scared or ashamed to go back home just because her brothers and father had tried to keep her from marrying the husband in the
first place. I believe it was just some more of that same kind of black-
complected and not extra-intelligent and pretty durn ruthless blood-
pride that them brothers themselves was waving around here for about
a hour that day. Anyway, there she was, and I reckon she knowed her
time was going to be short, and him saying to her, "Let's get married,"
and her saying, "I cant marry you. I've already got a husband." And her
time come and she was down then, on that shuck mattress, and him
feeding her with a spoon, likely, and I reckon she knowed she wouldn't
get up from it, and he got the midwife, and the baby was born, and
likely her and the midwife both knowed by then she would never get
up from that mattress and maybe they even convinced him at last, or
maybe she knowed it wouldn't make no difference nohow and said yes,
and he taken the mule Pap let him keep at the mill and rid seven miles
to Preacher Whitfield's and brung Whitfield back about daylight, and

Whitfield married them and she died, and him and Whitfield buried her. And that night he come to the house and told Pap he was quitting, and left the mule, and I went out to the mill a few days later and he was gone—just the shuck mattress and the stove, and the dishes and skillet Mammy let him have, all washed and clean and set on the shelf. And in the third summer from then, them two brothers, them Thorpes——'

'Thorpes,' Uncle Gavin said. It wasn't loud. It was getting dark fast now, as it does in our country, and I couldn't see his face at all any more. 'Tell,' he said.

'Black-complected like she was—the youngest one looked a heap like her—coming up in the surrey, with the deputy or bailiff or whatever he was, and the paper all wrote out and stamped and sealed all regular, and I said, "You cant do this. She come here of her own accord, sick and with nothing, and he taken her in and fed her and nursed her and got help to born that child and a preacher to bury her; they was even married before she died. The preacher and the midwife both will prove it." And the oldest brother says, "He couldn't marry her. She already had a husband. We done already attended to him." And I says, "All right. He taken that boy when nobody come to claim him. He has raised that boy and clothed and fed him for two years and better." And the oldest one drawed a money purse half outen his pocket and let it drop back again. "We aim to do right about that, too—when we have seen the boy," he says. "He is our kin. We want him and we aim to have him." And that wasn't the first time it ever occurred to me that this world aint run like it ought to be run a heap of more times than what it is, and I says, "It's thirty miles up there. I reckon you all will want to lay over here tonight and rest your horses." And the oldest one looked at me and says, "The team aint tired. We wont stop." "Then I'm going with you," I says. "You are welcome to come," he says.

'We drove until midnight. So I thought I would have a chance then, even if I never had nothing to ride. But when we unhitched and laid down on the ground, the oldest brother never laid down. "I aint sleepy," he says. "I'll set up a while." So it wasn't no use, and I went to sleep and then the sun was up and it was too late then, and about middle morning we come to that mailbox with the name on it you couldn't miss, and the empty house with nobody in sight or hearing neither, until we heard the axe and went around to the back and he looked up from the woodpile and seen what I reckon he had been expecting to see every time the sun rose for going on three years now. Because he never even stopped. He said to the little boy, "Run. Run to the field to Grandpap. Run," and came straight at the oldest brother with the axe already raised and the down-stroke already started, until I managed to catch it by the haft just as the oldest brother grabbed him and we lifted him clean off the ground, holding him, or trying to. "Stop it, Jackson!" I says. "Stop it! They got the law!" Then a puny something was kicking and clawing me about the legs; it was the little boy, not making a sound, just swarming around me and the brother both, hitting at us as high as he could reach with a piece of wood Fentry had been chopping. "Catch him and take him on to the surrey," the oldest one says. So the youngest one caught him; he was almost as hard to hold as Fentry, kicking and plunging even after the youngest one had picked him up, and still not making a sound, and Fentry jerking and lunging like two men until the youngest one and the boy was out of sight. Then he collapsed. It was like all his bones had turned to water, so that me and the oldest brother lowered him down to the chopping block like he never had no bones a-tall, laying back against the wood he had cut, panting, with a little froth of spit at each corner of his mouth. "It's the law, Jackson," I says. "Her husband is still alive."

"'I know it,' he says. It wasn't much more than whispering. "I been expecting it. I reckon that's why it taken me so by surprise. I'm all right now."

"'I'm sorry of it,' the brother says. "We never found out about none of it until last week. But he is our kin. We want him home. You done well by him. We thank you. His mother thanks you. Here," he says. He taken the money purse outen his pocket and puts it into Fentry's hand. Then he turned and went away. After a while I heard the carriage turn and go back down the hill. Then I couldn't hear it any more. I dont know whether Fentry ever heard it or not.

"'It's the law, Jackson,' I says. "But there's two sides to the law. We'll go to town and talk to Captain Stevens. I'll go with you." Then he set up on the chopping block, setting up slow and stiff. He wasn't panting so hard now and he looked better now, except for his eyes, and they was mostly just dazed looking. Then he raised the hand that had the money purse in it and started to mop his face with the money purse, like it was a handkerchief; I dont believe he even knowed there was anything in his hand until then, because he taken his hand down and looked at the money purse for maybe five seconds, and then he tossed it—he didn't fling it; he just tossed it like you would a handful of plow-dirt you had been examining to see what it would make—over behind the chopping block and got up and walked across the yard toward the woods, walking straight and not fast, and not looking much bigger than that little boy, and into the woods. "Jackson," I says. But he never looked back.

'And I stayed that night at Rufus Pruitt's and borrowed a mule from him; I said I was just looking around, because I didn't feel much like talking to nobody, and the next morning I hitched the mule at that gate and started up the path, and I didn't see Old Man Fentry on the gallery a-tall at first and when I did see him he was moving so fast I didn't even know what he had in his hands until it went "boom!" and I heard the shot rattling in the leaves overhead and Rufus Pruitt's mule trying his durn best either to break the hitch-rein or hang hisself from the gatepost. And one day about six months after he had located here to do the balance of his drinking and fighting and sleight-of-hand with other folks' cattle, Bucksnort was on the gallery here, drunk still and running his mouth, and about a half a dozen of the ones he had beat unconscious from time to time by foul means and even by fair on occasion, as such emergencies arose, laughing every time he stopped to draw a fresh breath. And I happened to look up, and Fentry was setting on his mule out there in the road. He was just setting there, with the dust of them thirty miles caking into the mule's sweat, looking at Thorpe. I dont know how long he had been there, not saying nothing, just setting there and looking at Thorpe; then he turned the mule and rid back up the road toward them hills he hadn't ought to never have left. Except maybe it's like the fellow says, and there aint nowhere you can hide from either lightning or love. And I didn't know why then. I hadn't associated them names. I knowed that Thorpe was familiar to me, but that other business had been twenty years ago and I had forgotten it until I heard about that hung jury of yourn. Of course he wasn't going to vote Bookwright free. . . . It's dark. Let's go to supper.'

But it was only twenty-two miles to town now, and we were on the highway now, the gravel; we would be home in an hour and a half, because sometimes we could make thirty and thirty-five miles an

hour, and Uncle Gavin said that someday all the main roads in Mississippi would be paved like the streets in Memphis and every family in
America would own a car. We were going fast now.

'Of course he wasn't,' Uncle Gavin said. 'The lowly and invincible of
the earth—to endure and endure and then endure, tomorrow and tomorrow and tomorrow. Of course he wasn't going to vote Bookwright free.'

'I would have,' I said. 'I would have freed him. Because Buck Thorpe
was bad. He—'

'No, you wouldn't,' Uncle Gavin said. He gripped my knee with one
hand even though we were going fast, the yellow light beam level on the
yellow road, the bugs swirling down into the light beam and ballooning
away. 'It wasn't Buck Thorpe, the adult, the man. He would have shot
that man as quick as Bookwright did, if he had been in Bookwright's
place. It was because somewhere in that debased and brutalised flesh
which Bookwright slew there still remained, not the spirit maybe, but
at least the memory, of that little boy, that Jackson and Longstreet
Fentry, even though the man the boy had become didn't know it, and
only Fentry did. And you wouldn't have freed him either. Dont ever
forget that. Never.'

AN ERROR IN CHEMISTRY

It was Joel Flint himself who telephoned the sheriff that he had killed his wife. And when the sheriff and his deputy reached the scene, drove the twenty-odd miles into the remote back-country region where old Wesley Pritchel lived, Joel Flint himself met them at the door and asked them in. He was the foreigner, the outlander, the Yankee who had come into our county two years ago as the operator of a pitch—a lighted booth where a roulette wheel spun against a bank of nickel-plated pistols and razors and watches and harmonicas—in a travelling street carnival and who when the carnival departed had remained, and two months later was married to Pritchel's only living child: the dim-witted spinster of almost forty, who until then had shared her irascible and violent-tempered father's almost hermit-existence on the good though small farm which he owned.

But even after the marriage, old Pritchel still seemed to draw the line against his son-in-law. He built a new small house for them two miles from his own, where the daughter was presently raising chickens for the market. According to rumor old Pritchel, who hardly ever went anywhere anyway, had never once entered the new house, so that he saw even this last remaining child only once a week. This would be when she and her husband would drive each Sunday in the second-hand truck in which the son-in-law marketed the chickens, to take Sunday dinner with old Pritchel in the old house where Pritchel now did his own cooking and housework. In fact, the neighbors said the only reason he allowed the son-in-law to enter his house even then was so that his daughter could prepare him a decent hot meal once a week.

So for the next two years, occasionally in Jefferson, the county seat, but more frequently in the little cross-roads hamlet near his home, the son-in-law would be seen and heard too. He was a man in the middle forties, neither short nor tall nor thin nor stout (in fact, he and his father-in-law could easily have cast that same shadow which later for a short time they did), with a cold, contemptuous intelligent face and a voice lazy with anecdote of the teeming outland which his listeners had never seen; —a dweller among the cities, though never from his own accounting long resident in any one of them, who within the first three months of his residence among them had impressed upon the people whose way of life he had assumed, one definite personal habit by which he presently became known throughout the whole county, even by men who had never seen him. This was a harsh and contemptuous derogation, sometimes without even provocation or reason or opportunity, of our local southern custom of drinking whiskey by mixing sugar and water with it. He called it effeminacy, a pap for children, himself drinking even our harsh, violent, illicit and unaged homemade corn whiskey without even a sip of water to follow it.

Then on this last Sunday morning he telephoned the sheriff that he had killed his wife and met the officers at his father-in-law's door and said: 'I have already carried her into the house. So you wont need to waste breath telling me I shouldn't have touched her until you got here.'

'I reckon it was all right to take her up out of the dirt,' the sheriff said. 'It was an accident, I believe you said.'

'Then you believe wrong,' Flint said. 'I said I killed her.'

And that was all. The sheriff brought him to Jefferson and locked him in a cell in the jail. And that evening after supper the sheriff came through the side door into the study where Uncle Gavin was supervising me in the drawing of a brief. Uncle Gavin was only county, not District, attorney. But he and the sheriff, who had been sheriff off and on even longer than Uncle Gavin had been county attorney, had been friends all that while. I mean friends in the sense that two men who play chess together are friends, even though sometimes their aims are diametrically opposed. I heard them discuss it once.

'I'm interested in truth,' the sheriff said.

'So am I,' Uncle Gavin said. 'It's so rare. But I am more interested in justice and human beings.'

'Aint truth and justice the same thing?' the sheriff said.

'Since when?' Uncle Gavin said. 'In my time I have seen truth that was anything under the sun but just, and I have seen justice using tools and instruments I wouldn't want to touch with a ten-foot fence rail.'

The sheriff told us about the killing, standing, looming above the table-lamp—a big man with little hard eyes, talking down at Uncle Gavin's wild shock of prematurely white hair and his quick thin face, while Uncle Gavin sat on the back of his neck practically, his legs crossed on the desk, chewing the bitt of his corn cob pipe and spinning and unspinning around his finger his watch-chain weighted with the Phi Beta Kappa key he got at Harvard.

'Why?' Uncle Gavin said.

'I asked him that, myself,' the sheriff said. 'He said, "Why do men ever kill their wives? Call it for the insurance." '

'That's wrong,' Uncle Gavin said. 'It's women who murder their spouses for immediate personal gain—insurance policies, or at what they believe is the instigation or promise of another man. Men murder their wives from hatred or rage or despair, or to keep them from talking since not even bribery nor even simple absence can bridle a woman's tongue.'

'Correct,' the sheriff said. He blinked his little eyes at Uncle Gavin. 'It's like he wanted to be locked up in jail. Not like he was submitting to arrest because he had killed his wife, but like he had killed her so that he would be locked up, arrested. Guarded.'

'Why?' Uncle Gavin said.

'Correct too,' the sheriff said. 'When a man deliberately locks doors behind himself, it's because he is afraid. And a man who would voluntarily have himself locked up on suspicion of murder. . . . .' He batted his hard little eyes at Uncle Gavin for a good ten seconds now while Uncle Gavin looked just as hard back at him. 'Because he wasn't afraid. Not then nor at any time. Now and then you meet a man that aint ever been afraid, not even of himself. He's one.'

'If that's what he wanted you to do,' Uncle Gavin said, 'why did you do it?'

'You think I should have waited a while?'

They looked at one another a while. Uncle Gavin wasn't spinning the watch-chain now. 'All right,' he said. 'Old Man Pritchel——'

'I was coming to that,' the sheriff said. 'Nothing.'

'Nothing?' Uncle Gavin said. 'You didn't even see him?' And the sheriff told that too—how as he and the deputy and Flint stood on the gallery, they suddenly saw the old man looking out at them through a window—a face rigid, furious, glaring at them through the glass for a second and then withdrawn, vanished, leaving an impression of furious exultation and raging triumph and something else. . . .

'Fear?' Uncle Gavin said.

'Fear?' the sheriff said. 'No. I tell you, he wasn't afraid——Oh,' he said. 'You mean Pritchel.' This time he looked at Uncle Gavin so long that at last Uncle Gavin said,

'All right. Go on.' And the sheriff told that too: how they entered the house, the hall, and he stopped and knocked at the locked door of the room where they had seen the face and he even called old Pritchel's name and still got no answer. And how they went on and found Mrs Flint on a bed in the back room with the shotgun wound in her neck, and Flint's battered truck drawn up beside the back steps as if they had just got out of it.

'There were three dead squirrels in the truck,' the sheriff said. 'I'd say they had been shot since daylight.'—and the blood on the steps and on the ground between the steps and the truck as if she had been shot from inside the truck, and the gun itself, still containing the spent shell, standing just inside the hall door as a man would put it down when he entered the house. And how the sheriff went back up the hall and knocked again at the locked door——

'Locked where?' Uncle Gavin said.

'On the inside,' the sheriff said.—and shouted against the door's blank surface that he would break the door in if Mr Pritchel didn't answer and open it, and how this time the harsh furious old voice answered, shouting:

'Get out of my house! Take that murderer and get out of my house!'

'I must talk to you,' the sheriff answered. 'You will have to make a statement.'

'I'll make my statement when the time comes for it!' the old man shouted. 'Get out of my house, all of you!' And how he (the sheriff) sent the deputy in the car to fetch the nearest neighbor, and he and Flint waited until the deputy came back with a man and his wife. Then they brought Flint on to town and locked him up and the sheriff telephoned back to old Pritchel's house and the neighbor answered and told him how the old man was still locked in the room, refusing to come out or even to answer save to order them all (several other neighbors had arrived by now, word of the tragedy having spread) to leave. But some of them would stay in the house, no matter what the seemingly crazed old man said or did, and the funeral would be tomorrow.

'And that's all?' Uncle Gavin said.

'That's all,' the sheriff said. 'Because it's too late now.'

'For instance?' Uncle Gavin said.

'The wrong one is dead.'

'That happens,' Uncle Gavin said. 'For instance?'

'That clay-pit business.'

'What clay-pit business?' Because the whole county knew about old Pritchel's clay-pit. It was a formation of malleable clay right in the middle of his farm, of which people in the adjacent countryside made quite serviceable though crude pottery—what times they could manage to dig that much of it up before Mr Pritchel saw them digging and reached there to drive them off. For generations, Indian and even aboriginal relics—flint arrow-heads, axes and dishes and skulls and thighbones and pipes—had been excavated from it by random boys, and a few years ago a party of archaeologists from the State University had dug into it until Old Man Pritchel got there, this time with a shotgun. But everybody knew this; this was not what the sheriff was telling, and now Uncle Gavin was sitting erect in the chair and his feet were on the floor now.

'I hadn't heard about this,' Uncle Gavin said.

'It's common knowledge out there,' the sheriff said. 'In fact, you might call it the local outdoor sport. It began about six weeks ago. They are three northern men. They're trying to buy the whole farm from Uncle Wes, to get the pit and manufacture some kind of road material out of the clay, I understand. The folks out there are still watching them trying to buy it. Apparently them northerners are the only folks in the country that dont know yet old Wes aint got any notion of selling even the clay to them, let alone the farm.'

'They've made him an offer, of course.'

'Probably a good one. It runs all the way from two hundred and fifty dollars to two hundred and fifty thousand, depending on who's telling it. Them northerners just dont know how to handle him. If they would just set in and convince him that everybody in the county is hoping he wont sell it to them, they could probably buy it before supper tonight.' He stared at Uncle Gavin, batting his eyes. 'So the wrong one is dead, you see. If it was that clay-pit, he's no nearer to it than he was yesterday. He's worse off than he was yesterday. Then there wasn't anything between him and his pa-in-law's money but whatever private wishes and hopes and feelings that dim-witted girl might have had. Now there's a penitentiary wall, and likely a rope. It dont make sense. If he was afraid of a possible witness, he not only destroyed the witness before there was anything he must have feared to have witnessed, before there was any witness to be destroyed, he has set up a signboard saying "Watch me and mark me" not just to this county and this state but to all folks everywhere who believe the Book where it says *Thou Shalt Not Kill*—and then went and got himself locked up in the very place created to punish him for this crime and restrain him from the next one. Something went wrong.'

'I hope so,' Uncle Gavin said.

'You hope so?'

'Yes. That something went wrong which has already happened, rather than that what has already happened is not finished yet.'

'How not finished yet?' the sheriff said. 'How can he finish whatever it is he aims to finish? Aint he already locked up in jail, with the only man in the county who might make bond to free him, being the father of the woman he as good as confessed he murdered?'

'It looks that way,' Uncle Gavin said. 'Was there an insurance policy?'

'I dont know,' the sheriff said. 'I'll find that out tomorrow. But that aint what I want to know. I want to know why he wanted to be locked up in jail. Because I tell you he wasn't afraid, then nor at any other time. You already guessed who it was out there that was afraid.'

But we were not to learn that answer yet. And there was an insurance policy. But by the time we learned about that, something else had happened which sent everything else temporarily out of mind. At daylight the next morning, when the jailer went and looked into Flint's cell, it was empty. He had not broken out. He had walked out, out of the cell, out of the jail, out of the town and apparently out of the country—no trace, no sign, no man who had seen him or seen anyone who might have been him. It was not yet sunup when I let the sheriff in at the side study door; Uncle Gavin was already sitting up in bed when we reached his bedroom.

'Old Man Pritchel!' Uncle Gavin said. 'Only we are already too late.'

'What's the matter with you?' the sheriff said. 'I told you last night he was already too late the second he pulled that wrong trigger. Besides, just to be in position to ease your mind, I've already telephoned out there. Been a dozen folks in the house all night, sitting up with the— with Mrs Flint, and old Wes still locked in his room and all right too. They heard him bumping and blundering around in there just before daylight, and so somebody knocked on the door and kept on knocking and calling him until he finally opened the door wide enough to give them all a good cussing and order them again to get out of his house and stay out. Then he locked the door again. Old fellow's been hit pretty hard, I reckon. He must have seen it when it happened, and at his age, and having already druv the whole human race away from his house except that half-wit girl, until at last even she up and left him, even at any cost. I reckon it aint any wonder she married even a man like Flint. What is it the Book says? "Who lives by the sword, so shall he die."?—the sword in old Wes's case being whatever it was he decided he preferred in place of human beings, while he was still young and hale and strong and didn't need them. But to keep your mind easy, I sent Bryan Ewell out there thirty minutes ago and told him not to let that locked door—or old Wes himself, if he comes out of it—out of his sight until I told him to, and I sent Ben Berry and some others out to Flint's house and told Ben to telephone me. And I'll call you when I hear anything. Which wont be anything, because that fellow's gone. He got caught yesterday because he made a mistake, and the fellow that can walk out of that jail like he did aint going to make two mistakes within five hundred miles of Jefferson or Mississippi either.'

'Mistake?' Uncle Gavin said. 'He just told us this morning why he wanted to be put in jail.'

'And why was that?'

'So he could escape from it.'

'And why get out again, when he was already out and could have stayed out by just running instead of telephoning me he had committed a murder?'

'I dont know,' Uncle Gavin said. 'Are you sure Old Man Pritchel——'

'Didn't I just tell you folks saw and talked to him through that half-opened door this morning? And Bryan Ewell probably sitting in a chair tilted against that door right this minute—or he better be. I'll telephone you if I hear anything. But I've already told you that too—that it wont be nothing.'

He telephoned an hour later. He had just talked to the deputy who had searched Flint's house, reporting only that Flint had been there sometime in the night—the back door open, an oil lamp shattered on the floor where Flint had apparently knocked it while fumbling in the dark, since the deputy found, behind a big, open, hurriedly ransacked trunk, a twisted spill of paper which Flint had obviously used to light his search of the trunk—a scrap of paper torn from a billboard——

'A what?' Uncle Gavin said.

'That's what I said,' the sheriff said. 'And Ben says, "All right, then send somebody else out here, if my reading aint good enough to suit you. It was a scrap of paper which was evidently torn from the corner of a billboard because it says on the scrap in English that even I can read——" and I says, "Tell me exactly what it is you're holding in your hand." And he did. It's a page, from a magazine or a small paper named Billboard or maybe The Billboard. There's some more printing on it but Ben cant read it because he lost his spectacles back in the woods while he was surrounding the house to catch Flint doing whatever it was he expected to catch him doing—cooking breakfast, maybe. Do you know what it is?'

'Yes,' Uncle Gavin said.

'Do you know what it means—what it was doing there?'

'Yes,' Uncle Gavin said. 'But why?'

'Well, I cant tell you. And he never will. Because he's gone, Gavin. Oh, we'll catch him—somebody will I mean, someday, somewhere. But it wont be here, and it wont be for this. It's like that poor, harmless, half-witted girl wasn't important enough for even that justice you claim you prefer above truth, to avenge her.'

And that did seem to be all of it. Mrs Flint was buried that afternoon. The old man was still locked in his room during the funeral, and even after they departed with the coffin for the churchyard, leaving in the house only the deputy in his tilted chair outside the locked door, and two neighbor women who remained to cook a hot meal for old Pritchel, finally prevailing on him to open the door long enough to take the tray from them. And he thanked them for it, clumsily and gruffly, thanking them for their kindness during all the last twenty-four hours. One of the women was moved enough to offer to return tomorrow and cook another meal for him, whereupon his old-time acerbity and choler returned and the kind-hearted woman suffered another complete reversal and was even regretting that she had made the offer at all. Then the harsh, cracked old voice from inside the half-closed door ruined that too by adding: 'I dont need no help. I aint had no darter nohow in two years,' and the door slammed in their faces and the bolt shot home.

Then the two women left, and there was only the deputy sitting in his tilted chair beside the door. He was back in town the next morning, telling how the old man had snatched the door suddenly open and kicked the chair out from beneath the dozing deputy before he could move and ordered him off the place with violent curses, and how as he (the deputy) peered at the house from around the corner of the barn a short time later, the shotgun blared from the kitchen window and the charge of squirrel shot slammed into the stable wall not a yard above his head. The sheriff telephoned that to Uncle Gavin too:

'So he's out there alone again. And since that's what he seems to want, it's all right with me. Sure I feel sorry for him. I feel sorry for anybody that has to live with a disposition like his. Old and alone, to have all this happen to him. It's like being snatched up by a tornado and whirled and slung and then slammed right back down where you started from, without even the benefit and pleasure of having taken a trip. What was it I said yesterday about living by the sword?'

'I dont remember,' Uncle Gavin said. 'You said a lot yesterday.'

'And a lot of it was right. I said it was finished yesterday. And it is. That fellow will trip himself again someday, but it wont be here.'

Only it was more than that. It was as if Flint had never been here at all—no mark, no scar to show that he had ever been in the jail cell in which for twenty-four hours now there had even been another prisoner—the meager group of people who pitied but did not mourn, departing, separating, from the raw grave of the woman who had had little enough hold on our lives at best, whom a few of us had known without ever having seen her and some of us had seen without knowing or even wondering who she was—the childless old man whom most of us had never seen at all, once more alone in the house where, as he said himself, there had been no child anyway in two years.

'As though none of it had ever happened,' Uncle Gavin said. 'As if Flint had not only never been in that cell, he had never existed at all: that triumvirate of murderer, victim, and bereaved not three flesh-and-blood people but just an illusion, a shadow-play on a sheet, not only neither men nor women nor young nor old but just three labels which cast two shadows for the simple and only reason that it requires a minimum of two in order to postulate the verities of injustice and grief. That's it. They have never cast but two shadows, even though they did bear three labels, names. It was as though only by dying did that poor woman ever gain enough substance and reality even to cast a shadow. Only her shadow still makes only two of them. And since Old Man Pritchel is still out there in that house, probably washing his dinner dishes now—provided he does wash them, Flint did not exist at all, did he?'

'But somebody killed her,' I said.

'Yes,' Uncle Gavin said. 'Somebody killed her.'

That was at noon. About five that afternoon I answered the telephone. It was the sheriff. 'Is your uncle there?' he said. 'Tell him to wait. I'm coming right over.' He had a stranger with him—a city man, in neat city clothes: 'This is Mr Workman,' the sheriff said. 'The adjustor. There was an insurance policy. For five hundred, taken out seventeen months ago. Hardly enough to murder anybody for.'

'If it ever had been a murder,' the adjustor said. His voice was cold too, cold yet at the same time at a sort of seething boil. 'That policy will be paid at once, without question or any further investigation. And I'll tell you something else you people here dont seem to know yet. That old man is crazy. It was not the man Flint who should have been brought to town and locked up.'

Only it was the sheriff who told that too: how yesterday afternoon the insurance company's Memphis office had received a telegram, signed with Old Man Pritchel's name, notifying them of the insured's death, and the adjustor arrived at Old Man Pritchel's house about two oclock this afternoon and within thirty minutes had extracted from Old Man Pritchel himself the truth about his daughter's death:—the facts of it which the physical evidence—the truck and the three dead squirrels and the blood on the steps and on the ground—supported. This was that while the daughter was cooking dinner, Pritchel and Flint had driven the truck down to Pritchel's woods lot to shoot squirrels for supper—'And that's correct,' the sheriff said. 'I asked. They did that every Sunday morning. Pritchel wouldn't let anybody but Flint shoot his squirrels, and he wouldn't even let Flint shoot them unless he was along.'—and they shot the three squirrels and Flint drove the truck back to the house and up beside the back steps and the woman came out to take the squirrels and Flint opened the door and picked up the gun to get out of the truck and stumbled, caught his heel on the edge of the running-board perhaps and perhaps flinging up the hand carrying the gun to break his fall, so that the muzzle of the gun was pointing right at his wife's head when it went off. And Old Man Pritchel not only denied having sent the wire, he violently and profanely repudiated any and all implication or suggestion that he even knew the policy existed at all. He denied to the very last that the shooting had been any part of an accident. He tried to revoke his own testimony as to what had happened when the daughter came out to get the dead squirrels and the gun went off, repudiating his own story when he realised that he had cleared his son-in-law of murder, snatching the paper from the adjustor's hand, which he apparently believed was the policy itself, and attempting to tear it up and destroy it before the adjustor could stop him.

'Why?' Uncle Gavin said.

'Why not?' the sheriff said. 'We had let Flint get away; Mr Pritchel knew he was loose somewhere in the world. Do you reckon he aimed to let the man that killed his daughter get paid for it?'

'Maybe,' Uncle Gavin said. 'But I dont think so. I dont think he is worried about that at all. I think Mr Pritchel knows that Joel Flint is not going to collect that policy or any other prize. Maybe he knew a little country jail like ours wasn't going to hold a wide-travelled ex-carnival man, and he expected Flint to come back out there and this time he was ready for him. And I think that as soon as people stop worrying him, he will send you word to come out there, and he will tell you so.'

'Hah,' the adjustor said. 'Then they must have stopped worrying him. Listen to this. When I got there this afternoon, there were three men in the parlor with him. They had a certified check. It was a big check. They were buying his farm from him, lock stock and barrel, and I didn't know land in this country was worth that much either, incidentally. He had the deed all drawn and signed, but when I told them who I was, they agreed to wait until I could get back to town here and tell somebody—the sheriff, probably. And I left, and that old lunatic was still standing in the door, shaking that deed at me and croaking: "Tell the sheriff, damn you! Get a lawyer, too! Get that Lawyer Stevens. I hear tell he claims to be pretty slick!" '

'We thank you,' the sheriff said. He both spoke and moved with that deliberate, slightly florid, old-fashioned courtesy which only big men can wear, except that his was constant; this was the first time I ever saw him quit anyone shortly, even when he would see them again tomorrow. He didn't even look at the adjustor again. 'My car's outside,' he told Uncle Gavin.

So just before sunset we drove up to the neat picket fence enclosing Old Man Pritchel's neat, bare little yard and neat, tight little house, in front of which stood the big, dust-covered car with its city license plates and Flint's battered truck with a strange Negro youth at the wheel—strange because Old Man Pritchel had never had a servant of any sort save his daughter, and no Negro at all on his land.

'He's leaving too,' Uncle Gavin said.

'That's his right,' the sheriff said. We mounted the steps. But before we reached the door, Old Man Pritchel was already shouting for us to come in—the harsh, cracked old man's voice shouting at us from beyond the hall, beyond the door to the dining-room where a tremendous old-fashioned telescope bag, strapped and bulging, sat on a chair and the three northerners in dusty khaki stood watching the door and Old Man Pritchel himself sat at the table. And I saw for the first time

(Uncle Gavin told me he had seen him only twice) the uncombed thatch of white hair, a fierce tangle of eyebrows above steel-framed spectacles, a jut of untrimmed moustache and a scrabble of short beard stained with chewing tobacco to the color of dirty cotton.

'Come in,' he said. 'That Lawyer Stevens, heh?'

'Yes, Uncle Wes,' the sheriff said.

'Hehm,' the old man barked. 'Well, Hub,' he said. 'Can I sell my land, or cant I?'

'Of course, Uncle Wes,' the sheriff said. 'We hadn't heard you aimed to.'

'Heh,' the old man said. 'Maybe this changed my mind.' The check and the folded deed both lay on the table in front of him. He pushed the check toward the sheriff. He didn't look at Uncle Gavin again; he just said: 'You, too.' Uncle Gavin and the sheriff moved to the table and stood looking down at the check. Neither of them touched it. I could see their faces. There was nothing in them. 'Well?' Mr Pritchel said.

'It's a good price, Uncle Wes,' the sheriff said.

This time he said 'Hah!' short and harsh. He unfolded the deed and spun it to face, not the sheriff but Uncle Gavin. 'Well?' he said. 'You, Lawyer?'

'It's all right, Mr Pritchel,' Uncle Gavin said. The old man sat back, both hands on the table before him, his head tilted back as he looked up at the sheriff.

'Well?' he said. 'Fish, or cut bait.'

'It's your land,' the sheriff said. 'What you do with it is no man's business else.'

'Hah,' Mr Pritchel said. He didn't move. 'All right, gentlemen.' He didn't move at all; one of the strangers came forward and took up the deed. 'I'll be out of the house in thirty minutes. You can take possession then, or you will find the key under the mat tomorrow morning.' I dont believe he even looked after them as they went out, though I couldn't be sure because of the glare on his spectacles. Then I knew that he was looking at the sheriff, had been looking at him for a minute or more, and then I saw that he was trembling, jerking and shaking as the old tremble, although his hands on the table were as motionless as two lumps of the clay which he had just sold would have been.

'So you let him get away,' he said.

'That's right,' the sheriff said. 'But you wait, Uncle Wes. We'll catch him.'

'When?' the old man said. 'Two years? Five years? Ten years? I am seventy-four years old; buried my wife and four children. Where will I be in ten years?'

'Here, I hope,' the sheriff said.

'Here?' the old man said. 'Didn't you just hear me tell that fellow he could have this house in thirty minutes? I own a automobile truck now; I got a nigger to drive it. I got money to spend now, and something to spend it for.'

'Spend it for what?' the sheriff said. 'That check? Even this boy here would have to start early and run late to get shut of that much money in ten years.'

'Spend it running down the man that killed my Ellie!' He rose suddenly, thrusting his chair back. He staggered, but when the sheriff stepped quickly toward him, he flung his arm out and seemed actually to strike the sheriff back a pace. 'Let be,' he said, panting. Then he said, harsh and loud in his cracked shaking voice: 'Get out of here! Get out of my house, all of you!' But the sheriff didn't move, nor did we, and after a moment the old man stopped trembling. But he was still holding to the table-edge. But his voice was quiet. 'Hand me my whiskey. On the sideboard. And three glasses.' The sheriff fetched them—an old-fashioned cut-glass decanter and three heavy tumblers—and set them before him. And when he spoke this time, his voice was almost gentle even and I knew what the woman had felt that evening when she offered to come back tomorrow and cook another meal for him: 'You'll have to excuse me. I'm tired. I've had a heap of trouble lately, and I reckon I'm wore out. Maybe a change is what I need.'

'But not tonight, Uncle Wes,' the sheriff said.

And then again, as when the woman had offered to come back and cook, he ruined it. 'Maybe I wont start tonight,' he said. 'And then maybe again I will. But you folks want to get on back to town, so we'll just drink to goodbye and better days.' He unstoppered the decanter and poured whiskey into the three tumblers and set the decanter down and looked about the table. 'You, boy,' he said, 'hand me the water-bucket. It's on the back gallery shelf.' Then, as I turned and started toward the door, I saw him reach and take up the sugar-bowl and plunge the spoon into the sugar and then I stopped too. And I remember Uncle Gavin's and the sheriff's faces and I could not believe my eyes either as he put the spoonful of sugar into the raw whiskey and started to stir it. Because I had not only watched Uncle Gavin, and the sheriff when he would come to play chess with Uncle Gavin, but Uncle Gavin's father too who was my grandfather, and my own father before he died, and all the other men who would come to Grandfather's house who drank cold toddies as we call them, and even I knew that to make a cold toddy you do not put the sugar into the whiskey because sugar will not dissolve in raw whiskey but only lies in a little intact swirl like sand at the bottom of the glass; that you first put the water into the glass and dissolve the sugar into the water in a ritual almost, then you add the whiskey, and that anyone like Old Man Pritchel who must have been watching men make cold toddies for seventy-four years and had been making and drinking them himself for at least fifty-three, would know this too. And I remember how the man we had thought was Old Man Pritchel realised too late what he was doing and jerked his head up just as Uncle Gavin sprang toward him, and swung his arm back and hurled the glass at Uncle Gavin's head, and the thud of the flung glass against the wall and the dark splash it made and the crash of the table as it went over and the raw stink of the spilled whiskey from the decanter and Uncle Gavin shouting at the sheriff: 'Grab him, Hub! Grab him!'

Then we were all three on him. I remember the savage strength and speed of the body which was no old man's body; I saw him duck beneath the sheriff's arm and the entire wig came off; I seemed to see his whole face wrenching itself furiously free from beneath the makeup which bore the painted wrinkles and the false eyebrows. When the sheriff snatched the beard and moustache off, the flesh seemed to come with it, springing quick and pink and then crimson, as though in that last desperate cast he had had to beard, disguise, not his face so much as the very blood which he had spilled.

It took us only thirty minutes to find old Mr Pritchel's body. It was under the feed-room in his stable, in a shallow and hurried trench, scarcely covered from sight. His hair had not only been dyed, it had been trimmed, the eyebrows trimmed and dyed too and the moustache and beard shaved off. He was wearing the identical garments which Flint had worn to the jail and he had been struck at least one crushing blow on the face, apparently with the flat of the same axe which had split his skull from behind, so that his features were almost unrecognisable and, after another two or three weeks underground, would perhaps have been even unidentifiable as those of an old man. And pillowed carefully beneath the head was a big ledger almost six inches thick and weighing almost twenty pounds and filled with the carefully pasted clippings which covered twenty years and more. It was the record and tale of the gift, the talent, which at the last he had misapplied and betrayed and which had then turned and destroyed him. It was all there: inception, course, peak, and then decline—the handbills, the theatre programs, the news clippings and even one actual ten-foot poster:

SIGNOR CANOVA
Master of Illusion
He Disappears While You Watch Him
Management offers One
Thousand Dollars in Cash
To Any Man or Woman or Child

Last of all was the final clipping, from our Memphis-printed daily paper, under the Jefferson date-line, which was news and not press-agentry. This was the account of that last gamble in which he had cast his gift and his life against money, wealth, and lost—the clipped fragment of news-sheet which recorded the end not of one life but of three, though even here two of them cast but one shadow: not only that of the harmless dim-witted woman, but of Joel Flint and Signor Canova too, with scattered among them and marking the date of that death too, the cautiously-worded advertisements in *Variety* and *Billboard*, using the new changed name and no takers probably, since Signor Canova the Great was already dead then and already serving his purgatory in this circus for six months and that circus for eight—bandsman, ringman, Bornean wild man, down to the last stage where he touched bottom: the travelling from country town to country town with a roulette wheel wired against imitation watches and pistols which would not shoot, until one day instinct perhaps showed him one more chance to use the gift again.

'And lost this time for good,' the sheriff said. We were in the study again. Beyond the open side door fireflies winked and drifted across the summer night and the crickets and tree-frogs cheeped and whirred. 'It was that insurance policy. If that adjustor hadn't come to town and sent us back out there in time to watch him try to dissolve sugar in raw whiskey, he would have collected that check and taken that truck and got clean away. Instead, he sends for the adjustor, then he practically dares you and me to come out there and see past that wig and paint—'

'You said something the other day about his destroying his witness too soon,' Uncle Gavin said. 'She wasn't his witness. The witness he destroyed was the one we were supposed to find under that feed-room.'

'Witness to what?' the sheriff said. 'To the fact that Joel Flint no longer existed?'

'Partly. But mostly to the first crime, the old one: the one in which Signor Canova died. He intended for that witness to be found. That's why he didn't bury it, hide it better and deeper. As soon as somebody found it, he would be at once and forever not only rich but free, free not only of Signor Canova who had betrayed him by dying eight years ago, but of Joel Flint too. Even if we had found it before he had a chance to leave, what would he have said?'

'He ought to have battered the face a little more,' the sheriff said.

'I doubt it,' Uncle Gavin said. 'What would he have said?'

'All right,' the sheriff said. 'What?'

'"Yes, I killed him. He murdered my daughter." And what would you have said, being, as you are, the Law?'

'Nothing,' the sheriff said after a time.

'Nothing,' Uncle Gavin said. A dog was barking somewhere too, not a big dog, and then a screech-owl flew into the mulberry tree in the back yard and began to cry, plaintive and tremulous, and all the little furred creatures would be moving now—the field mice, the possums and rabbits and foxes and the legless vertebrates—creeping or scurrying about the dark land which beneath the rainless summer stars was just dark: not desolate. 'That's one reason he did it,' Uncle Gavin said.

'One reason?' the sheriff said. 'What's the other?'

'The other is the real one. It had nothing to do with the money; he probably could not have helped obeying it if he had wanted to. That gift he had. His first regret right now is probably not that he was caught, but that he was caught too soon, before the body was found and he had the chance to identify it as his own;—before Signor Canova had had time to toss his gleaming top-hat vanishing behind him and bow to the amazed and storm-like staccato of adulant palms and turn and stride once or twice and then himself vanish from the pacing spotlight— gone, to be seen no more. Think what he did: he convicted himself of murder when he could very likely have escaped by flight; he acquitted himself of it after he was already free again. Then he dared you and me to come out there and actually be his witnesses and guarantors in the consummation of the very act which he knew we had been trying to prevent. What else could the possession of such a gift as his have engendered, and the successful practicing of it have increased, but a supreme contempt for mankind? You told me yourself that he had never been afraid in his life.'

'Yes,' the sheriff said. 'The Book itself says somewhere, *Know thyself.* Aint there another book somewhere that says, *Man, fear thyself, thine arrogance and vanity and pride*? You ought to know; you claim to be a book man. Didn't you tell me that's what that luck-charm on your watch-chain means? What book is that in?'

'It's in all of them,' Uncle Gavin said. 'The good ones, I mean. It's said in a lot of different ways, but it's there.'

KNIGHT'S GAMBIT

I.

One of them knocked. But the door opened in the middle of it, swinging right out from under the rapping knuckles, so that the two callers were already in the room when he and his uncle looked up from the chessboard. Then his uncle recognised them too.

Their name was Harriss. They were brother and sister. At first glance they might have been twins, not just to strangers but to most of Jefferson too. Because there were probably not half a dozen people in Yoknapatawpha County who actually knew which one was the oldest. They lived six miles from town on what twenty years ago had been just another plantation raising cotton for the market and corn and hay to feed the mules which made the cotton. But now it was a county (or for that matter, a north Mississippi) landmark: a mile square of white panel and rail paddock- and pasture-fences and electric-lit stables and a once-simple country house transmogrified now into something a little smaller than a Before-the-War Hollywood set.

They came in and stood, rosy, young, delicate and expensive-looking, flushed from the December night. His uncle rose. 'Miss Harriss, Mr Harriss,' he said. 'But you are already in, so I cant——'

But the boy didn't wait for that either. Then he saw that the boy held his sister, not by the arm or elbow, but by the forearm above the wrist like in the old lithographs of the policeman with his cringing captive or the victory-flushed soldier with his shrinking Sabine prey. And that was when he saw the girl's face.

'You're Stevens,' the boy said. He didn't even demand it. He stated it.

'That's partly correct,' his uncle said. 'But let it pass. What can I——'

Nor did the boy wait for that. He turned to the girl. 'That's Stevens,' he said. 'Tell him.'

But she didn't speak. She just stood there, in the evening dress and a fur coat which had cost a good deal more than any other girl (or woman either) in Jefferson or Yoknapatawpha County had to spend for such, staring at his uncle with that frozen sickness of dread or terror or whatever it was on her face, while the knuckles of the boy's hand grew whiter and whiter on her wrist. 'Tell him,' the boy said.

Then she spoke. You could hardly hear her. 'Captain Gualdres. At our house——'

His uncle had taken a few steps toward them. Now he stopped too, standing in the middle of the floor, looking at her. 'Yes,' his uncle said. 'Tell me.'

But it seemed as if that one expiring rush was all of it. She just stood there, trying to tell his uncle something, whatever it was, with her eyes; trying to tell both of them for that matter, since he was there too. But they found out quickly enough what it was, or at least what it was the boy wanted her to say, had dragged her in to town by the arm to say. Or at least what he thought it was she wanted to say. Because he should have known then that his uncle probably knew already more than the boy or the girl either intended to say yet; perhaps, even then, all of it. But it would be a little while yet before he would realise that last. And the reason he was so slow about it was his uncle himself.

'Yes,' the boy said, in exactly the same tone and voice which had declined to address the older man by any title of courtesy or deference to age; he—Charles—watched the boy staring at his uncle too—the same delicate face which the sister had, but with nothing delicate about the eyes. They—the eyes—stared at his uncle without even bothering to be hard: they just waited. 'Captain Gualdres, our so-called house-guest. We want him out of our house and out of Jefferson too.'

'I see,' his uncle said. He said, 'I'm on the draft board here. I dont remember your name in the registration.'

But the boy's stare didn't change at all. It was not even contemptuous. It just waited.

Then his uncle was looking at the sister; his voice was quite different now. 'Is that what it is?' his uncle said.

But she didn't answer. She just stared at his uncle with that urgent desperation, her arm hanging at her side and her brother's knuckles white around her wrist. Now his uncle was speaking to the boy too though he still watched the girl and his voice was even still gentle too or at least quiet:

'Why did you come to me? What makes you think I can help you? That I should?'

'You're the Law here, aren't you?' the boy said.

His uncle still watched the sister. 'I'm the County Attorney.' He was still talking to her too. 'But even if I could help you, why should I?'

But again it was the boy: 'Because I dont intend that a fortune-hunting Spick shall marry my mother.'

Now it seemed to him that his uncle really looked at the boy for the first time. 'I see,' his uncle said. Now his uncle's voice was different. It was no louder, there was just no more gentleness in it, as though for the first time his uncle could (or anyway had) stop speaking to the sister: 'That's your affair and your right. I ask you again: why should I do anything about it, even if I could?' And now the two of them—his uncle and the boy—spoke crisply and rapidly; it was almost as though they stood toe to toe, slapping each other:

'He was engaged to marry my sister. When he found out that the money would still be our mother's as long as she lived, he ratted.'

'I see. You wish to employ the deportation laws of the Federal government to avenge your sister on her jilter.'

This time even the boy didn't answer. He just stared at the older man with such cold, controlled, mature malevolence that he—Charles—watched his uncle actually pause for a moment before turning back to the girl, speaking—his uncle—again in the gentle voice, though even then his uncle had to repeat the question before she answered:

'Is this true?'

'Not engaged,' she whispered.

'But you love him?'

But the boy didn't even give her time, didn't give anybody time. 'What does she know about love?' he said. 'Will you take the case, or do I report you to your superiors too?'

'Can you risk being away from home that long?' his uncle said in the mild voice which he—Charles—knew anyway and, if it had been addressed to him, would have leaped at once to hold his hat. But the boy didn't even pause.

'Say it in English if you can,' he said.

'I wont take your case,' his uncle said.

For a moment still the boy stared at his uncle, holding the girl by the wrist. Then he—Charles—thought the boy was going to jerk, fling her bodily through the door ahead of him. But he even released her, himself (not the host, the owner of the door which he had already passed through once without even waiting for permission, let alone invitation) opening the door, then standing aside for the girl to precede him through it—a gesture, a pantomime of courtesy and deference even when automatic from habit and early training, as his was: automatic: and from long habit and the best of training under the best masters and tutors and preceptors in what the ladies of Yoknapatawpha County anyway would call the best of company. But there was no deference in it now: only arrogance: swaggering, insulting not just to whom offered but to everyone watching it too, not even looking at the sister for whom he held the door but still staring at the man twice his age whose domicile he had now violated twice.

'All right,' the boy said. 'Dont say you were not warned.'

Then they were gone. His uncle closed the door. But for a second his uncle didn't move. It was a pause, a check, an almost infinitesimal instant of immobility so quick and infinitesimal that probably nobody but he, Charles, would have remarked it. And he noticed it only because he had never before seen his uncle, that quick and nervous man garrulous in speech and movement both, falter or check in either once he had begun them. Then his uncle turned and came back toward where he, Charles, still sat at his side of the chessboard, not even realising yet, so rapid and staccato the whole thing had been, that he not only hadn't risen himself, he would hardly have had time to even if he had thought about it. And maybe his mouth was open a little too (he was not quite eighteen yet and even at eighteen there were still a few situations which even a man of his uncle's capacity for alarms would have to admit you might not be able to assimilate at the drop of a hat or the slam of a door, or at least hadn't needed to yet), sitting at his side of the half-played game watching his uncle come back to his chair and begin to sit back down and reach for the overturned cob pipe on the smoking stand all in the same motion.

'Warned?' he said.

'So he called it,' his uncle said, finishing the sitting down and approaching the bitt of the pipe to his mouth and already taking a match from the box on the smoking stand, so that the actual relighting of the pipe would be merely a continuation of the coming back from the door: 'I'd call it a threat, myself.'

And he repeated that too, with his mouth still open probably.

'All right,' his uncle said. 'What would you call it then?'—striking the match and in the same sweep of the arm bringing the flame to the cold ash in the pipe, and still talking around the stem into the vain shape of the invisible puffing so that it would be a second or two yet before he would realise that all he had to smoke now was the match.

Then his uncle dropped the match into the ashtray and with the other hand made the move which without doubt he had already planned out long before the knock came on the door which he had been too late or at least too slow to answer or even say 'Come in.' He made the move without even looking, moving the pawn which exposed his, Charles's, castle to the rook which his uncle had probably been convinced even longer back than the plan that he, Charles, had forgotten to watch, and then sat there with his thin quick face and his shock of premature white hair and his Phi Beta Kappa key and the dime corncob pipe and the suit which looked as if he had slept in it every night since the day he bought it, and said, 'Move.'

But he, Charles, wasn't that stupid even if his mouth was open a little. In fact, he wasn't really surprised, after the first shock of that entrance, that abrupt and that informal, at this hour, this late at night and this cold: the boy without doubt dragging the girl by the arm right on through the front door without bothering to ring or knock there at all, on down the strange hall which, if he had never seen before, would have been seventeen or eighteen years ago as an infant at nurse, to a strange door and knocking this time true enough but not waiting for any response, and so into a room where for all he knew (or cared) his, Charles's, mother might have been undressing for bed.

What surprised him was his uncle: that glib and talkative man who talked so much and so glibly, particularly about things which had absolutely no concern with him, that his was indeed a split personality: the one, the lawyer, the county attorney who walked and breathed and

displaced air; the other, the garrulous facile voice so garrulous and
facile that it seemed to have no connection with reality at all and presently hearing it was like listening not even to fiction but to literature.

Yet two strangers had burst not only into his home but into his private sitting room, and delivered first a peremptory command and then
a threat and then burst out again, and his uncle had sat calmly back to
an interrupted chessgame and an interrupted pipe and completed a
planned move as though he had not only not noticed any interruption
but hadn't actually been interrupted. This in the face of what should
have supplied his uncle with food and scope for garrulity for the rest
of the night, since of all possible things which might have entered this
room from the whole county's remotest environs, this one concerned
him least: the domestic entanglements or impasses or embroilments
of a family a household six miles from town whose four members or
at least inhabitants not a dozen people in the county knew more than
merely to speak to on the street—the wealthy widow (millionairess,
the county stipulated it), the softly fading still softly pretty woman in
the late thirties, and the two spoiled children a year apart somewhere
under twenty-one, and the Argentine army captain house-guest, the
four of them like the stock characters in the slick magazine serial, even
to the foreign fortune-hunter.

For which reason (and maybe that was why, though it would take
a good deal more than even his uncle's incredible taciturnity to convince him, Charles, of this) his uncle didn't really need to talk about
it. Because for twenty years now, long before there were any children
even, let alone anything to draw the foreign fortune-hunter, the county
had been watching it unfold as the subscribers read and wait and watch
for the serial's next installment.

Which—the twenty years—was before his, Charles's, time too. But
it was his nevertheless; he had inherited it, heired it in his turn as he
would heir in his turn from his mother and father who had heired them
in their turn, the library shelf in the room just across the hall from this
one where he and his uncle sat, containing not the books which his
grandfather had chosen or heired in his turn from his father, but the
ones which his grandmother had chosen and bought on the semi-yearly
trips to Memphis—the sombre tomes before the day of gaudy dust-
jackets, the fly leaves bearing this grandmother's name and address and

even that of the store or shop where she purchased them and the date in the nineties and the early nineteen hundreds in her fading young women's seminary script, the volumes to be exchanged and lent and returned to be the subject of the leading papers at the next meeting of the literary clubs, the yellowed pages bearing even forty and fifty years later the imprint of pressed and vanished flowers and through which moved with the formal gestures of shades the men and women who were to christian-name a whole generation: the Clarissas and Judiths and Marguerites, the St Elmos and Rolands and Lothairs: women who were always ladies and men who were always brave, moving in a sort of immortal moonlight without anguish and with no pain from birth without foulment to death without carrion, so that you too could weep with them without having to suffer or grieve, exult with them without having to conquer or triumph.

So the legend was his too. He had even got some of it direct from his grandmother by means of childhood's simple inevitable listening, by-passing his own mother, who in a sense had had a part in it. And until tonight it had even remained as harmless and unreal as the old yellowed volumes: the old plantation six miles from town which had been an old place even in his grandmother's time, not so big in acreage but of good land properly cared for and worked, with the house on it which was not large either but was just a house, a domicile, more spartan even than comfortable, even in those days when people wanted needed comfort in their homes for the reason that they spent some of their time there; and the widower-owner who stayed at home and farmed his heritage and, with a constant tumbler of thin whiskey-and-water at his elbow and an aged setter bitch dozing at his feet, sat through the long summer afternoons in a home-made chair on the front gallery, reading in Latin the Roman poets; and the child, the daughter, the motherless girl who grew up in that almost conventual seclusion without companions or playmates, with nobody in fact except a few Negro servants and the middle-aged father who paid (again by the town's and the county's postulation) little or no attention to her and who therefore, without ever once saying so to anyone of course, certainly not to the child, perhaps never even to himself, still charged against the life of the daughter, the death of the wife who apparently had been his own life's one monogamous love; and who (the child) at seventeen and without

warning to anyone, not to the county anyway, married a man whom
nobody in that part of Mississippi had ever heard of before.

And there was something else: an appendix or anyway appendage;
a legend to or within or behind the actual or original or initial legend;
apocryphal's apocrypha. He not only couldn't remember whether it was
from his mother or his grandmother that he had heard it, he couldn't
even remember whether his mother or grandmother had actually seen
it, known it at first hand, or had themselves heard it from someone else.
It was something about a previous involvement, prior to the marriage:
an engagement, a betrothal in form in fact, with (so the legend said) the
father's formal consent, then broken, ruptured, voided—something—
before the man she did marry ever appeared on the scene;—a betrothal
in form according to the legend, yet so nebulous that even twenty years
after, with twenty years of front gallery gossip for what his uncle called
the Yoknapatawpha County spinster aunts of both sexes to have cast
that romantic mantle over the shoulders of every male under sixty who
had ever taken a drink or bought a bale of cotton from her father, the
other party to it had not only no name but no face too—which at least
the other man had, the stranger, for all that he appeared without warning out of nowhere and (as it were) married her all in one burst, one
breath, without any space between for anything called by so leisurely
a name as betrothal, let alone courtship. So it—the first, the other one,
the true betrothal, worthy of the word for the simple reason that nothing came of it but apocrypha's ephemeral footnote, already fading: a
scent, a shadow, a whisper; a young girl's trembling Yes in an old garden at dusk, a flower exchanged or kept; and nothing remained unless
perhaps the flower, the rose pressed between the pages of a book as
the successors to his grandmother's generation occasionally did—was
probably, without doubt, it had to be, the aftermath of some boy-and-
girl business of her schooldays. But indubitably it was to someone in
Jefferson or at least in the county. Because until now she had never
been anywhere else to have involved or pledged her inclinations and
then lost them.

But the man (or the boy) had no face, no name. He had no substance
at all, in fact. He had no past, no yesterday; protagonist of a young girl's
ephemeride: a shade, a shadow; himself virgin as the untried passions
of that cloistered and nunlike maiden. Not even the five or six girls (his,

Charles's mother, was one of them) who had been the nearest thing she had to friends during the three or four years she attended the female half of the Academy, even knew for certain that an engagement really existed, let alone the mortal partner in it. Because she never spoke of it herself, and even the rumor, legend's baseless legend, was born rather of a chance remark of her father's one day, and now its own part of the legend, to the effect that for a girl of sixteen to be partner in a betrothal was like a blind man being a partner in the ownership of an original Horatian manuscript.

But at least his uncle had a reason for not talking about this part of it because his uncle didn't even know about the first engagement except by second hand two or three years later. Because he—his uncle—was not there then; that was 1919 and once more Europe—Germany—was open to students and tourists too with student visas, and his uncle had already gone back to Heidelberg to finish his Ph.D., and when he returned five years later, she was already married to the other man, the one who did have a name and a face even if nobody in the town or the county had heard the one nor seen the other until they came up the church aisle almost, and had borne the two children and then herself departed with them for Europe and the old other thing which had never been more than a shadow anyway, had been forgotten even in Jefferson, unless maybe on fading occasions over cups of coffee or tea or ladies' punch (and then more fading still over their own bassinets) by the six girls who had been her only friends.

So she married the stranger not only to Jefferson but to all north Mississippi and perhaps to all the rest of Mississippi too as far as anyone knew, about whom the town knew nothing except that he was not the materialisation at last of the nameless shadow of the other affair which had never emerged far enough into the light to have two actual people in it. Because there was no engagement prolonged or deferred here waiting for her to get another year older; his—Charles's—mother said you had only to look at Harriss once to know that he would never abate one jot—or acquiesce one jot to the abatement—of anything he considered his.

He was more than twice her age, old enough himself to be her father—a big florid affable laughing man about whom you noticed at once that his eyes were not laughing too; noticed so quickly that his eyes were not laughing too that you realised only later that the laughter never had gone much further than his teeth;—a man who had what his uncle called the Midas touch, who as his uncle said, walked in an aura of pillaged widows and minors as some men walk in that of failure or death.

In fact, his uncle said that the whole pattern was upside down. He— his uncle—was home again now, for good this time, and his sister and mother, Charles's mother and grandmother (and all the other women he couldn't help but listen to probably) had told him about the marriage and about the other shadowy betrothal too. Which itself should have unbraked his uncle's tongue when the violation of his home didn't, for the very reason that it was not merely no concern of his but so little concerned with any reality at all that there would have been nothing in it anywhere to confound or restrict him.

And he, Charles, of course hadn't been in his grandmother's sitting room yet by about two years, but in his imagination he could see his uncle looking exactly as he always had since and before too and always would, sitting there beside his (Charles's) grandmother's footstool and rocker, with white folks' tobacco once again in the cob pipe and drinking the coffee (his grandmother wouldn't abide tea; she said it was for sick people) which his mother brewed for them, with his thin quick face and the wild shock of hair which had already begun to turn white when he got home in 1919 after three years as a stretcher-bearer in the French army, and spent that spring and summer doing nothing whatever that anyone knew of, before going back to Heidelberg to finish the Ph.D., and the voice which talked constantly not because its owner loved talking but because he knew that while it was talking, nobody else could tell what he was not saying.

The whole plot was hind-part-before, his uncle said; all the roles and parts mixed-up and confused: the child acting and reading what should have been the parent's lines and character—assuming of course that the father's cryptic remark about the Horatian manuscript meant anything at all; not the parent but the child putting aside the childhood sweetheart (no matter how thin and ephemeral had been that entanglement, his uncle said, asking, so his, Charles's, mother told, for the second time if anyone had ever learned the sweetheart's name or what had become of him) in order to lift the mortgage on the homestead; the child herself choosing the man twice her age but with the Midas touch whom it should have been the father's role to pick and, if necessary, even bring pressure to bear to the end that the old romance (and his mother told how his uncle said again, No matter how worthless and ephemeral) be voided and forgotten and the marriage done: and worse: even if it had been the father who chose the husband, the plot would still have been upside down because the money (and his mother told how his uncle asked this twice too: if the man Harriss was already rich or if he just looked like, given enough time and enough people, he would be) was already the father's even if there wasn't much of it, because, as his uncle said, the man who read Latin for pleasure wouldn't have wanted any more than he already had.

But they were married. Then for the next five years what his uncle called that whole broad generation of spinster aunts who, still alive seventy-five years after the Civil War, are the backbone of the South's social and political and economic solidarity too, watched it as you watch the unfolding story in the magazine installments.

They went to New Orleans on the wedding journey, as everyone in that country at that time did who considered his marriage legal. Then they returned and for about two weeks were seen daily in town in an old battered victoria (her father had never owned an automobile and never would) drawn by a team of plow-horses and driven by a Negro plowhand in overalls and stained where the chickens had roosted in it or over it and maybe owls too. Then it—the victoria—was seen occasionally in the Square for another month with just the bride in it before the town found out that the husband was gone, back to New Orleans, to his business: which was the first anybody knew that he had a business and where it was. But even then, and for the next five years too, they wouldn't know what it was.

So now there was only the bride for the town and the county to watch, alone in the old victoria, coming the six miles in to town, maybe to call on his, Charles's, mother or another of the six who had been her friends, or maybe just to drive through the town, the Square, and then back home. And then for another month it was just to drive through the Square, and that maybe once a week when it had used to be almost every day. Then a month passed and not even the victoria was seen in town. It was as if she had realised at last, it had finally occurred to her,

what for two months now the whole town and the county too had been
believing and saying; —only eighteen then and his mother said how she
didn't even look that—a slight, dark-haired, dark-eyed girl who didn't
look much bigger than a child perched alone in the cave-like opening
of the victoria's hooded back seat which would have held five or six of
her—who, his mother said, hadn't been any too bright even in school
and had never tried to be anything else, and who, his uncle said, maybe
didn't need to be bright, having been created for simple love and grief;
that is it must have been for love and grief because it was certainly not
for haughtiness and pride, since she had failed (if she had ever really
tried even that) at assurance without even accomplishing bravado.

So there were more than just what his uncle called the spinster
aunts who now believed they knew what sort of business Harriss's
was, and that it had taken him long since a good deal further than New
Orleans,—four or five hundred miles further probably, since although
this was in the twenties when absconders still considered Mexico far
and safe enough, this one could hardly have found enough money in
that family and that plantation to have made Mexico a solvent necessity, let alone have got there—or in fact to have found flight at all a
necessity, and that it was probably only his own fears which had sent
him even the three hundred miles which New Orleans represented.

But they were wrong. He came back Christmas. And once he was
actually back, where they could see him again, unchanged—the same
man, a little ageless, affable, high-colored, bland, without grace and
without imagination, it was all right again. In fact, it had never been
wrong; even the very ones who had said soonest and most positively
that he had deserted her, were now the most convinced that they had
never really believed it; when he left again after New Year's like any
other husband unlucky enough to have his work, business, in one place
and his family in another, nobody even marked the day. They didn't
even bother about his business anymore. They knew what it was now:
bootlegging: and no petty furtive peddling of pint bottles in hotel bar-
bershops either, because when she drove through the Square now
alone in the victoria, it was in a fur coat: at which—the coat—as soon
as they saw it, the man himself rose in the town's and the county's
opinion and respect too. Because he was not only successful, but in
the best tradition he spent it on his womenfolks. And more than that:

his was a still older and firmer American tradition; he was successful not even despite the Law but over the Law as though the Law itself and not failure were his vanquished adversary, moving among them on his returns home now, in an aura not merely of success, not solely of romance and bravado and the odor of spent cordite, but of delicacy too since he had had the taste to conduct his business in another state three hundred miles away.

And it was big business. He came back that summer in the biggest and shiniest car that had ever stayed overnight within the county's boundaries, with a strange Negro in a uniform who did nothing but drive and wash and polish it. And the first child came and then there was a nurse too: a light-colored Negress a good deal smarter, or at least snappier-looking, than any other woman white or black either in Jefferson. Then Harriss was gone again, and now every day the four of them—the wife, the infant, the uniformed chauffeur and the nurse—would be seen in the big glittering car, in and out of the Square and the town two and three times a day and not even always stopping anywhere, until pretty soon the county and the town knew also that it was the two Negroes who decided where and perhaps when too they would drive.

And Harriss came back that Christmas, and the next summer, and the second child came and then the first one was walking and now even the rest of the county besides his, Charles's, mother and the other five who had been the girlhood companions, knew at last whether it was a boy or not. And then the grandfather was dead and that Christmas Harriss took command of the plantation, making in his wife's name— or rather in that of his own absentee-landlordship—an arrangement, trade, with the Negro tenants for the next year's farming of the land which everybody knew would not possibly work, which—so the county believed—Harriss himself didn't even bother to want not to work. Because he didn't care; he was making the money himself, and to have stopped merely to run a modest cotton-plantation even for one year would have been like the hot horse-player quitting the tracks in mid-season to run a milk-route.

He was making the money and waiting, and so sure enough one day he didn't have to wait any longer. When he came home that summer, he stayed two months, and when he left there were electric lights and running water in the house, and the day-long night-long thump and hum of the pump and dynamo were the mechanical sounds where there used to be the creak of the hand-turned well-pulley and of the ice-cream freezer on Sunday mornings; and now there was nothing left of the old man who had sat on the front gallery with his weak toddy and Ovid and Horace and Catullus for almost fifty years, except his home-made hickory rocking chair and the finger-prints on the calf bindings of his books and the silver goblet he drank from, and the old setter bitch which had dozed at his feet.

His, Charles's, uncle said that the impact of the money had been stronger even than the ghost of the old stoic, the sedentary and provincial cosmopolite. Maybe his uncle thought it was even stronger than the daughter's capacity for grief. The rest of Jefferson did, anyway. Because that year passed and Harriss came for Christmas and then for a month in the summer, and both children were walking now; that is, they must have been though nobody in Jefferson could vouch for it since nobody ever saw them except in the passing moving car, and the old setter was dead now and in that year Harriss rented all the farm-land in one lump to a man who didn't even live in the county, who drove seventy miles from Memphis each Sunday night during planting and harvest time, and camped in one of the abandoned Negro cabins until time to go back to Memphis the next Saturday noon.

And the next year came and that spring the renter brought his own Negro farm-hands, and so even the Negroes who had lived and dropped their sweat on the old place longer than she was old, were gone now and now there wasn't anything at all of the old owner left because his home-made chair and his silver goblet and the boxes containing the finger-worn calf-bound books were in his, Charles's, mother's attic, and the man who rented the farm-land was living in the house as the caretaker.

Because Mrs Harriss was gone too. She didn't notify Jefferson in advance about that either. It was even a conspiracy, since his, Charles's, mother knew both that she was going, and where, and if his mother knew, then the other five did too.

One day she was there, in the house which Jefferson thought she would never have wanted to escape from, no matter what he did to it, no matter if the house where she had been born and lived all her life except for the two weeks' honeymoon in New Orleans, was now a kind of mausoleum of electric wires and water pipes and automatic cooking and washing machines and synthetic pictures and furniture.

Then the next day she was gone: herself, the two children, the two Negroes who even after four years in the country were still city Negroes, and even the long glittering hearselike car,—to Europe, for the children's health it was said, and nobody knew who said that either, because it was not his, Charles's, mother nor any of the other five who of all Jefferson and all the county had known she was going, and certainly it wasn't she who had said it. But she was gone, running from what, the town maybe thought it knew. But hunting for what or if hunting for anything, this time not even his uncle, who always had something to say (and something that quite often made sense) about anything which wasn't particularly his business, didn't know or at least didn't say.

And now not only Jefferson but the whole county watched it, not only what his uncle called the spinster aunts who watched by hearsay and supposition (and maybe hope) from their front galleries, but the men too, and not just men from the town who had only six miles to go, but farmers who had the whole county to cross.

They would come by whole families in battered dusty cars and wagons, or singly on horses and mules taken last night from the plow, to stop along the road and watch gangs of strange men with enough machinery to have built a highway or a reservoir, disc and terrace the old fields once dedicated to simple profit-producing corn and cotton, and sow them to pasture grass costing more per pound than sugar.

They would ride past mile after mile of white-painted panel fence, to sit in the cars and wagons or on the horses and mules, and watch long rows of stables being built of better material than was in most of their houses, with electric lights and illuminated clocks and running water and screened windows such as most of their homes didn't have; they would come back on the mules, maybe without saddles even, with the plow-gear merely looped up over the hames to keep it from dragging, and watch van after van unload the fine pedigreed stallions and colts and mares whose ancestors for fifty generations (as his, Charles's, uncle might have said but didn't since this was the year during which his uncle seemed to have stopped talking very much about anything) would have blenched at a trace-gall like a housewife at a hair on the butter-dish.

He (Harriss) rebuilt the house. (He was making flying trips up every week now, in an aeroplane; they said it was the same aeroplane which ran the whiskey up from the Gulf to New Orleans.) That is, the new house was going to occupy the same ground the old one would have covered if there had been four of them just alike nailed together. It had been just a house, of one storey, with the gallery across the front where the old master would sit in his home-made chair with his toddy and his Catullus; when Harriss got through with it, it looked like the Southern mansion in the moving picture, only about five times as big and ten times as Southern.

Then he began to bring friends up from New Orleans with him, for week-ends and longer, and not just at Christmas and in the summer now, but four and five times during the year, as though the money was coming in so fast and smooth now that he didn't even have to stay there and watch it. Sometimes he wouldn't even come himself, but would just send them. He had a caretaker who lived in the house all the time: not the old one, the first renter, but a new one from New Orleans whom he called his butler: a fat Italian or Greek collarless in white silk shirt sleeves and a pistol loose in his hip pocket until the guests arrived. Then he would shave and put on a four-in-hand tie of soft scarlet silk, and a coat too when it was very cold: who they said in Jefferson wore the pistol even when he was serving meals, though nobody from town or the county either had ever eaten there to see.

So sometimes Harriss would just send his friends up for the butler to take care of them: the men and women with a hard, sleek, expensive unmarried air and look about them even when now and then some of them really were married to each other perhaps: the strange outlanders driving big shining sports cars fast through town and fast along the road which was still just a country road for a while a distance, no matter what he had built at one end of it, where chickens and dogs lay in the dust for coolness, and hogs and calves and mules strayed: a burst and whirl of feathers, a jolt or yelp or squeal (and if it were a horse or mule or cow or, deadliest of all, a hog, a bent bumper or fender too), the car not even slowing: until after a while the butler kept a mass of coins and banknotes and a few of Harriss's checks signed in blank, in a canvas sack hanging from the inside knob of the front door, the farmer or his wife or his child riding up to the front door and saying 'hog' or 'mule' or 'hen' and the butler would not even have to leave the door to reach down the sack and count out the money or fill in the check and pay them and they would go away: because that had become a secondary source of rural income for that whole six miles of road like the gathering and selling of blackberries or eggs.

There was a polo field too. It was beside the road, the highway; the men from town, the merchants and lawyers and deputy sheriffs, could drive out now and watch the riding without even getting out of their cars. And the men from the countryside too—the farmers, the land-holders and the tenants and renters and croppers—who wore boots only when walking in mud was unavoidable, and who rode horses only to get from one place to another without having to walk, and that in the same clothes they had put on to eat breakfast in, would come too on horses and mules taken from the plow, to stand along the fence and look at the fine horses a little but mostly at the clothes—the women and the men too who couldn't ride a horse except in shiny boots and special pants, and the others in the pants and boots and derby hats who didn't even ride horses.

And presently to watch something else. They had heard about polo and they even believed it before they ever saw it. But the other they still did not believe even while they were watching it and its preparation too: gangs of workmen cutting out whole panels of the costly plank-and-rail fences and the outermost and still costly wire fences too, then in the resulting gaps setting lower makeshift barriers of brush-tops and laths a little stouter than matchsticks, which wouldn't have stopped a serious dog, let alone a calf or a mule; and, at one place, a section of something molded and painted to resemble a stone wall (It was said to be paper, though naturally the county didn't believe this—not that they didn't believe that paper could be made to look like that, but simply because they did not believe any of it; they knew that the thing was not stone for the very reason that it looked like stone, and they were already prepared to be lied to about what it really was.) which a man at each end could pick up and carry to one side like two housemaids moving a canvas cot; and at another place, in the middle of a forty-acre pasture as bare and empty as a baseball diamond, a section of hedgerow not even growing in the ground but in a wooden box like a hog-trough, and behind it, an artificial pit filled with water pumped through a galvanised pipe from the house almost a mile away.

And after it had happened two or three times and the news had got around, half the men in the county would be there to watch it: the two Negro boys laying the trail of torn paper from one jump to the next, and then the men (one in a red coat, with a brass horn) and the women in the pants and boots on the thousand-dollar horses riding it.

And the next year there was an actual pack of hounds, fine ones, a little too fine to be simple dogs just as the horses were a little too fine to be simple horses, a little too clean, a little too (somehow) unaccustomed, living in weather-proof hutches with running water and special human beings to wait on them too like the horses did and had. And now, instead of two Negroes with two long cotton-pickers' sacks of shredded paper, just one rode a mule, dragging along the ground at the end of a rope something tied up in a burlap sack, dragging it with tedious care up to each jump, then dismounting and tying the mule to something handy while he dragged the bag carefully up to the jump and across the middle of it and then mounted the mule again and dragged the bag on to the next one, and so completing the long looping circle back to the starting-place in the home pasture, the one nearest the highway and the fence where the tethered trace-galled mules and plow-horses stood and the motionless men who had ridden them.

Whereupon the Negro would rein up the mule and sit on it, his eyes rolling a little white, while one of the watchers who had seen it before and followed by the six or ten or fifteen who had not, would climb the fence and, without even looking at the Negro, pass the mule and go and pick up the bag and hold it while one by one the six or twelve or fifteen bent down and sniffed it. Then he would put the bag back down, and with still no word, no sound, they would go back and climb the fence and stand once more along it—men who would squat all night with a jug of corn whiskey around a smoldering stump or log, and call correctly to one another the names of the running hounds by the tone and pitch of their voices a mile away, watching not only the horses which didn't need a quarry to run at, but the frantic clamor of dogs themselves pursuing not even a phantom but a chimaera, leaning their elbows on the white fence, immobile, sardonic and contained, chewing tobacco and spitting.

And each Christmas and New Year's, his, Charles's, mother and the other five who had been the girlhood friends, would receive the seasonal cards. They would be postmarked from Rome or London or Paris or Vienna or Cairo, but they hadn't been bought there. They hadn't been bought anywhere within the last five or ten years, because they had been chosen and purchased and saved from a quieter time than this one, when the houses that people were born in didn't always even know they lacked electric wiring and water pipes.

They even smelled like that. There were not only the fast ships, there was airmail crossing the ocean now, and he, Charles, would think of the pouches of letters from all the world's capitals, postmarked one day and delivered and read and forgotten almost the next, with among them the old-timey cards out of the old time, giving off the faint whisper of old sentiment and old thought impervious to the foreign names and languages, as if she had carried them across the ocean with her from a bureau drawer in the old house which these five and ten years had no longer existed.

And between the cards, on his mother's and the five other birthdays, the letters that even after ten years had not changed—letters constant in sentiment and expression and uncertain spelling, written in the hand of a girl of sixteen and still talking not only of the old homely things but in the old unchanged provincial terms, as if in ten years of the world's glitter she still hadn't seen anything she had not brought with her: talking not about names or places but about the children's health and schooling, not of the ambassadors and millionaires and exiled kings, but of the families of the porters and waiters who had been kind or at least gentle with her and the children, and of the postmen who delivered the mail from home; she didn't always remember to name, let along underline, the fine fashionable schools the children attended, as if she didn't even know they were fine and fashionable. So that the taciturnity was really not new; he would watch his uncle sitting even then, holding one of the letters his mother had received, incorrigible and bachelor, faced for the only time in his life with something on which he apparently had nothing to say, exactly as he sat here across the chessboard ten years later, still speechless, or certainly still taciturn.

But his uncle nor anybody else could have called Harriss's pattern upside down. And he, Harriss, followed it, and fast: marry a girl a child half your age and in ten years tentuple the dowry, then one morning your lawyer's secretary telephones your wife long distance in Europe and says you just died sitting at your desk.

Maybe he really did die at the desk; maybe it was even a desk in an office, as the message implied. Because you can be shot just as discreetly across a desk in an office as anywhere else. And maybe he really did just die sitting at it, because prohibition was even legally dead by then and he was already rich when it ended, and the casket wasn't opened again after the lawyer and eight or ten of the butlers in their sharp clothes and arm-pitted pistols brought him home to lie in state for a day in his ten-year-old ancestral baron's hall, with a butler cum pistol in each downstairs room as far as the butlers went, so that now anybody in Jefferson that wanted could pass the casket with a neat white card engraved in script $5500 propped among the flowers against it, and examine the inside of the house, before the lawyer and the butlers took him back to New Orleans or anyhow away and buried him.

That was in what was going to be the first year of the new war in Europe, or rather the second phase of that old one his uncle had gone to; the family would have had to come back home anyway in another three months.

They were back in less than two. So he saw them at last, for the first time, or the boy and girl, that is. He didn't see Mrs Harriss then. But then he didn't need to see her; he had listened to his mother too long; he already knew how she would look; it was as if he had not only seen her before, but had known her as long as his mother had—the slight dark-haired woman still looking like a girl even at thirty-five, not looking very much older in fact than her own children, maybe because she had the power or capacity, whatever it was, or maybe the gift, the fortune, to have spent ten years among what his great-aunt would have called the crowned heads of Europe, without ever really knowing she had left Yoknapatawpha County; not so much looking older than her children but just softer, more constant, quieter; maybe just stiller.

He never saw any of them but just a few times—nor did anybody else that he knew of. The boy rode the horses, but only out there, in the paddock or the polo field, and not for pleasure it appeared, but simply to pick out a few of the best ones to keep, because within a month they had held an auction sale in one of the smaller paddocks and sold off all but about a dozen. But he seemed to know horses, because the ones they kept were good ones.

And the people who saw him said that he could ride too, though in a curious, foreign, high-kneed fashion which was new to Mississippi or at least to Yoknapatawpha County, which—the county—presently heard that he was even better at something else still more foreign than he was at riding; that he had been the star pupil of some famous Italian fencing-master. And they would see the sister now and then in town in one of the cars, in and out of the stores as girls will, who can seem to find something they want or at least will buy in any store, no matter how small, no matter if they grew up in Paris and London and Vienna, or just Jefferson and Mottstown and Hollyknowe, Mississippi.

But he, Charles, never saw Mrs Harriss that time. And so he would imagine her moving about that incredible house which she probably recognised only by its topographical location, not like a ghost, because—to him—there was nothing at all wraithlike about her. She was too— too— and then he found the word: tough. Toughness: that constancy, that imperviousness, that soft still malleableness which had lived ten years in the glittering capitals of Europe without even having to be aware that she had completely resisted them;—merely soft, merely malleable: a breath say of an old sachet, as if one of the old bureau drawers or such from the old house had remained stubborn and constant against all change and alteration, not only impervious but not even aware that it had resisted change, inside the parvenue's monstrous mushroom, and somebody passing had jarred open the drawer——and then suddenly and without warning he saw the true juxtaposition, the true perspective: it was not she which was the ghost; the wraith was Harriss's monstrous house: one breath one faint waft of sachet from that disturbed drawer, and all the vast soar of walls, the loom and sweep of porticoes, became at once transparent and substanceless.

But he never saw her this time. Because two months later they were gone again, to South America this time, since Europe was interdict. So for another year the cards and the letters came back to his mother and the other five, telling no more still of foreign lands than if they had been written from the next county, talking not only about the children now but about home: not the monstrosity Harriss had changed it into, but as it had been before, as if, seeing again its site in space, she remembered its shape in time; and, absent from it, it existed intact again as though it had merely bided and waited for that; it was still as though, even approaching forty, she had less than ever any capacity for novelty, for experiencing any new thing or scene.

Then they were back. There were four of them now: the Argentine cavalry captain too, pursuing or following or anyway drawn by not the daughter apparently but the mother, and so that pattern was upside down too since Captain Gualdres was no more senior to the girl than her father had been to his bride; and so at least the pattern was consistent.

So one morning he and his uncle were crossing the Square, thinking (he anyway) of anything but that, when he looked up and saw her. And he was right. She looked exactly as he had known she would, and then and even before they stopped, he could smell it too: the scent of old sachet, lavender and thyme and such, which, you would have thought, the first touch of the world's glitter would have obliterated, until in the next second you realised that it—the scent, the odor, the breath, the whisper—was the strong and the enduring, and it was the inconstant changing glitter which flashed and passed.

'This is Charles,' his uncle said. 'Maggie's boy. I hope you'll be happy.'

'I beg your pardon?' she said.

His uncle said it again: 'I hope you'll be very happy.' And already he, Charles, knew something was wrong with it, even before she said:

'Happy?'

'Yes,' his uncle said. 'Didn't I see it in your face? or shouldn't I?'

And then he knew what was wrong. It was his uncle; it was as though that year ten years ago when his uncle had stopped talking, had already been too long. Because probably talking was like golf or wing-shooting; you couldn't afford to miss a day; and if you ever missed a whole year, you never got your game or your eye back.

And he stood there too, watching her while she stood looking at his uncle. Then she blushed. He watched it start and move up and cover her face as the moving shadow of a cloud crosses a patch of light. Then it even crossed her eyes too, as when once the cloud-shadow reaches the water, you can not only see the shadow, you can even see the actual cloud too, while she still looked at his uncle. Then she sort of ducked her head, his uncle stepping aside to let her pass. Then his uncle turned too and bumped into him and then they went on and even after he and his uncle had gone a hundred feet or more, it seemed to him that he could still smell it.

'Sir?' he said.

'Sir what?' his uncle said.

'You said something.'

'Did I?' his uncle said.

'You said "less oft is peace." '

'Let's hope not,' his uncle said. 'I dont mean the peace, but the quotation. But then, suppose I did say it. What's the good of Heidelberg or Cambridge or Jefferson High or Yoknapatawpha Consolidated, except to furnish a man a certain happy glibness with which to be used by his myriad tongues.'

So maybe he had been wrong. Perhaps his uncle had not lost that year after all, like the old golfer or wing-shot who, a little slack and off and even consistently missing shot after casual shot, can still bear down at last not even when the pressure comes but merely when he wants to. Because almost before he had even had time to think that, this uncle said, striding on, glib, familiar, quick, incorrigibly garrulous, incorrigibly discursive, who had always something curiously truthful yet always a little bizarre to say about almost anything that didn't really concern him:

'No, we'll let it stand. The least we can wish Captain Gualdres, the stranger in our midst, is that peace be not less oft or indeed not oft at all.'

Because by that time the whole county knew Captain Gualdres, by hearsay, and most of them even by sight. Then one day he, Charles, saw him too. Captain Gualdres was crossing the Square on one of the Harriss horses, and his, Charles's, uncle said what it was. Not who the man was nor even what, but what they were, the man and the horse together: not a centaur, but a unicorn. He looked hard, not that flabby hardness of too much living which Harriss's butlers had had, but the hardness of metal, of fine steel or bronze, desiccated, almost epicene. And as soon as his uncle had said it, he, Charles, could see it too: the horse-creature out of the old poetry, with its single horn not of bone but of some metal so curious and durable and strange that even the wise men could not name it; some metal forged out of the very beginning of man's dreams and desires and his fears too, and the formula lost or perhaps even deliberately destroyed by the Smith himself; something far older than steel or bronze and stronger than all the power for suffering and terror and death in mere gold or silver. That was how, his uncle said, the man seemed a part of the horse he rode; that was the quality of the man who was a living part of the living horse: the composite creature might die, and would, and must, but only the horse would leave bones: in time the bones would crumble to dust and vanish into the earth, but the man would remain intact and impervious where they had lain.

But the man himself was all right. He spoke a hard, rigid sort of English that was not always clear in context, but he spoke it to everybody, anybody; soon he was not only known, but well known, not only in town but through the county too. Within a month or two he seemed to have been everywhere in the county that a horse could go; he must have known back roads and lanes and paths which even his, Charles's, uncle, politicking the county yearly to hold his constituency together, probably had never seen.

He not only knew the county, he had made friends in it. Soon all sorts of people were going out there to see, not the Harrisses but the stranger; as guests not of the woman who owned the place and whose family name they had known all her life and her father's and grandfather's too, but of the stranger, the foreigner who six months ago they had never heard of and even a year later they would not be able to understand all he said;—out-of-doors men, usually bachelors: farmers, mechanics, a locomotive fireman, a civil engineer, two young men on the highway maintenance crew, a professional horse-and-mule trader—going out there on his invitation to ride the horses belonging to the woman who was his hostess known and whose lover (the whole county was convinced before they ever saw him that his interest, or at least intentions, was in the older woman, the mother, who already controlled the money, because he could have married the girl, the daughter, at any time, long before they left South America) he already probably was and whose husband he could be at any time he wished —which would be when he finally had to, since, being not only a foreigner but a Latin too, he would have sprung from a long line of bachelor Don Juans and would be adulterous not even through preference but simply in the same way that a leopard is spotted.

In fact, it was presently said of him that if Mrs Harriss had been a horse instead of a human, he would have married her at once long ago. Because it was soon realised that horses were his heart's love just as drink or dope or gambling are other men's. The county heard how he would go to the stables alone at night, moon or dark, and saddle a half-dozen of them and ride them in relays into dawn and sunup; and that summer he build a steeple-chase course in comparison to which that one Harriss had built was an obstacle race for crawling infants: sections of rail or wall not set into the fences but higher than the fences by a foot or two feet, not matchwood this time but solid beams capable of supporting roofs, not papier-mâché this time but the actual living rock freighted all the way from eastern Tennessee and Virginia. And now many people from town too would go out there, because that was something to see: the man and the horse fusing, joining, becoming one beast, then passing on beyond even that point, that juncture: not daring, but testing, almost physically palping at that point where even at mutually-compounding ultimate, concorded at absolute's uttermost, they must become violently two again, like the rocket pilot at his *mach* *1* then *2* then *3* and toward (himself and the machine) their own finitive apex where the iron craft explodes and vanishes, leaving his tender and naked flesh still hurtling forward on the other side of sound.

Though in this case (the man and the horse) the thing was in obverse. It was as if the man knew that he himself was invulnerable and unbreakable, and of their two, only the horse could fail, and that the man had laid out the course and built the jumps just to see where the horse must ultimately falter. Which, by all the tenets of that agrarian and equestrian land, was exactly right; that was exactly the way to ride a horse; Rafe McCallum, one of his constant watchers, who had bred and raised and trained and sold horses all his life and who knew more about horses probably than any man in the country, said so: that when it was in the stall, treat it like it cost a thousand dollars; but when you were using it for something you had, or you and it both liked, to do, treat it like you could have bought ten like it for that many cents.

And one thing more happened or at least began about three months ago now, which the whole county had had to know about, or at least form an opinion about, for the very reason that this was the only phase or side of Captain Gualdres' Mississippi life which he ever tried to keep, if not secret, at least private.

It had a horse in it of course because it had Captain Gualdres in it too. In fact, the county even knew specifically what horse. It was the one animal—or creature, including Captain Gualdres—in all those broad paneled manicured acres which didn't belong even titularly to the Harrisses.

Because this one belonged to Captain Gualdres himself. He had bought it on his own selection and with his own money—or what he used for his own money: and the fact that he bought a horse with what the county believed was his mistress's money was one of the best, perhaps the best North American stroke Captain Gualdres ever made or could have made. If he had used Mrs Harriss's money to buy himself a girl, which, being younger than Mrs Harriss, they had expected all the time that sooner or later he would, the county's contempt and disgust for him would have been exceeded only by their contempt and shame for Mrs Harriss. While, having decently spent her money for a horse, the county absolved him in advance by accepting the prima facie; he had gained a kind of male respectability by honorableness in adultery, fidelity and continence in pimphood; continuing (Captain Gualdres) to enjoy it for almost six weeks in fact, going himself all the way to St Louis and buying the horse and coming back in the truck with it.

It was a mare, a filly, sired by a famous imported steeple-chaser and going blind from trauma, purchased of course, the county believed, to be a brood mare (which was proof to them that Captain Gualdres anyway considered his tenure on North Mississippi worth a year's purchase at least) since there was obviously nothing else that anyone could do with the mare, no matter what the breeding, which in another year would be totally blind. Which the county continued to believe for the next six weeks, even after they discovered that he was doing something with the mare besides simply waiting on nature, discovering this—not what he was doing with the mare, but that he was doing something with it—for that same reason that this was the first one of his horse activities which he ever tried to keep private.

Because there were no watchers, spectators this time, not only because whatever it was Captain Gualdres was doing with the mare took place at night and usually late, but because Captain Gualdres

himself asked them not to come out and watch, asking them with
that Latin passion for decorum and courtesy become instinctive from
dealing with its own hair-triggered race, which shone even through
the linguistic paucity:

'You will not come out to see because, my honor, there is nothing
now to see.'

So they didn't. They deferred, not to his Latin honor perhaps, but
they deferred. Perhaps there really was nothing to see, since there
couldn't have been very much out there at that hour worth going that
distance to see; only occasionally someone, a neighbor on his way
home, passing the place in the late silence, would hear hooves in one
of the paddocks beyond the stables at some distance from the road—a
single horse, at trot then canter then for a few beats at dead run, the
sound stopping short off into complete silence while the listener could
have counted two or perhaps three, then beginning once more in the
middle of the dead run, already slowing back to canter and trot as if
Captain Gualdres had snatched, jerked, wrenched the animal from full
speed into immobility in one stride and held it so for the two or three
beats, then flung it bodily into full run again,—teaching it what, nobody
knew, unless as a barber-shop wit said, since it was going to be blind,
how to dodge traffic on the way to town to collect its pension.

'Maybe he's learning it to jump,' the barber said—a neat dapper man
with a weary satiated face and skin the color of a mushroom's belly, on
whom the sun shone at least once every day because at noon he would
have to cross the open street to get from the barber-shop to the All
Nite Inn and eat his dinner, who if he had ever been on a horse, it was
in his defenseless childhood before he could protect himself.

'At night?' the client said. 'In the dark?'

'If the horse is going blind, how does it know it's night?' the barber said.

'But why jump a horse at night?' the client said.

'Why jump a horse?' the barber said, slapping the brush around the
foaming mug. 'Why a horse?'

But that was all. It didn't make sense. And if, in the county's opinion,
Captain Gualdres was anything, he was sensible. Which—the sensible-
ness or at least practicalness—even proved itself by the very action
which smirched his image in another phase of the county's respect.
Because they knew the answer now, to the mare, the blind mare and

the night. He, the matchless horseman, was using a horse not as a horse but as a disguise; he, the amoral preyer on aging widows, was betraying the integrity of his amorality.

Not his morals: his morality. They had never had any illusions about his—a foreigner and a Latin—morals, so they had accepted his lack of them already in advance before he could have demanded, requested it even. But they themselves had foisted on, invested him with a morality, a code which he had proved now was not his either, and they would never forgive him.

It was a woman, another woman; they were forced at last to the acceptance of that which, they realised now, they had always expected of a foreigner and a Latin, knowing now at last why the horse, that horse, a horse going blind, the sound and reason for the sound of whose feet late at night nobody would understand probably, but at least nobody would bother enough about to investigate. It was a Trojan horse; the foreigner who as yet barely spoke English, had gone all the way to St Louis to find and buy with his own money, one meeting the requirements: blindness to establish an acceptable reason for the night absences, a horse already trained or that he himself could train to make on signal—perhaps an electrical sound every ten or fifteen minutes operated from a clock (by this time the county's imagination had soared to heights which even horse-traders didn't reach, let alone mere horse-trainers)—those spurts of galloping around an empty paddock, until he got back from the assignation and threw a switch and put the horse up and rewarded it with sugar or oats.

It would be a younger woman of course, perhaps even a young girl; probably was a young girl, since there was a hard ruthless unimaginative maleness to him which wore and even became the Latin formality like a young man's white tie and tails became him and stood him in good stead, with no real effort on his part at all. But this didn't matter. In fact, only the concupiscent wondered who the partner might be. To the others, the rest, the most of them, the new victim was no more important than Mrs Harriss. They turned the stern face of repudiation not on a seducer, but simply on another buck of the woods running the land, as though the native domestic supply were not enough. When they remembered Mrs Harriss, it was as the peers and even superiors of her million dollars. They thought, not 'Poor woman' but 'Poor fool.'

And for a while, during the first months of that first year after they all came home from South America, the boy would ride with Captain Gualdres. And he, Charles, had already known that the boy could ride, and the boy did ride; it was when you watched him trying to follow Captain Gualdres over the steeple-chase course that you actually realised what riding was. And he, Charles, thought that, with a Spanish-blooded guest in the house, maybe the boy would have someone to fence with. But whether they did or not, nobody ever knew, and after a while the boy even stopped riding with his mother's guest or lover or his own prospective father-in-law or whatever, and when the town saw the boy at all, it would be passing through the Square in the supercharged sports car with the top back and the rumble full of luggage, either going somewhere or just coming back. And after the six months, when he did see the boy close enough to look at his eyes, he would think: *Even if there were just two horses in the world and he owned both of them, I would have to want to ride one mighty bad before I would ride with him, even if my name was Captain Gualdres.*

II.

Yet these were the people—the puppets, the paper dolls; the situation, impasse, morality play, medicine show, whichever you liked best—dropped out of a clear sky into his uncle's lap at ten oclock on a cold night four weeks before Christmas, and all his uncle saw fit or felt inclined or even needful to do, was to come back to the board and move the pawn and say 'Move' as though it had never happened, never been; not only dismissed but repudiated, refused.

But he didn't move yet. And this time he repeated himself, stubbornly: 'It's the money.'

And this time his uncle repeated himself too, still abrupt, short, even harsh: 'Money? What does that boy care about money? He probably hates it, is put into a rage each time he has to carry a wad of it around with him simply because he wants to buy something or go somewhere. It if was just the money, I'd never have heard about it. He wouldn't have had to come here bursting in on me at ten oclock at night, first with a royal ukase then with a lie then with a threat, just to keep his mother from marrying a man who has no money. Not even if the man had no money at all, which in Captain Gualdres' case may not even be the fact.'

'All right,' he said, quite stubbornly. 'He doesn't want his mother or sister either to marry that foreigner. Just not liking Captain Gualdres is plenty enough for that.'

Now his uncle really had finished talking, sitting opposite him across the chessboard, waiting. Then he discovered that his uncle was looking at him, steady and speculative and quite hard.

'Well well,' his uncle said. 'Well well well:'—looking at him while he found out that he hadn't forgot how to blush either. But he should have been used to that by now—or at least to the fact that his uncle would still remember it, whether it had slipped his mind or not. But at least he stuck to his guns, holding his head up, hot suffusion and all, staring as steadily back as his uncle stared, answering that too:

'Not to mention dragging his sister along to make her tell the lie.'

His uncle was looking at him, not quizzical now, not even staring: just looking.

'Why is it,' his uncle said, 'that people of seventeen——'

'Eighteen,' he said. 'Or almost.'

'All right,' his uncle said. 'Eighteen or almost—are so convinced that octogenarians like me are incapable of accepting or respecting or even remembering what the young ones consider passion and love?'

'Maybe it's because the old ones can no longer tell the difference between that and simple decency, like not dragging your sister six miles at ten oclock on a cold December night to make her tell a lie.'

'All right,' his uncle said. '*Touché* then. Will that do? Because I know one octogenarian of fifty who will put nothing past seventeen and eighteen and nineteen—and for that matter, sixteen too—, least of all, passion and love or decency or dragging your sister six or twenty-six miles at night to make her tell a lie or break a safe or commit a murder either——if he had to drag her. She didn't have to come; at least, I saw no shackles.'

'But she came,' he said. 'And she told the lie. She denied she and Captain Gualdres were ever engaged. But when you asked her right out if she loved him, she said Yes.'

'And got dismissed from the room for saying it,' his uncle said. 'That was when she told the truth—which incidentally I dont put past seventeen and eighteen and nineteen either when there is a practical reason for it. She came in here, the two of them did, with the lie all rehearsed to tell me. But she lost her nerve. So they were each trying to use the other to accomplish a purpose. Only it's not the same purpose.'

'But at least they both quit when they saw it had failed. He quit pretty quick. He quit almost as hard as he started. I thought for a minute he was going to throw her out into the hall like she might have been a rag doll.'

'Yes,' his uncle said. 'Too quick. He quit that plan to try something else as soon as he found out he couldn't depend on her. And she had already quit before then. She quit as soon as she began to believe, either that he was getting out of hand, or that I was not going to swallow it and so maybe I would get out of hand too. So they have both already decided to try something else, and I dont like it. Because they are dangerous. Dangerous not because they are stupid; stupidity (your pardon, sir) is to be expected at that age. But because they have never had anybody to tell them they are young and stupid whom they had enough respect for or fear of to believe.—Move.'

And that seemed to be all of it as far as his uncle was concerned; at least on this subject he was going to get no more change from him apparently.

It seemed to be all of it indeed. He moved. He had planned it a long time back too, a longer time back than his uncle, counting as airmen do by contiguous and not elapsed time, because he had not had to make a landing long enough to repel an invading force and then get airborne again, as his uncle had. He checked his uncle's queen and her castle both with the horse. Then his uncle fed him the pawn which only he, Charles, seemed to have believed that nobody had forgotten about, and he moved and then his uncle moved and then as usual it was all over.

'Maybe I should have taken the queen twenty minutes ago when I could, and let the castle go,' he said.

'Always,' his uncle said, starting to separate the white and the black pieces as he, Charles, reached for the box on the lower shelf on the smoking stand. 'You couldn't have taken them both without two moves. And a knight can move two squares at once and even in two directions at once. But he cant move twice'—shoving the black pieces across the board toward him. 'I'll take the white this time and you can try it.'

'It's after ten,' he said. 'It's almost ten thirty.'

'So it is,' his uncle said, setting up the black pieces. 'It often is.'

'I thought maybe I ought to be going to bed,' he said.

'Maybe you ought,' his uncle said, still absolutely immediate and absolutely bland. 'You dont mind if I stay up, do you?'

'Maybe you would have a better game then,' he said. 'Playing against yourself, at least you'd have the novelty of being surprised at your opponent's blunders.'

'All right, all right,' his uncle said. 'Didn't I say *touché*? At least put the pieces back on the board whether you use them or not.'

That was all he knew then. He didn't even suspect any more. But he learned fast—or caught on fast. This time they heard the feet first— the light sharp brittle staccato clapping that girls make, coming up the hall. He had already learned, from the time he had spent in his uncle's quarters, that you really never actually hear the sound of feet in any house or building containing at least two more or less separate establishments. So he realised in the same moment (which was before she even knocked, even before his uncle said, 'Now it's your time to be too late to open it') that not only had his uncle known all the time that she would come back, but that he must have known it too. Only he thought at first that the boy had sent her back; it wasn't until afterward that he thought to wonder how she had managed to get away from him that quick.

She looked as if she had been running ever since, anyway, stand- ing in the door for a moment after he opened it, holding the fur coat together at her throat with one hand and the long white dress flowing away from beneath it. And maybe the terror was still in her face, but there wasn't anything dazed about her eyes. And she even looked at him this time, good, when on the other one, as near as he could tell, she never had seen that he was in the room.

Then she quit looking at him. She came in and crossed the room fast to where his uncle (this time) stood beside the chessboard.

'I must see you alone,' she said.

'You are,' his uncle said. 'This is Charles Mallison, my nephew.' His uncle turned one of the chairs away from the chessboard. 'Sit down.'

But she didn't move.

'No,' she said. 'Alone.'

'If you cant tell me the truth with three here, you probably wont with just two,' his uncle said. 'Sit down.'

Still she didn't move for a space. He, Charles, couldn't see her face because her back was toward him. But her voice had changed completely.

'Yes,' she said. She turned toward the chair. Then she stopped again, already bending to sit down, half-turned and looking at the door as if she not only expected to hear the brother's feet coming up the hall, but as if she were on the point of running back to the front door to look up and down the street for him.

But it was hardly a pause, because she sat down, collapsing on down into the chair in that rapid swirling of skirts and legs both, as girls do, as if their very joints were hinged differently and at different places from men's.

'Can I smoke?' she said.

But before his uncle could reach for the box of cigarettes which his uncle himself didn't smoke, she had produced one from somewhere— no platinum-and-jewel case as you expected, but a single cigarette bent and crumpled and already shedding tobacco like it had lain loose in her pocket for days, holding her wrist in the other hand as though to steady it while she leaned the cigarette to the match his uncle struck. Then she expelled that one puff and laid the cigarette in the ashtray and put her hands in her lap, not clenched, just lying tight and small and still against the dark fur.

'He's in danger,' she said. 'I'm afraid.'

'Ah,' his uncle said. 'Your brother is in danger.'

'No no,' she said, almost pettishly. 'Not Max: Sebas—Captain Gualdres.'

'I see,' his uncle said. 'Captain Gualdres is in danger. I've heard he rides hard, though I've never seen him on a horse myself.'

She took up the cigarette and drew on it twice rapidly and mashed it into the tray and put her hand back into her lap and looked at his uncle again.

'All right,' she said. 'I love him. I told you that. But it's all right. It's just one of those things. That you cant help. Mother saw him first, or he saw her first. Anyway, they belong to the same generation. Which I dont, since S— Captain Gualdres is a good eight or ten years older than I am, maybe more. But no matter. Because that's not it. He's in danger. And even if he did give me the run-around for Mother, I still dont want to see him hurt. At least I dont want my brother locked up in jail for doing it.'

'Especially as locking him up wouldn't undo the deed,' his uncle said. 'I agree with you: much better to lock him up before.'

She looked at his uncle. 'Before?' she said. 'Before what?'

'Before he does what he might be locked up for having done,' his uncle said in that bland immediate quick fantastic voice which lent not only a perspicacity but a sort of solid reasonableness to the most fantastic inconsequence.

'Oh,' she said. She looked at his uncle. 'Lock him up how?' she said. 'I know that much about law, myself: that you cant keep anybody locked up just because of what they are planning to do. Besides, he'd just give some Memphis lawyer two or three hundred dollars and be out again the next day. Isn't that true?'

'Isn't it?' his uncle said. 'Remarkable how hard a lawyer will work for three hundred dollars.'

'So that wouldn't do any good at all, would it?' she said. 'Deport him.'

'Deport your brother?' his uncle said. 'Where? What for?'

'Stop it,' she said. 'Stop it. Dont you know that if I had anyone else to go to, I wouldn't be here? Deport Seb— Captain Gualdres.'

'Ah,' his uncle said. 'Captain Gualdres. I'm afraid immigration authorities lack not only the will-to-succeed but the scope of movement too, of Memphis or three-hundred-dollar lawyers. It would take weeks, maybe months, to deport him, which if there is food for your fears, two days would be too much. Because what would your brother be doing all that time?'

'Do you mean that you, a lawyer, couldn't keep him locked up somewhere until Sebastian is out of the country?'

'Keep who?' his uncle said. 'Locked up where?'

She stopped looking at his uncle, though she hadn't moved.

'Can I have a cigarette?' she said.

His uncle gave her one from the box on the table and held the match and she sat back again, puffing rapidly at it and talking through the puffs, still not looking at his uncle.

'All right,' she said. 'When things finally got so bad between Max and him, when I finally realized that Max hated him so much that something bad was going to happen, I persuaded Max to agree to——'

'—to save your mother's fiancé,' his uncle said. 'Your prospective new father.'

'All right,' she said through the rapid smoke, holding the cigarette between two fingers with pointed painted nails. 'Because there was nothing really settled between him and Mother—if there ever had been anything to settle. And so at least it wasn't Mother who wanted anything settled about it because. . . . And he would have had the horses or at least the money to buy new ones, no matter which one of us . . .' She puffed rapidly at the cigarette, not looking at his uncle nor at anything. 'So when I found out that sooner or later Max was going to kill him if something wasn't done about it, I made a trade with Max that if he would wait twenty-four hours, I would come with him to you and persuade you to have him deported, back to the Argentine——'

'—where he wouldn't have anything but his captain's pay,' his uncle said. 'And then you would follow him.'

'All right,' she said. 'Yes. So we came to you, and then I saw that you didn't believe us and were not going to do anything about it and so the only thing I could think to do was to let Max see with you watching that I loved him too, so that Max would do something to make you believe that at least Max meant what he was saying. And he did it and he does mean it and he's dangerous and you've got to help me. You've got to.'

'And you've got to do something too,' his uncle said. 'You've got to start telling the truth.'

'I have. I am.'

'But not all of it. What's wrong between your brother and Captain Gualdres. Not—as they say—chewing gum this time.'

She watched his uncle for just a second through the rapid smoke. The cigarette was almost gone now, right down to the painted finger-tips.

'You're right,' she said. 'It's not the money. He doesn't care any-thing about money. There's plenty of that for Se——all of us. It wasn't even because of Mother. It was because Sebastian always beat him. At everything. Sebastian came without even a horse of his own, and Max rides well too but Sebastian beat him, beat him on Max's own horses, the very horses that Max knew Sebastian was going to be the owner of as soon as Mother came to taw and said Yes. And Max had been the best pupil Paoli had had in years and one day Sebastian took a hearth-broom and parried through two ripostes until Max jerked the button off and went at him with the bare point and Sebastian used the hearth-broom like a sabre and beat down the lunge until somebody grabbed Max——'

She was breathing, not hard so much as fast, rapid, panting almost, still trying to draw on the cigarette which would have been too short to smoke even if her hand had been steady enough to hold it steady, sitting huddled in the chair in a kind of cloud of white tulle and satin and the rich dark heavy sheen of little slain animals, looking not wan so much as delicate and fragile and not even fragile so much as cold, evanescent, like one of the stalked white early spring flowers bloomed ahead of its time into the snow and the ice and doomed before your eyes without even knowing that it was dying, feeling not even any pain.

'That was afterward,' his uncle said.

'What? After what?'

'That happened,' his uncle said. 'But it was afterward. You dont want a man dead just because he beat you, on a horse or with a rapier either. At least, you dont take actual steps to make the wish a fact.'

'Yes,' she said.

'No,' his uncle said.

'Yes.'

'No.'

She leaned and put the cigarette stub into the ashtray as carefully as if it was an egg or maybe a capsule of nitroglycerin, and sat again, her hands not even shut now but lying open on her lap.

'All right,' she said. 'I was afraid of this. I told—knew you wouldn't be satisfied. It's a woman.'

'Ah,' his uncle said.

'I thought you would,' she said, and now her voice had changed again, for the third time since she entered the room not ten minutes ago yet. 'Out there, about two miles from our back door. A farmer's daughter.—Oh yes,' she said, 'I know that one too: Scott or Hardy or somebody else three hundred years ago: the young lord of the manor and the villeins: *droit du seigneur* and all the rest of it. Only this time it wasn't. Because Max gave her a ring.' Now her hands were lying on the chair arms, clenched again, and she wasn't looking at his uncle now either. 'A good deal different this time. Better than Hardy or Shakespeare either thought of. Because there were two city lads this time:

not only just the rich young earl but the young earl's foreign friend or anyway house-guest: the dark romantic foreign knight that beat the young earl riding the young earl's own horses and then took the young earl's sword away from him with a hearth-broom. Until at last all he had to do was ride at night up to the young earl's girl friend's window, and whistle——. Wait,' she said.

She got up. She was already walking before she got onto her feet. She crossed the room and jerked the door open before he could even move, her heels clapping hard and fast in the hall. Then the front door banged. And still his uncle just stood there looking at the open door.

'What?' he said. 'What?'

But his uncle didn't answer; his uncle was still watching the door and then almost before his uncle could have answered, they heard the front door again and then the hard brittle girl-heels in the hall, two pairs of them now, and the Harriss girl came in fast and crossed the room and flipped one hand backward behind her and said,

'There she is,' and went on and swirled down into the chair again while he and his uncle looked at the other girl—a country girl, because he had seen her face before in town on Saturday, but that was the only way you could tell them now because their mouths and faces were painted too and sometimes their fingernails and the Sears and Roebuck clothes didn't look like Sears and Roebuck now and sometimes they were not even Sears and Roebuck even if they were not trimmed off in thousand-dollar mink; —a girl about the same age as the Harriss girl but not quite as tall, slender yet solid too, as country-bred girls can look, with dark hair and black eyes, looking at him for a second and then at his uncle.

'Come in,' his uncle said. 'I'm Mr Stevens. Your name is Mossop.'

'I know it,' the girl said. 'No, sir. My mother was a Mossop. My father is Hence Cayley.'

'She's got the ring too,' the Harris girl said. 'I asked her to bring it because I knew you wouldn't believe it any more than I did when I heard it. I dont blame her for not wearing it. I wouldn't wear anybody's ring either that said to me what Max said to her.'

The Cayley girl looked at the Harriss girl—a look level and black and unwinking and quite calm—for about a minute while the Harriss girl took another cigarette from the box, though this time nobody went to strike a match for her.

Then the Cayley girl looked at his uncle again. Her eyes were all right so far. They were just watchful.

'I never did wear it,' she said. 'On account of my father. He dont think Max is any good. And I'm not going to even keep it, as soon as I can find him to give it back. Because I dont think so too now——'

The Harriss girl made a sound. It didn't sound to him like anything she would have learned in Swiss convent either. The Cayley girl gave her another of the hard black contemplative looks. But her eyes were still all right. Then she looked at his uncle again.

'I didn't mind what he said to me. I didn't like the way he said it. Maybe that was the only way he could think of to say it at the time. But he ought to have been able to think of a different way. But I wasn't mad because he felt he had to say it.'

'I see,' his uncle said.

'I wouldn't have minded his having to say it, anyway,' she said.

'I see,' his uncle said.

'But he was wrong. He was wrong from the beginning. He was the one that said first that maybe I better not wear the ring out where folks could see it for a while yet. I never even had time to tell him I already knew better than to let Papa find out I even had it——'

The Harriss girl made the sound again. This time the Cayley girl stopped and turned her head quite slowly and looked at the Harriss girl for five or six seconds while the Harriss girl sat with the unlighted cigarette between her fingers. Then the Cayley girl looked at his uncle again.

'So he was the one that said we better not be engaged except in private. So since I wasn't to be engaged except in private, I didn't see any reason why Captain Golldez——'

'Gualdres,' the Harriss girl said.

'Golldez,' the Cayley girl said.— or anybody else couldn't ride up and sit on our gallery and talk to us. And I liked to ride horses that didn't have trace-galls for a change too, so when he would bring one along for me——'

'How could you tell whether it had a trace-gall or not, in the dark?' the Harriss girl said.

Now the Caley girl, and still without haste, turned her whole body and looked at the Harriss girl.

'What?' she said. 'What did you say?'

'Here,' his uncle said. 'Stop it.'

'You old fool,' the Harriss girl said. She wasn't even looking at his uncle. 'Do you think that any man except one like you with one foot already in the grave, would spend half the night every night riding a horse up and down an empty polo field by himself?'

Then the Cayley girl moved. She went fast, stooping and hiking up the hem of her skirt and taking something from the top of her stocking as she went, and stopped in front of the chair and if it had been a knife, he and his uncle would still have been too late.

'Stand up,' she said.

Now the Harris girl said 'What?' looking up, the hand still holding the unlighted cigarette in front of her mouth. The Cayley girl didn't speak again. She just rocked back onto her heels, slender and solid too, and swung her arm back and his uncle was moving now, hollering 'Stop it! Stop it!' but the Cayley girl had already swung, slapping the Harriss girl's face and the cigarette and the hand that held it, all together, and the Harriss girl jerked in the chair and then sat with the broken cigarette dangling between her fingers and a long thin scratch down her cheek; and then the ring itself, a big diamond, tumbled winking down the front of her coat and onto the floor.

The Harriss girl looked at the cigarette a moment. Then she looked at his uncle. 'She slapped me!' she said.

'I saw her,' his uncle said. 'I was just about to, myself——' and then jumped too; he had to: the Harriss girl coming fast out of the chair and the Cayley girl already rocked back onto her heels again. But his uncle got there first, between them this time, flinging the Harriss girl back with one arm and the Cayley girl with the other , until in another second they both stood there crying, bawling, exactly like two three-year-olds who have been fighting, while his uncle watched them for a moment and then stooped and picked up the ring.

'That'll do now,' his uncle said. 'Stop it. Both of you. Go to the bathroom and wash your faces. Through that door yonder'—saying quickly 'Not together' as they both moved. 'One at a time. You first,' to the Harriss girl. 'There's styptic in the cabinet if you want it, fear hydrophobia rather than merely believe in it. Show her the way, Chick.'

But she had already gone on into the bedroom. The Cayley girl stood wiping her nose on the back of her hand until his uncle handed her his handkerchief.

'I'm sorry,' she said, sniffling, snuffling, that is. 'But she ought not to have made me do it.'

'She ought not to have been able to,' his uncle said. 'I suppose she had you waiting out there in the car all the time. Drove out to your house and got you.'

The Cayley girl blew her nose into the handkerchief. 'Yes sir,' she said.

'Then you'll have to drive her home,' his uncle said to him, not looking back. 'They both cant——'

But the Cayley girl was all right now. She gave her nose a good hard wipe right and then left and started to hand the handkerchief back to his uncle and then stopped, letting the hand drop at her side.

'I'll go back with her,' she said. 'I'm not afraid of her. It wont be but two miles home even if she wont take me any further than her gate.'

'All right,' his uncle said. 'Here': holding out the ring. It was a big diamond; it was all right too. The Cayley girl didn't hardly look at it.

'I dont want it,' she said.

'I wouldn't either,' his uncle said. 'But you owe yourself the decency of letting your own hand be the returner.'

So she took the ring and then the Harriss girl returned and the Cayley girl went to bathe her face, still carrying the handkerchief. The Harriss girl looked all right again, with a glazed swipe of styptic on the scratch; and she had the platinum-and-jewel box now, but it was powder and such. She didn't look at either of them. She looked into the mirror in the box's lid, finishing her face.

'I should apologise, I suppose,' she said. 'But I imagine lawyers see all sorts of things in their trade.'

'We try to avoid bloodshed,' his uncle said.

'Bloodshed,' she said. She forgot her face then and the platinum-and-jewel box too and the flipness and the hardness both went and when she looked at his uncle, the terror and dread were in her eyes again; and he knew that, whatever he and his uncle might think about what her brother could or would or might do, at least she didn't have any doubts. 'You've got to do something,' she said. 'You've got to. If I had known anybody else to go to, I wouldn't have bothered you. But I——'

'You told me he made a pact with you to do nothing for twenty-four hours,' his uncle said. 'Do you think he will hold himself still bound to it, or will he do what you did—make an effort of his own behind your back too?'

'I dont know,' she said. 'If you could just lock him up until I——'

'Which I cant do, any more than I can have the other one deported before breakfast. Why dont you deport him yourself? You said that you——'

Now there was terror and despair both in her face.

'I cant. I tried. Maybe Mother is a better man than I am, after all. I even tried to tell him. But he's like you: he doesn't believe either that Max is dangerous. He says it would be running from a child.'

'That's just exactly what it would be,' his uncle said. 'That's just exactly why.'

'Exactly why what?'

'Nothing,' his uncle said. Then his uncle was not looking at her, not looking at any of them, not at anything as far as he could tell, just standing there rubbing the ball of his thumb against the bowl of the cob pipe. Then she said,

'Can I have another cigarette?'

'Why not?' his uncle said. She took the cigarette from the box and this time he lit it for her, passing his uncle to the smoking stand, stepping carefully among the scattered chessmen to strike the match as the Cayley girl came in, not looking at anybody either, saying to his uncle:

'It's on the mirror.'

'What?' his uncle said.

'Your handkerchief,' the Cayley girl said. 'I washed it.'

'Oh,' his uncle said, and the Harriss girl said,

'Just talking to him wont do any good either. You tried that once, you know.'

'I dont remember,' his uncle said. 'I dont recall hearing anything but him. But you are right about the talking. I have an idea this whole business started because somebody has already talked too much.'

But she wasn't even listening. 'And we'll never get him in here again either. So you'll have to come out there——'

'Good night,' his uncle said.

She was not listening at all. '—in the morning before he can get out of bed and go somewhere. I'll telephone you in the morning when will be the best time——'

'Good night,' his uncle said again.

Then they were gone: through the sittingroom door, leaving it open of course; that is, the Harriss girl did, though when he went to close it the Cayley girl had turned back to do it until she saw he was already there. But when he started to shut it, his uncle said, 'Wait' so he stood holding it and they heard the hard brittle girlheels in the hall and then, sure enough, the front door too.

'That's what we thought the other time,' his uncle said. 'Go and make sure.'

But they were gone. Standing in the open front door in the vivid chill windless December dark, he heard the over-revved engine and watched the big supercharged roadster lurch almost into full speed with a whine a squeal of tires on pavement, then around the next corner, the tail-lights sucking from view too fast there too, so that long after it must have crossed the Square, it seemed to him that he could still smell the outraged rubber.

Then he went back to the sitting-room where his uncle now sat among the scattered chessmen, filling the pipe. He went on without stopping and picked up the chessboard and set it back on the table. Luckily all the fighting had taken place in the other direction, so none of the pieces had been stepped on. He gathered them up from around his uncle's feet and set them back in place on the board again, even advancing the white queen's pawn in the orthodox opening which his uncle insisted on. His uncle was still filling the pipe.

'So they were right about Captain Gualdres after all,' he said. 'It was a girl.'

'What girl?' his uncle said. 'Didn't one of them drive six miles twice tonight just to make sure we understood that she wanted her name coupled with Captain Gualdres', no matter what the conditions; and the other one not only resorted to fisticuffs to refute the aspersion, she cant even spell his name?'

'Oh,' he said. Then he didn't say it. He drew his chair up and sat down again. His uncle watched him.

'You had a nice sleep?' his uncle said.

He was a little slow on that one too. But all he had to do was to wait, because the only time when his uncle absolutely refused to diagram his wit was when it was really witty, really brilliant; never when it merely had an edge.

'Thirty minutes ago you were on your way to bed. I couldn't even stop you.'

'And I almost missed something,' he said. 'I dont intend to this time.'

'There will be no more to miss tonight.'

'I thought that too,' he said. 'That Cayley girl——'

'—is safe at home,' his uncle said. 'Where, I hope and trust, she will stay. And the other one too. Move then.'

'I already have,' he said.

'Then move again,' his uncle said, matching the white pawn. 'And watch what you are doing this time.'

He thought he did, was, had, always had every time. But all watching what he was doing seemed to accomplish was to show him a little sooner than ordinary that this one too was going to end just like the other did: until suddenly his uncle swept the board clean and set up a single problem with the horses and rooks and two pawns.

'It stops being a game then,' he said.

'Nothing by which all human passion and hope and folly can be mirrored and then proved, ever was just a game,' his uncle said. 'Move.'

And this time it was the telephone, and this time he knew it was going to be the telephone and he even knew what the telephone was going to say, not even really having to listen to the one audible side of it: nor did that take his uncle long:

'Yes? Speaking ... When? ... I see. When you got home they just told you he had packed his bag and taken his car and said he was going to Memphis. ... No no, never prescribe for a physician nor invite a postman to a walk': and put the receiver back into the cradle and sat there with his hand still on it, not moving, not even breathing apparently, not even rubbing the thumb against the bowl of the pipe; sitting there so long that he was getting ready to speak, when his uncle raised the receiver and asked for the number, nor did this take long either: to Mr Robert Markey in Memphis, a lawyer and in city politics too, who had been at Heidelberg with his uncle:

'No no, not the police; they couldn't hold him. I dont want him held anyway; I just want him watched, so he cant leave Memphis without me knowing it. A good private man, just to keep an eye on him without him knowing it—unless he tries to leave Memphis. ... What? I never really authorise actual bloodshed, at least not with witnesses. ... Yes, until I come up and put my own hand on him, tomorrow or next day. ... At the hotel. ... There's only one: the Greenbury. Did you ever hear

of a Mississippian who has learned yet there is another one? (Which
was true enough: there was a saying in North Mississippi that the state
began in the lobby of the Greenbury hotel). . . . Assumed name? Him?
The last thing he is running from is notoriety. He will probably call all
the newspapers to be sure they have his name and location right, and
that they record it. . . . No no, just wire me in the morning that you have
him safely under surveillance and keep him so until you hear from me
again': and put the telephone down and got up, but not to return to
the chessboard but instead went to the door and opened it and stood
holding the knob, until finally he did catch up. He got up and picked
up the book he had started upstairs with three hours ago. But this time
he spoke, and this time his uncle answered him:

'But what do you want with him?'

'I dont,' his uncle said. 'I just want to know he's in Memphis, and
that he stays there. Which he will do; he will want me and the rest of
the world too to be convinced he is safely and harmlessly in Memphis,
or anywhere else except Jefferson, Mississippi, ten times more than I
want to know it.'

But he was slow on that too; he had to ask that too.

'His alibi,' his uncle said.

And that too.

'For whatever he is planning to do—whatever trick he has invented
to frighten his mother's fiancé into leaving the country.'

'Trick?' he said. 'What trick?'

'How do I know?' his uncle said. 'Ask yourself; you're eighteen, or
so near it doesn't matter; you know what a child of nineteen will do;
a Black Hand letter maybe, or even a reasonably careful shot fired
through the bedroom window at him. I'm fifty; all I know is that people
nineteen years old will do anything, and that the only thing which
makes the adult world at all safe from them is the fact that they are so
preconvinced of success that the simple desire and will are the finished
accomplishment, that they pay no attention to mere dull mechanical
details.'

'Then if the trick's not going to work, you dont need to worry,' he
said.

'I'm not worrying,' his uncle said. 'I'm being worried. Worse;
annoyed. I just want to keep my—or Mr Markey's—finger on him until I

can telephone his sister tomorrow and she—or their mother, or anyone else in the family who have or hope to have any control over him or either or both of them—can go up there and get him and do whatever they want to with him; I would suggest that they tie him up in one of the stalls and let his prospective father (this might even be enough reason to Captain Gualdres for him to give over his maiden hesitancy and consent to an immediate marriage) work on him with his riding-crop.'

'Oh,' he said. 'Anyway, there's nothing wrong with that Cayley girl. Maybe if he'd just been here tonight and seen her when his sister——'

'Nobody ever believed there was, except his sister,' his uncle said. 'She was the one who even convinced him in the first place that there was, started this whole thing. To get her own man. Maybe she thought that, as soon as her brother reached for that foil again, Gualdres would leave the country. Or maybe she hoped that simple discretion and good sense would be enough to move him; in either case, all she would have to do would be to follow him, to some or any other place in the United States or even back to the Argentine (where of course there are no other women) and, by surprise envelopment or perhaps simple compromise, gain the victory, render him at least monogamous. But she underestimated him; she aspersed his character with the crime of maturity too.'

His uncle held the door open, looking at him.

'There's nothing actually wrong with any of them except youth. Only—as I believe I mentioned a moment ago—the possession of youth is a good deal like the possession of smallpox or bubonic plague.'

'Oh,' he said again. 'Maybe that's what's the matter with Captain Gualdres too. We were wrong about him. I thought he was about forty. But she said he's not but eight or ten years older than she is.'

'Which means she believes he is about fifteen years older,' his uncle said. 'Which means he is probably about twenty-five older.'

'Twenty-five?' he said. 'That would put him right back where he used to be.'

'Had he ever left it?' his uncle said. His uncle held the door open. 'Well? What are you waiting for?'

'Nothing,' he said.

'Then good night too,' his uncle said. 'You go home too. This kinder-garten is closed for the day.'

III.

So that was that. He went upstairs to his room. He went to bed too, taking off the uniform, 'shedding the brown' as the Corps called it. Because this was Thursday, and the battalion always drilled on Thursday. And he was not only cadet lieutenant colonel this year, but nobody ever missed drill because, although the Academy was only a prep school, it had one of the highest R.O.T.C. ratings in the country; at the last review, the inspector-general himself told them that when war came, every one of them who could prove he was eighteen years old would be almost automatically eligible for officer-candidate school.

Which included him too, since he was already so near eighteen that you could put the difference in your eye. Except that it wouldn't matter now whether he was eighteen or eight or eighty; he would be too late even if he were going to wake up eighteen tomorrow morning. It would be over and people would already have begun to be able to start forgetting about it before he could even reach officers' school, let alone finish the course.

It was already over even now as far as the United States was concerned: the British, the handful of boys, some no older than he and some probably not even as old, who flew the Royal Air Force's fighter command, had stopped them on the west and so now there was nothing left for that whole irresistible tide of victory and destruction to do but vanish away into the plumbless depths of Russia like the mop-thrust push of dirty water across a kitchen floor: so that each time during the fifteen months since that fall of 1940 that he took the uniform down or hung it back up in the closet—the khaki serge true enough such as real officers wore but without even the honest stripes of N.C.O.'s but instead, the light-blue tabs and facings of R.O.T.C. like the lapel badges of fraternity pledges, and the innocent pastless metal lozenges such as you might see on the shoulders of a swank hotel doorman or the leader of a circus band, to divorce it still further from the realm of valor and risk, the heart's thirst for glory and renown;—each time he looked at it, in the eyes of that heart's thirst (if that's what it was), certainly in the irremediable regret which had been his these last months after he realised that it was too late, that he had procrastinated, deferred too long, lacking not only the courage but even the will and the desire and the thirst, the khaki altered transmogrified dissolved like the moving-picture shot, to the blue of Britain and the hooked wings of a diving falcon and the modest braid of rank: but above all the blue, the color the shade which the handful of Anglo Saxon young men had established and decreed as such visual synonym of glory that only last spring an association of American haberdashers or gent's outfitters had adopted it as a trade slogan, so that every lucky male resident of the United States who had the price could walk into church that Easter morning in the authentic aura of valor yet at the same time safe from the badges of responsibility and the candy-stripes of risk.

Yet he had made a little something resembling an attempt (and he thought a little better of it for the very fact that remembering he had done so gave him no comfort). There was Captain Warren, a farmer a few miles from town, who had been a flight commander in the old Royal Flying Corps before it because the RAF; he had gone to see him that day going on two years ago now when he was only just past sixteen.

'If I could get to England some way, they would take me, wouldn't they?' he said.

'Sixteen's a little young. And getting to England's a little hard to do too now.'

'But they would take me if I could get there, wouldn't they?' he said.

'Yes,' Captain Warren said. Then Captain Warren said, 'Look. There's plenty of time. There'll be plenty and more for all of us before its over. Why not wait?'

So he did. He waited too long. He could tell himself that he had done that at the advice of a hero, which at least did this much for the heart's thirst: having accepted and followed it from a hero would forever prevent his forgetting that, no matter how deficient he might be in courage, at least he wasn't in shame.

Because it was too late now. In fact, as far as the United States was concerned, it had never begun at all and so all it would cost the United States was just money: which, his uncle said, was the cheapest thing you could spend or lose: which was why civilization invented it: to be the one substance man could shop with and have a bargain in whatever he bought.

So apparently the whole purpose of the draft had been merely to establish a means for his uncle to identify Max Harriss, and since the identification of Max Harriss had accomplished no more than the interruption of a chess-game and a sixty-cent telephone toll to Memphis, even that was not worth its cost.

So he went to bed and to sleep; tomorrow was Friday so he would not have to put on the pseudo khaki in order to shed the brown and, for another week, the heart's thirst, if that's what it was. And he ate breakfast; his uncle had already eaten and gone, and he stopped at his uncle's office on the way to school to pick up a notebook he had left yesterday, and Max Harriss wasn't in Memphis; the wire came from Mr Markey while he was still in the office:

Missing prince missing here too now what

and he was still there while his uncle told the boy to wait and wrote the answer:

No what just thanks

and so that was that too; he thought that was all; when he came back at noon to where his uncle waited on the corner to walk home to dinner, he didn't even think to ask; it was his uncle who voluntarily told him how Mr Markey had even telephoned and said how Harriss seemed to be well known not only to all the clerks and telephone girls and the Negro doormen and bellboys and waiters in the Greenbury, but to all the liquor stores and taxi-drivers in that part of town too, and that he, Mr Markey, had even tried the other hotels just on the impossible supposition that there was one Mississippian who had heard there were others in Memphis.

So he said, like Mr Markey, 'Now what?'

'I dont know,' his uncle said. 'I would like to believe that he had dusted the whole lot of them from his feet and was a good five hundred miles away by now, and still travelling, except that I wouldn't asperse him either behind his back with an accusation of judgment.'

'Maybe he has,' he said.

His uncle stopped walking.

'What?' his uncle said.

'You just said last night that people nineteen years old are capable of anything.'

'Oh,' his uncle said. 'Yes,' his uncle said. 'Of course,' his uncle said, walking on again. 'Maybe he has.'

And that was all: eating his dinner: walking back with his uncle as far as the office corner: in school that afternoon, through the history class which Miss Melissa Hogganbeck now called World Affairs with capitals on both, which, coming twice a week, should have been worse for the heart's thirst than the inevitable next Thursdays when he would have to tote the brown again—the sabre and the pastless shoulder-pips— and posture through the spurious the straight-faced the make-believe of command, but which was not at all: the tireless cultured educated 'lady's' voice talking with a kind of frantic fanaticism of peace and security: of how we were safe because the old worn-out nations of Europe had learned their lesson too well in 1918; they not only did not dare outrage us, they couldn't even afford to, until the world's whole staggering and savage mass was reduced to that weightless interminable murmuring not even echoed within the isolate insulate dusty walls of a prep-school classroom and having a hundred times less connection with any reality than even the sword and the pips. Because at least the sabre and pips were a make-believe of what they parodied, while to Miss Hogganbeck the whole establishment of national R.O.T.C. was an inescapable inexplicable phenomenon of the edifice of education, like the necessity for having children in the junior courses.

And it was still all even when he had seen the horse. It was in a muddy horse-van standing in an alley behind the Square when he passed after school, with a half dozen men standing around looking at the van from a definitely respectful distance, and only afterward did he actually see the horse shackled into the van not with ropes but with steel chains as if it were a lion or an elephant. Because he hadn't really looked at the van yet. In fact, he hadn't even got as far as affirming, accepting that there was a horse in it, because at that moment he saw Mr Rafe McCallum himself coming up the alley and he crossed the street to speak to him because he and his uncle would go out to the McCallum farm fifteen miles from town to shoot quail in season, and, until they enlisted last summer, he used to go out there by himself to spend the night in the woods or the creek bottom running fox or coon with the twin McCallum nephews.

So he recognised the horse, not by seeing it, because he had never seen it, but by seeing Mr McCallum. Because everybody in the county knew the horse or knew about it—a stallion of first blood and pedigree but absolutely worthless; they—the county—said that this was the only time in his life that Mr McCallum had ever been beaten in a horse-trade, even if he had bought this one with tobacco- or soap-coupons.

It had been ruined either as a colt or a young horse, probably by some owner who had tried to break its spirit by fear or violence. Only its spirit had refused to break, so that all it had got from whatever the experience had been, was a hatred for anything walking upright on two legs, something like that abhorrence and rage and desire to destroy it which some humans feel for even harmless snakes.

It was unrideable and unmanageable even for breeding. It was said to have killed two men who just happened to get on the same side of a fence with it. Though this was not very probable, or the horse would have been destroyed. But Mr McCallum was supposed to have bought it because its owner wanted to destroy it. Or maybe he believed he could tame it. Anyway, he always denied that it had ever killed anyone, so at least he must have thought he could sell it, since no horse was ever quite as bad as the man who bought it claimed, or as good as the man who sold it contended.

But Mr McCallum knew that it could kill a man, and the county believed that he thought it would. For although he would go into the lot where it was (though never into a stall or pen where it would be cornered), he would never let anyone else do it; and it was said that once a man had offered to buy it from him, but he had refused. Which had an apocryphal sound too, since Mr McCallum said himself that he would sell anything which couldn't stand up on its hind legs and call his name, because that was his business.

So here was the horse roped and chained and blanketed into a horse-box fifteen miles from its home paddock, and so he said to Mr McCallum:

'You finally sold it.'

'I hope so,' Mr McCallum said. 'A horse aint ever sold until the new stall door is shut behind it though. Sometimes not even then.'

'But at least it's on the way,' he said.

'At least it's on the way,' Mr McCallum said.

Which didn't mean much, didn't mean anything in fact except that Mr McCallum would have to hurry like billy-O just to prove he hadn't even sold it. Which would be in the dark and a good while into it: four oclock now, and anyone who had engaged to buy that horse would have to have lived a long way off not to have heard about it.

Then he thought how anybody who bought that horse would live too far away to be reached in just one daylight even if it were the twenty-second of June, let alone the fifth of December, so maybe it didn't matter what time Mr McCallum started, and so he went to his uncle's office and that was all except the postscript and even that was not too long away; his uncle had the practice brief all laid out for him on the desk and the list of references beside it and he got to work and it seemed almost at once when the light began to fail and he switched on the desk lamp and then the telephone rang. The girl's voice was already talking when he lifted the receiver and it never did stop, so that it was a second or two before he could recognise it:

'Hello! Hello! Mr Stevens! He was here! Nobody even knew it! He just left! They called me from the garage and I ran down and he was already in the car with the engine running and he said if you want to see him, to be on your corner in five minutes; he said he wouldn't be able to come up to your office, for you to be on the corner in five minutes if you want to see him, otherwise you can call and maybe get an appointment with him at the Greenbury hotel tomorrow——' and still talking when his uncle came in and took the receiver and listened for a moment, and probably still talking even after his uncle put the receiver back up.

'Five minutes?' his uncle said. 'Six miles?'

'You never saw him drive,' he said. 'He's probably already crossing the Square.'

But that would be a little too fast even for that one. He and his uncle went down to the street and stood on the corner in the cold dusk for what seemed like ten minutes to him, until at last he began to believe that here was some more of the same hurrah and hokum and uproar they had been in the middle of or at least on the edge of, since last night, in which the last thing they would expect would be not only what they might have expected, but what they had been warned to look for.

But they did see him. They heard the car, the horn; the heel of the Harriss boy's palm on the button or maybe he had simply reached inside the dash or the hood and jerked the ground connection loose, and probably if the boy was thinking about anything at all then, he was being sorry he didn't have an old-time muffler cutout. And he, Charles, thought of Hampton Killegrew, the night marshal, running out of the pool room or the Allnite Inn or wherever he would be at this time and already too late too, the car howling and wailing up the street toward the Square with all the lights burning, parking driving and fog, then blatting and crashing between the brick walls and the street narrowed into the Square; and afterward he remembered a cat leaping in silhouette across the rushing lights, looking ten feet long one second then the next one high and narrow as a fleeing fence post.

But luckily there wasn't anybody else but him and his uncle at the crossing and the boy saw them then, the lights swinging down at them as if he was going to drive right up onto the curb. Then they swung away at the last second and he could have touched the boy—the face, the teeth glinting in it—as the car shot past into the Square and crossed it and slewed skidding, the tires squealing against the pavement, into the Memphis highway, the horn and the tires and the engine growing fainter and fainter, until at last he and his uncle could even hear Hampton Killegrew running toward the corner cursing and yelling.

'Did you pull the door to?' his uncle said.

'Yes sir,' he said.

'Then let's go home to supper,' his uncle said. 'You can stop at the telegraph office on the way.'

So he stopped in the telegraph office and sent the wire to Mr Markey exactly as his uncle had worded it:

He is now Greenbury tonight use police per request Jefferson chief if necessary

and came out and overtook his uncle at the next corner.

'Why the police now?' he said. 'I thought you said——'

'To escort him on through Memphis toward wherever he is going,' his uncle said. 'In any direction except back here.'

'But why is he going anywhere?' he said. 'You said last night that the last place he will want to be is out of sight; the last place he will want to be is where nobody can see him, until after his joke——'

'Then I was wrong,' his uncle said. 'I maligned him too. Apparently I attributed to nineteen not only more ingenuity than it is capable of, but even malice too. Come along. You're late. You've not only got to eat supper, you've got to get back to town.'

'To the office?' he said. 'The telephone? Cant they call you at home? Besides, if he's not even going to stop in Memphis, what will they have to telephone you about——'

'No,' his uncle said. 'To the picture show. And before you can ask that, the reason is, that's the one place where nobody nineteen or twenty-one named Harriss nor going on eighteen named Mallison either, can talk to me. I'm going to work. I shall spend the evening in the company of scoundrels and felons who have not only the courage of their evil, but the competence for it too.'

He knew what that meant: the Translation. So he didn't even go to his uncle's sitting-room. And his uncle left the supper table first, so he didn't see him again.

And if he, Charles, hadn't gone to the picture show, he wouldn't have seen his uncle at all that evening: eating his supper without haste since there was plenty of time despite his uncle and only his uncle seemed to want to avoid the human race: walking still without haste, since there was still plenty of time, through the cold vivid dark toward the Square and the picture show, not knowing what he was going to see and not even caring; it might be another war picture he was walking toward and it didn't even matter, thinking remembering how once a war picture should, ought, to have been the worst thing of all for the heart's thirst to have to endure, except that it was not, since there lay between the war movie and Miss Hogganbeck's world events a thousand times even the insuperable distance which lay between Miss Hogganbeck's world events and the R.O.T.C. pips and the sword: thinking how if the human race could just pass all its time watching moving pictures, there would be no more wars nor any other man-made anguishes, except for the fact that man couldn't spend that much time watching moving pictures since boredom was the one human passion that movies couldn't cope with and man would have to spend at least eight hours a day watching them since he would have to sleep for another eight and his uncle said the only other thing man could stand for eight continuous hours was work.

So he went to the show. And if he hadn't gone to the show, he wouldn't have been passing the Allnite Inn where he could see, recognise the empty horse-van at the curb before it with the empty chains and shackles looped through the side-planks, and, turning his head toward the window, Mr McCallum himself at the counter, eating, the heavy white-oak cudgel he always carried around strange horses and mules, leaning against the counter beside him. And if he hadn't had fourteen minutes yet before the week-night hour (except Saturday or unless there was a party) when he was supposed to be back home and indoors, he wouldn't have entered the Inn and asked Mr McCallum who had bought the horse.

The moon was up now. Once the lighted Square was behind him, he could watch the chopping shadows of his legs chopping off the shadows of the leafless branches and then finally of the fence pickets too, though not for long because he climbed the fence at the corner of the yard and so saved the distance between there and the gate. And now he could see the shaded down-glow of the desk lamp beyond the sitting-room window and, himself not walking hurrying but rather being swept along on the still-pristine cresting of the astonishment and puzzlement and (most of all, though he didn't know why) haste, his instinct was to stop, avoid evade—anything rather than violate that interdiction, that hour, that ritual of the Translation which the whole family referred to with a capital T—the rendering of the Old Testament back into the classic Greek into which it had been translated from its lost Hebrew infancy—which his uncle had been engaged on for twenty years now, a few days over two years longer than he, Charles, had lived, retiring to the sitting-room once a week always (and sometimes two and three times provided that many things happened to displease or affront him), shutting the door behind him: nor man woman nor child, client well-wisher or friend, to touch even the knob until his uncle turned it from inside.

And he, Charles, thought how if he had been eight instead of almost eighteen, he wouldn't have paid any attention even to that student lamp and that shut door; or how if he had been twenty-four instead of eighteen, he wouldn't have been here at all just because another boy nineteen years old bought a horse. Then he thought how maybe that was backward; that he would have been hurrying faster than ever at twenty-four and at eight he wouldn't have come at all since at eighteen all he knew to do was just the hurrying, the haste, the astonishment, since, his uncle to the contrary or not, his was one eighteen anyway which couldn't begin to anticipate how Max Harriss's nineteen hoped to circumvent or retaliate on anybody with even that horse.

But then he didn't need to; his uncle would attend to that. All required of him was the hurry, the speed. And he had supplied that, holding the steady half-walk half-trot from that first step through the Inn door where he could turn the corner, to the yard and across it and up the steps into the hall and down the hall to the closed door, not pausing at all, his hand already reaching for the knob, then into the sitting-room where his uncle sat in shirtsleeves and an eyeshade at the desk beneath the lamp, not even looking up, the Bible propped open in front of him and the Greek dictionary and the cob pipe at his elbow and the better part of a ream of yellow copy paper strewn about the floor at this feet.

'He bought a horse,' he said. 'What can he do with the horse?'

Nor did his uncle look up yet nor even move. 'Ride it, I hope,' his uncle said. Then his uncle looked up, reaching for the pipe. 'I thought it was understood——'

His uncle stopped, the pipe too, the stem already turned to approach his uncle's mouth, the hand holding it just clear of the desk, motionless. And he had seen this before and it seemed for a moment that he was watching it now: the instant during which his uncle's eyes no longer saw him, while behind them shaped the flick and click of the terse glib succinct sentence sometimes less than two words long, which would blast him back out of the room.

'All right,' his uncle said. 'What horse?'

He answered, succinct too. 'McCallum's. That stallion.'

'All right,' his uncle said again.

And this time he was not slow; he didn't need the diagram.

'I just left him at the Inn, eating supper. He took it out there this afternoon. I saw the truck in the alley on the way from school this afternoon, but I didn't——'

His uncle was not seeing him at all; the eyes were as empty as the Harriss girl's had been when she came through the door the first time last night. Then his uncle said something. It was in Greek, the old Greek, like his uncle was back there in the old time when the Old Testament had first been translated or even written. Sometimes his uncle would do that: say something for him in English that neither of them would have intended for his, Charles's, mother to hear, then again in the old Greek, and even to him who couldn't understand the Greek, it sounded a lot stronger, a lot more like whoever was saying it meant exactly that, even to the ones who couldn't understand it or at least hadn't understood it until now. And this was one of them and neither did this sound like anything that anybody had got out of the Bible, at least since the Anglo-Saxon puritans had got hold of it. His uncle was up now too, snatching off the eyeshade and flinging it away, and kicked the chair backward and snatched his coat and vest from the other chair.

'My overcoat and hat,' his uncle said. 'On the bed. Jump.'

And he jumped. They went out of the room exactly like an automobile with a scrap of paper being sucked along behind it, up the hall with his uncle in front in the flapping coat and vest now and still holding his arms extended back for the overcoat, and he, Charles, still trying to gain enough to shove the overcoat sleeves over his uncle's hands.

Then across the moonlit yard to the car, he still carrying the hat, and into the car and without warming the engine at all, his uncle rushed it backward on the choke at about thirty miles an hour, out of the drive into the street and dragged the tires and whirled it around and went up the street still on the choke and took the corner on the wrong side, crossing the Square almost as fast as Max Harriss had done, and slammed in beside Mr McCallum's truck in front of the Inn and jumped out.

'You wait,' his uncle said, running on across the pavement into the Inn, where through the window he watched his uncle run up to where Mr McCallum still sat at the counter drinking coffee with the stick still leaning beside him until his uncle ran up and snatched up the stick and turned without even stopping, sucking Mr McCallum along behind and out of there just like he had sucked him, Charles, out of the sitting room two minutes ago, back to the car where his uncle jerked the door open and told him, Charles, to move over and drive and flung the stick in and shoved Mr McCallum in and got in himself and slammed the door.

Which was all right with him, because his uncle was worse even than Max Harriss, even when he wasn't in a hurry or going anywhere. That is, the speedometer only showed about half as much, but Max Harriss had an idea he was driving fast, while his uncle knew he wasn't.

'Step on it,' his uncle said. 'It's ten minutes to eight. But the rich eat late so maybe we'll be in time.'

So he did. Soon they were out of town and he could let the car out some even though the road was just gravel; building himself a concrete driveway six miles in to town was the only thing Baron Harriss had forgot to do or anyway died too quick to do. But they went pretty fast, his uncle perched forward on the edge of the seat and watching the speedometer needle as if the first time it flickered he intended to jump out and run ahead.

'Howdy Gavin, hell,' his uncle said to Mr McCallum. 'Wait and howdy me after I indict you as an accessory.'

'He knew the horse,' Mr McCallum said. 'He came all the way out home and insisted he wanted to buy it. He was there at sunup, asleep in the car at the front gate, with four or five hundred dollars loose in his overcoat pocket like a handful of leaves. Why? Does he claim to be a minor?'

'He dont claim either,' his uncle said. 'He seems to hold the entire subject of his age interdict from anybody's meddling—even his uncle in Washington. But never mind that. What did you do with the horse?'

'I put him in the stable, the stall,' Mr McCallum said. 'But it was all right. It was the little stable, with just one stall in it, with nothing else in it. He told me I wouldn't need to worry, because there wouldn't be anything else in it. He had it already picked out and ready when I got there. But I looked, myself, at the doors and fences both. The stable was all right. If it hadn't been I wouldn't have left the horse, no matter how much he paid me for it.'

'I know that,' his uncle said. 'What little stable?'

'The one that's off to itself, that he built last summer, behind some trees, away from the other stables and the paddocks too. With a pad-dock of its own, and nothing else in the stable but the one big stall and a tack room and I looked in the tack room too: just a saddle and bridle and blankets and a curry-comb and brush and some feed. And he said that anybody that touched that saddle and bridle or the feed either, was going to already know about the horse and I told them they had certainly better, because if anybody walked into that lot and opened that stall door expecting to find just an ordinary horse behind it, it would not only be a considerable worry to the one that did the walking and the opening, but to the one that owned the horse too. And he said that at least that let me out, because I was just the one that sold it. But the stable was all right. There was even an outside window where a man could climb into the loft and throw down feed until the horse got used to him.'

'And when would that be?' his uncle said.

'I learned how to do it,' Mr McCallum said.

'Then maybe in a minute now we can watch you,' his uncle said.

Because they were almost there. They hadn't gone out as quick as Max Harriss had come in, but already they were running between the white fences which, in the moonlight, didn't look any more substantial than cake-icing, with the broad moon-filled pastures beyond them where his uncle could probably remember cotton growing—or at least his uncle would probably claim he did—while the old owner sat in his home-made chair on the gallery, to look out over them for a while, then turn back to his book and his toddy again.

Then they turned through the gates, with his uncle and Mr McCallum both sitting on the edge of the seat now, and ran fast up the drive between the combed and curried lawns, the bushes and shrubs and trees as neat as laid-by cotton, until they could see what had been the old owner's house too: the tremendous sprawl of columns and wings and balconies that must have covered half an acre.

And they were in time. Captain Gualdres must have come out the side door just in time to see their lights in the drive. Anyway, he was already standing there in the moonlight when they saw him and he was still standing there when the three of them got out of the car and approached, bareheaded, in a short leather jacket and boots and a light crop dangling from his wrist.

It began in Spanish. Three years ago he had reached optional Spanish in High School and he didn't remember now, in fact he never had really understood, how or why he started taking it; just exactly what his uncle had done, as a result of which he, Charles, found himself committed to taking the Spanish which he had never really intended to commit himself to. It wasn't persuasion and it wasn't a bribe, because his uncle said you didn't need to be bribed to do something you wanted to do, needed to do, whether you knew at the time you needed it, would ever need it, or not. Perhaps his mistake was in dealing with a lawyer. Anyway, he was still taking Spanish and he had read *Don Quixote* and he could keep up with most Mexican and South American newspapers and he had started the *Cid* only that was last year and last year was 1940 and his uncle said, 'But why? It should be easier than *Quixote* because the *Cid* is about heroes.' But he couldn't have explained, to anyone, least of all a man fifty years old, even his uncle, how to assuage the heart's thirst with the dusty chronicle of the past when not fifteen hundred miles away in England men not much older than he was were daily writing with their lives his own time's deathless footnote.

So most of the time he could understand them; only a little of the Spanish went too fast for him. But then, some of the English was too fast for Captain Gualdres too, and at one time he was even about to believe there were two of them who were not keeping up with his uncle's Spanish too.

'You go to ride,' his uncle said. 'In the moonlight.'

'But certainly,' Captain Gualdres said, still courteous, still only a little startled, his black eyebrows up only a little—so courteous that the voice never showed the surprise at all and not even the tone of it was actually saying, in whatever way a Spaniard would say it, *So what?*

'I'm Stevens,' his uncle said, in that same rapid voice—which to Captain Gualdres, he realised, was much worse than just rapid since to a Spaniard the rapidity and abruptness would be the worst crime of all; which (the Spanish), he realised also, was the trouble; there had not been time; his uncle had not had time to do anything but just talk in it. 'This is Mr McCallum. And this is my sister's son, Charles Mallison.'

'Mr McCallum I know well,' Captain Gualdres said in English, turning; they could see his teeth for a second too. 'He has one much horse too. A pity.' He shook hands with Mr McCallum, sudden and brief and hard. But even doing that he still looked like bronze, for all his soft worn moon-gleamed leather and brilliantined hair, as if he had been cast from metal, hair boots jacket and all, in one jointless piece. 'The young gentleman, not so well.' He shook hands with him, Charles, quick and brief and hard too. Then he stepped back. And this time he didn't shake hands. 'And Mr Stevens, not so well. A pity too, perhaps.' And still even the tone of the voice didn't say, *You may now present the apologies for consideration*. It didn't even say, *Yes, gentlemen?* Only the voice itself said, perfectly courteous, perfectly heatless, with no inflection whatever:

'You come out for ride? Is no horse up for now, but plenty on the little campo. We go to catch.'

'Wait,' his uncle said in Spanish. 'Mr McCallum has had to look at the ends of too many horses every day to need to ride one tonight, and my sister's son and I do not have to look at enough of them to want to. We have come to do you a favor.'

'Ah,' Captain Gualdres said, in Spanish too. 'And that favor?'

'All right,' his uncle said, still in the rapid voice, in that quick splatter of Captain Gualdres' native tongue resonant, not quite musical, like partly detempered metal: 'There was a great haste. Perhaps I came so fast that my manners could not keep up.'

'That politeness which a man can outride,' Captain Gualdres said, 'was it ever his to begin with. With deference: what favor?'

And he, Charles, thought too: *What favor?* Captain Gualdres hadn't moved. There had never been doubt, disbelief in his voice; now there wasn't even astonishment, surprise in it. And he, Charles, was ready to agree with him; that there could be anything anything could do to him that his uncle or anybody else would need to warn him against or save him from: thinking (Charles) of not only Mr McCallum's horse but a whole drove like it cracking their cannons and crowns on him, maybe rolling him in the dust and getting him dirty even and maybe even chipping his edges or possibly even denting him a little, but that was all.

'A wager then,' his uncle said.

Captain Gualdres didn't move.

'A request then,' his uncle said.

Captain Gualdres didn't move.

'A favor to me then,' his uncle said.

'Ah,' Captain Gualdres said. Nor did he move even then: only the one word not even Spanish nor even English either because it was the same in all the tongues that he, Charles, had ever heard of.

'You ride tonight,' his uncle said.

'Truth,' Captain Gualdres said.

'Let us go with you to the stable where you keep your night riding-horse,' his uncle said.

Again Captain Gualdres moved, even though it was only the eyes, he—Charles—and Mr McCallum watching the gleam of the whites as Captain Gualdres looked at him then at Mr McCallum then back to his uncle and then no more, no more at all, apparently not even that of breathing, while he, Charles, could have counted sixty almost. Then Captain Gualdres did move, already turning.

'Truth,' he said, and went on, the three of them following, around the house that was too big, across the lawn where the bushes and shrubs were too many, past the garages that would have held more cars than just four people could ever have used and the conservatories and hothouses of too many flowers and grapes for just four people ever to have eaten or smelled, crossing that moon-still moon-blanched moon-silent barony with Captain Gualdres leading the way on the hard bowed pistons of boot-gleamed and glinted legs, then his uncle then himself then Mr McCallum carrying the white-oak cudgel, the three of them in single file behind Captain Gualdres like three of his family *gauchos* if Captain Gualdres had a family and they were not *gauchos* instead or maybe even something else altogether ending in *ones*.

But not toward the big stables with the electric clocks and lights and gold-plated drinking fountains and mangers, nor even toward the lane which led to them. Instead, they crossed the lane, climbing the white fence and crossing the moonlit pasture, on to and around and then beyond a small patch of woods and there it was and he could even still hear Mr McCallum talking almost: the small paddock inside its own white fence, and a single stable about the size of a two-car garage, all new since last September without doubt and neat and fresh with paint and the upper half of the single stall door open; a black square in the dazzling white; [37] and suddenly behind him Mr McCallum made a kind of sound.

And this was where it began to go too fast for him. Even Captain Gualdres went Spanish now, turning, his back to the fence, compact, durable, even somehow managing to look taller, saying to his uncle what until now even the tone of the voice had not said, the two of them facing one another in the rapid splatter of Captain Gualdres' native language so that they sounded like two carpenters spitting tacks at each other's handsaw. Though his uncle began in English and at first Captain Gualdres followed, as if his uncle anyway felt that Mr McCallum was at least entitled to this much:

'Now, Mr Stevens. You explain?'

'With permission?' his uncle said.

'Truth,' Captain Gualdres said.

'This is where you keep your night horse, the blind one.'

'Yes,' Captain Gualdres said. 'No horse here but the little mare. For night. Is left in the stable by the negrito each afternoon.'

'And after supper—dinner—midnight, whenever it's dark enough, you come out here and go into that paddock and walk across to that door and open it, in the dark, like now.'

And at first he had thought how there were too many people here, one too many, anyway. Now he realised that they were short one: the barber: because Captain Gualdres said,

'I set first up the jumps.'

'The jumps?' his uncle said.

'The little mare does not see. Soon she will not see forever. But she can still jump, not by seeing but by the touch, the voice. I teach her the—how you say it?—faith.'

'I think the word you want is invulnerability,' his uncle said. Then it went into Spanish, fast, the two of them, except for the rigidity, like boxers. And he might have kept up with Cervantes just writing it, but having the Batchelor Sampson and the chief of the Yanguesians trading a horse right before his face, was too much for him until his uncle explained it afterward when (or so he thought) it was finally all over—or came as near to explaining it as he, Charles, ever really expected.

'Then what?' he said. 'What did you say then?'

'Not much,' his uncle said, 'I just said, "That favor." And Gualdres said, "For which, naturally, I thank you beforehand." And I said, "But which, naturally, you do not believe. But of which, naturally, you wish to know the price." And we agreed on the price, and I performed the favor, and that was all.'

'But what price?' he said.

'It was a bet,' his uncle said. 'A wager.'

'A wager on what?' he said.

'On his fate,' his uncle said. 'He called it. Because the only thing a man like that believes in is his destiny. He doesn't believe in a fate. He doesn't even accept one.'

'All right,' he said. 'The bet. Bet him what?'

But his uncle didn't even answer that, just looking at him, sardonic, whimsical, fantastical and familiar still, even though he, Charles, had just discovered that he didn't know his uncle at all. Then his uncle said:

'A knight comes suddenly out of nowhere—out of the west, if you like—and checks the queen and the castle all in that same one move. What do you do?'

At least he knew the answer to that by now. 'You save the queen and let the castle go.' And he answered the other one too: 'Out of western Argentina.' He said: 'It was that girl. The Harriss girl. You bet him the girl. That he didn't want to cross that lot and open that stable door. And he lost.'

'Lost?' his uncle said. 'A princess and half a castle, against some of his bones and maybe his brains too? Lost?'

'He lost the queen,' he said.

'The queen?' his uncle said. 'What queen? Oh, you mean Mrs Harriss. Maybe he realised that queen had been moved the same instant he realised he would have to call the bet. Maybe he realised that the queen and the castle both had been gone ever since the moment he disarmed the prince with that hearth-broom. If he ever wanted her.'

'Then what was he doing here?' he said.

'Why was he waiting?' his uncle said.

'Maybe it was a pleasant square,' he said. 'For the pleasure of being able to move not only two squares at once but in two directions at once.'

'Or indecision, since he can,' his uncle said. 'And almost fatal for this one, because he must. At least, he'd certainly better. His threat and his charm are in his capacity for movement. This time, he forgot that his safety lay in it too.' But that was tomorrow. Right now he couldn't even keep up with what he was watching. He and Mr McCallum just stood there looking and hearing while his uncle and Captain Gualdres stood facing each other, rapping out the brittle splattering syllables, until at last Captain Gualdres made a motion, not quite a shrug and not quite a salute, and his uncle turned to Mr McCallum.

'What about it, Rafe?' his uncle said. 'Will you walk over there and open that door?'

'I reckon so,' Mr McCallum said. 'But I dont see——'

'I've made a bet with Captain Gualdres,' his uncle said. 'If you wont do it, I'll have to.'

'Wait,' Captain Gualdres said. 'I think it is for me to——'

'You wait yourself, Mister Captain,' Mr McCallum said. He shifted the heavy stick to the other hand and stood looking across the white fence into the empty moon-filled lot, at the silent white wall of the stable with its single black square of half-door, for almost a half minute. Then he shifted the cudgel back to the other hand and climbed up onto the fence and put one leg over it and turned his head and looked back down at Captain Gualdres. 'I just found out what all this is about,' he said. 'And so will you in a minute.'

Then they watched him climb, still without haste, down into the paddock: a compact light-poised deliberate man with about him something of the same aura, sense of horses which Captain Gualdres had, walking steadily on in the moonlight, toward the blank white stable and the single black square of emptiness, of utter of absolute silence, in the center of it, reaching the stable at last and lifting the heavy wrought-iron latch and opening the closed lower half of the door; only then moving with unbelievable speed, jerking the half-door quickly back and out on its hinges and already moving with it, swinging it all the way back to the wall until he stood slightly behind it, between it and the wall, the heavy cudgel clutched in his other hand; swinging the door back barely an instant before the stallion, itself the same color as the inky blackness of the inside, exploded out into the moonlight as if it had been tied to the door itself with a rope no longer than a watch-chain.

It came out screaming. It looked tremendous, airborne even: a furious mass the color of doom or midnight in a moonward swirling of mane and tail like black flames, looking not merely like death because death is stasis, but demoniac: the lost brute forever unregenerate, bursting out into the moonlight, screaming, galloping in a short rushing circle while it flung its head this way and that, searching for the man until it saw Mr McCallum at last and quit screaming and rushed toward him, not recognising him until he stepped out from the wall and shouted at it.

Then it stopped, its fore feet bunched and planted, its body bunching against them, until Mr McCallum, again with that unbelievable quickness, walked to it and swung the cudgel with all his strength across its face, and it screamed again and whirled, spun, already galloping, and Mr McCallum turned and walked toward the fence. He didn't run: he walked, and although the horse galloped two complete circles around him before he reached the fence and climbed it, it never quite threatened him again.

And during another time Captain Gualdres didn't move, metal-hard, inviolable, not even pale. Then Captain Gualdres turned to his uncle; it was in Spanish still, but now he could follow it.

'I have lost,' Captain Gualdres said.

'Not lost,' his uncle said.

'Truth,' Captain Gualdres said. 'Not lost.' Then Captain Gualdres said, 'Thanks.'

IV.

Then Saturday, no school: the whole unchallengeable day in which to have sat around the office and attended the little rest of it, the cleaning up; the what little rest of it remained, or so he thought, who even at that late hour of December afternoon had not yet known his own capacity to be astonished and amazed.

He hadn't even really believed that Max Harriss would come back from Memphis. Mr Markey, in Memphis, hadn't believed it either apparently.

'Memphis city police cant transport a prisoner back to Mississippi,' Mr Markey said. 'You know that. Your sheriff will have to send someone——'

'He's not a prisoner,' his uncle said. 'Tell him that. Tell him I just want him to come back here and talk to me.'

Then for almost half a minute there was nothing on the telephone at all except the faint hum of the distant power which kept the line alive, which was costing somebody money whether voices went over it or not. Then Mr Markey said:

'If I gave him that message and told him he could go, would you really expect to see him again?'

'Give him the message,' his uncle said. 'Tell him I want him to come back here and talk to me.'

And Max Harriss came back. He arrived just ahead of the others, just far enough ahead of them to have got through the anteroom and into the office while the other two were still mounting the stairs; and he, Charles, shut the anteroom door and Max stood in front of it, watching his uncle, delicate and young and expensive-looking still and a little tired and strained-looking too as if he hadn't slept much last night, except for his eyes. They didn't look young or tired either, watching his uncle exactly as they had looked at him night before last; looking anything but all right by a good long shot. But at least there wasn't anything cringing in them, whatever else there might be.

'Sit down,' his uncle said.

'Thanks,' Max said, immediate and harsh, not contemptuous: just final, immediate, negative. But he moved in the next second. He approached the desk and began to peer this way and that about the office in burlesque exaggeration. 'I'm looking for Hamp Killigrew,' he said. 'Or maybe it's even the sheriff himself. Where've you got him hidden? in the water cooler? If that's where you put either one of them, they are dead of shock by now.'

But still his uncle didn't answer, until he, Charles, looked at his uncle too. His uncle wasn't even looking at Max. He had even turned the swivel chair sideways and was looking out the window, motionless except for the almost infinitesimal stroking of the thumb of the hand which held it, on the bowl of the cold cob pipe.

Then Max stopped that too and stood looking down at his uncle's profile with the hard flat eyes in which there was little of youth or peace or anything else that should have been in them.

'All right,' Max said. 'You couldn't prove an intention, design. All you can prove, you wont even have to. I already admit it. I affirm it. I bought a horse and turned it into a private stable on my mother's property. I know a little law too, you see. I probably know just exactly the minor and incorrect amount of it to make a first-class small-town Mississippi lawyer. Maybe even a state legislator, though probably a little too much ever to be elected governor.'

Still his uncle didn't move, except for the thumb. 'I'd sit down, if I were you,' he said.

'You'd do more than that right now if you were me,' Max said. 'Well?'

Now his uncle moved. He swung the chair around with the pressure of his knees against the desk until, he faced Max.

'I dont need to prove it,' his uncle said. 'Because you are not going to deny it.'

'No,' Max said. He said it immediately, contemptuously. It wasn't even violent. 'I dont deny it. So what? Where's your sheriff?'

His uncle watched Max. Then he put the stem of the cold pipe into his mouth and drew at it as if it had fire and tobacco in it; he spoke in a voice mild and even almost inconsequential:

'I suppose that when Mr McCallum brought the horse out and you had him put it into Captain Gualdres' private stable, you told the grooms and the other Negroes that Captain Gualdres had bought it himself and wanted it let alone. Which wasn't hard for them to believe, since Captain Gualdres had already bought one horse which he wouldn't let anyone else touch.'

But Max no more answered that than he had answered the other night when his uncle asked him about not being registered for draft. There was not even contempt in his face while he waited for his uncle to go on.

'All right,' his uncle said. 'When are Captain Gualdres and your sister to be married?'

And that was when he, Charles, found out what else it was in the hard flat eyes. It was despair and grief. Because he watched the rage blaze up and burn, scour, sear them out until there was nothing left in them but the rage and the hatred, and he thought how maybe his uncle was right and there are more ignoble things than hatred and how if you do hate anyone, it must surely be the man you have failed to kill even if he doesn't know it.

'I've been doing some trading lately,' his uncle said. 'I'll know soon whether I did so bad at it or not. I'm going to make another trade with you. You are not nineteen years old, you are twenty-one, but you haven't even registered yet. Enlist.'

'Enlist?' Harriss said.

'Enlist,' his uncle said.

'I see,' Harriss said. 'Enlist, or else.'

Then Harriss began to laugh. He stood there in front of the desk, looking down at his uncle and laughing. But it never had touched his eyes in the first place, so it didn't need to leave them: it was just his face which the laughter left, laughing itself gradually away from his eyes even if it hadn't ever been there, until at last they looked like his sister's had two nights ago: the grief and the despair, but without the terror and fear, while his uncle's cheeks went through the motion of drawing at the cold pipe as though there were smoke in it.

'No,' his uncle said. 'No "else." Just enlist. Look. You are playing poker (I assume you know poker, or at least—like a lot of people—anyway play it). You draw cards. When you do that, you affirm two things: either that you have something to draw to, or you are willing to support to your last cent the fact that you have not. You dont draw and then throw the cards in because they are not what you wanted, expected, hoped for; not just for the sake of your own soul and pocket-book, but for the sake of the others in the game, who have likewise assumed that unspoken obligation.'

Then they were both motionless, even the void similitude of his uncle's smoking. Then Harriss drew a long breath. You could hear it: the inhale and the suspiration.

'Now?' he said.

'Yes,' his uncle said. 'Now. Go back to Memphis now and enlist.'

'I . . . . .' Harriss said. 'There are things——'

'I know,' his uncle said. 'But I wouldn't go out there now. They will allow you a few days after you are enlisted to come back home and say——put your affairs in order. Go back now. Your car is downstairs, isn't it? Go back to Memphis now and enlist.'

'Yes,' Harriss said. He drew another of the long breaths and let it go. 'Go down those steps and get in the car by myself, and leave. What makes you think you or the army or anybody else will ever catch me again?'

'I hadn't thought about it at all,' his uncle said. 'Would it make you feel better to give me your word?'

And that was all. Harriss stood there for another moment by the desk, then he went back to the door and stood there, his head bent a little. Then he raised his head and he, Charles, thought that he would have done that too: gone back through the anteroom where the others were. But his uncle spoke in time.

'The window,' his uncle said, and got up himself from the swivel chair and went and opened it, onto the outside gallery from which the stairs descended to the street, and Max stepped through it and his uncle closed the window and that was all: the feet on the stairs for a moment, but no shriek of tires now nor fading wail of the horn either this time, and if Hampton Killegrew or anybody else ran after him yelling this time, he and his uncle never heard that either. Then he went to the anteroom door and opened it and asked Captain Gualdres and the sister to come in.

Captain Gualdres still looked like bronze or metal of some sort even in the double-breasted dark suit any man might have worn and most men owned. He even still looked like horses too. Then he, Charles, realised that this was because the horse was missing: and that was when he first noticed that Captain Gualdres' wife was a little taller than Captain Gualdres. It was as if, without the horse, Captain Gualdres was not only incomplete as regarded mobility, but in height too, as if his legs had not been intended for him to be seen and compared with others while standing on them.

She was in a dark dress too, the dark blue in which brides 'go away,' travel, with the fine rich fur coat with a corsage (Orchids, of course. He had heard of orchids all his life, so he realised that he had never seen them before. But he knew them at once; on that coat and that bride they could be nothing else.) pinned to the collar and the thin thread from the Cayley girl's fingernail still showing on her cheek.

Captain Gualdres wouldn't sit down, so he and his uncle stood too.

'I come to say goodbye,' Captain Gualdres said in English. 'And to receive your—how you say——'

'Felicitations,' his uncle said. 'And to you, congratulations. You have them a thousand times. May I ask since when?'

'Since—' Captain Gualdres looked quickly at his wrist—'one hour. We just leave the padre. Our mama has just return home. We decide not to wait. So we come to say goodbye. I say it.'

'Not goodbye,' his uncle said.

'Yes. Now. By one—' again Captain Gualdres looked at his wrist '—five minutes we are no more for here.' (Because, as his uncle had said, there was one thing about Captain Gualdres: he not only knew exactly what he thought he was going to do, he quite often did it.) 'Back to my country. The *Campo*. Maybe I do not ought to have left him to begin. This country. Is magnificent, but too strong for simple *gaucho, paysano*. But for now, no matter. For now, is done. So I come to say one more goodbye and one hundred more *gracias*.' Then it was Spanish again. But he kept up. 'You have Spanish. My wife, having been educated only in the best of European convents for rich young American ladies, has no language at all. In my country, the campo, there is a saying: Married; dead. But there is another saying: To learn where the rider will sleep tonight, ask the horse. So no matter about that either; that's all finished too. So I have come to say goodbye, and thanks, and to congratulate myself that you had no stepchildren also to be placed for life. But I really have no confidence even in that condition because nothing is beyond a man of your capacity and attainments, not to mention imagination. So we return to my—our—country in time, where you are not. Because I think you are a very dangerous man and I do not like you. And so, with God.'

'With God,' his uncle said in Spanish too. 'I wouldn't hurry you.'

'You cant,' Captain Gualdres said. 'You dont even need to. You dont even need to wish you could.'

Then they were gone too: back through the anteroom; he and his uncle heard the outer door, then watched them pass across the gallery window, toward the stairs, and his uncle took from his vest the heavy watch with its loop of chain and the dangling golden key and laid it face-up on the desk.

'Five minutes,' his uncle said. Which was time enough, moment enough for him, Charles, to have asked exactly what was the other side of that bet his uncle had made last night with Captain Gualdres, except that he knew now he didn't need to ask; in fact, he realised now he had begun not to need to ask that at that instant Thursday night when he shut the front door after Max Harriss and his sister and came back to the sitting room and found that his uncle had no intention of going to bed.

So he said nothing, merely watching his uncle lay the watch on the desk, then stand over it, his arms spread a little and braced on either side of the watch, not even sitting down.

'For decency. For moderation,' his uncle said, then, already moving and even in the same breath, his uncle said, 'Or maybe I've already had too much of both,' taking up the watch and putting it back into his vest, then through the anteroom, taking up the hat and overcoat, and through the outer door, not even saying backward over his shoulder: 'Lock it,' then down the stairs and already standing beside the car, holding the door open, when he, Charles, reached it.

'Get in and drive,' his uncle said. 'And remember this is not last night.'

So he took the wheel and drove on through across the crowded Saturday Square, still having to dodge among the homeward-bound cars and trucks and wagons even after they were clear of downtown. But the road itself was still open for a little speed—a lot of it if he had been Max Harriss going home instead of just Charles Mallison driving his uncle backward.

'Now what?' his uncle said. 'What's wrong with it? Or has your foot gone to sleep?'

'You just said it's not last night,' he said.

'Of course it's not,' his uncle said. 'There's no horse waiting to run over Captain Gualdres now, even if the horse was necessary. He's got something this time a good deal more efficient and fatal than just an insane horse.'

'What's that?' he said.

'A dove,' his uncle said. 'So what are you poking along for? Are you afraid of motion?'

So they went then, almost half as fast as Max Harriss, over the road which the baron hadn't had time to concrete but which he probably would have dropped other things to do if he had just been warned in time, not for his own comfort because he didn't travel it; he went and came from New Orleans in his own airplane so that when Jefferson saw him it went out there to do it; but for the uniqueness of spending that much money on something not only not his but which all who knew him would not even expect him to use, just as Huey Long in Louisiana had made himself founder owner and supporter of what his uncle said was one of the best literary magazines anywhere, without ever once looking inside it probably nor even caring what the people who wrote and edited it thought of him any more than the baron did what the farmers thought of him whose straying livestock leaped and shrieked and demised under the speeding wheels of his guests; they were going fast now through the early December afternoon—the winter afternoon, the sixth day of winter the old folks called it, who counted from the first of December.

And it (the road) was older than gravel too, running back into the old time of simple dirt red and curving among the hills, then straight and black where the rich land flattened, alluvial and fertile; niggard in width since the land was too rich, too fecund in corn and cotton, to allow room for men to pass one another almost, marked only by the thin iron of carriage- and wagon-rims and the open O's of horses and mules when the old owner, the baron's father-in-law, would leave the Horace and the weak toddy long enough to come in to town the two or three or four times a year, to vote or sell the cotton or pay the taxes or attend a funeral or a wedding, and then be driven back to the toddy and the Latin pages again, along the simple dirt in which even hooves, unless running, made no noise, let alone the wheels or anything other than the creak of harness; back to the acres which were hardly bounded then except in his own recollection and holding and belief and that of his neighbors, not even fenced always, let alone in carefully paneled and railed oak and hickory designed in Virginia and Long Island and handicrafted in Grand Rapids factories, the lawn which was a yard of shabby oaks then, innocent of shears and pruners and clippers and borderers in a light mist of gasoline fumes, to the house which was just a house to back a front gallery for him to sit on with the silver cup and the worn calf; a garden which was just a garden, overgrown, shabby too, of old permanent perennial things: nameless roses and lilac bushes and daisies and phlox and the hard durable dusty bloom of fall, itself in the tradition of the diluted whiskey and the Horatian odes: unassertive, enduring.

It was the quiet, his uncle said. This, the first time, the only time his uncle actually said it, was twelve years ago when he, Charles, was not even quite six yet, just old enough to listen: which in fact his uncle even mentioned: 'Not that you are old enough to hear it, but that I'm still young enough to say it. Ten years from now, I wont be.' And he said,

'You mean ten years from now it wont be true?' And his uncle said,

'I mean that ten years from now I wont say it because ten years from now I will be ten years older and the one thing age teaches you is not fear and least of all more of truth, but only shame. —That spring of 1919 like a garden at the end of a four-year tunnel of blood and excrement and fear in which that whole generation of the world's young men lived like frantic ants, each one alone against the instant when he too must enter the faceless anonymity behind the blood and the filth, each one alone' (which at least proved one of his uncle's points, the one about truth anyway) 'with his constant speculation whether his fear was as plain to others as to himself. Because the groundling during his crawling minutes and the airman during his condensed seconds have no friends or comrades any more than the hog at the trough or the wolf in the pack has. And when the corridor ends at last and they come out of it—if they do—they still have none. Because' (but at least he, Charles, hoped his uncle was right about the shame) 'they have lost something, something of themselves dear and irreplaceable, scattered now and diffused and become communal among all the other faces and bodies which also survived: I am no more just John Doe of Jefferson, Mississippi; I am also Joe Ginotta of East Orange, New Jersey, and Charley Longfeather of Shoshone, Idaho, and Harry Wong of San Francisco; and Harry and Charley and Joe are all John Doe of Jefferson, Mississippi too. But that composite is each still us, so we cant repudiate it. And that's why America Legions. And though we may have been able to face and lie down what we had seen Harry and Joe and Charley do in the person of John Doe of Jefferson, we cant face down and lie away what we saw John Doe do as Charley or Harry or Joe. And that's why, while they were still young and had faith in breath, American Legions got mass-drunk.'

Because only the point about the shame was right, since his uncle only said that twelve years ago and never again since. Because the rest of it was wrong, since even twelve years ago, when his uncle was only in the late thirties, he had already lost touch with what was the real truth: that you went to war, and young men would always go, for glory because there was no other way so glorious to earn it, and the risk and fear of death was not only the only price worth buying what you bought, but the cheapest you could be asked, and the tragedy was, not that you died but that you were no longer there to see the glory; you didn't want to obliterate the thirsting heart: you wanted to slake it.

But that was twelve years ago; now his uncle only said, first: 'Stop. I'll drive.'

'No you wont,' he said. 'This is fast enough.' Within a mile now they would begin to pass the white fence; in two they would reach the gate and even see the house.

'It was the quiet,' his uncle said. 'At first I couldn't even sleep at night for it. But that was all right, because I didn't want to sleep; I didn't want to miss that much of silence: just to lie in bed in the dark and remember tomorrow and tomorrow and all the colored spring, April and May and June, morning noon and evening, empty, then dark again and silence to lie in because I didn't need to sleep. Then I saw her. She was in the old stained victoria with the two mis-matched plow-horses drawing it and the plow-hand on the box who didn't even have on shoes. And your mother was wrong. She didn't look like a parading doll at all. She looked like a little girl playing grown-up in the carriage-house, but playing it in deadly seriousness; like a child of twelve say, orphaned by sudden catastrophe, upon whom has devolved the care of a whole litter of younger brothers and sisters and perhaps even an aged grandparent, supervising the diet and changing and washing out the garments of infants; too young to have a vicarious interest in, let alone the conception of and kinship with the passion and mystery which created them alive into the world, which alone could have made the drudgery of feeding them bearable or even explicable.

'Of course it wasn't that. There was only her father, and if anything, the situation was reversed: the father who not only farmed the land and supervised the household, but did it in such a way that a plow-team and its driver from the field could be spared always to draw those six miles back and forth to town, the old carriage against the tremendous expanse of whose cushions she could resemble an archaic miniature, sober and sedate and demure ten years beyond her age and fifty years beyond her time. But that was the impression I got: a child playing house in that windless and timeless garden at the red and stinking corridor's end: and so one day I knew suddenly and irrevocably that just silence was not peace. It was after I saw her the third or the tenth or the thirtieth time, I dont remember which, but one morning I stood beside the halted carriage with the barefoot nigger on the box and she like something preserved from an old valentine or a 1904 candy-box against that faded soiled expanse of back seat (when the carriage passed, all you saw was just her head, and from behind you couldn't even see that though obviously the hand and the team wouldn't have been taken from the plow just to give the plowman a ride to town and back);—one morning I stood beside the halted carriage while on all sides rushed and squawked the bright loud glittering new automobiles because the war was won and every man would be rich and at peace forever.

"'I'm Gavin Stevens,' I said. "And I'm going on thirty years old."

"'I know it,' she said. But I felt thirty, even if I wasn't quite. She was sixteen. And how could you say to a child (as we said then): "Give me a date?" And what would you (at thirty) do with it? And you dont just simply invite the child: you ask the child's parents if it can come. So it was just dusk when I stopped your grandmother's car at the gate and got out. There was a garden then, not a florist's landscaping dream. It was a good deal bigger than even five or six rugs spread side by side, with old bushes of roses and callicanthus and paintless collapsing arbors and trellises and beds of perennials re-seeding themselves without outside meddling help or let, and she standing in the middle of it watching me as I entered the gate and went up the walk until she couldn't see me anymore. And I knew she would not have moved from where she stood, and I mounted the steps to where the old gentleman sat in his hickory chair with the setter pup at his feet and the silver cup and the marked book at his elbow, and I said,

"'Let me be betrothed to her' (mark how I put it: me to her). "I know," I said. "I know: not now. Not now. Just let us be betrothed, and we wont even have to think about it again."

'And she hadn't moved from where she stood, not even for listening. Because it was too far for listening, and besides she didn't need to: just standing there in the dusk the twilight, not moving: not shrinking, just not anything at all; it was even I who tilted up her face though it took no more strength than to raise a strand of honeysuckle. It was like tasting sherbet.

"'I dont know how,' she said. "You'll have to teach me."

"'Dont learn then,' I said. "It's all right. It doesn't even matter. You dont have to learn." It was like sherbet: the rest of spring, and summer and the long rest of summer: the darks and silence to lie in, remembering sherbet: not retasting it because you dont need to retaste sherbet; it doesn't take much sherbet because you dont forget it. Then it was time for me to go back to Germany and I took the ring out to her. I had already looped it onto the ribbon myself.

"'You dont want me to wear it yet?' she said.

'"Yes," I said. "No," I said. "All right. Loop it over the bush here if you want to. It's just a little piece of glass and colored iron; it probably wont even last a thousand years." And I went back to Heidelberg and every month the letters would come, talking about nothing. Because how could they? She was just sixteen; what can have happened to just sixteen to write about, even talk about? And each month I answered, talking about nothing too, because how could just sixteen have translated it if I had, translated it to? And that's what I never did understand, never did find out,' his uncle said.

Now they were almost there; he was already slowing the car to enter the gate.

'Not how she got the German translated,' his uncle said. 'But how whoever translated the German for her, translated the English too.'

'German?' he said. 'You wrote her in German?'

'There were two letters,' his uncle said. 'I wrote them at the same time. I sealed and mailed them in the wrong envelopes.' Then his uncle cried, 'Look out!' and even reached for the wheel. But he caught the car in time.

'The other one was for a woman too,' he said. 'Yes. So that——'

'She was a Russian,' his uncle said. 'She had escaped from Moscow. For a price, paid by installments, over a long time, to different collectors. She was through a war too, O my Philistine. I knew her in Paris in 1918. When I left America in the fall of '19 to go back to Heidelberg, I thought, believed I had forgotten her. That is, one day in mid-ocean I discovered that I hadn't thought about her since spring. And so I knew I hadn't forgot. I changed my booking and went to Paris first; she was to follow me to Heidelberg as soon as someone would visé what papers she had. I would write to her each month too while we waited. Maybe while I waited. You must bear in mind my age. I was a European then. I was in that menopause of every sensitive American when he believes that what (if any) future Americans' claim not even to human spirit but to simple civilization has, lies in Europe. Or maybe that was wrong. Maybe it was simply, sherbet, and I was not even allergic to sherbet nor even impervious to it but simply incapable of sherbet; writing the two letters at the same time because it didn't even demand any cerebral process to compose one of them, that one flowing from somewhere around, amid the intestines, out to the fingertips, the penpoint, the ink without detour via the brain: as a result of which I was never even able to recall what could have been in the one which went where I had not written it to go, though there couldn't have been much doubt; never occurred to me to remember to be careful with them because they did not exist in the same world although the same hand wrote them at the same desk upon successive sheets of paper with the same one unbroken pen-stroke beneath the same two pfennigs' worth of electricity while the same space on the clock's dial crept beneath the moving hand.'

Then they were there. His uncle didn't have to say stop; he had already parked the car in the empty drive too wide too suave and too neatly raked and graveled for even a station wagon and a convertible or two and a limousine and something for the servants, his uncle not even waiting for that but already out of the car and walking toward the house while he, Charles, was still saying,

'I dont have to come in too, do I?'

'Haven't you come a little far to quit now?' his uncle said.

So he got out too and followed, up the flagged walk too wide and with too many flagstones in it, toward the side portico which, merely a side one, would have held a president and cabinet or a supreme court all right though a little cozy for Congress, and the house itself like something between a gargantuan bride's cake and a freshly whitewashed circus tent, his uncle still going fast and still talking:

'We are strangely apathetic toward some very sound foreign customs. Think what a blaze it would have made, with this coffin on stacked gasoline-soaked cross-ties high in the middle of it: its (the house's) amortization one with its creator's suttee.'

Then inside; the Negro butler opened the door and immediately vanished and he and his uncle stood in the room in which Captain Gualdres (assuming he was or had been cavalry) could have paraded his troops, horses too, though he noticed little else because it was the orchid again: recognised at once, immediately, without surprise nor even attention. Then he even forgot the pleasant savor, titillation of simple tremendousness, because she came in: her feet in the hall and then into the room, though he had already smelled it, as if somebody had opened an old drawer by gaucherie, clumsiness, mistake and forty servants in rubber soles jumping frantically through the long corridors and rooms of flash and glitter to hurry it shut again; coming into the room and stopping and beginning to put her hands up palm-out in front of her without even having time to look at him since his uncle, who had never really stopped at all, was already walking toward her.

'I'm Gavin Stevens and now I'm almost fifty,' his uncle said, walking on toward her even after she began to retreat, fall back, bringing the hands higher and still palm-out toward his uncle, his uncle walking right on into the hands too and still walking right on while she was still trying to hold him away long enough to at least give herself time to change her mind about wanting to turn and run: too late now, assuming that was what she wanted or anyway thought she ought to do: but too late now, so that his uncle could stop too, looking back at him.

'Now what?' his uncle said. 'You can say something, cant you? Even good afternoon Mrs Harriss will do.'

He started to say 'Excuse me.' But already he had thought of something better than that.

'Bless you, my children,' he said.

V.

That was Saturday. The next day was December seventh. But even before he left, the store windows were already bright with toys and tinsel and artificial snow like any other December in any other year, the air bright and merry with the taste and smell of Christmas even with gunfire in it, the gunfire and the whine of bullets and the sound they made on flesh getting ready to echo right here in Jefferson before many more weeks or months.

But when he saw Jefferson next, it was spring. The wagons and pick-ups of the hill farmers and the five- and ten-ton trucks of the bot-tomland planters and operators had already backed up to the loading platforms of the seed stores and the fertilizer warehouses, and tractors and spanned and tripled mules would be moving across the dark shear-ing of the land's winter sleep: plow and middlebuster, harrow and drag and disc; dogwood would bloom soon and soon the whippoorwills, but this was only 1942 and there would be a little time yet before the party-line telephones would begin to carry the War and Navy Department telegrams, and on Thursday mornings the RFD carrier would leave in the lonely post-perched boxes the weekly *Yoknapatawpha Clarion* bearing the reproduced photograph and the brief obit already too familiar yet still cryptic as Sanscrit or Chinese—the country-boy face not really old enough yet to be a man's photograph, the uniform still showing the creases of the quartermaster shelves, the place-names which those who had created that face and flesh apparently in order that it might die in agony there, had never even heard of before, let along pronounce.

Because the inspector-general had been right. In fact, Benbow Sartoris, who had been only nineteenth in the class, had his commission and was already in England on something hush hush. Which, first and cadet colonel on the battalion list, he might have been doing too before it was too late, except that as usual he had exchanged the devil for the witch: not even the Sam Browne and the sabre and the trick insigne now, but only the blue hat-band and, even though being a cadet colonel or maybe that particular cadet colonel had shortened preflight some, probably a year yet before the winged badge on the cap would move down to just above the left pocket (with the shield of a pilot in the middle he hoped or at least a navigator's globe or anyway a bomb dropper's bomb).

And not even coming home really but just passing it on the way from preflight to basic, airplanes at last, only stopping in the station long enough for his mother to get on the train and ride with him down to the mainline junction where he would get a train for Texas and she would come back on the next local; approaching, passing, beginning to pass the familiar land: the road crossings he knew, the fields and woods where he had hiked as a cub then a scout and, old enough at last for a gun, hunted rabbits first and then quail on the wing.

Then the shabby purlieus themselves timeless and durable, familiar as his own voracious omnivorous insatiable heart or his body and limbs or the growth of his hair and fingernails: the first Negro cabins weathered and paintless until you realised it was more than just that and that they were a little, just a little awry: not out of plumb so much as beyond plumb: as though created for, seen in or by a different perspective, by a different architect, for a different purpose or anyway with a different past: surviven or even impervious to, unaware of, harder air or weather, whatever it was, each in its fierce yet orderly miniature jungle of vegetable patch, each with a shoat hog in a pen too small for any hog to thrive in yet this one did and would, and usually a tethered cow and a few chickens, the whole thing—cabin outhouse washpot shed and well—having a quality flimsy and makeshift, alien yet inviolably durable like Crusoe's cave; then the houses of white people, no larger than the Negro ones but never cabins, not to their faces anyway or you'd probably have a fight on your hands, painted or a least once-painted, the main difference being that they wouldn't be quite so clean inside.

Then he was home: a paved street-crossing not very far from the house he had been born in, and now he could see above the trees the water tank and the gold cross on the spire of the Episcopal church and then no more: his face pressed to the grimy glass as if he were eight years old, the train slowing over a clash and clatter of switch-points among the box- and cattle-cars and the gondolas and the tanks, and there they were, seen as the child of eight sees them: with something of shock, set puny yet amazingly durable against the perspective of the vast encompassable earth: his mother: his uncle: his new aunt: and his mother had been married to one man for twenty years and had raised another one, and his new aunt had been married to two in about that same time and had watched two more in her own house fighting each other with hearth-brooms and horses, so he was not surprised nor did he even really know how it happened: his mother already in the train and his new aunt already gone back to the waiting car while he and his uncle had the one last word together:

'Well, Squire,' he said. 'You not only went once too many to the well, you threw the pitcher in and then jumped in after it. I've got a message from your son.'

'My who?' his uncle said.

'All right,' he said. 'Your son-in-law. Your daughter's husband. The one that dont like you. He came out to camp to see me. He's a cavalry-man now. I mean a soldier, an American'—tediously, himself recapitulant: 'You understand? One night an American acquaintance had tried to kill him with a horse. The next day he married the American's sister. The day after that a Jap dropped a bomb on another American on a little island two thousand miles away. So on the third day he enlisted, not into his own army in which he already held a reserve commission, but into the foreign one, renouncing not only his commission to do so but his citizenship too, using an interpreter without doubt to explain both to his bride and to his adopted government what he was trying to do'—remembering, still recapitulant, not amazed or if amazed, the tireless timeless amazement of the child watching tireless and timeless the repetitive Punch and Judy booth: that afternoon and no warning whatever until the summons to the orderly room, and there Captain Gualdres was '—in a private's uniform, looking more like a horse than ever, maybe because of the fact that he had got himself into the one situation or condition above earth—a 1942 United States Army cavalry regiment—where as long as the war lasted he would have no contact whatever with horses—' himself (Charles) repetitive too: 'He didn't look brave, he just looked indomitable, not offering a life or a limb to anyone, any government in gratitude for or protest against anything, as if in this final and serious moment neither would he assume any sentimental pretence regarding the vain and idle pattering of bullets against him any more than he had used to about the vain and fragile hooves of horses; not hating Germans or Japs or even Harrisses, going to war against Germans not because they had ruined a continent and were rendering a whole race into fertilizer and lubricating oil, but because they had abolished horses from civilised cavalry, getting up from the chair when I came in and saying,

'"I come here so you can see me. Now you have seen me. Now you will return to your uncle and say to him, Perhaps you are satisfied now."'

'What?' his uncle said.

'I dont know either,' he said. 'That's what he said: that he had come all the way there from Kansas so I could see him in that brown suit and then come back to you and say, "Now maybe you're satisfied." '

And now it was time to go; they had already pulled the express hand-truck away from the baggage car door, and the express clerk was even leaning out the door looking back, and Mr McWilliams, the conductor, was standing at the vestibule steps with his watch in his hand, but at least he was not hollering at him, Charles, yet, because he, Charles, wore a uniform and this was still early in 1942 and civilians hadn't got used to war yet. So he said,

'And one more thing. Those letters. Two letters. Two wrong envelopes.'

His uncle looked at him. 'You dont like coincidence?'

'I love it,' he said. 'It's one of the most important things in life. Like maidenhead. Only, like maidenhead, you only use it once. I'm going to save mine a while yet.'

His uncle looked at him, quizzical, fantastical, grave. 'All right,' his uncle said. 'Try this. A street. In Paris. Within, as we Yoknapatawphians say, a medium spit of the Bois de Boulogne, so recent in nomenclature that its name is no older than the last battles of 1918 and the Versailles peace table—less than five years then; so select and so discreet that its location was known only to garbage collectors and employment bureaus for upper servants and the under secretaries of embassys. But no matter; it doesn't exist anymore now, and besides, you'd never get there to see it if it did.'

'Maybe I will,' he said. 'Maybe I'll look at where it used to be.'

'You can do that here,' his uncle said. 'In the library. Simply by opening the right page in Conrad: the same waxed red-and-black tiled floor, the ormolu, the faience, the buhl; even to the long mirror which seemed to hold as in a silver dish the whole condensation of light, of afternoon, in whose depths seemed to float, like the lily upon its own concordant repetition, that forehead innocent and smooth of thought, ravaged only by grief and fidelity——'

'How did you know she was there?' he said.

'I seen it in the paper,' his uncle said. 'The Paris *Herald*. The United States government (given a little time) did very well in keeping up with its own first American Expeditionary Force in France. But theirs was nothing to how the Paris *Herald* kept cases on the second one which began to land in Europe in 1919.— But this one was not ravaged at all by anything: just sitting there looking still exactly like a little girl whom all the world was helping now in the make-believe that she was a queen; and no caller this time come to do justice to a dead man because the man, creature, whose message this caller bore was anything but dead; he had sent his envoy all that distance from Heidelberg not to deliver a message but a demand: he wanted to know. So I asked it.

'"But why didn't you wait for me?" I said. "Why didn't you cable?"'

'Did she answer it?' he said.

'Didn't I say that brow was unravaged, even by indecision?' his uncle said. 'She answered it. "You didn't want me," she said. "I wasn't smart enough for you." '

'And what did you say?'

'I answered correctly too,' his uncle said. 'I said, "Good afternoon, Mrs Harriss." Will that one do?'

'Yes,' he said. And now it was time. The engineer even blew the whistle at him. Mr McWilliams had never once shouted, 'Come on here, boy, if you're going with us' as he would have five years ago (or for that matter, five months ago); only the two short deep impatient blasts of steam; simply because of the yet untried uniform he wore, a creature whose constant waking habit was talk, who would not even have missed or been aware of the breath passing over his vocal cords necessary to holler at him, had made no sound; instead, simply because he wore the uniform, a trained expert in a hundred-ton machine costing a hundred thousand dollars had expended three or four dollars' worth of coal and pounds of hard-earned steam to tell an eighteen-year-old boy that he had spent enough time gossiping with his uncle: and he thought how perhaps that country, that nation, that way of living really was invincible which could not only accept war but even assimilate it in stride by compromising with it; with the left hand so to speak, without really impeding or even deflecting, aberrating, even compelling the attention of the right hand still engaged in the way's old prime durable business.

'Yes,' he said. 'That's better. I might even buy that one. And that was twenty years ago. And it was true then or at least enough then or at least enough for you then. And now it's twenty years later and it's not true now or at least not enough now or at least not enough for you now. How did just years do all that?'

'They made me older,' his uncle said. 'I have improved.'

APPENDIX

The following provides a representative sample of variations between the text of this edition and previous editions. The reading to the left of the first bracket is the text of the current edition with a brief parenthetical explanation of the basis for the change. The reading farthest to the right, unless otherwise marked, is the text of the first edition of *Knight's Gambit*. In a very few places, I overrule typescript evidence in favor of volume consistency or to correct typos; such occasions are explained at greater length in the introduction. At times there are readings between the left and right. These additional variants are marked parenthetically with their sources.

I have also marked places where there are missing pages in the late typescript of "Hand Upon the Waters," which serves as the basis of my edition of the story; for the missing typescript pages, I rely on the first edition but retain Faulkner's preferred spellings as found in this typescript and all other manuscript material relating to *Knight's Gambit*.

In a few instances where the manuscript material and the first edition agree, I have nevertheless felt the need to provide clarifying notes.

ABBREVIATIONS

DM	*Doctor Martino and Other Stories*
EQMM	*Ellery Queen's Mystery Magazine*
H	*Harper's*
MS	"Smoke" manuscript; see Texts Consulted under "Smoke" in introduction for details
S	*Scribner's*
SEP	*Saturday Evening Post*
ts	typescript used as basis for a particular story; see Texts Consulted for each story in the introduction for more detailed information
UG	uncorrected galleys
VI	Vintage International

"SMOKE"

Page 3, line 13: Negro (volume consistency; see introduction)] negro (MS, *H*, *DM*, UG, 1st ed)

Page 4, line 26: Negro (1st ed)] negro (MS, *H*, *DM*, UG)

Page 5, line 29: dont (MS)] don't [Same change in all subsequent instances.]

Page 6, line 11: wont (MS)] won't [Same change in all subsequent instances.]

Page 6, line 15: civilised (MS)] civilized

Page 7, line 28: Negroes (volume consistency; see introduction)] negroes (MS, *H*, *DM*, UG, 1st ed)

Page 7, line 35: Negro (volume consistency; see introduction)] negro (MS, *H*, *DM*, UG, 1st ed)

Page 8, line 9: Negroes (volume consistency; see introduction)] negroes (MS, *H*, *DM*, UG, 1st ed)

Page 8, lines 12–13: its wording (*H*, *DM*, *EQMM*)] it wording

Page 8, line 17: The other two (*DM*, *EQMM*, 1st ed)] The two other (*H*)

Page 8, line 35: pay Anse's fine that time, (*H*, *DM*, *EQMM*)] pay Anse's fine that,

Page 9, line 21: Negroes (volume consistency; see introduction)] negroes (MS, *H*, *DM*, UG, 1st ed)

Page 9, lines 30–31: ten minutes past eight oclock (Faulkner's consistent usage in all other typescripts)] 10 minutes past 8 (MS)] ten minutes past eight o'clock

Page 9, line 31: Negro (volume consistency; see introduction)] negro (MS, *H*, *DM*, UG, 1st ed)

Page 9, line 34: Negro (1st ed)] negro (MS, *H*, *DM*, UG)

Page 10, line 1: Negro (volume consistency; see introduction)] negro (MS, *H*, *DM*, UG, 1st ed)

Page 10, line 9: or of hips (*H*, *DM*, *EQMM*)] or hips

Page 10, line 10: a little after five oclock (Faulkner's consistent usage in all other typescripts)] a little after 5 (MS)] a little after five o'clock

Page 10, line 15: Negro (volume consistency; see introduction)] negro (MS, *H*, *DM*, UG, 1st ed)

Page 10, line 21: Negro (volume consistency; see introduction)] negro (MS, *H*, *DM*, UG, 1st ed)

Page 10, line 26: Negro (volume consistency; see introduction)] negro (MS, *H*, *DM*, UG, 1st ed)

Page 10, line 27: Mr (MS)] Mr. [Same change in all subsequent instances.]

Page 10, line 31: Negro (volume consistency; see introduction)] negro (MS, *H*, *DM*, UG, 1st ed)

Page 10, line 32: Negro (volume consistency; see introduction)] negro (MS, *H*, *DM*, UG, 1st ed)

Page 11, line 10: Negro's (volume consistency; see introduction)] negro's (MS, *H*, *DM*, UG, 1st ed)

Page 15, line 32: realised (MS)] realized [Same change in all subsequent instances.]

Page 16, line 17: Negro (volume consistency; see introduction)] negro (MS, *H*, *DM*, UG, 1st ed)

Page 17, line 8: bed (*DM*, *EQMM*, 1st ed.)] bed, (*H*)

Page 17, line 25: Negro (volume consistency; see introduction)] negro (MS, *H*, *DM*, UG, 1st ed)

Page 17, line 36: dont (MS)] don't (*H*, *DM*, *EQMM*)] didn't

Page 19, lines 31–32: No, sir. (MS, *H*, *DM*, *EQMM*)] No sir.

Page 20, line 1: standardised (MS)] standardized [Same change in all subsequent instances.]

Page 21, lines 25–26: We watched him. (*H*, *DM*, *EQMM*)] We watched him:

Page 23, line 32: sanctuary (*H*, *DM*, *EQMM*)] sanctuaries

Page 24, line 15: Negro (1st ed)] negro (MS, *H*, *DM*, UG)

Page 24, line 21: Negro (volume consistency; see introduction)] negro (MS, *H*, *DM*, UG, 1st ed)

Page 25, line 12: Negro (volume consistency; see introduction)] negro (MS, *H*, *DM*, UG, 1st ed)

Page 26, line 26: Negro (volume consistency; see introduction)] negro (MS, *H*, *DM*, UG, 1st ed)

Page 26, line 29: Negro (volume consistency; see introduction)] negro (MS, *H*, *DM*, UG, 1st ed)

Page 26, line 29: Negro (volume consistency; see introduction)] negro (MS, *H*, *DM*, UG, 1st ed)

"MONK"

Page 28, line 13: dont (submitted ts)] don't [Same change in all subsequent instances.]

Page 28, line 26: him, (submitted ts)] him

Page 29, lines 35–36: hard bright metallic city hair (submitted ts)] hard, bright, metallic, city hair

Page 29, line 36: hard blonde city face (submitted ts)] hard, blonde, city face

Page 30, line 2: deadly too but (submitted ts)] deadly, too, but

Page 30, line 2: like a snake (submitted ts)] as a snake

Page 30, line 11: born there again (submitted ts)] born there—again

Page 30, line 13: Mrs (submitted ts)] Mrs. [Same change in all subsequent instances.]

Page 30, line 27: had been greased and fled (submitted ts)] had been greased, and fled

Page 30, line 35: him at least (submitted ts)] him, at least

Page 31, line 15: back room (submitted ts)] backroom

Page 32, line 5: not of good, use (submitted ts)] not of good nor use

Page 32, line 7: realise (submitted ts)] realize [Same change in all subsequent instances.]

Page 32, line 7: current, (submitted ts)] current

Page 32, lines 17–18: free himself of it, (submitted ts)] free himself of,

Page 32, line 20: old fecund ponderable travailing earth (submitted ts)] old, fecund, ponderable, travailing earth

Page 32, line 21: tell it (submitted ts)] tell about

Page 32, line 27: wilfully (submitted ts)] willfully

Page 32, line 31: aint (submitted ts)] ain't [Same change in all subsequent instances.]

Page 33, lines 21–22: still pristine gaudy-banded imitation panama hat (submitted ts)] still pristine, gaudy-banded, imitation Panama hat

Page 33, line 31: behind him and never (submitted ts)] behind him, never

Page 33, lines 32–33: glass yet wearing (submitted ts)] glass, yet wearing

Page 34, line 1: My uncle Gavin (submitted ts)] My Uncle Gavin

Page 34, line 11: like (submitted ts)] as

Page 34, line 18: like (submitted ts)] as

Page 36, line 20: Negro (volume consistency; see introduction)] negro (ts, *S*, UG, 1st ed)

Page 37, line 1: wont (submitted ts)] won't [Same change in all subsequent instances.]

Pages 37–38, lines 37; 1–3: Terrel, Bill. Manslaughter. Twenty years. Served since May 9, 19--. Applied for pardon January, 19--. Vetoed by Warden C. L. Gambrell. Applied for pardon September, 19--. Vetoed by Warden C. L. Gambrell. Record: Troublemaker. (submitted ts)] *Terrel, Bill. Manslaughter. Twenty years. Served since May 9, 19--. Applied for pardon January, 19--. Vetoed by Warden C. L. Gambrell. Applied for pardon September, 19--. Vetoed by Warden C. L. Gambrell. Record: Troublemaker.*

Page 38, line 20: Mr (submitted ts)] Mr. [Same change in all subsequent instances.]

Page 38, line 37: trap.' Still (submitted ts)] trap.'⁋ Still

Page 38, line 37: all. ⁋ (submitted ts)] all.

Page 40, line 14: bitched me up (submitted ts)] crossed me up

Page 40, line 20: spoken them: (submitted ts)] spoken;

Page 41, lines 3–8: speaking in that half-whining singsong. 'Send that son of a bitch away.'⁋ 'Son of a bitch yourself, fellow,' the guard said. 'You aint out of here yet.' But Terrel paid no more attention to the guard. He was looking at Uncle Gavin, speaking again in that voice in which the abjectness was completely false. 'What do you want to keep me locked up in here for? (submitted ts)] speaking in that half-whining singsong. 'What do you want to keep me locked up in here for? [Note: This cut was made at Morton Goldman's office on the carbon typescript intended for final author corrections; it was returned to *Scribner's* and used for final copyediting. On this carbon, along with the deletions, the following instruction to the copy editor appear holographically in the left margin: 'run in paragraph preceding.' The copy editor followed this instruction on the copyedited typescript used for typesetting.]

Page 41, lines 28–29: in that striped overall (submitted ts)] in those striped overalls

Page 42, line 2: have to done (submitted ts)] have to do

Page 42, line 29: go free.' For (submitted ts)] go free.'⁋ For

Page 42, line 30: he said, ⁋ 'Free (submitted ts)] he said, 'Free

Page 42, line 37: kinfolks (submitted ts)] kinsfolk

Page 43, line 7: paused and (submitted ts)] paused,

Page 43, line 16: Have you?' Now (submitted ts)] Have you?'⁊ Now

Page 43, line 17: Then he said, ⁊ 'No (submitted ts)] Then he said, 'No

Page 43, line 18: I hadn't (submitted ts)] I haven't

Page 43, line 29: broad heat-miraged (submitted ts)] broad, heat-miraged

Page 43, line 30: acres which (submitted ts)] acres, which

"HAND UPON THE WATERS"

The editing of "Hand Upon the Waters" at *The Saturday Evening Post* was so exten-sive that it is possible only to provide a few representative samples of the significant differences between the late typescript and the story as it always previously has been published.

Pages 44–45, lines 20–25; 1–4: They went on in single file, following the path, the youth, who was in front, glancing downward from time to time. A blue crane crossed the river, flying deliberately, its long legs trailing. Presently they came in sight of their destination. The bank rose to a cleared point almost like a headland—a point cleared apparently not so much by design and any labor as found comparatively free of undergrowth and further cleared by subsequent usage. In it sat a conical hut of such a harlequin appear-ance as to be almost camouflaged—generally round, with a pointed roof, built partly of mildewed canvas and odd-shaped boards and partly of oil tins hammered out flat. A section of stovepipe (late ts)] Presently the ground rose to a cleared point almost like a headland. Upon it sat a conical hut with a pointed roof, built partly of mildewed canvas and odd-shaped boards and partly of oil tins hammered out flat. A rusted stovepipe

Page 45, lines 31–32: So the older one followed too, for fifteen or twenty feet along the bank, to where the youth leaned eagerly (late ts)] The older one followed. The youth was leaning eagerly

Page 46, lines 4–7: slanted sharply down into the water from either end, with a heavy indicated downstream sag, and even the older man admitted to the youth's excited reiteration that the cord had more of movement than the current should have given it. (late ts)] slanted down into the water from either end, with a heavy downstream sag, and even the older man could feel the movement on it.

Page 47, lines 17–19: country doctor, with a snuffy moustache and the blurred eyes of an old man behind steel spectacles. (later ts)] country doctor.

Page 47, lines 21–26: Later, in his own car—that car which contrived somehow to look exactly like him: never quite new, always a little shabby, a little light-looking, yet always sturdy and serviceable enough even though he did drive it too fast—he never once thought that actually he had no business there, could have had no business there merely as County Attorney (late ts)] As county attorney he had no business there

Page 48, lines 4–11: It was still early afternoon. The distances were blue with heat, the land itself rich and heavy with the imminent harvest. Hay was already being cut and the corn stood in full tassel. Soon it would begin to fire, and the cotton was laid-by, square bloom and boll, which in another month would begin to open. Then, across the long flat where the road began to parallel the river bottom, he saw the store. By ordinary it should have stood as solitary and lonely as a milepost beside the empty road, (late ts)] It was early afternoon. The distances were blue with heat. Then, across the long flat where the road began to parallel the river bottom, he saw the store. By ordinary it would have been deserted,

Page 50, lines 26–31: So he did not return to town. He moved aside with the others, with his thin face and his thoughtful nose and his mop of hair more white than brown and his bright dark eyes which read Descartes and Plato and the Latin poets for pleasure, and watched four men enter, carrying their hats and looking at nobody, and move toward the quilt, walking stiffly; he saw that they were walking on tiptoe. (late ts)] Stevens moved aside with the others and watched the four men cross toward the quilt.

Page 56, line 26: Negro (*SEP*, UG, 1st ed)] negro (late ts)

Page 56, line 35: Negroes (*SEP*, UG, 1st ed)] negroes (late ts)

Page 57, line 34: Page 24 of the ts ends with "Put your"; since ts 25 and 26 are missing, this edition largely follows the text of the first edition but retains Faulkner's preferred spelling conventions as exhibited in both the early and late tss. However, following the early ts, I eliminate (here and in the subsequent missing late ts pages), certain paragraph breaks that appear in the first edition; Faulkner preferred longer paragraphs, but since the *Post* published in columns, the copy editor often added paragraph breaks so that readers would not encounter an entire column with no breaks.

Page 58, line 2: off." He (early ts)] off."¶ He

Page 59, line 1: Page 27 of late ts begins with this new paragraph; this edition again follows the late ts.

Page 59, line 20: Last word of ts 27 is "in"; since ts 28 is missing, this edition follows the text of the first edition until late ts 29 picks up but retains Faulkner's preferred spelling conventions as exhibited in both the early and late tss.

Page 60, line 2: Page 29 of late ts begins with "as"; this edition again follows the late ts.

Page 60, lines 19–22: The doctor kept him in the hospital only one day, though Tyler Ballenbaugh would be there longer than that. That evening, his unruly hair bursting above the neat surgeon's bandage about his head, he was sitting with two friends on the veranda (late ts)] He was sitting on the veranda

Page 60, line 26: bothered you at all. (late ts)] bothered you.

Page 60, lines 27–29: "We'll go inside," Stevens said.¶ "No no," both the men said. "We'll walk down to the gate and see if the weather's changed." So they departed, and the Sheriff lowered (late ts)] The sheriff lowered

Page 61, line 2: just as inscrutably (late ts)] just as blankly

Pages 61–62, lines 26–37; 1–5: Now the Sheriff bit the end from the cigar and took a match from his pocket. "It's too bad though he dont know about last night. It might make him feel better. It ought to make somebody feel better." ¶ "Maybe it does," Stevens said. "You dont get a whole lot out of this earth except the privilege of going back into it quiet and lying quiet after you get there. All men deserve that."¶ "Oh; Lonnie," the Sheriff said. "What about the men who are killed in wars?"¶"There's always a lot of them at one time, all together, all victims at one time of one general injustice, one roman holiday of lust and greed and folly; there were eight million of them, all with one set of emperors and kings and presidents and admirals and generals to curse. But Lonnie was by himself. Those others died to make the earth safe for Lonnie and his lot. They made all the earth safe for everybody else but Lonnie. It's like all the lepers jeering at the man who lost his leg, you see."⏍ "Ah," the Sheriff said. He rose, and struck the match. "Did that bullet (late ts)] "Did that bullet

Page 62, line 8: skiff (late ts)] paddle ["skiff" becomes "paddle" in next paragraph as well]

"TOMORROW"

Page 63, line 1: My Uncle, Gavin Stevens, had not always been County Attorney. (ts)] Uncle Gavin had not always been county attorney.

Page 63, lines 6–7: State University (ts)] state university

Page 63, line 7: Grandfather (ts)] grandfather [Same change in all subsequent instances.]

Page 63, lines 8–9: Heidelberg, and he had voluntarily taken the case (ts)] Heidelberg; and he had taken the case voluntarily

Page 63, lines 10–12: because, due to the victim's known character and the circumstances, the trial would be a mere formality even if the defendant had not had self-defense to plead. (ts)] everyone believed the trial would be a mere formality.

Page 63, line 16: Though actually (ts)] Actually

Page 63, line 17: autumn (ts)] fall

Page 63, lines 24–27: known (Uncle Gavin learned this only while preparing his case, since into that corner of the county even sheriffs seldom penetrated and in it people were born and died and were buried without certificates from county authorities) to be (ts)] known to be

Page 64, line 4: name which was signed to it. (ts)] name signed to it.

Page 64, line 4: it. And (ts)] it.⏍ And

Page 64, line 4: tawdry story (ts)] story

Page 64, lines 6–7: proven physical prowess and the daring and the tongue glib with explanations, (ts)] prowess and the daring and the glib tongue;

Page 64, line 11: Beat (ts)] district

Page 64, lines 11–12: handed his pistol butt-first to Varner (ts)] handed Varner his pistol

Page 64, lines 14–15: And that was all he said or would say, even after Uncle Gavin saw him in jail and arranged his bond. It was a neighbor (ts)] And a neighbor

Page 64, line 18: all that Bookwright would say even when, a week after (ts)] and a week after

Page 64, lines 22–23: left, so that not even Uncle Gavin ever discovered how Bookwright had managed to learn about the wife. (ts)] left.

Page 64, line 24: remember yet our surprise (ts)] remember our surprise

Page 64, lines 26-27: District Attorney (ts)] district attorney [Same change in all subsequent instances.]

Page 64, line 27: himself did not even appear but conducted (ts)] even conducted

Page 64, line 29: at the (ts)] the

Page 64, line 30: , and at the (ts)] and the

Page 64, lines 34-35: And I can still hear Uncle Gavin's voice, quiet, (ts)] Uncle Gavin's voice was quiet,

Page 65, line 2: Negroes (*SEP*, UG, 1st ed)] negroes (ts)

Page 65, lines 4-8: 'I wont talk anymore about the deceased. He is dead; let the dead bury him. And I'm not talking about self-defense. The defendant did not have to force this issue to the point of taking a life. He could have stayed at home that night and let what he could not otherwise stop, come to pass. All of us (ts)] 'All of us

Page 65, line 32: Court (ts)] court [Same change in all subsequent instances.]

Page 65, line 32: again, and the jury (ts)] again. The jury

Page 65, line 33: Judge (ts)] judge [Same change in all subsequent instances.]

Page 65, line 35: Bench (ts)] bench

Page 65, line 36: then it passed (ts)] then passed

Page 66, line 3: And I remember how I hurried (ts)] I hurried

Page 66, lines 3-4: through the dry vivid heat of that September noon and ate (ts)] and ate

Page 66, line 12: hair that was already (ts)] hair already

Page 66, lines 16-17: on the outside stairs that led down to the hot Square, (ts)] on the stairs

Page 66, lines 25-26: And there was the hot dry afternoon wind shaking the mulberry leaves too. I looked out through the windy leaves (ts)] But I could look through the windy mulberry leaves

Page 66, line 27: I could see and hear them too— (ts)] and see and hear, both—

Page 67, line 2: turned up here (ts)] turned up

Page 67, line 11: court in the spring. (ts)] court.

Page 67, line 13: breakfast. (ts)] breakfast.¶

Page 67, lines 16-17: bright, quick, not baffled (ts)] bright, not baffled

Page 67, line 29: *J.A. Fentry* (ts)] G. A. FENTRY

Page 67, line 31: broken gate, then (ts)] gate.¶ Then

Page 68, line 2: harried and badgered (ts)] badgered and harried

Page 68, line 5: said quietly. (ts)] said.

Page 68, line 6: We drove again, not fast now (ts)] We did not drive fast now

Page 68, lines 7-8: painted, neat and white, (ts)] painted,

Page 68, line 13: me.' (ts)] me.'¶

Page 68, line 19: gallery.' (ts)] gallery.'¶

Page 68, line 22: Stevens, Ma, (ts)] Stevens,

Page 68, line 24: 'Yes,' Uncle Gavin said again. 'Tell me.' So we (ts)] So we

Page 68, line 27: never seen (ts)] didn't see

Page 69, line 9: 'Yes,' he said. 'Tell me.' (ts)] 'Yes,' he said.

Page 69, line 10: 'All right,' Pruitt said. '—A day-wage job. Not (ts)] 'A day-wage job.' Pruitt said. 'Not

Page 69, line 17: right— (ts)] right.

Page 69, lines 19–20: his fields (ts)] the field

Page 69, line 25: hoe or drive nails with" (ts)] hoe

Page 69, line 28: years, then (ts)] years. Then

Page 69, line 32: sawmill——' (ts)] sawmill.'

Page 69, line 37: cypress logs through it again (ts)] logs through it

Page 70, line 3: baby——' (ts)] baby.'

Page 70, line 5: We didn't know how he come home (ts)] We never knew how he got home

Page 70, line 7: baby——' (ts)] baby.'

Page 70, line 8: said. And they (ts)] said.¶ They

Page 70, lines 10–11: Gavin's bright intent eyes. They (ts)] Gavin. His eyes

Page 70, line 14: going. 'Yes,' (ts)] going.¶ 'Yes,'

Page 70, line 17: goat-milk——' (ts)] goat's milk—'

Page 70, line 20: just had (ts)] had

Page 70, line 22: made him some cloths (ts)] made some cloths

Page 70, line 25: have it, Jackson. (ts)] take it.

Page 70, line 25: it (ts)] he

Page 70, line 36: Frenchman's Bend (ts)] Frenchman Bend

Page 70, line 36: "Nome," (ts)] "No'm,"

Page 71, line 12: and then take (ts)] and take

Page 71, line 15: thigh-deep (ts)] middle-thigh

Page 71, line 22: baptised (ts)] baptized

Page 71, line 35: night.' We (ts)] night.'¶ We

Page 72, line 10: whirled and snatched (ts)] snatched

Page 72, line 22: dinner. Uncle (ts)] dinner.¶ Uncle

Page 72, lines 26–27: Frenchman's Bend village (ts)] Frenchman's Bend Village

Page 72, line 28: car. It (ts)] car.¶ It

Page 72, line 30: a vague, dreamy (ts)] a dreamy

Page 72, line 32: water-haul (ts)] water haul

Page 72, line 34: tell me sooner? (ts)] tell me?

Page 73, lines 2–3: trees and the frogs boomed and brunted and the lightning-bugs (ts)] trees and the lighting bugs

Page 73, line 11: Pap (ts)] pap [Same change in all subsequent instances.]

Page 73, line 23: Until in the late fall, (ts)] Until late fall,

Page 74, line 10: I'm telling this (ts)] I'm going to tell

Page 74, line 23: husband in (ts)] husband, in

Page 74, lines 25–26: blood-pride (ts)] blood pride

Page 74, line 27: Anyway, (ts)] ¶ 'Anyway,

Page 75, line 5: Mammy (ts)] mammy

Page 75, line 37: axe (ts)] ax

Page 76, line 4: Grandpap (ts)] grandpap
Page 76, line 8: law!" Then (ts)] law!"ꟻ 'Then
Page 76, line 25: of it (ts)] for it
Page 76, line 33: Then (ts)] ꟻ 'Then
Page 77, line 4: plow-dirt (ts)] dirt
Page 77, line 12: Old Man Fentry (ts)] old man Fentry
Page 77, line 13: first and when (ts)] first.ꟻ 'When
Page 77, line 16: hitch-rein (ts)] hitch rein
Page 77, line 17: And (ts)] ꟻ 'And
Page 77, line 24: road. He (ts)] road. ꟻ 'He
Page 78, line 14: brutalised (ts)] brutalized

"AN ERROR IN CHEMISTRY"

Page 80, line 19: wont (final ts)] won't [Same change in all subsequent instances.]
Page 80, line 24: all. The sheriff (final ts)] all.ꟻ The sheriff
Page 80, line 36: aint (final ts)] ain't [Same change in all subsequent instances.]
Page 81, line 8: bitt (final ts; Faulkner's recurring variant spelling of "bit")] bit
Page 81, line 21: wanted (final ts)] *wanted*
Page 81, line 28: ten seconds now while (final ts)] ten seconds while
Page 82, line 15: Mrs (final ts)] Mrs. [Same change in all subsequent instances.]
Page 82, line 28: Mr (final ts)] Mr. [Same change in all subsequent instances.]
Page 83, line 18: what times (final ts)] those times
Page 83, lines 19–20: saw them digging and reached there to drive them off (final ts)] saw them and drove them off
Page 83, line 34: them Northerners (early ts and sheriff's subsequent usage)] the Northerners
Page 83, line 35: dont (final ts)] don't [Same change in all subsequent instances.]
Page 84, lines 13–16: he not only destroyed the witness before there was anything he must have feared to have witnessed, before there was any witness to be destroyed, he has set up a signboard saying "Watch me and mark me" (final ts)] he not only destroyed the witness before there was anything to be witnessed but also before there was any witness to be destroyed. He set up a signboard saying "Watch me and mark me," [Note: Dannay deletes some words as he breaks Faulkner's sentence into two separate ones. This edit decouples what the sheriff in Faulkner's sentence sees as Flint's two linked actions: not only 1) destroying the witness, but also 2) putting people on notice ("setting up a signboard") about how dangerous he is.]
Page 84, line 31: wanted (final ts)] *wanted*
Page 85, line 12: old Wes still locked (final ts)] old Pritchel's still locked
Page 87, lines 11–14: the kind-hearted woman suffered another complete reversal and was even regretting that she had made the offer at all. Then the harsh, cracked old voice from inside the half-closed door ruined that too by adding: (final ts)] the kind-hearted

woman was even regretting that she had made the offer at all when the harsh, cracked old voice from inside the half-closed door added:

Pages 87–88, lines 36; 1–2: jail cell in which for twenty-four hours now there had even been another prisoner—the meager (final ts)] jail cell. The meager

Page 88, lines 5–6: without knowing or even wondering who she was— (final ts)] without ever knowing her . . .

Page 88, lines 10–11: cell, he had never existed at all: that (final ts)] cell but had never existed at all. That

Page 88, lines 18–22: cast a shadow. Only her shadow still makes only two of them. And since Old Man Pritchel is still out there in that house, probably washing his dinner dishes now—provided he does wash them, Flint did not exist at all, did he?' (final ts)] cast a shadow.

Page 88, line 28: clothes: (final ts)] clothes.¶

Page 88, line 31: ever had been (final ts)] ever was

Page 89, line 5: oclock (final ts)] o'clock

Page 89, line 18: running-board perhaps and perhaps flinging (final ts)] running-board and flinging

Page 89, line 26: realised (final ts)] realized [Same change in all subsequent instances.]

Page 90, line 28: his daughter, and no Negro at all on his land. (final ts)] his daughter.

Page 91, line 3: moustache (final ts)] mustache [Same change in all subsequent instances.]

Page 91, line 6: Uncle Wes (final ts)] Mr. Pritchel [Dannay changes every instance where the sheriff addresses Flint disguised as Pritchel as "Uncle Wes" to "Mr. Pritchel."]

Page 91, line 35: clay which he had just sold would (final ts)] clay would

Page 92, lines 7–8: truck now; I got a nigger to drive it. (final ts)] truck now.

Page 92, line 24: gentle even and (final ts)] gentle and

Page 94, line 1: axe (final ts)] ax

Page 94, lines 16–18: Management offers One¶ Thousand Dollars in Cash¶ To Any Man or Woman or Child (final ts)] Management offers One Thousand Dollars¶ in Cash To Any Man or Woman or¶ Child Who . . .

"KNIGHT'S GAMBIT"

Page 100, line 15: no deference (ts)] no difference (error introduced in typesetting)

Page 101, line 3: bitt (ts, 1st edition: Faulkner's alternative spelling of "bit")

Page 102, line 7: chessgame (ts)] chess game (copy editor change)

Page 105, line 31: older; (ts, UG)] older,

Page 105, line 31: his—Charles's—mother (ts)] his—Charles's mother (change introduced in galleys)

Page 110, line 31: Mrs Harriss (ts)] Mrs. Harriss (error introduced in galleys)

Page 114, line 28: pick up the bag] pick the bag (uncorrected error in ts, UG) [Note: Faulkner originally typed "pick of the bag," saw the error, and x-ed out "of." Because this mistake happened on the last line of the page, Faulkner likely was unable to roll the page back a line in the typewriter, as he normally did, to correct the idiom to "up" and missed it later, as did the copy editor.]

Page 116, line 13: <u>$5500</u> (ts underlines, indicating italics)] $5500

Page 121, line 7: steeple-chase (ts)] steeplechase (copy editor's change)

Page 122, line 23: steeple-chaser (ts)] steeplechaser (copy editor's change)

Page 125, line 5: steeple-chase (ts)] steeplechase (copy editor's change)

Page 125, line 10: father-in-law (ts)] stepfather (the copy editor writes in the left margin "step-father" and "brother-in-law" and changes the text to "stepfather"; while the change is more accurate, "brother-in-law" would also emphasize the ambiguity of Gualdres's position)

Page 129, line 18: like (ts)] as if (copy editor's change)

Page 133, line 21: Sears and Roebuck (ts)] Sears, Roebuck (copy editor's change here and in the two subsequent instances in this sentence)

Page 138, line 3: girlheels (ts, 1st edition)] girl-heels (VI)

Page 138, line 10: a whine a squeal (ts and 1st edition)] a whine, a squeal (VI)

Page 138, line 14: sitting-room (ts)] sittingroom (copy editor's change)

[Note: this word is handled inconsistently by the copy editor. Twice earlier in the typescript, Faulkner correctly uses "sitting room," and it is unchanged. Subsequently, Faulkner uses "sitting-room" (ts 90), and it is also unchanged. The one time Faulkner runs the two words together without a hyphen is when he uses it as an adjective.]

Page 138, line 36: on your way to bed.] on your way to be. (uncorrected typo in ts, UG) [Context demands that the word be "bed," but Faulkner and the copy editor missed this error.]

Page 141, line 11: even convinced him] ever convinced him (uncorrected typo in ts, UG) ["Ever" does not make sense but "even" does; Faulkner and the copy editor missed this error.]

Page 143, line 33: Note: Although Faulkner typically uses the British spelling for "civilization," the ts in this instance uses the US spelling.

Page 145, line 26: Square (uncorrected typo)] square [The ts refers to Jefferson's "Square" twenty times. Nineteen of these are capitalized, which argues that Faulkner intended to capitalize the twentieth instance as well.]

Page 149, line 18: sitting-room (ts)] sittingroom (copy editor change on ts)

Page 150, line 30: sitting-room (ts)] sittingroom (copy editor change on ts)

Page 151, line 15: sitting-room (ts)] sittingroom (copy editor change on ts)

Page 152, line 4: like his uncle (ts)] as his uncle (copy editor change on ts)

Page 152, line 23: into the car and without warming (ts)] into the car; and without warming (copy editor change on ts)

Page 152, lines 31–32: watched his uncle run up to where Mr McCallum still sat (ts, UG)] watched Mr McCallum still sitting

Page 152, lines 33–34: snatched up the stick (ts, UG)] snatched it up

Page 152, line 35: just like he (ts)] just as he (copy editor change on ts)

Page 152, line 35: Note: copy editor inconsistently allows "sitting room" to stand as two words.

Page 153, line 7: ten minutes to eight (ts, UG)] ten minutes to ten

Page 153, line 8: we'll be in time (ts, UG)] we'll still be in time

Page 154, line 36: High School (ts)] high school (copy editor change on ts)

Page 155, line 29: Spanish), he realised also (ts)] Spanish), realised also (error introduced during typesetting)

Page 156, line 5: *Yes* (ts)] *yes* (changed during typesetting)

Page 156, line 19: 'was it ever his to begin with. With deference: what favor?' (ts, UG)] 'was it ever his to begin with.' With deference: 'what favor?'

Page 157, lines 30–31: upper half of the single stall door open; a black square in the dazzling white; (1st ed)] lower half of the single stall door shut; (ts, UG) [Note: This is one of two instances where I privilege the first edition over the typescript. Faulkner must have made this change and addition on his copy of the galleys, which are lost.]

Page 158, line 8: the blind one.' (ts, 1st ed.)] the blind one?' (VI)

Page 163, line 31: You are not nineteen years old, you are twenty-one, (1st ed)] You are twenty-one years old, (ts, UG) [Note: This is the second of two instances where I privilege the first edition over the typescript. Faulkner must have made this change and addition on his copy of the galleys.]

Page 165, line 24: goodbye (ts)] good-bye [copy editor changes word here and in all subsequent instances.]

Page 166, line 29: sitting room (ts)] sittingroom (copy editor change)

Page 167, line 25: Note: although Faulkner uses "aeroplane" earlier in ts, he uses the US spelling here.

Page 167, lines 33–34: shrieked and demised (ts, UG)] shrieked and died

Page 170, line 7: mis-matched (ts)] mismatched (copy editor change on ts)

Page 171, line 16: anymore (ts)] any more (copy editor incorrectly changes ts).

Page 173, lines 32–33: without surprise nor even attention] without surprise not even attention (uncorrected typo in ts, UG) ["Without X nor even Y" is a common rhetorical pattern in Faulkner's writing. Faulkner and the copy editor both missed the error.]

Page 174, line 1: flash and glitter (uncorrected typo in ts and UG)] glash and glitter [Faulkner elsewhere uses "flash and glitter": in *Absalom, Absalom!*, for example, when speaking of Charles Bon introducing Henry Sutpen to the sensual pleasures of New Orleans: "the flash and glitter of myriad carriage wheels, in which women, enthroned and immobile and passing rapidly across the vision, appeared like painted portraits. . . ." (VI, 87–88)]

Page 175, line 4: Sanscrit (alternative spelling appears in ts and 1st edition)

Page 176, line 4: makeshift (hyphenated in ts because it comes at a line break; elsewhere [see *Sanctuary* and *Pylon*], Faulkner always uses "makeshift" as an unhyphenated word)] make-shift

Page 177, line 14: anything] any thing (uncorrected typo in ts, UG) [In every other instance throughout *Knight's Gambit*, Faulkner always uses "anything"; Faulkner and the copy editor miss this.]

Page 178, line 10: embassys (Faulkner's variant spelling in ts and 1st ed)

Page 178, line 11: anymore (ts)] any more (copy editor incorrectly changes on ts)

Page 179, line 25: that?' (dropped quotation mark in ts, UG)] that? [A quotation mark does end Chick's dialogue in the carbon of the setting ts, but apparently after copyediting, Faulkner crossed out the original ending, reinserted the last page of the story in his typewriter, and made Charles's last piece of dialogue longer and forgot to close the quotation. Here are Chick's final words on the carbon: 'Yes,' he said. 'That's better. But if it was true then or at least enough, how could just years make it not enough now?']

ALSO BY

WILLIAM FAULKNER

ABSALOM, ABSALOM!

In *Absalom, Absalom!*, Faulkner's epic tale of Thomas Sutpen, an enigmatic stranger comes to Jefferson, Mississippi, in the early 1830s to wrest his mansion out of the muddy bottoms of the north Mississippi wilderness. He was a man, Faulkner said, "who wanted sons and the sons destroyed him."

Fiction

AS I LAY DYING

As I Lay Dying is Faulkner's harrowing account of the Bundren family's odyssey across the Mississippi countryside to bury Addie, their wife and mother. Narrated in turn by each of the family members—including Addie herself—the novel ranges in mood, from dark comedy to the deepest pathos. Considered one of the most influential novels in American fiction in structure, style, and drama, *As I Lay Dying* is a true twentieth-century classic.

Fiction

BIG WOODS

Some of Nobel Prize–winning author William Faulkner's most famous stories are collected in this volume—"The Bear," "The Old People," "A Bear Hunt," and "Race at Morning." In these stories, he observed, celebrated, and mourned the fragile otherness that is nature, as well as the cruelty and humanity of men.

Fiction

Forty-two stories make up this magisterial collection by the writer who stands at the pinnacle of modern American fiction. Compressing an epic expanse of vision into hard and wounding narratives, Faulkner's stories evoke the intimate textures of place, the deep strata of history and legend, and all the fear, brutality, and tenderness of the human condition. These tales are set not only in Yoknapatawpha County, but in Beverly Hills and in France during World War I. They are populated by such characters as the Faulknerian archetypes Flem Snopes and Quentin Compson, as well as by ordinary men and women who emerge so sharply and indelibly in these pages that they dwarf the protagonists of most novels.

Fiction

A FABLE

This novel won both the Pulitzer Prize and the National Book Award in 1955. An allegorical story of World War I set in the trenches in France and dealing ostensibly with a mutiny in a French regiment, it was originally considered a sharp departure for Faulkner. Recently it has come to be recognized as one of his major works and an essential part of the Faulkner oeuvre. His descriptions of the war "rise to magnificence," according to *The New York Times*, and include, in Malcolm Cowley's words, "some of the most powerful scenes he ever conceived."

Fiction

FLAGS IN THE DUST

The complete text of Faulkner's third novel was published for the first time in 1973. In 1919, young Bayard Sartoris returns to Yoknapatawpha from the war. But unlike his heroic Civil War great-grandfather and great-uncle, Sartoris's war experiences leave him aimless and bitter, a walking casualty of how the lost ideals and abiding memory of the antebellum South have crippled the present.

Fiction

GO DOWN, MOSES

Go Down, Moses is composed of seven interrelated stories, all of them set in Faulkner's mythic Yoknapatawpha County. From a variety of perspectives, Faulkner examines the complex, changing relationships between blacks and whites, between man and nature, weaving a cohesive novel rich in implication and insight.

Fiction

THE HAMLET

The Hamlet, the first novel of Faulkner's Snopes trilogy, is both an ironic take on classical tragedy and a mordant commentary on the grand pretensions of the antebellum South and the depths of its decay in the aftermath of war and Reconstruction. It tells of the advent and the rise of the Snopes family in Frenchman's Bend, a small town built on the ruins of a once-stately plantation. Flem Snopes—wily, energetic, a man of shady origins—quickly comes to dominate the town and its people with his cunning and guile.

Fiction

INTRUDER IN THE DUST

A classic Faulkner novel that explores the lives of a family in the South. In this work, an aging black man who has long refused to adopt the black's traditionally servile attitude is wrongfully accused of murdering a white man.

Fiction

LIGHT IN AUGUST

Light in August features some of Faulkner's most memorable characters: guileless, dauntless Lena Grove, in search of the father of her unborn child; Reverend Gail Hightower, who is plagued by visions of Confederate horsemen; and Joe Christmas, a desperate, enigmatic drifter consumed by his mixed ancestry.

Fiction

THE MANSION

The Mansion completes Faulkner's great trilogy of the Snopes family in the mythical county of Yoknapatawpha, Mississippi, which also includes *The Hamlet* and *The Town*. Beginning with the murder of Jack Houston, and ending with the murder of Flem Snopes, it traces the downfall of this indomitable postbellum family, who managed to seize control of the town of Jefferson within a generation.

Fiction

MOSQUITOES

Wealthy Mrs. Maurier, the widowed heiress of an old New Orleans family, likes to collect "artistic types." When she plans a multi-day outing on her yacht and manages to corral aboard a group that includes a melancholic poet, a brooding sculptor, a self-important writer, her unconventional young niece, and assorted other odd characters, the results are both disastrous and hilarious. When the ship runs aground near an overheated swamp, the pretensions and frustrations of its various passengers reach a fever pitch. Faulkner's lyrical descriptions, witty dialogue, and forays into fluid stream of consciousness demonstrate in lighter form the literary techniques that the young author later came to be so celebrated for.

Fiction

REQUIEM FOR A NUN

This sequel to Faulkner's most sensational novel, *Sanctuary*, was written twenty years later but takes up the story of Temple Drake eight years after the events related in *Sanctuary*. Temple is now married to Gowan Stevens. The book begins when the death sentence is pronounced on the nurse, Nancy, for the murder of Temple and Gowan's child. Told partly in prose, partly in play form, *Requiem for a Nun* is a haunting exploration of the impact of the past on the present.

Fiction

THE SOUND AND THE FURY

The Sound and the Fury is the tragedy of the Compson family, featuring some of the most memorable characters in literature: beautiful, rebellious Caddy; the man-child Benjy; haunted, neurotic Quentin; Jason, the brutal cynic; and Dilsey, their black servant. Their lives fragmented and harrowed by history and legacy, the characters' voices and actions mesh to create what is arguably Faulkner's masterpiece and one of the greatest novels of the twentieth century.

Fiction

SANCTUARY

Sanctuary is a powerful novel examining the nature of evil, informed by the works of T. S. Eliot and Freud, mythology, local lore, and hard-boiled detective fiction. *Sanctuary* is the dark, at times brutal, story of the kidnapping of Mississippi debutante Temple Drake, who introduces her own form of venality into the Memphis underworld where she is being held.

ALSO AVAILABLE
Pylon
The Reivers
Soldiers' Pay
The Town
The Uncollected Stories of William Faulkner
The Unvanquished
The Wild Palms
AND OTHERS